THE FINAL HOMESTEAD

JAMES HUNT

❀ Created with Vellum

"*P*ete, you have to give me a better price than that." The sound of boot heels paced the hallway in front of the pharmacy of the San Antonio's Children Medical Center. "You and I have always had a good relationship, and that's why I told you I didn't have a problem with the verbal agreement."

Mary Bowers was thirty-three, her jet-black hair pulled back into a ponytail to keep it out of her face. She had olive skin and a pair of stunningly green eyes that sat between clusters of freckles on her high cheekbones. She wore a light blue blouse that flowed down over blue jeans tucked into worn and dusty boots.

"No, Pete." Mary stood her ground. The man was always looking for a bargain, and while he was one of their ranch's biggest buyers, he was slipperier to deal with than his father. She sandwiched the phone between her cheek and her shoulder and reached into her purse to find the notes she had written down for the call. "It was four dollars a pound, not three."

A pair of nurses walked by, one of them pressing a finger to her lips, hushing Mary on her way past.

Mary covered the mouthpiece of the phone. "Sorry." She walked closer to the wall, trying to keep her voice down.

"Fine. If you don't want to honor our agreement, then I'll give Charles Mathers a call and see if he'll be interested." Charles was Pete's biggest competitor, and the only reason Pete hadn't gone belly up was his business with Bowers Ranch.

Mary smiled, and Pete's stubbornness melted away like butter on a hot roll. "I'll be on the lookout for the paperwork this afternoon. Always a pleasure, Pete." She hung up, rolling her eyes as she pocketed her phone.

"Mrs. Bowers?" A young woman in a long white coat two sizes too big held up a paper bag from behind the pharmacy's counter.

Mary walked over, grabbing her wallet from her purse to show her RX card. "Sorry if I was too loud."

"It's fine." The young woman smiled kindly as she took the card, typing its information into her computer. "This place is always loud, but people seem to only enjoy their own noise." She winked at Mary and handed her RX card back. "You're all set. Do you have any questions about the medications?"

"No," Mary said, cramming the paper bags into her purse. "It's not my first rodeo. Thanks."

With her prescription filled, Mary hurried down the hallway and returned to the children's surgical ward, where she found her son Jake still reading in the waiting room.

Mary sat next to Jake, brushing some bangs out of her eyes that had broken loose from her ponytail.

"Is everything all right?" Jake remained focused on his book and turned the page of the flimsy paperback, the spine crinkled from its folded position.

Jake Bowers was only twelve, but going on forty. The boy had gone through more hardship in his young life than most people would experience in two lifetimes. He had the same dirty blond hair as his father, but Mary's green eyes. He was in the middle of a growth spurt and Mary knew that by next year, she would be the one looking up at him during their conversations.

Mary rubbed her eyes. "Oh, you know, just feeding the world, one head of cattle at a time." She dropped her hands. "Unless you're a vegetarian."

"Or a vegan," Jake said, still reading.

Mary smirked, and then moved her son's hands so she could read the title of his book. She arched her eyebrows. "The Rainmaker? When did you start reading John Grisham?"

Jake pulled the book away from his mother's reach. "Since the library sent me the wrong book by mistake." He settled back into his chair and continued reading. "He's not bad."

"I'm sure he'll be relieved to hear it." Mary checked the time on her phone and grimaced. "Have any of the nurses come out yet?"

"Nope."

Mary sighed, leaning her head back. "It's already been an hour."

"Maybe they're upgrading me to the premium operating room," Jake said, feigning elation.

"Hey." Mary covered the page Jake was reading with her palm, forcing her son's eyes to meet her own. "I still get three more months before you become a snarky teenager. That's the deal."

Jake shrank in his seat. "Sorry."

Caught between the worlds of child and man, Jake leaned his head against Mary's shoulder. She could tell that he was worried. Having gone through this dozens of times already, she would have thought they'd be used to it by now. But when it came to his condition, there was never anything routine.

"What's that?" Jake asked.

"Hmm?" Mary frowned when she saw the top of the prescription bag sprouting from her purse. "Oh, it's nothing." She quickly shoved it down and zipped the compartment. "Something for your dad."

Mary wasn't in the habit of lying to her son, but before Jake could ask any more questions, a nurse stepped into the waiting room, staring at the clipboard in her hands.

"Jake Bowers?"

"Finally," Mary said.

The nurse was an older woman, short and round, with a head of grey hair that had just been permed. She quickly scribbled something down on her clipboard, never looking up as she turned back toward the hallway. "Follow me, please."

Mary kept her arm around Jake as they passed into the surgical unit, the pair of double doors flapping back and forth after they entered.

"Room seventeen. Change, and the doctor will be in shortly." The nurse placed a file in the folder by the door and then disappeared, still navigating the hallways without ever looking up.

Mary stepped toward the door, but Jake blocked her path. She frowned. "What's wrong?"

"Nothing." Jake rubbed his arm and folded into himself, his changing body providing the awkward angles of puberty. "It's just…" He finally looked up. "I wanted to go in alone this time."

"Oh." Mary arched her eyebrows in surprise. "Okay, sure."

"I just think it would be good for me to handle it by myself," Jake said, clearing his throat. "Now that I'm getting older."

"I understand." Mary smiled and then kissed the top of Jake's head. "I love you."

Jake smiled, but he no longer resembled the boy she drove here this morning. "I love you too, Mom."

The door shut, and Mary lingered in the hallway. She knew that it was normal for him to want his independence, but that didn't lessen the sting.

Mary returned to the waiting room where more families had arrived. Most of the chatter in the waiting room was a combination of nervous whispers, casual conversations, and the news from the television hoisted in the right-hand corner near the ceiling.

You could always spot the regulars with their calm demeanor who had learned to pass the time by reading or watching videos on their laptops.

Newcomers always fidgeted in their seats. Nothing held their attention for long, and their search for a distraction only worsened their anxiety.

Mary found an empty seat next to a woman who sat with her purse clutched in her lap, knee bouncing a mile a minute.

The woman was young, pretty, dressed in a faded print skirt with polka dots and a white blouse that exposed her pale and freckled shoulders. Her hair was a mess, tied up in a bun that rested on the very top of her head with a 'leaning-tower-of-Pisa' attitude. A string of sleepless nights had made their mark beneath her eyes, and she had twisted a packet of tissues to the point of tearing.

Having been in that same seat before, Mary wanted to help. "Boy or girl?"

The young mother arched her eyebrows and froze. "I'm sorry?"

"Your patient," Mary answered. "Boy or girl?"

"Oh." The woman exhaled, and a little color returned to her cheeks as she smiled. "Girl."

"How old?" Mary asked.

"Two."

Mary nodded. "It's always hard to bring them here. Especially when they're that little. I'm Mary."

The young mother released the tight twisted spiral of

tissues and clasped Mary's hand firmly. "Kelly." She relaxed a little when she let go and returned the crumpled tissues to her purse as she leaned back, mirroring Mary's posture.

"I'm waiting on my son," Mary said.

"Is it serious?" Kelly asked.

"It can be, but he has a mild case of AVS." Mary rolled her thumb against the pages of Jake's novel, and then explained more when she saw the confusion on Kelly's face. "Aortic valve stenosis. It's a genetic heart condition. It causes blood to clog in his heart chambers. Every six months he needs to have a procedure done to drain the blood to relieve pressure."

Kelly frowned. "That must be so hard having to come in here so frequently."

Mary nodded, staring at her purse, remembering that first day with her son, and how instead of holding him, he was placed in the ICU until he was strong enough to be taken home. "You want to protect them from everything when they're little. But no amount of baby books can prepare you for that unexpected speech from your doctor after nine hours of labor explaining to you that they're doing everything they can to keep your child alive."

Kelly was quiet for a moment, only nodding along, but then fell into the rhythm of conversation. "Iris, my daughter, kept getting sick, so we took her to our family physician. He couldn't figure out what was wrong so they had some blood work drawn. Her white blood cell count was practically non-existent. They're not sure if it's cancer, but we're waiting on the test results and—" The tears came quickly, and she covered her mouth to muffle her whimper.

Mary instinctively reached for Kelly's hand, squeezing tight, the young mother reciprocating the embrace of strength.

A few eyes glanced their way, each of them with varying

expressions of empathy. Everyone here had reached the breaking point at one time or another.

After a minute, Kelly regained her composure, making use of the crinkled tissue package as she wiped her eyes and blew her nose. "I'm sorry."

"You don't have anything to be sorry for, love," Mary said. "I hope that the news is good, or at least as good as it can be in a place like this."

"Kelly Ronan?" A nurse entered, holding a blue folder and staring directly at Kelly. "We're ready for you."

Kelly exhaled, her breath trembling as she gathered her purse and stood, Mary rising with her. "Thank you." She wrapped her arms around Mary's neck and squeezed.

"Hang in there, mamma," Mary said.

Kelly let go and followed the nurse out of the waiting room. Once Kelly was out of eyeshot, Mary sat down and bowed her head, quietly praying for the young mother and her little girl to be cancer free, and if not, then to have the strength to bear what came next.

Mary opened her eyes, the hospital still buzzing with activity, and in the next instance the world went dark, bringing with it a stunned silence.

No lights, no hum of A/C, no chatter of patients or staff or visitors. The waiting room had transformed into a dark hole of which there was no escape, and Mary would float aimlessly for the rest of her life.

But the silence lasted only for a moment, broken by panicked voices that ricocheted around the darkness

"What was that?"

"The power's out."

"I can't see anything."

"My phone's not working."

"What is going on?"

Mary remained seated, processing her surroundings.

Blind, she fumbled her fingers into her purse until she felt the outline of her phone. She pressed the power button, her heart sinking to the pit of her stomach, anchoring her in her chair while she heard others shuffling around in the darkness.

Mary dropped her phone back into her purse and then removed a hand-powered kinetic flashlight. She squeezed the handle on the side, and light flooded the waiting room, blinding anyone within range.

"Everyone, just remain calm." Mary stood and maneuvered her way to the hallway. "Find a nurse, locate your family member, and if they can leave the hospital, then do it as quickly as possible."

A slew of questions followed Mary out the door, but she didn't stop to explain. Every second counted now.

Mary passed through the double doors of the surgical unit, the scene chaotic as nurses and doctors scrambled to save patients crippled by the loss of the power.

"All operating rooms are dark, I've got twelve kids on the table right now, and the doctors are blind."

"All life support in the ICU is offline, we need as many nurses there for CPR that we can spare."

"I need a crash cart in room twelve!"

Mary hastened her pace, finding Jake's room, and she shouldered the door open. She found her son still dressed in his regular clothes, holding his hands up to block the light.

"Thank God." Mary lowered the light and hugged her son.

"What's going on?" Jake asked.

Mary held his face, keeping him still. "Do you remember the rendezvous location where we're supposed to meet your father if something happens when we're separated?"

Jake nodded.

"That's where we're going," Mary said, her voice teetering on the edge of panic. "It's going to be very chaotic when we leave the hospital, but we need to keep moving forward. We don't stop for anything, and we always stay together. Got it?"

"Y-yeah," Jake answered, his voice dry. "Stay together. Always."

Mary fisted a bunch of Jake's hair and then kissed his forehead. "Don't let go of my hand, and keep close."

Mary led them from the room. Beyond the beam of the flashlight, screams echoed from deeper in the building, the cries growing more horrific the longer the hospital was engulfed in darkness.

Eventually, windows provided enough sunlight for her to pocket the flashlight. Pushing her way through the crowded hallways, she found the stairwell, which was already packed with people on a mass exodus toward the first floor.

The river of bodies on the staircase flowed in both directions, people either fighting to get out, or fighting to go deeper in search of their loved ones. Mary and Jake hugged the walls, avoiding the worst of the foot traffic. One misstep and both of them could be trampled.

"Mom, what's going on?" Jake asked, struggling to keep up.

"We just need to keep moving," Mary answered.

Both she and her husband James had talked about something like this, how the world could be flipped upside down with the snap of a finger. And if this was what she thought it was, then things were going to get worse.

When Mary and Jake reached the bottom of the stairwell, she shouldered open the door that led them to the outside, their senses bombarded by the harsh light and heat of summer.

And while Mary couldn't see, it was what she didn't *hear* that confirmed her fears.

The normal sounds of city life, the cars, the horns, the hum of power lines and the chatter of folks on phones, all of it had vanished. And when her vision adjusted to the sunlight, Mary's heart skipped a beat.

The cars along the highway nearby were gridlocked.

Motorists were outside of their vehicles, scratching their heads at why everything had suddenly come to a stop.

The folks in the hospital parking lot stared at their blank phones, whispering to one another in concern.

"Mom?" Jake asked, still concerned. "What's going on?"

"It happened," Mary said, speaking more to herself.

No phones. No cars. No power. The rug had been pulled out from beneath their feet, and just like the confusion in the hospital that spread throughout the darkened halls, Mary knew that fear would infect every citizen of San Antonio, a city of more than one point three million residents who had just been affected by an EMP.

2

---

*S*unshine was in large supply as hooves thundered over the grassy fields. The herd of five hundred steer clustered together, moving lethargically toward the holding pen at the front of the property where they would be tagged and prepared for the long trip toward the rail carts in three days.

James Bower rode alongside the herd on his mare. The wide and worn brim of his Stetson and the bandana just below his eyes shielded him from the hot Texas sun. A long-sleeve denim shirt, dirty jeans, and boots rounded out the rest of the attire.

Broad-shouldered and muscular, he sat comfortably in the saddle, conditioned by a lifetime of riding, and broke the animal out into a full gallop.

The wind whipped at James's shirt, the sweaty fabric clinging tight to his chest and arms as he leaned forward in the saddle, enjoying the open space. Out here they were free to roam, free to play, free to live.

When James reached the front of the herd, he pulled back on the reins, slowing the horse and ending both their fun.

James dismounted from the mare and lowered the red

bandana that revealed the grizzled face of a man who had made his living outdoors. He opened one of the saddlebags and took a long pull from his water bottle. It was warm.

The mare huffed for attention, and James removed his right glove and placed a calloused hand along the animal's soft neck.

The bond between man and horse possessed a mythological connection, and he wished he could have been a part of those old Western days, exploring the world on horseback and discovering new, untouched land.

It was a romantic sentiment, but it was one that was instilled into James by his father, along with his love of old time Westerns. The Rifleman, Bonanza, Gunsmoke, the Virginian. He bet Wyoming in 1890 was a sight to behold. Nothing but open lands as far as the eye could see. So much untapped potential just waiting to be enjoyed by those brave, strong, and skilled enough to harvest it.

Covered in sweat and dirt, James tipped his Stetson up to the top of his forehead and watched the herd catch up.

At forty-five, his job wasn't getting any easier, but despite the long hours, hard labor, and increasingly harsh conditions in both environment and business, James couldn't imagine doing anything else.

"Boss!" Luis Martinez rode up alongside Ken, both men covered in dust from watching the back of the herd. "How many are we circling up?"

"Two hundred for Calvert, fifty for John Stenner, and one hundred for Pete Hamper," James answered.

"I didn't think we closed the deal on Pete yet?" Luis asked.

"Mary had a call scheduled with him for this morning to straighten him out." James grinned. "Knowing my wife, I'd say the paperwork on that deal is already dry."

"You'd have thought the poor bastard would have learned his lesson by now," Ken said.

"You two handle the rest of the trip," James said. "And

make sure Mickey got everything unloaded from the shipment. He should be done by now, but I know his back's been bothering him, and the stubborn mule won't stay home to rest."

"You got it, boss." Luis nodded and then heeled his horse, Ken following suit.

James watched his ranch hands guide the herd toward the pens and helped a few stragglers in the back find their way before he led his mare to a nearby tree.

The temperature dropped ten degrees in the shade, and James tethered the horse to a nearby branch and let her graze while he stepped to the edge of the shade and gazed out onto the horizon.

The Bowers Ranch was one thousand acres of land that had been in James's family for the past four generations. His great-grandfather had bought the land when it was dirt cheap during the Great Depression.

It was a long hard road before they made any profit, but after the Japanese bombed Pearl Harbor to trigger the United States into the start of World War II, the demand for meat skyrocketed as the Army needed to provide food for their soldiers. And since then, through feast and famine, the Bowers Ranch had stood the test of time.

The west side of the property butted up against the highway, which put them in a prime position for transportation, and the train depot was only five miles east. The east border was marked by the Nueces River, which acted as the ranch's water source. The north end backed into thick woods teeming with game and helped protect the land's topsoil from any storms making their way from the northwest.

The long days were made more palpable by the beautiful scenery, and the work gave him a purpose. He wasn't just providing for his own family out here, but countless others. He was helping feed his country.

A breeze blew from the east, and James's mare whinnied

in distress. James walked over, placing both hands on the animal's mane. "Easy, girl."

It was rare for the horse to startle. James had been riding with her for the past two years, and the pair had settled into a nice rhythm. They could read each other's thoughts and moods, and James knew something was wrong.

One hundred miles east was San Antonio, where his wife and son had traveled this morning. Anxious, James untethered the horse and rode back toward the house, stealing glances toward San Antonio along the way. And while the sun was still shining and there wasn't a cloud in the sky, James sensed a darkness forming in the distance.

Grass and dust trailed the mare as James stretched the animal's legs, and the horse's hastened pace matched James's growing anxiousness.

Slowly, the house and the barn came into view on the horizon, along with the herd that Luis and Ken had brought in, but while the animals were in the pen, his farm hands were standing around in a circle. All three of them held up their arms, catching James's attention.

James headed toward his workers, the horse stopping near the group as he pulled back on the reins, a cloud of dust engulfing all of them.

"What happened?" James asked.

Mickey kept his hands on his hips, a light stoop in his upper back, but still the tallest among them. "Trucker never showed. Been waiting here all morning. I tried to call Luis, but my phone died."

A sour pit formed in James's stomach as he dismounted the horse. "Luis, Ken, either of your phones working?"

Both men had the devices in their hands, and they shook their heads.

"It was fully charged this morning," Ken said.

Gloved hands on his hips, James stared at the soil he'd worked on all his life, a northern breeze flapping his shirt and cooling the sweat that soaked his body. With his head tilted down, the brim of his cowboy hat concealed his worried expression from his crew.

"Start packing up," James said, leading his horse toward the barn.

"You sure, boss?" Luis asked. "There's still plenty to do—"

"I'm sure." James tied off the horse to one of the posts in the barn, but didn't remove the saddle.

While Luis and the other hands started finishing up with the herd as if they were done for the day, James headed toward the house, the same home that his family had lived in since the land was purchased all those years ago.

It was a two-story building, plenty of room for a large family. The wraparound porch provided views of the land, sunrises, and sunsets. The large windows could be opened to let the cool breeze flow through on a hot summer day. It was the perfect home to raise a family.

And while the integrity of the building hadn't been compromised since its construction, there had been a few updates.

James lined the top of the roof with floodlights that circled the entire house, and large solar panels had been installed. The electricity they generated were stored in batteries that could be used as back-up power in case of an emergency. Rain collectors were also set up on the roof and funneled water into large bins at the corners of the house.

The water wasn't potable, but it was used for watering the plants in the garden or for sewage. They had well water for all of their drinking, bathing, and cooking needs.

Inside the house, James paused for a moment, listening for the hum of the air conditioner, but heard none. He stared at the light switch in the house's foyer, which should have turned on the light above his head. But when he flicked it up, there was nothing.

The rest of the house was in the same condition. No television. No computer. No appliances. Everything was shut off. He found his cell phone on the kitchen counter, he never carried it with him in the fields, and saw that it was also off like Luis's and Ken's.

Finally, James walked toward the radio, the old device consisting of nothing but tubes with an antenna, very old technology.

The solar panels provided enough juice for James to turn it on, and when he scanned the channels, the static he heard confirmed what he didn't want to believe.

The back door to the kitchen opened, and Luis led Ken and Mickey inside.

James flicked off the radio and then turned toward his ranch hands.

"What's going on, boss?" Luis asked.

James shifted his weight from his left heel to his right and cleared his throat. "There's been an incident. Most likely an attack."

"By who?" Luis asked.

"I don't know who, but I know what they used," James answered. "It's called an EMP."

James went through the scenario, slow and calm, and studied the expressions of the men that had worked for his family for years. They all knew about his family's lifestyle choice, and he'd even managed to convince them to start prepping themselves. But he wasn't sure if any of them were prepared for what they were about to face.

"Nothing works?" Luis asked. "How is that even possible?"

"There are a few theories about how something like this could happen," James answered. "An EMP detonated in the atmosphere in the middle of the country, several smaller EMP devices detonated at strategic locations... I'm not sure about the how or the why, but I know what comes next. You need to go home, collect your families, and gather as much non-perishable food and water as you can, along with any medications that your family needs. If you have cash, use it at the store if they'll still take it, but do it quickly."

Ken and Mick exchanged a glance, but Luis kept his attention on James.

"How long?" Luis asked.

James looked at him, frowning.

"How long is this going to last?" Luis asked, elaborating.

"It depends," James said. "If the outage is restricted to something local like the San Antonio area, maybe a couple of months. The state? Maybe a year before things return to normal. But the whole country? An entire nation without food and water or basic necessities and with no way to communicate?"

The crew filled in the blanks for themselves.

"Go home," James said. "Take the horses. Be with your family tonight, tell them what I told you. And be back here tomorrow morning, same time, to start your shift. We can talk more about it then."

Ken frowned. "We're still working?"

"The world doesn't stop just because the power goes out," James answered.

Ken and Mick lingered for a little bit, the shock of the news still settling in their minds, but James marched past them and outside, heading back to the barn.

"And where are you going?" Luis asked, stepping from the backside of the house.

"I need to grab a few things," James answered, and then he untethered his horse, mounted, and galloped off toward the fields and to a place he'd hoped he'd never have to go.

One of the joys that James had always experienced when riding was the freedom of the open space. He could clear his mind and be present in the moment. But this ride was plagued with thoughts of the unknown. Despite his worries, the sun still shone in the sky and the grass still grew from the ground. And while James pushed the horse toward the center of the property, he mentally prepared himself for what was to come.

James and his family had practiced for something like this but up until today, everything was done in a controlled environment. And while James was confident in his skills and those of his family, no one could ever prepare for every possible outcome. Adaptability was key.

"Whoa, girl." James eased back on the reins, and the horse slowed to a trot.

At the center of the Bowers' ranch was nothing but open fields as far as the eye could see. Unless you knew what to look for, the small stack of brush blended seamlessly with the field, but beneath it was a last resort should his family ever need it.

James dismounted and let the animal trot and graze. He knew she wouldn't wander far, and he wouldn't be here long.

James walked to the middle of the brush and shoved his hand through one of the bushes, feeling around for the metal lever. He pressed it down and then heaved the hidden metal door open, the hinges groaning.

James stared down into the black hole and the ladder that dropped thirty feet into the soil. He descended into the darkness, his boots triggering a thud with every step down onto the next metal rung.

At the bottom of the ladder, James reached for a crank handle and turned it a few rotations, lighting up the bunker's interior as the kinetic battery charged with every rotation.

The bunker was shaped like a cylinder measuring one hundred feet in length and twenty feet wide. It would allow three individuals to survive for three months.

A second tank was buried less than one hundred feet away, providing a water supply, and the shelves that lined the walls contained MREs and other provisions.

But James walked past the food, water, and medical supplies, past the small bunks and the tiny corner carved out for entertainment and games, and reached for a bin near the air filters that helped with the ventilation chutes.

Among the normal dry storage boxes, James searched for a particular box, one that he had built just for this occasion. A Faraday cage.

It was a special container used to protect electronic devices from an EMP. Inside, James had placed a few minor electronics that would come in handy during the outage. Walkie talkies, flashlights, and a small tablet that Jake had wanted stored inside should the world end and he still wanted to play games.

Having what he needed, James returned to the ladder and glanced back on the cylinder tube. Most people viewed their lifestyle as something that was for fanatics, people who lived in mud huts or tents in the middle of the woods with nothing but the clothes on their back and a hunting knife. And while James happened to be good friends with some folks who trained for such a lifestyle, most preppers didn't fall into that same category. They came in all shapes and sizes. They lived in big cities and small towns. They were mechanics, soldiers, doctors, and teachers. They were anyone who understood that when push came to shove, you had to know how to take care of yourself. Because in the end, *you* were your most valuable resource.

He ascended the ladder, and the battery on the hand-cranked light finally ran out, sealing the bunker in darkness until it was needed again.

Topside, James quickly mounted his horse and headed back toward the house where he found his ranch hands already gone.

James headed upstairs, grabbing his personal go-bag from the closet, which housed a few essentials, including the map that contained the route he'd take to meet with his family.

Part of their preparation involved scenarios if the family had been separated. They figured the most likely scenario for a separation during a disaster would be during a trip to San Antonio for one of Jake's treatments, so they had a predetermined location where they would meet outside of the city in case communications were down. Like they were now.

The family ran the route a few times a year during different weather conditions to ensure they wouldn't run into any big surprises along the way. But that didn't eliminate every threat.

People would be confused and scared, desperate to survive. And desperation bred poor choices.

James flattened the map on the bed. He'd committed most of the trip to memory but with his family stuck in the city, he wasn't going to take any chances. He'd need to keep off the main roads because most people wouldn't have a working vehicle, and he'd stick out like sore thumb with his ride.

Confident about the route, James refolded the map and headed downstairs where Luis was there to meet him at the front door.

"I thought I told everyone to go home," James said.

"I am home," Luis replied. "You going after Mary and Jake?"

James passed Luis, his ranch foreman following. "This trip won't be easy."

"And you know this because you've been through it before?" Luis asked, stepping into the same stride as James on their way to the barn. "No way I'm letting you go out here alone."

James stopped, pressing a firm hand against Luis's chest. The pair had been like brothers ever since they were little. And while James had always considered himself the big brother, he knew that the man in front of him was stubborn as a mule.

"I can't let anyone slow me down," James said.

"I can keep up," Luis said.

Deep down, James knew that it wasn't a bad idea to have someone come along for backup. After all, it wasn't like James had eyes in the back of his head.

"You really think people are going to lose their cool over something like this?" Luis asked.

"Most people don't live like we do. Out here, we can make it on our own." James stopped, blocking Luis's path. "It will be violent, Luis."

Luis held James's gaze and then swallowed, that cocky arrogance sliding off of him. "All the more reason for you to have someone watching your back."

James grinned. "You really like learning things the hard way, don't you?"

Luis caught up to James and opened the other side of the

barn door. "It makes for a more lasting impression, and you know how short my memory is."

James walked to the back of the barn and heaved a stack of feed bags off the floor, which covered a hidden panel that James had installed a few years back. The property was marked with dozen of the secret caches.

Each cache was filled with different supplies. Some held food, others water, and a few were medicine and bartering items like whisky and cigarettes, soap and toothpaste, floss and deodorant. Items that people took for granted every day.

But the cache buried in the back of the barn was a different commodity, one that might grow to become the most important of anything that James had stored on the ranch. Weapons.

James lifted the first crate from the hole and set it on the ground with a heavy thud, and he used the crowbar that sat on top to pry the lid open.

Inside were an assortment of assault weapons. AR-15s, M-16s, and AK-47s, all of them fully automatic, with the capacity to fire dozens of rounds in seconds.

James picked the AR-15, the weapon most comfortable for him, and reached for the box of ammunition and started to load magazines as Luis approached.

"So how are we going to make it all the way to San Antonio? We taking the horses like the rest of the crew?"

James finished loading his weapon and then handed one to Luis as he put on a Kevlar vest and motioned for Luis to do the same. "It'd take too long on horseback." James walked over to a large object covered by a tarp. "I need to get Mary and Jake out of there fast." He flung the cover off, revealing the off-road, armored plated Humvee that his father had bought when he was a kid.

Luis shook his head, confused. "I thought you said nothing worked? No phones, no power, no cars?"

"Any vehicle made prior to 1974 didn't have a microchip

used for fuel injection." Inside the back of the Humvee were two go-bags, and James loaded some of the other rifles in the back along with the radios and a few spare cans of fuel. "This baby came off the line back in 1964." He slammed the rear hatch shut. "I started fixing it up a few years ago." He knocked on the doors and windows. "Armor plating. Bullet-proof glass up to fifty caliber rounds. Four-wheel drive. This thing can go anywhere." James walked around to the driver side, Luis heading to the passenger side.

James pressed down the clutch, and the old Humvee cranked to life. He revved the engine a few times, letting it warm up.

After a minute, James placed both hands on the wheel, staring out the barn doors through the thick plated glass, lowering his voice. "I'm not coming back without my family."

"Neither am I," Luis said.

James nodded and released the clutch.

4

"*Mom?*" Jake tugged at Mary's sleeve, and she finally peeled her eyes away from the chaos outside the hospital. "Should we go?"

Mary nodded, pulling Jake toward the parking garage, and found the entrance blocked from a wreck, the pair of drivers arguing over who was at fault.

Sunlight streamed in from the open sides of the parking garage, and Mary breathed a sigh of relief when she found her van unharmed.

"Keep an eye out for me." Mary lifted the rear door and then fumbled her fingers over the false bottom of the van's rear hatch. Inside was her bag filled with two days' worth of rations, plus their first aid kit.

Mary slid the pack's straps over her shoulders, removed what cash she had from her purse, and turned her back as she stuffed the money in her left boot. She then checked the .38 special revolver concealed in her right boot.

The weapon was fully loaded, but Mary didn't want to pull it out until it was absolutely necessary. The idea was to blend into the crowd and move amongst the masses until they were safely out of the city. With everything situated, she stood and shut the trunk's door.

Mary glanced around her and saw more people flooding into the parking garage, heading toward their vehicles, which she knew wouldn't work. And even if it did, there would be too many other vehicles clogging the road to make a clear path. People were stuck, and a crowd unable to get where they needed to go was always dangerous. "We're going to meet Dad at that spot. And if something happens to me—"

"I won't leave you," Jake said.

"You need to listen," Mary said, her voice calm. "If I get hurt, or I can't be moved, then you have to meet your father, okay? Promise me."

Jake nodded. "I promise."

Mary kissed Jake's forehead. "Good boy." She adjusted the pack on her back and led Jake out of the parking garage to a growing chorus of frustration and confusion.

But unlike the people she passed, Mary held the confidence of preparation and knowledge, and she would need every bit of it if she and Jake were to make it out of the city alive.

The children's hospital was clustered in a building complex right next to the I-10 and the I-35, and both were gridlocked in all directions.

In the heart of San Antonio's downtown, Mary and Jake were currently in the hotbed of what would soon turn into an explosive situation. And her first priority was to move them out of this densely populated area.

On their exit from the medical complex, Mary moved quickly beneath the overpass, knowing that they had to cover a lot of ground in a short period of time. While they moved, Mary kept a sharp eye out for anyone nearby. She wasn't sure how quickly things would turn violent, but she saw people slowly realizing the severity of the situation.

"My phone isn't working!"

"All of the cars are just stopped."

"The power's out, look, even the traffic lights aren't working."

"What the hell is going on?"

Buildings emptied as people walked out, everyone chatting amongst themselves, the groups growing larger and larger and leading towards one inevitable outcome. Panic.

The first crash of glass hushed the crowds. The second crash of glass triggered a scream, and the motionless crowd erupted in a one convulsing mob.

Bodies slammed against Mary, and she tightened her grip on Jake's hand. The bodies pressed tighter and tighter against them as she shouldered her way through the crowd. She looked behind her, the crowd so thick that she saw Jake's arm, but not his face.

With all her strength, Mary pulled Jake closer, searching for any path out of the stampede before she and her son were trampled.

A break in the crowd opened ahead, and Mary sprinted toward it before it closed, and she and Jake escaped into an alley.

Jake paused to catch his breath, but Mary forced him to keep moving.

"We can't stop," Mary said, her legs slowly turning to jelly from the exertion. "We have to keep moving."

The plan for their original escape route was to keep to the side streets and off the main drag. With the alley empty, Mary kept to their path, knowing that so long as they continued their journey west, she would be able to find her way out of the back alley maze.

Mary led them through the alleys for as long as she could, but eventually the paths led them back to the streets. Back to the chaos.

The road was congested with broken-down cars, most of

them abandoned, but a few motorists had their hoods up, still peeking into the engines to determine what was wrong.

However, the crowds had thinned. Mary remained close to the buildings and sidewalks where she could quickly duck for cover. After a few blocks without incident, Mary thought that they would make it, that they would be home free.

But those thoughts ended with the series of explosions nearby.

5

The Humvee bounced over the rough terrain, James avoiding the paved roads of the highway, cruising at a steady twenty-five miles per hour.

"How long is the drive?" Luis asked.

"We're about three hours away," James answered.

The sun shone down on the highway, reflecting off the cars that were at a standstill.

"You think the whole country is like this?" Luis asked.

"I don't know," James answered.

The Humvee hit a divot, bouncing the vehicle up and rocking the pair of men inside, the shocks absorbing most of the blow.

Luis sat quietly for a while, digesting James's words, and then he frowned. "Who would do something like this?"

"Our country has enemies, Luis," James said.

"Yeah, but this is some high-tech stuff, right?" Luis asked, growing excited. "I mean for some group of terrorists to have organized something like this, I just… I didn't think they'd be capable of something like this."

"Never underestimate an enemy," James said. "Anyone can

be a threat, no matter their background." He checked his heading and then pointed ahead. "We're almost there."

Luis leaned forward. "Is that Ruckins? I thought you said we were meeting your family outside of San Antonio."

"We will," James answered. "But we need to stop for fuel first. The cans I have in the back are only for an emergency. It's not enough for a full round trip."

Luis cocked an eyebrow up. "But if nothing is working, how are we supposed to get gas from the pumps? I mean, don't they run on computers and—"

"It'll be fine." James glanced at his partner. "I planned for this."

James slowed on his approach toward the town, which brought them closer to the highway where they caught the eyes of everyone that was stranded.

"I don't like the look of this," Luis said.

The rumble of the Humvee's engine emptied people from the shops and buildings along Ruckins' dusty main street. The congestion from the disabled vehicles forced the Humvee to a crawl, allowing the gathering crowds to move close.

Luis eyed the dozens of faces peering into their window. "Now I know how those tigers at the zoo feel."

James rolled the Humvee into the gas station without incident and then shut off the engine as he stepped out, staring back at the wake of bodies that had followed him to the fuel pumps. He studied the faces. They were scared.

Finally, one of the men stepped forward from the group, but James didn't recognize him. He was dressed in business attire, but he wore gloves, which James thought was odd. He gestured to the Humvee. "How come it's working?"

The group behind him leaned forward, as if James's answer was some kind of gospel.

"EMP," James said, seeing if the letters registered with anyone, but found no such understanding. "Electromagnetic pulse. It renders all microchip processors obsolete, and because nearly everything is run by computers, it's why you've seen everything shut down."

A quiet murmur spread through the crowd, everyone leaning into each other, all of them conversing about what it meant, all of them but the man who asked the question.

Instead, he walked up to James, the pair of men eye to eye, and he moved so close that James could smell the stench of the man's aftershave.

"Where are you going?" the gloved man asked.

"Away from here," James answered, unwilling to share anything with this stranger.

The man cracked a smile, exposing very white teeth, his gaze so intense that it looked like he was trying to burn a hole into James's forehead.

"James!" Larry Darvish hobbled out of the gas station, accompanied by his son.

Distracted by Larry, James missed the gloved man as he dissolved back into the crowd, their greeting leaving a sour aftertaste.

"Everything's set up out back." Larry was pushing sixty, but years of smoking had aged him as a man in his nineties. He could barely stand on his own two feet, and he was forced to wheel an oxygen tank around with him. Each time he coughed, it sounded like his lungs were disintegrating, and he leaned against his son to keep from collapsing.

Mavis Darvish was a few years younger than James, but the pair had crossed paths in high school on the football team. While his father looked two steps from the grave, Mavis was built like a bear. He was six foot six inches and pushing three hundred pounds. He nearly broke James's hand when he shook it. "Good to see you, James."

"You too, Mavis."

"Hey!" Larry shouted to the crowd still lingering. "If you ain't buying, then you're loitering."

"Oh, come on, Larry," Jon Carven said. "We just want to know what's going on."

"He told you what was going on," Larry said. "Standing around gaping like a bunch of dead fish isn't going to change that! Now, go on!" He stomped his foot, and the crowd slowly dispersed.

Ruckins didn't have a mayor, but Larry Darvish was the closest thing, and when he spoke, people listened.

"People," Larry said, covering his mouth as he coughed. "Soon as they see something they don't have, they want it. That's one thing that's never going to change, no matter if the power comes back on or stays off." He looked to James. "I had Mavis set up those hand pumps like you suggested." He inhaled some oxygen. "I'd hope we'd never have to use them."

"So it finally happened," Mavis said when they stepped inside the garage. "It's the end of the world."

"The world has ended before," Larry said, raising his oxygen mask to his face again, but paused and stared at James. "Our arrangement is still secure?"

James nodded. "You kept your end of the bargain, and I'll keep mine."

"Good." Larry exhaled relief, and then coughed into his palm a few more times. "Go on and help them, Mavis."

"Okay, Pop."

James and Luis followed Mavis around back to the hand pump. James had paid for the installation in exchange for free fuel, and he knew that it would come in handy should an EMP event occur. James had prepared a manual backup for everything that he might need should the power shut off. It was important to remember the old ways.

The three men all took turns working the pump until they had enough fuel to carry James the full round trip.

With the Humvee topped off, James hung back to speak with Mavis alone.

"How's he holding up?" James knew that Larry was on his

last leg. He had finally quit smoking, but it was a case of too little too late. And judging by how the man looked one step away from death, he wasn't sure how much more time the old man had left.

Mavis had always been a stoic man, never revealing much of what was happening behind his pair of almond-colored eyes. Mary had always described him as a gentle giant. It suited him.

"It's not good," Mavis said, hands planted on his hips as he shook his head. "We got those extra tanks like you suggested, so it'll last him a good while, but…"

James placed a hand on the man's boulder-like shoulder. "Just make sure he gets plenty of rest. And tell him to keep taking his meds if you can convince him. I know how he gets though."

Mavis laughed. "Saying that Pops is strong-willed would be an understatement."

"Listen, I need to stop and have a chat with Nolan," James said. "When we're done, I can have him come take a look at your dad if you want."

"Thanks, James, I'd appreciate that," Mavis said.

Luis finished loading the gas cans, and James instructed him to wait by the Humvee, telling him what he'd told Mavis about checking in with Nolan.

James walked down Main Street, ignoring the stares as he passed the storefronts. Nearly everyone here knew who James was, at least by name and his ranch, but aside from Larry and Mavis, he'd separated himself and his family from the rest of the town.

He wasn't sure why he'd done it. Maybe deep down, he always knew that a day like this would come and it would just be easier if he didn't have to be connected with so many people.

A bell chimed when James stepped through Nolan's front office door, and despite the chaos outside and the uncertainty that had gripped the community, James wasn't surprised to find Doris Huggins at the reception desk where she had sat for the past forty years looking after Nolan's day-to-day business needs.

"James." Doris brightened with a smile and adjusted her glasses as she pushed herself out of her chair and stepped around the desk to give him a hug. "Good to see you, boy."

"Good to see you too, Doris."

She laughed and then slapped James's stomach. She was a short woman, barely five feet with her shoes on, but even at seventy, she could get around just fine and her mind was sharper than folks half her age.

"Doc!" Doris shouted. "James is here! C'mon out of that darkness, you old hermit." She cackled and then squeezed James once more before returning to her chair, her gaudy necklaces jingling together as she moved. "He's been back there since the lights went out." Doris lifted the old ledger that she used to keep track of appointments. "That's why I never used that hunk of plastic." She gestured to the laptop that Nolan had given her a few years back as he tried to push her into the digital age. "I don't know why people even bother with those."

James only smiled. "You still have me down for my check-up next spring?"

Doris flipped right to the page on the first try. "Thursday morning at eight a.m. Bright and early." She smiled back.

"James." Doctor Nolan Springer emerged from the darkened hallway, holding an old gas lamp, which he set on Doris's desk. "What brings you in today? Not feeling under the weather, I hope?"

"I'm fine," James answered. "I just wanted to see how you guys were holding up, and to see if you could go and have a quick look at Larry."

Doris groaned, rolling her eyes. "Getting that man to visit

the doctor is like trying to get a little boy to eat his vegetables."

And while Doris didn't sound worried, Nolan frowned. "Is he all right?"

"I don't know," James answered. "But Mavis is worried, and I'm going more off of how he feels than how Larry feels."

Nolan nodded. "That's probably smart. Well, I can go and take a look at him, see what I can find, but he really needs to go and see a specialist." He paused, glancing up at the non-working light bulbs above him. "Though I'm not sure how much they'd be able to help him now."

"I know Mavis would appreciate it," James said. "You still keep your meds in the back?"

"Yeah, and good thing our shipment came in yesterday." Nolan exhaled in relief. "Lord knows it might be a while before we get any more refills."

"That's what I wanted to talk to you about," James said. "The power isn't coming back on anytime soon. And anyone looking to score meds who's lived in this town will know what I know. So make sure you keep your lock on it, and I would hide any of the high-powered painkillers or antibiotics. Those are going to be in high demand."

Nolan frowned and then stepped forward, and even Doris stepped from around her reception desk. "You really think this is going to last a while?" His voice was hushed.

"I do." James glanced back out onto the street and then retreated for the door. He'd spent enough time in the town already.

"I'll move the meds to the safe," Nolan said.

"Be safe out there, James," Doris said.

Back at the gas station, Luis was standing near the Humvee when James returned. "Everything all right?"

"For now." James walked past Luis and met with Mavis. "Doc will come take a look at him. Just make sure that Larry doesn't give him too much grief."

"I will," Mavis said. "Thanks, James."

James climbed back behind the wheel and started the Humvee, giving one final glance at Ruckins in the rearview mirror before he headed out of town, again sticking to the fields and off the main highway, which was becoming more congested with broken-down vehicles the closer they moved toward the city.

"You all right?" Luis asked.

James peeled his eyes away from the rearview mirror and then glanced ahead. "I don't know how long things are going to hold together."

Luis turned and looked at Ruckins, now nothing more than a small mound on the horizon behind them. "Maybe people will surprise you?"

But while Luis maintained his optimism, the rising plumes of black smoke on the horizon only doused more water on James's remaining flames of hope.

6

---

*I*t was the ringing in Mary's ear that woke her, combined with the sound of her son's voice breaking through the high-pitched whine from the explosions.

On her back, body aching, Mary sat up. At first she thought that something was wrong with her eyes, but the more she blinked, the more she realized that it was the world that had blurred, not her vision.

A cloud of dust cast a hazy filter over the city streets, limiting visibility to only a few feet in front of her face. Once on her feet, Mary grabbed hold of her son's hand and saw that he was covered from head to toe in dust.

Mary spun in half circles, disoriented from the explosion. Screams penetrated the clouds of dust, and she reached for her revolver, only to realize that she had lost it after the explosion.

Mary scoured the ground, stumbling around, bumping into bodies that emerged from the dust like apparitions and then evaporated a few feet later in the distance as they sprinted in random and chaotic directions.

Gunshots echoed in the distance, and Mary flinched,

ducking and bringing Jake down to the ground with her. She leaned them both up against a nearby vehicle, staying low, the gunfire growing louder. Closer.

Mary's heart pounded wildly, her lungs choked with dust. She scanned the ground for the weapon, not wanting to move forward into the unknown until she had the revolver.

Another gunshot. Another scream. The violence was made more terrible by the cloak of haze that had befallen the city. It sounded like the fighting was right on top of them, and just when Mary thought she was about to run out of time, she saw the revolver camouflaged in the grey dust.

Mary reached for the weapon, but another gunshot echoed and a body fell from the dust, landing on top of the revolver with a heavy thud. Mary recoiled her outstretched hand. The man's face was tilted toward Mary, his lifeless eyes locking with Mary's own.

Another gunshot broke Mary from her paralysis. She thrust her hand beneath the dead body, feeling around for the weapon, her fingertips scraping against the handle. She tried to pull it out, but it wouldn't budge.

The hammer was caught on the body's shirt. Mary pulled harder, breaking the corpse's hold on the weapon and ripping a piece of cloth from the shirt.

Not bothering to stay still any longer, Mary grabbed Jake's hand and pulled him through the cloud of dust that had descended upon the city and then picked a direction she believed was west.

"Just stay close, Jake." Mary kept the revolver aimed in front of her, finger on the trigger as she moved forward through the haze.

People sprinted past her and in front of her, the scene growing more chaotic.

Finally, at a cross street, Mary confirmed she was still headed in the right direction. She hastened her pace, but Jake tugged at her arm, slowing Mary down, and she turned to find him hunched over and coughing.

"Jake," Mary said, placing her hands on his shoulders and trying to pull him forward. "We need to move, we can't stay here."

"I can't... breathe." Jake clutched his chest, his eyes wide, his breaths raspy and painful. He dropped to his knees, and Mary knelt with him, finally lowering the gun.

Mary placed his hand over his chest, trying to calm him. "Jake, we need—"

Gunfire erupted behind her, and Mary turned just in time to watch the flashes from the muzzle of the rifles only a few feet away. The gunmen were aiming to the left of Mary and Jake, their figures nothing more than a hazy outline. There were at least six of them.

Mary lifted her son to his feet, holding him upright. "Jake, I need you to push through and be strong. Or we will die. Do you understand?"

Mary's tone was harsher than she intended, but she needed to make him see that this was life or death. He nodded, still struggling for air, but started moving forward.

Mary led them away from the figures in the dust, keeping low, using the vehicles in the street as cover. Bullets ricocheted off the vehicles, shattering glass that rained over their heads.

But as she pulled both of them through the lingering haze brought on by the explosions, the further they walked, the quieter it became. The gunfire faded, the screams dissipated and silence shrouded the street, but it wasn't until Jake yelped that she realized why.

Mary stared at the ground and saw the first body, face down, lifeless and Mary saw the wake of corpses that the terrorists had left behind.

Not wanting to disturb the dead, the pair carefully

stepped around the tangle of limbs and torsos that stretched the length of the road.

At the next crossroads, Mary turned west. She glanced back only once to see if anyone had followed her, but she saw nothing but the bodies and cars along the road.

Away from the explosion, the streets were barren, and Mary figured that the gunfire had sent everyone back into the buildings for cover, hoping to wait out the storm.

Seeing the skyscrapers along the street, Mary realized that they were still on the edge of the center of downtown. She'd forgotten how big the city was, and with the streets empty, dust settling on the broken-down cars in the middle of the road, she never thought that she could feel alone in a city this big.

Some of the cars had veered off the road when they'd lost power, crashing into storefronts, trees, benches, and signs. Wind kicked up the trash from overturned waste bins, spreading it across the streets and slapping against her shins.

She kicked an old magazine off of her bare leg, which was wet with some garbage, when she finally noticed the faces in the windows.

Noses and foreheads were pressed up against the dirty glass, staring at Mary and Jake as they walked down the street.

They approached another crossroads, one of the final intersections before the skyscrapers ended and they moved out of the city's epicenter. But with her attention on the faces staring at her from the first-floor windows, it was Jake who alerted her to the danger ahead.

"Mom!"

Mary pivoted, aiming the gun in the same motion, poised to shoot, but when she saw what Jake had seen, a breathless whisper escaped her lips. "Oh my god."

Two dozen gunmen, all of them with their faces

concealed with bandanas, carrying AK-47s, marched down the middle of the street like an army of death.

The gunmen turned their weapons at the storefronts, fingers pressed over the triggers, and unleashed hundreds of rounds into glass and flesh.

Mary pulled Jake down behind the nearest car and searched for the closest building. She found a door on the south side of the street in one of the skyscraper's lobbies, and she turned to Jake, surprised at how steady her voice sounded as she pointed to the door where they would run. "On three. Ready?"

Jake nodded.

"One. Two. Three!"

Mary pushed Jake forward, and she made the conscious effort to keep herself between the gunmen and her son, using herself as a human shield.

Jake reached the door first, Mary exhaling with relief as it opened without incident.

"Get inside! Go! Go! Go—" Mary was still on the run when the sting bit at her lower back, the pain hot and sharp. She only made it one step farther on her right leg before she collapsed, sliding across the hot tile as she passed through the door.

Mary's vision blurred when she hit the floor, and she watched Jake's feet skid to a stop as he spun around and returned to his mother's side.

"Mom?" Jake held her hand, tears squeezing from his eyes as blood stained her shirt.

"It's all right, sweetheart," Mary said, her voice cracking. She became cold and clammy, her complexion piqued. "You need to hide."

"I'm not leaving you."

But Mary saw the soldiers moving closer toward the building, killing anyone in their path.

Mary shoved Jake back, twisting her face into a snarl.

"Go!" She screamed with what strength remained. "Now, Jacob!" She watched him hesitate, but he finally sprinted deeper into the building.

With Jake gone, Mary used what strength she had left to aim the revolver at the door. She struggled to keep the revolver steady, but despite the concentrated effort, she dropped the weapon.

The pain in her lower back multiplied tenfold, and she laid her head back, finding it hard to breathe. Darkness descended, but before she completely lost consciousness, a pair of silhouettes hovered over her, and then she heard the screams drowned out by gunshots.

7

*O*nce James neared San Antonio's suburbs, he was forced to use the paved roads, his open fields now blocked by houses. James recognized the street names of the community of Rio Medina.

But the situation in the city looked to be deteriorating. The columns of smoke within the city had grown thicker and multiplied from two to six.

"Hey," Luis said. "They know how to take care of themselves. You guys have run drills like this before, right? Going in and out of the city?"

James nodded, adjusting his grip on the steering wheel as he mounted the curb to bypass a wreck, taking notice of the people stepping from their homes at the sight of the Humvee.

"How much farther?" Luis asked, anxious from the growing crowd.

James veered back onto the road. "We're close." He wanted to slam the accelerator down and plow through the busted vehicles. But he knew that it would cause more damage than good, and he still needed the Humvee to survive the trip home.

A fist smacked against the driver-side window, startling both James and Luis.

"Hey!" The woman's face had sharp features, the angles so extreme along her cheeks, chin, and nose that it looked like she could carve out her name on the glass. "You with the military?"

"No," James answered, his voice deep and loud as he made sure to keep the windows up. The doors were locked so there wasn't any chance of her being able to get inside, but the longer she walked along with the Humvee, the closer other people started to approach, boxing the vehicle in.

"Where are you going? Do you know what's happening?" The woman stayed close to the window, her face sweaty and red from the sun. She glanced into the back. "You got any water in there?"

"James." Luis spoke with a sense of foreboding, and James looked over to find another six people walking along the side of the Humvee, all of them peering into the vehicle, searching for what they might have inside.

The woman pounded her fist on the window, this one angrier.

"You think you're better than us?" the woman shouted, and the growing crowd murmured the same discontent.

With the amount of blockage ahead, James knew that he couldn't drive his way out of this until the road cleared, but he didn't want to lead these people to the rendezvous location. Nor did he want any of the residents to be harmed.

"Come out of there, you coward!" The woman spit on the window, and that one simple act triggered the rest of the crowd to break out in a frenzied attack, pounding their fists against the glass, kicking and stomping and rocking the vehicle from side to side as best they could, but it was too heavy to flip, even with the large crowd.

Luis leaned back from the window as rocks were tossed

against the glass, along with anything else that the bystanders could pick up and throw with their hands.

"They won't get through the armor," James said, his voice remaining steady in the chaos that surrounded him, though he felt his heart rate quicken.

Up ahead James had spied an open lane, and it would give them enough open space to put some distance between themselves and the growing mob. James just hoped that none of them decided to step in front of the vehicle when that happened. It wasn't a choice he was ready to make. Not yet.

James ignored the angry faces peering into the windows, still screaming, still beating their fists against the glass and doors, though most of them had stopped throwing things at the vehicle once they realized they weren't going to break through.

It was all about intimidation now. They wanted James to know that they were still there, that they were still a threat. Nearing the end of the road, James sped up, forcing the mob to follow in a jog, and the increased speed caused most of the residents to end their pursuit. All save for the woman who first approached.

The woman landed one last punch on the window before the road opened completely and James pulled away, the engine rumbling with ferocity as he stole one last glance in the rearview mirror of the mob.

James saw the woman's brazen anger give way to fear, to the cold hard truth of knowing that they wouldn't be able to survive on their own.

Years from now, James would remember those faces. Not necessarily the individual details of each person, but the collective energy of everyone that chased him. It was heightened by fear and loss and pain and uncertainty. It was the petulant anger of a child who didn't understand why they were being left behind.

James kept their pace up, the Humvee scraping the sides

of a few vehicles as they passed. Luis tensed, slamming his foot into the imaginary brake in the floorboard.

James swerved down side streets and over yards, turning left and right on a serpentine path to ensure that the mob wouldn't find them, and then finally, when they were out of the neighborhood, James slowed, confident they were out of harm's way.

"Christ," Luis said, catching his breath, relaxing once the Humvee slowed down. "I think I saw my life flash before my eyes."

"There," James said, pointing to a large abandoned building in the forgotten and bankrupt industrial sector outside of San Antonio. "That's where we'll meet them."

"Place looks like it could use a new coat of paint," Luis said.

James had bought the building a few years ago, and while the outside looked dilapidated, the barbed wire fence that protected it was brand new, along with the gate's chain and lock.

James gave Luis the key, who unlocked it, and then James passed through, letting Luis close and relock the gate after he was inside. He drove around to the north side of the building where there was a garage door and gestured for Luis to open it.

The inside of the building was an open floor plan, like a warehouse. The windows were high on the walls next to the ceiling, and aside from the garage door, there were only two other entrance points into the rectangular-shaped building.

James shut off the engine and stepped out of the Humvee, Luis shutting the garage door behind them.

"They haven't gotten here yet?" Luis asked, stating the obvious.

"It's at least at six-hour hike from the hospital to here," James answered, still scanning the darkened interior as if his wife and son would be hiding from him. He shook his head and walked back to the Humvee. "It took us three hours to get here, but I'm sure they knew about the EMP blast before we did. Hopefully they'll be here soon."

While they waited, James refueled the Humvee, wanting to be able to head out at a moment's notice and not stop until they made it home. After that, he checked the weapons and his rations, but when the housekeeping was finished, James became restless.

Restlessness had always plagued James Bowers's life. At times it drove him wild, and most of the time it drove his wife insane, but it was always there, always prodding him to get up and do something, to keep moving, because James Bowers could do anything but sit still.

He paced the inside of the warehouse, checking the pocket watch that was one of the old wind-up devices that belonged to his grandfather. It was given as a present from his great-grandmother to his great-grandfather after he purchased the ranch.

Unable to stand the silence of the warehouse any longer, James walked to the ladder on the west end, taking a set of binoculars with him.

"Where are you going?" Luis asked, his voice echoing in the empty space.

"Stay with the Humvee," James answered.

James climbed the ladder attached to the inside wall, which led to a small panel at the top of the roof that could be removed.

Sunlight seeped into the open panel as James climbed onto the roof. He walked to the roof's edge, the old warehouse giving him a bird's eye view of the surrounding area.

James turned toward the neighborhood where they'd driven through the mob and found that most people had returned to their homes, then turned his attention toward the city.

It was an eerie sight, watching the smoke drift upward

and into the blue sky, but what was more concerning was the silence. He heard no screams, no sirens, no signs of life at all. There was over a million and a half citizens in that city.

James lowered the binoculars, thinking about what his wife and son might be caught in. He started to think about the enemy who did this to their country, crippling hundreds of millions in the blink of an eye. He thought about what caused those pillars of black smoke. Bombs? Fires?

After ten minutes, James found no sign that his family was close, and he lowered the binoculars and rested his elbows on the raised perimeter wall of the roof.

He was about to head back inside when a bright streak of red broke through the smoke, cutting across the blue sky.

James's first instinct was to sprint back to the ladder, but he forced himself to stay put and tracked the red flare to the location where it was set off. The binoculars got him close, but it wasn't exact. The flare was just meant to give a general vicinity. But it was also a signal that meant Jake and Mary were in trouble.

Once James located a landmark nearby the source of the flare, he lowered his binoculars and then shimmied down the ladder and back inside the warehouse.

James jumped the last four rungs and landed with a heavy smack from his boot heels that caught Luis's attention as James sprinted toward the Humvee.

"What's wrong?" Luis asked.

"I'm going into the city." James slipped one of the back-packs in the trunk over his shoulders and secured it tightly.

Luis watched James for a moment and then reached for the other bag, but James stopped him.

"No," James said.

"Why the hell not?" Luis asked.

"Because I need someone here to protect and watch the Humvee. It's the only way we're going to make it home, and I don't need it destroyed or stolen." James reached for the AR-

15 and loaded a magazine, then he grabbed the radios he pulled from the Faraday cage and handed one to Luis, keeping the other for himself. "The range on these are shit, but we should be able to communicate to one another when we're within a half mile. I'll be on channel one."

Luis jogged to catch up to James before he made it out the door. "Why not just use the Humvee? Get in there quick and get out—"

"The roads will be too clogged, and the moment people see that I have a working vehicle, I'll be swamped." James stopped at the door, facing his friend. "You saw what happened back in that neighborhood."

Luis placed his hands on his hips and nodded. He wiped the sweat from his forehead and then looked back at the Humvee before finding James's eyes again. "You sure you want to go into that place alone? I know I'd feel better having your back out there. I think you would too."

"I'd be able to move quicker on my own," James said.

Unlike James, Luis had put himself through extensive training, logging countless hours at the gun range. Luis was a good man, but he wasn't ready for what James was about to encounter. "Whatever you do, don't leave."

Luis spread his arms wide, his shirt already starting to get soaked with sweat. "Where else would I rather be?" He smiled. "Stay safe out there, brother."

James opened the door, stepping out into the sunlight as he prepared himself mentally for what came next. The fact was, in order to save his family, he might have to end someone else's life. But he wasn't leaving without his family. No matter what.

---

8

*W*ith both of his gloved hands gripped firmly over the assault rifle, James moved swiftly and purposefully through the clogged city streets. But unlike during his time in the Humvee, no one stopped to chat, not with the rifle in plain view.

It was dangerous to display the rifle so blatantly, because James wasn't sure the average police officer would be able to differentiate James from the bad guys. They would only see him as a man with a deadly weapon, moving tactically through city streets.

Every storefront window that James passed was smashed, glass littered the ground, the store's goods strewn about the sidewalk like guts. If people weren't sprinting up and down the street in some random direction, then they were running into the open stores, grabbing anything they could carry.

No one stopped them, not even the store owners. It had been only hours since the EMP had been detonated, and society had completely devolved.

Storefronts weren't the only thing that was looted. Nearly every car that had been stranded on the road had its windows smashed, or their doors were open, the insides looted for whatever they could find in the glove box or the center console compartments. Footprints covered the hoods and roofs of the cars.

Like the people, the summer heat was trapped in the city, and James was soaked through to his undershirt, sweat dripping from his forehead and stinging his eyes. He swiped at it angrily but never lost his focus. He was at least another hour from the location of the flare, and while he would eventually need to stop and rehydrate, he'd push himself to the brink. Time was working against his family.

"HELP! PLEASE HELP!"

The bloodcurdling cry broke through James's tunnel vision and he glanced left down an alleyway, pausing at the sight of a woman being knocked around and then pinned up against the wall, two men holding her arms flat, while a third had shimmied her pants and underwear down at her ankles.

The sight was so horrendous, so disturbing, so unconceivable in the bright of day, that it took James a few moments to realize what was happening. And even more concerning was the fact that James was the only person that stopped, as more and more people passed the alleyway, ignoring the woman's screams. But James couldn't.

Before he realized it, James was already halfway down the alley. He said nothing on his approach, and the three animals pinning the woman down were too engrossed by their own sickening pleasure that they didn't notice him.

"Don't go too rough on her, Sal, I want to make sure I have— GAH!"

James struck the back of the skull of the closest man to him, the force quick and powerful, the contact between rifle and bone eliciting a nasty crack before the man collapsed to his knees, and the other two turned toward James with the surprised expression of teenage boys that had been caught doing something they knew to be wrong.

"Fuck!" The man with his pants down had a mangy beard

and greasy bangs stuck to his forehead. When he tried to reach for his pants and pull them up to run, James caught him in the forehead with the butt of the rifle as well, sending him down on his ass in the same dazed confusion as the first man.

The third man had already started to run down the alleyway, but James flipped the rifle around and brought the man between his crosshairs. He squeezed the trigger and something crashed into his right arm, causing the bullet to miss. James turned, surprised to find that the woman who'd been under attack was the one who'd stopped him.

"No!" Red-faced, sweating, and still trembling, she struggled to pull her pants up, both of her spaghetti straps slipping from her shoulders. "Please, no."

James caught his breath, staring at the pair of men still in a foggy, pain-induced haze as they wallowed over the hot concrete, and lowered his weapon.

The woman walked over to the pair of attackers on the ground and swung her leg back as far as it would go and then landed a square shot to each of their groins that triggered a yelp so high-pitched that only dogs could hear it.

The woman spit on both of them and then stumbled to James's side, staring at them with a contempt reserved for the vilest of living creatures. "Remember that! Both of you!" Her face was still red, but she managed to fix her hair as she looked back to James. "Thank you." She leaned forward and kissed him on the lips, the gesture more ceremonial than passionate, but again James blushed.

With both rapists down for the count, James turned back for the road.

"Wait!" the woman shouted, jogging to catch up with James before he reached the front of the alley. "Let me come with you—"

"I can't help you. I need to find my wife and son. You would only slow me down. If you have a place to stay outside of the city, then go there now." James reached around to the side pouch of his pack with his left hand and removed a small blade that he kept as a spare. He flipped the blade around so the handle faced the woman. "Take it."

The woman regarded the knife as if it might hurt her, but eventually she slowly curled her fingers around the black composite handle and removed it from James's grip.

"You flash that the next time someone starts hassling you," James said. "Be direct and aggressive with them. Most people will just turn and run. But if they don't, then you can't hesitate."

The woman turned the blade over in her hand, becoming more familiar with it, staring at it with a sense of awe.

"Why did you stop me?" James asked.

The woman's face was slack, but her eyes were wide, a rich dark-brown color. "Because you were going to kill him."

"But they were going to rape you," James said. "They had you pinned down—"

"And you stopped them," the woman said. "You don't look like a man who enjoys killing. So you should probably stay that way." She took one last glance down the alleyway at the pair of men who were still clutching their privates on the ground and then headed west, the same direction where James had just come from.

Once the woman disappeared, more screams pulled James's attention deeper into the city, and he aimed his rifle to the east, where he heard the distant pop of gunfire. He moved toward the danger without hesitation, but when he neared an intersection blocked with wrecked vehicles, more gunfire transformed a nearby car into Swiss cheese.

James hit the pavement, and glass from the car's windows rained over his head and shoulders. He hadn't realized the shooters were so close, but when the gunfire died down, James slowly glanced through the now-windowless doors and saw a masked enemy marching down the street.

James ducked back below the cover of the sedan. He needed to move, and he knew he could use the vehicles as cover.

James squat-walked to the trunk of the sedan and then hurried toward the next closest vehicle. The progress was slow until he heard shouts followed by gunfire that chased him behind a mini-van.

James cursed beneath his breath and retreated to the mini-van's rear bumper as the voices grew louder. They were speaking a foreign language, but James couldn't pinpoint the accent.

Outnumbered, James knew that evasion was still his best chance of survival. But when he pivoted toward the van's bumper, he noticed something in his peripheral view.

A young boy peered through one of the van's busted windows. With his head covered by a blanket, James could only see the bright blue of his eyes.

Immediately, James knew that his plans had changed. This was someone he couldn't leave behind.

James jiggled the door handle, but it was jammed. If he tried to reach for the boy over the broken window, then both of them would be exposed to the gunman's fire, which were getting closer.

"Hey!" James whispered as loud as possible without the masked terrorists picking up his voice. "If you can hear me, I'm going to count and when I reach three, I want you to climb out of the back window. But you need to be quick."

James waited, his heart pounding in his throat as he prayed the boy heard him.

"One." James positioned himself at the edge of the van, rifle at the ready and finger on the trigger. He would emerge from cover and then shoot as many of them as he could to distract them while giving the boy time to climb out of the van.

"Two." At the very least James would be able to provide a

distraction, giving the boy enough time to flee, even if he was shot down. And he was banking on the gunfire to scare him to sprint.

"Three." James emerged from the back of the van, targeting the first group of three masked terrorists weaving between the cars like they were tall grass out in the plains.

None of them had their weapons up in a firing position when James emerged, and all it took was one squeeze of the trigger to bring down the first man and send the next for cover while they fired blindly in James's vicinity, their bullets missing by a mile.

With the enemy cowering, James glanced over and saw the boy had climbed out. He scooped the boy up in one arm and sprinted down the street.

More screams preceded the echo of gunfire that chased James between the alleys of vehicles as he searched for a way out of the danger.

a sour taste flooded Mary's mouth, and a throbbing ache in her lower back was accompanied by a tingling sensation in her legs. She tossed and turned for a while, lost in darkness, but when she opened her eyes, she still couldn't see.

Mary panicked, jostling on the floor until several pairs of hands calmed her down and silhouettes were thrust into her field of vision.

"Shhh," a voice said. "You need to be quiet."

Mary blinked, rapidly, hoping that her eyes would adjust so she could see the features of the people hovering above her. But while she couldn't see them, she did calm down.

"You've been shot," a voice said. "Your son is—"

"Jake?" Mary lifted her head, but pain pulled her back down.

"You need to take it easy," the voice said.

A door opened and light was cast inside, momentarily illuminating the faces above her. Two women and one man. She caught only glimpses of them. The man, the one who was speaking, looked Asian. One of the two women was Asian, and the other was black.

"Mom?"

Mary whimpered at the sound of her son's voice, and then cried when she felt his arms wrap around her neck. "Thank God you're all right." He was warm, or maybe she was cold. But either way, she was thankful he was alive.

"Are you okay?" Jake asked. "I poured the powder on your back. There wasn't an exit wound. I know that's bad."

Mary grimaced, and then fragments of what happened came back quickly. She remembered that she'd been shot on their way inside the building.

"Those men," Mary said, her mouth suddenly dry. "Did they—"

"We managed to get you to the back room." It was the Asian man speaking. "It's a break room for building staff."

Jake helped his mother drink from a water bottle, and then gave her a quick recap of the events that transpired after she was shot.

When she blacked out on the tile, Jake had tried to pull her himself, but she was too heavy, and with the wound, he didn't think it was best to drag her.

Stevie, the Asian male that Mary got a quick look at when the door opened, had been stuck on the first floor when the tenants on the second floor had blocked the door to the stairs. And his pass only worked on the first two, so he ran here, grabbing Maya and Zi on the way over.

The trio was heading for the closet when Maya saw Mary get shot, and then they rushed over to help them get to cover before the gunmen finished them off.

"Thank you," Mary said, her gratitude overwhelming. She raised a shaky hand and gently pressed it against Jake's cheek, which he cupped with his own hand. "You did good."

"So what do we do now?" Zi asked, her hair starting to take shape like a cloud in the darkness. "Do we just stay here?"

Jake turned to his mother, smiling. "I fired the flare from the roof, just like we're supposed to when we got stuck."

"You went to the roof?" Mary asked. "When?"

"It's been at least an hour," Stevie answered.

"How long do you think it will take before Dad finds us?" Jake asked.

"What building are we in?" Mary asked, avoiding answering Jake's question and hoping the boy didn't notice.

"The TD Waterhouse building," Maya answered. "It's a mix of businesses and apartments. We all work in some of the shops on the first floor."

Mary shut her eyes, trying to concentrate on how far they made it from the hospital. They walked for at least an hour, and if she'd been passed out for an hour, that would barely give James enough time to arrive at the rendezvous site to see the flare.

"Mom, how long do you think it will take before Dad comes and finds us?" Jake asked, repeating the question with urgency.

Mary knew that the flare was meant more to let the other party know that they were in danger, and while it did help narrow down the search area, it was far from being pinpoint accurate.

"Mom!" Jake screamed, his voice cracking from the strained effort. "When is Dad coming?" It was the fear that was starting to break through now, as hope burned out.

"Jake—" Mary reached for his hand, but he pulled it away, retreating to a corner of the room where he kept his back to her.

"Maybe you should just give him a minute," Zi said.

"Right." Mary adjusted herself on the blanket and pillow that they'd laid down as a buffer from the tile. "One of you should send another flare up. There should be more in the bag."

"I can go," Stevie said. "I know the building well, and I

went with the boy earlier." He walked to the corner and grabbed the flare. "I'll be back in a bit."

The door opened, the room once again flooding with light, allowing Mary to get a better look at Zi and Maya's faces before they were shrouded in darkness again. She was surprised to see how young they were.

"Um, we didn't know what to do with this." Maya slid something across the tile, which scraped and then bumped into Mary's hand.

It was the revolver. Mary lifted it, her hand still shaking, and then lost the grip, sending it to the ground, causing the other two women to jump.

"It's fine," Mary said, looking to her son, who was still huddled in the corner. "It's going to be difficult for my husband to find us. Especially in this room."

"I didn't think it was a good idea to move you," Zi said. "You could have internal injuries." She cleared her throat, trying to explain. "I'm going to nursing school. Night classes. I saw the prescription in your purse and I wasn't sure—"

"It's okay," Mary said before the woman revealed too much. "Thank you."

Mary had already rifled through the options. With the pain in her body, she knew that she wouldn't be walking anywhere, not even with assistance. She couldn't sit up, so a wheelchair wouldn't work.

"Jake, do you remember those medical drills we did last spring?" Mary asked.

"Yes," Jake answered.

"I need a stretcher. It's the only way you're going to be able to move me."

"I can help him look for supplies," Zi said. "We have a bunch of stuff in the kitchen."

"That's good," Mary said, nodding quickly. "Jake, take the revolver with you."

Jake picked up the weapon and led Zi to the door, disappearing like the light from the room.

It was quiet after they left, and Mary couldn't tell if Maya was staring at her in the darkness or not. The pain gripping her body was keeping her busy though. She might slip back into unconsciousness if it kept it up at this pace.

"Are we going to die?" Maya's voice was quiet and solemn, and it sounded like it was coming from a little girl as opposed to the grown woman in the room with Mary.

Mary saw the woman was scared, but she wasn't sure she had the strength to give the woman a pep talk. "Do you have family in the city, Maya?"

"Just Stevie," she answered, maintaining that sheepish tone. "He's my husband."

"How long have—Shit." A muscle spasm caught in the left side of Mary's ribs and she palmed the spot where it was originated, breathing quickly and heavy until it passed.

Mary exhaled in a series of exhausting coughs until she grew so tired that she couldn't keep her eyelids open anymore, but the aching in her back refused to let her rest.

"Why is this happening?" Maya asked, silently sobbing through the question, which Mary was unsure was directed at her, or if the woman was just asking it aloud.

Mary suspected that everyone was asking that question, trying to determine just how this could happen to them, in their city, in their state, in their country. How could everything just stop?

Mary opened her mouth, almost telling her about the ranch, about their supplies, about how they had enough to take care of her and Stevie, but she stopped herself. She knew that they already had their hands full with the ranch workers and their families. Not to mention the number of people that James had made deals with. They had all worked so hard to prepare for the storm. And while they didn't wish anyone ill, they couldn't fit everyone on the ark.

More light flooded the room and Stevie returned. "I did

it." Panting, he crouched by Mary's side. "Things are getting worse out there." He sniffled and wiped his brow. "There's still a lot of shooting around our building. I think those guys with the guns are fortifying their position."

Maya whimpered.

"Do you think that your husband is really going to be able to get through all of that?" Stevie asked. "It's like a warzone out there."

Mary grinned, cracking her eyes open. "He'll come. James doesn't know how to quit."

The pair waited in silence until both Zi and Jake returned.

Jake had found some old drywall that they could reinforce with some of the sturdier legs of chairs they'd been able to detach. It was a crude set-up, but if they reinforced the drywall with enough of the steel pieces, then it should hold Mary. She wasn't that heavy. Not yet at least.

While Jake instructed Stevie, Maya, and Zi on how to tie the most secure knots to attach the steel pieces to the back of the drywall so it wouldn't buckle, Mary busied herself with trying to manage the pain that was becoming increasingly difficult to handle.

But the pain was a welcome distraction, because it didn't allow her to obsess over what might be happening to the life inside of her. A life that she hadn't told her family about, because she had been waiting for the right time. She had to stay alive, not just for herself, but for the child she hoped was still growing inside.

Voices echoed from the lobby and all eyes drifted to the barricaded door.

Maya whimpered, and she quickly covered her mouth with both hands as Stevie held her shoulders, pulling him into his chest. Zi retreated to the farthest back corner, crouching low into a ball and brandishing what looked like a knife, the steel blade glowing in the darkness.

Mary took the revolver from her son and aimed it at the door. She knew that they were grossly unprepared to face the enemy in the streets, and she knew that these men wouldn't be deterred by the flash of a pistol or the threat of violence. These men *were* violence. They were killers, murderers, thieves.

Voices and footfalls grew louder on the enemy's sweep through the first floor. Mary adjusted her grip on the revolver, hoping that she'd have enough strength to at least prolong the inevitable. To give them one fighting chance before they were gunned down.

The voices stopped just outside the door. The exchange was quick, the back and forth causing Mary's stomach to tighten, and the pain in her back worsened.

The door handle jiggled, the bodies on the other side grunting in frustration. A heavy, angry thud from the person elicited a shudder through the entire room.

The door started to shake more violently, the shouts and demands on the other side growing considerably tenser and more hurried.

The door buckled, the table that they used to brace the door nearly rattling out of place.

Jake dropped to his mother's side, lying alongside her, and Mary raised the revolver toward the door, a surge of strength providing the necessary grit to perform her last stand.

But before Mary could make the decision to fire, the pounding ended and the voices faded from the door.

Everyone exhaled relief, and Mary relaxed, lowering the weapon. She knew that they couldn't stay any longer, and she wasn't willing to leave her son's future to chance.

"Mom?" Jake asked, sitting up. "You smell that?"

The rest of the room leaned forward, and when Mary finally noticed the fumes, there was already smoke coming through the cracks of the door.

10

*D*renched in sweat from the run, the heat, and carrying the boy in his arms, James collapsed to his hands and knees nearly ten blocks from his contact with the enemy.

The little boy stood off to the side, staring at James with a sense of calm wonder. He hadn't cried the entire run, and even now, standing in the middle of a warzone with a stranger, the boy showed no signs of fear.

Once James managed to collect himself, he stood and adjusted the rifle in his hands, glancing around to get his bearings. He had run in the right direction, keeping his wits about him even under the stress of the fight.

James glanced up at the skyscrapers. The building where he saw the flare was close. But with the windows above, he was exposed for an ambush, and he quickly pulled himself and the boy under the cover of a concrete overhang.

James spied the blood on the boy's shirt and shorts, along with some specks on his cheeks, and he examined the boy for any injury. "Are you hurt?" It wasn't the boy's blood. "What's your name?"

The boy stood there, gazing at James with those blue eyes.

With the heat of the day they looked cold as ice, which was a stark contrast to the boy's fiery red hair that was tangled and messy.

"Was that your family's van?" James asked. "Do you live in the city?"

The longer the boy's silence dragged on, the more the city deteriorated around them. It wouldn't be long before the final implosion buried millions under a pile of rubble and dust, leaving anyone that survived to pick through the wreckage of the collapse.

"My parents died." The boy spoke softly, speaking such horrible news with such a fragile innocence. "The bad people killed them."

James brushed his fingers through the boy's tangled mane. "I'm sorry."

James removed a small wraparound Kevlar vest from his pack. The device was originally designed for a quick means of providing extra cover over any exposed areas of the neck and face, which were prone for targets by sniper fire, but the material was so bulky that it restricted movement of the head and made a soldier more susceptible to ambush, so it was rarely used in the field.

But the device fit perfectly around the torso of a child, and James knew that the boy wouldn't need to be mobile, not so long as James carried him.

"What's your name?" James asked, securing the device and making sure it wouldn't slip once they started moving. "I know you have one of those."

The little red head stared down at the Kevlar strip that James had nearly finished securing. "Teddy."

"Like Roosevelt," James said, smiling as he finished up with the Kevlar. "You know, he was a very brave man. Led a group of soldiers into battle. He was fearless."

Teddy looked up, running his hands over the material that now stretched from his chest down to just below his waist. Aside from putting the boy into a bulletproof box, this was the best way to help keep him safe. But a bullet could still do considerable damage to the boy even without penetrating the Kevlar. Depending on the caliber of the bullet, it could shatter his ribs, bruise his organs, and cause internal bleeding.

James glanced around, spotting random people jogging through the wreckage of the city. From what he'd seen, most of the big groups had dissipated, leaving behind the few lone wolves in the streets.

James slung the rifle's strap over his shoulder before he scooped the boy up with his left arm and grabbed his pistol with his right hand. He flicked the safety off the big .45 ACP. Most folks would have difficulty handling the big pistol with one hand, but James had practiced for just such an occasion.

James moved forward, paying close attention to the activity in his peripherals as he maneuvered through the streets to the next intersection where he veered right, his head tilted up as he searched for the building where he saw the first flare.

It was nearly time for another one to pop up, knowing that they would keep to a schedule of continuing to fire a flare every hour until their rescue, or until they couldn't fire them anymore.

But James forced those thoughts out of his head. He wasn't going to allow himself to get sucked into that vortex of doubt and unanswerable questions. Until he found them, he couldn't guess their condition, so he fought those doubts with hope.

James watched the sky, which had darkened from the huge columns of smoke, until he saw a streaking flare of red, challenging the dark haze that had engulfed the city, and this time he spotted the rooftop from which it spiraled into the sky.

The sight of the flare provided a boost of energy, and

James sprinted toward the building where it had been fired from. But on his run, he heard a growing roar coming from behind him.

James turned at the waist to find another flood of people sprinting down the street, pushed forward by the roar of gunfire, sending the horde into a crazed stampede, charging at full speed and ready to trample anyone in their path.

James faced forward, focusing on the evasion of the coming storm. The building where the flare had been shot was on the corner of an intersection up ahead, and he saw smoke spweing out of the sides from some of the broken windows.

"No." The disbelief departed James's lips in a whisper, and his heart skipped a beat when he saw the masked terrorists flee from the bottom of the building, three of them standing back and staring at the building as it caught fire.

James aimed his path directly at the three men standing near the closest entrance, and he saw that they had their guns aimed at the exit. They were smoking people out.

Still wild with adrenaline, James forgot that the boy was still in his arms and skidded to a stop, his gaze shifting between the fire raging ahead of him and the wide-eyed boy in his arms.

James couldn't take the child into the building with him - the smoke inhalation would kill him. But leaving him out in the open like this was just as dangerous, especially with the stampede of people sprinting toward them, chased by more men with guns.

James scanned the street and found a truck that hadn't been torn to shreds with windows too high for fists or crow-bars to smash. And it also meant that the windows were too high for anyone to see inside.

James lifted Teddy into the truck, the boy still sporting that wide-eyed stare, but remaining completely still. The kid was like pond water on a breezeless summer day. "Stay there, and don't make a sound until I get back." He slammed the door shut, not bothering to wait for a response, and gripped the pistol with both hands, allowing him better aim and control as he moved to the building.

Between the roar of the crowd behind James and the growing crackle of the fire ahead of him, the three masked terrorists couldn't hear James's heavy footfall or even his screams as he aimed for the back of their heads on the run, the first two shots missing wide left as he adjusted for shooting on the move. But when he planted his foot and readjusted his aim, the first two men were down before the third had a chance to spin around. The first bullet smacked into the gunman's chest, and the second connected to his left cheek and dropped him permanently to the floor.

The heat blasted James before he even made it to the door. Black smoke billowed out of any exit it could find, rising into the sky and adding to the orange haze that had engulfed all of San Antonio.

But James never broke stride as he raised the bandana to cover his nose and mouth and sprinted headfirst into the fire raging through the building.

The heat was so intense that James thought his skin was melting from his bones, and despite the bandana that he placed over his mouth and nose, he still choked from the smoke and oxygen-starved atmosphere.

"Jake! Mary!" James kept low to avoid the smoke, then maneuvered around the flames, the ceiling dripping liquid fire. "Mary! Jake!" He screamed, but the roar of the fire drowned out his voice, and it was so hot that all of the moisture in his throat had burned away, making it difficult to breathe, let alone speak.

James followed the natural pathway from the door deeper into the building and holstered the weapon, knowing that whatever he'd encounter next couldn't be fixed by bullets. With both hands raised to fend off the encroaching flames,

James's vision blurred, drifting back and forth through the haze of the fire that distorted his vision like the heat coming off the black asphalt during a hot summer day.

It grew so hot that the fire sucked the moisture from James's eyes, drying them like raisins as he pushed deeper into the building until he dropped to his knees, collapsing from exhaustion, his lungs clogged with smoke.

James retched on the floor, thrusting forward with his palms and striking the melting tile with the palms of his gloved hands. The vomit that splashed against the tile was black like tar, and James trembled as much from the sight of it as he did the exhaustion that riddled his body.

He had come so close, only to burn in the end.

James collapsed to his side, the fires burning brighter, when through his half-closed eyelids, he saw a door buckle up ahead. At first he thought it was just more of the heat waves playing tricks on him, but he realized there was someone on the other side.

James rolled to his hands and knees, then forced himself to stand. He remained hunched over, barely able to place one shaky foot in front of the other as he reached for the door and yanked it open at the same time his own son had been reaching for the handle.

Jake's face was smeared with soot, his eyes bloodshot red. He was exhausted, his body poisoned from the smoke. Behind him he saw three others, lifting Mary on some kind of stretcher and struggling to carry her from the room.

When James returned his attention to his son, he saw the boy's eyes roll to the back of his head and his body go limp as he collapsed.

James lunged forward, catching Jake before he hit the floor, and then waved the others carrying his wife toward the exit, through the building that had transformed into a raging inferno.

Too tired to speak and barely able to hold his son in his

arms, James's vision tunneled into a tiny circle, the rest turning to black. He knew he would pass out soon. Exhaustion would finally force its hand. But he needed to get them to a safe place to recover before he collapsed.

The narrow hole that was James's vision helped guide him and the others trailing him to the front door, which had collapsed from the fire, blocking their exit.

James turned, his muscles shivering from exhaustion, his mind just as sluggish. To the left, he saw one of the windows blown out and he charged toward it, able to see into the streets through the smoke and through that small pinhole of vision that was left to him. He charged forward with his remaining strength and vigor.

The moment that James stepped from the building the world went black, but he didn't pass out. He trudged forward, slamming his knee into a car. He spun around, coughing, his lungs still choking for fresh air, his body and mind ravaged from the fire. He opened his mouth to call out for his wife, but again his throat was so dry and hot that James was convinced that his throat had been charred to a crumbly crisp.

"—ary!" James coughed, his voice finally breaking through with a crack. "Mary!"

"She's here!" It was a man's voice, close, shouting above the roar of the fire. "She's passed out, where do we take her?"

James's vision had yet to fully return but there was some light, and he just kept blinking, kept breathing, because in those moments, it was all he could do. "Find cover." He drew in another rattled breath that sounded like his lungs were crunching glass, and then that pinwheel of vision returned, and he was able to see the clogged streets and raging inferno that they'd just escaped. "Anywhere close."

"There!" The man who had carried his wife from the building pointed to a door across the street, and James followed.

One of the women held the door while James carried Jake inside, making it three steps before he collapsed to his knees. He gently laid his son down on the floor. It was carpet, soft beneath James's aching knees, but he knew that the relief was short-lived as he made his way back to the door until a hand grabbed his shoulder and pulled him back.

"What are you doing?" the man asked.

James frowned, squinting. "The boy."

The man pointed to Jake, who was still on the ground, unconscious. "Your son is right here! You can't go back out there. They're just shooting anyone that they come across! You don't hear that gunfire?"

James couldn't hear the gunfire. He could barely hear the man in front of him, but he had to move quickly because he wasn't sure how much consciousness he had left before he passed out. His muscles had turned to jelly and every breath he took filled his lungs with daggers.

Without another word, James spun back around toward the door, removing the pistol from his holster, which he was forced to hold with two hands so he wouldn't drop it.

Staggering down the street and weaving between the cars on the road, James's right side was warmed by the fire from the building.

The only good thing about the fire was that it had completely evacuated the street, everyone running away from the flames, which allowed James to walk down the street unhindered.

James wasn't sure how he found the truck where he'd stashed Teddy, but he did. He reached for the handle and opened the door. He blinked, staring into the cab. It was empty.

James checked behind the seats and under the dash, but the boy was gone, leaving behind the small Kevlar vest. He stepped out into the street, looking around the truck and into the adjacent vehicles. "Teddy!" His voice was drowned out by gunfire, pushing him back toward the building.

James blacked out briefly, twice, only for a half second each time. Unsure of how he found the building again, he stumbled inside and collapsed to his knees and face-planted onto the carpet.

Before he lost consciousness, James saw his son and wife on the ground ahead of him, both of them sleeping, and he wasn't even sure if they were still alive. But they were together, and if this was to be their end, he was thankful that he had seen them one last time.

11

---

*T*he dreams were vivid despite the burnt orange haze that covered the images like a film, dulling all the colors except for the blood.

The crimson splashed vividly on the streets, a stark contrast to the black asphalt, and everywhere James looked, there was nothing but fighting. But the people that were attacking others were wearing the masks that James had seen during his trek through San Antonio. They were all citizens.

People used knives, rocks, any blunt instruments that they could carry in their hands. And those that didn't have a weapon used their bare hands, beating and choking the life out of anyone that opposed them.

The fighting stretched for miles in every direction. It was savage and desperate. People were stealing food, water, medical supplies. And amongst it all, James stood in the center, coated in blood, screaming for people to stop, but they were so overcome by bloodlust that he couldn't get them to listen.

"Dad?"

The voice sucked James from the nightmare. Light

blinded him and he was painfully aware of the aching of his own body.

Disoriented, James rolled to his side, coughing badly, then dry heaved as the white canvas of his vision slowly filled in the world around him. He saw Jake's smoke-smeared face smiling over him, and the boy hugged his father tightly.

Jake finally pulled back, wiping tears from his eyes. "Mom's not doing good." He then looked to his right where Mary lay on the stretcher that they used to carry her out of the building.

The three other people that they were with when James found them coming out of that room were hovering over Mary, staring down at her with the worried expressions of people unable to help.

James stood, planting one shaking foot in front of the other until he was by his wife's side. He ripped the left glove from his hand and pressed his fingers against her cheek. He lowered his gaze to her abdomen, which was covered with a bandage, and then turned back to Jake. "What happened?"

Jake went through the scenario, how the gunmen had chased them into the building, shooting Mary in the back and how Stevie, Maya, and Zi helped Jake move Mary deeper into the building so they could hide from the terrorists.

James stood, limping more from exhaustion and fatigue than injury, and shook each of their hands. "Thank you. Thank you for saving my family."

Each of them muttered what anyone in their position would have said. That they were happy to help, that they couldn't sit by and do nothing. And he was incredibly grateful for such kindness directed to his family.

"The bullet didn't have an exit wound," Zi said. "Your son applied some clotting powder, but the bullet needs to come out. She needs professional medical care."

Jake shook his head and lowered his gaze. "I didn't know how else to stop the bleeding other than the clot powder. I wasn't sure if giving her any of the pain meds would make her heart rate come down, so I—"

James placed his large palm on his son's shoulder and made the boy look up at him. "You did everything right."

Two red blotches formed at the top of Jake's cheeks and his eyes watered as he nodded.

James kissed the top of his son's head and then walked to the window. The smoke from the fires had made the air outside silky, like James was looking through a screen.

Cars, light posts, garbage cans, benches, bus signs, all of it was covered in the residue from the fires that ravaged the city. But most of the fires had burned themselves out, leaving behind the blackened and crumbling skeletons of the buildings that could collapse at any moment. The streets were empty. Now was the time to move.

James found his pack and the guns that the others had stacked on top after they had carried James and his family inside. "We need to get out of the city before whoever burned those buildings sets fire to the entire downtown area." He removed a hydration packet from one of the pouches of his bag and chewed on it, and it helped break through the fog of fatigue as he donned the pack and picked up his rifle. "It's at least another two hours to get out of the city, maybe longer if we have to stop and evade the people hunting us—"

"They're hunting us?" Maya scrunched up her face in disgust. "Why? Why is this happening?"

"Can't we just go to the police?" Stevie asked. "I mean, going to a police station would probably be the safest place we could be, right? They're supposed to help us."

"How did this happen?" Zi asked. "Do you know? Is that how you were prepared? Did you know this was going to happen?"

James didn't have time to explain everything, because he knew that most of their questions were just based out of fear.

They wanted reassurance that they would survive, but after everything he'd seen on his way into the city, James wasn't sure they would be. He walked over to his son. "I need you to look after your mother while we head to the Humvee. Make sure she—"

"Humvee?" Stevie asked, an eager look of surprise on his face. "Are you military? Is that how you—"

"I'm not military," James answered, facing Stevie, who was a good six inches shorter than James.

Stevie slunk backward, huddling together with the other two, separating themselves from James's family, and he realized that they were all frightened of him. He glanced down at his attire and the tactical nature of his clothes, the rifle, the gun, the blood and dirt smeared over his body.

James had wanted to avoid putting himself in this situation, having to take care of people he didn't know, who he knew would latch onto him like shipwreck survivors on a life raft stuck out at sea. They would do anything to keep themselves from drowning, but if too many people jumped on, then the raft would sink. And James wasn't about to let his family die for strangers.

But these people had saved his family, and it was a debt that he would repay.

"I have transportation," James said. "But it's outside the city boundaries. My first priority is getting my wife to a doctor, and it'll be a long drive to get there. But once my wife is stabilized, I can help you. Food, water, shelter. If you need to go somewhere, I can get you there. But we need to get out of the city first."

The three exchanged glances, and with a wordless consensus, they all nodded and Zi stepped forward. "What do we need to do?"

James removed the pistol from his holster. "Has anyone fired a gun before?"

Zi raised her hand. "I dated a cop for a few months." She

stared at the gun, swallowing her hesitation. "He took me to the range a few times, showed me firearm safety, but it's been a long time since I've shot anything."

With no one else speaking up, James placed the weapon in Zi's palm. "Safety is here, magazine is full, and there is one in the chamber." With her one hand on the weapon already, he forced the other hand on it to keep it steady. "Keep the safety off, but your finger doesn't go on the trigger unless you're going to shoot, understand?"

Zi nodded quickly, still staring at the weapon.

"And you aim it at the ground unless you're aiming to shoot, and you don't aim to shoot unless you're ready to pull the trigger." James squeezed her hands, forcing Zi's gaze up to his eyeline. "You cannot hesitate to shoot once you've committed. You hesitate out there, and you die." James released his hand from the weapon and then turned to Stevie and Maya. "I'll need both of you to carry the stretcher."

"We don't get a weapon?" Maya asked. "How will we defend ourselves?"

"I'll be on point," James said, and then slid the rifle from his shoulder and into his hands. "Anything that comes into my field of vision that I assess as a threat, I take down. Zi, you're watching our backs and making sure that no one sneaks up on us." He stepped back, addressing all of them. "Everyone needs to keep their guard up. Everyone needs to have eyes in the back of their heads. Right now, we are a perfect target for anyone who is looking for a quick and easy kill. But I'm going to do everything I can to make sure we aren't put in a position like that."

James knew that it wasn't much of a pep talk, but he didn't have the luxury to sugarcoat their situation.

"And no matter what, do not stop moving," James said. "If you need a break, then tell me. But we need to push as fast and as far as we can, and a stop is only of absolute necessity."

James stared down at his wife, who was still unconscious

and wheezing with every breath. He couldn't lose her. He *wouldn't* lose her.

"Everyone ready?" James asked.

Nervous nods bobbed quickly in response, and while Stevie and Maya walked over to pick Mary up, James took a knee by Jake.

"You all right?" James asked.

"I'm okay," Jake answered. "I'm glad you're here."

James kissed Jake's forehead. "Keep an eye on your mother's vitals. And stay between me and Mom, okay? Right on my heels."

"Okay," Jake said.

James waited until both Stevie and Maya had a good grip on the stretcher before he moved toward the door. He paused. "Remember, keep your eyes open, keep together, and do not stop moving. And above all, do exactly what I tell you. I say jump, you jump. I say duck, and you hit the floor. I say run, and you sprint as fast as your legs will carry you. Got it?"

A unanimous and confident 'yes' rang out, and it gave James a flicker of hope that they might be able to escape the city before it added their bodies to the piles in the streets.

$\mathcal{T}$he first hour after James had left, Luis had walked the building's interior perimeter at least a half dozen times and discovered a few hidden caches of supplies along the walls and through false bottoms in the flooring.

They were well-hidden, and it took Luis a few times before he was able to see the cracks from the cutouts. He found food, ammunition, and medical supplies. It wasn't much, but Luis gathered everything he found and loaded it into the Humvee, knowing that James would want to bring it back.

Luis suspected that once they left here and returned to the ranch, they wouldn't be returning for a long time. And after how nervous he'd seen James become during their ride here and for his departure into the city, Luis thought that the effects of today would ripple for months. Maybe even years.

Once the heat had become unbearable, Luis ascended the ladder to the roof where he could at least catch a breeze. He didn't like being locked up.

Years working outside at the ranch had spoiled him, giving him the freedom of being out in the open. It was hard work, but it was honest work. And in a world where right and wrong had blurred together, it was priceless.

Luis lowered the binoculars and turned away from the darkening skies, fires, smoke, gunshots, and screams that had carried over to him on the wind.

With his friend nowhere in sight, Luis returned to the ground floor and stepped outside, but he quickly retreated behind the door when he glanced down the street.

Three other Humvees moved steadily down the street, each vehicle surrounded by a dozen soldiers.

The vehicles had been retrofitted with large bumpers, and the steady speed and power of the Humvees pushed the idle cars and trucks from its path, forging its way through the streets.

A trail of people had followed the soldiers, all of them shouting questions, but the military personnel didn't answer. And Luis noticed that while the civilians followed, they made sure to keep their distance.

Luis slunk back into the warehouse, not wanting to draw any attention to himself, and then quickly climbed the ladder to the roof so he could get a better look at where the military was heading.

The convoy turned right when the road reached a cross section at the warehouse and traveled one more block before stopping in an open parking lot where they set up a mobile command station.

Luis couldn't hear what was said, but the tone was aggressive, and the crowd dispersed.

Once the crowds had vanished, Luis returned his attention to the military, finding a tent set up with men coming in and out of the cover quickly and often.

Luis sat there on the roof, waiting for the military to mobilize and go deeper into the city, to help secure the area, but once they sat there at the end of the street, they didn't move. He lowered his binoculars and then descended the ladder before creeping out of the warehouse on the first floor.

Luis left the rifle in the warehouse, but kept the pistol tucked behind his back.

The parking lot where the soldiers set up camp had a building nearby. Like the warehouse, the building adjacent to where the soldiers had camped was also abandoned. The signage outside along with the broken ice maker marked the old brick building as a convenience store.

There was no ladder to the roof, but Luis found a dumpster that gave him enough of a step to climb onto the top of the single-story building. The old flat roof was sagging in a few areas brought on by neglect and water damage over the years from heavy rainfall. Luis stuck to the perimeter where the roof was strongest, but had to stay low on all fours as he made his way toward the east side of the roof that was closest to the empty parking lot.

He paused at the roof's edge and then slowly raised his eyes and peeked over the top, where he saw the roof of the tent and the lower half the soldiers that stood beneath it, their voice drifting upwards with the breeze.

At first it was nothing but scrambled nonsense, but the longer that Luis sat there and concentrated on listening, the more he was able to decipher.

"Command has three other units in place at the north, east, and south ends of the city," a man said. "Units have identified that enemy strongholds have developed in the city's epicenter and spread west to our location."

"What about rescue units?" A second man asked.

"We're pulling out who we can, but if the area isn't cleared in less than an hour, then our units are going to use artillery shells to bombard the enemy and clear the path for our ground forces to enter."

Luis's pulse increased and he rolled onto his back, still able to hear most of the conversation, which had moved onto the more monotonous details of the operation. But Luis knew that if they were planning on bombing the area before they went into the city to fight the people who did this, then the possibility of civilian casualties would greatly increase, which meant that James and the others would be caught in the crossfire.

"And what about the evacuation routes?" one of the soldiers asked. "How are people getting out of the city now?"

Luis turned back toward the wall, making sure that he heard what came next, because he might be able to help in pulling James and his family out of danger.

"The enemy has blockaded all known escape routes from the city except one," the soldier answered. "They are funneling all the citizens to the north end of the city, but our forces have been unable to secure the area."

"So that means… what?"

Luis became nervous the longer the soldier's silence stretched, and he finally peered over the edge, exposing himself. He couldn't miss what came next.

"It means that the only exit out of the city is being held by the enemy, and they've created a kill box. Anyone that walks into that area will be blown away. Period."

Luis rolled away from the wall and laid there for a moment on his back, staring up at the orange haze of the sky above, the clear blue toward the west fighting against the smoke and fires radiating from the city.

A kill box.

The phrase repeated in Luis's mind, like a record caught on a terrible scratch. He knew that James was capable, more prepared than even the most capable resident in San Antonio. But if either Jake or Mary were hurt and if he couldn't move with the same agility as he normally would, Luis knew that it would be difficult for him with the amount of forces that had even the military worried.

Unable to bake with worry any longer on top of the roof,

Luis retreated to the warehouse, going out the same way he had come in.

Back at the warehouse, Luis found the radio that James had left him. "James? Do you copy? James!" Only static blared back, and Luis tossed the radio back in the Humvee out of frustration.

After everything Luis had just heard, he knew that he had a choice to make. If he decided to go after James at the entry point north of the city, then he could risk being blown off the face of the earth like the rest of the military.

Luis glanced at the Humvee, remembering how adamant James had been about staying put. But the Humvee wouldn't do James and the others any good if they died in a hail of gunfire when they walked into an ambush.

13

*J*ames struggled to keep a pace that was acceptable for the number of people and the condition of his group.

But they didn't stop. They couldn't stop.

The few hours that had passed since their departure from the burning building had been without any excitement.

Farther west, the streets became more desolate, and the gunshots and explosions became less frequent. The eerie silence was a stark contrast to the roars of fear and confusion that had plagued James's journey since his departure from the ranch, but they couldn't escape the long reach of death.

Hundreds of bodies lined the streets. They looked like dummies made out of clay or straw instead of the flesh and blood that had begun to rot under the hot summer sun.

Buzzards and flies were already calling, swooping down to collect their pound of rotten flesh. They circled the sky above the city streets, more and more of them collecting by the hour. And the longer they circled overhead, the more he wished for the return of gunfire. Because there was something ominous about those birds flying overhead. It was like they were waiting for James and his group to join the dead that they avoided. But he wasn't going to become a meal today, and neither was his family.

When James caught sight of a few people along the roads, they were no longer running like the frenzied hordes that James had escaped from in the city's epicenter.

Most folks were traveling in small groups like theirs, but the rare moments where they found themselves in close contact with others, both parties approached hesitantly. No questions were asked, but each of their eyes studied one another with the piercing gaze of a frightened animal.

Both were waiting for the others to make a move, keeping an eye on one another until both parties had put a considerably safe distance between themselves, and then moved forward like nothing had happened.

The longer that James moved west, the more he noticed a disturbing trend. More and more people of larger groups were heading in the opposite direction. It was like they were being turned back, but James didn't understand how that was possible until he was forced to return to the main city roads to finish his route out of the city and found the exit blocked.

"Holy hell," Stevie said, walking up next to James, who had stopped, the others lining up next to him.

To call it a roadblock was an understatement. An entire building had collapsed, and tar had been dumped over the mounds and set afire, letting it burn slowly and preventing anyone from trying to cross over.

"How are we supposed to climb over that thing?" Zi asked, still gripping the pistol with both hands, being mindful of their surroundings. She had grown comfortable in her position as watchdog, and James was glad to see that she'd kept her guard up even when they stopped. It made him feel better about choosing her to watch their backs.

"We don't," James answered, and he turned north, hoping

that they could find another crossroads somewhere up ahead.

But every street was exactly the same, blocked by an impassible structure. And the farther James traveled north, the more he realized why he had seen so many people turn around.

All of those explosions, all of the crowds running in circles, people desperate to escape the city, but they couldn't. The terrorists had collapsed the city into itself.

Wanting to avoid pushing his people to the point of collapse, James found a nearby alleyway and let them rest while he tried to come up with a way out of this mess.

The number of people attached to James's group forced him to change his approach on exactly how he was going to navigate through the city. Moving by himself and moving with a group was completely different. It wouldn't take much to cause them harm, which meant that James was forced to stick to the tried-and-true method of evasion.

Avoiding gunfire, crowds, and staying off the beaten path would force James to take routes that he would have normally skipped because it was slower. But slower was better than dead.

Conversation was minimal, everyone sipping from the canteen as they passed it around. A quick check on Mary's fading vitals made James more nervous than he'd hoped. Her breathing was sporadic, and raspy, and her abdomen had swollen. She was barely holding on, and as James took her hand, he whispered his encouragement.

"You're strong, Mary," James said, keeping a firm grip on her hand. "You've always been a fighter. I just need you to keep fighting for a little while longer. I know you can do it. I love you."

James kissed her forehead, the skin salty with sweat, and Mary stirred at his touch. He paused, hoping that she might wake up, but she remained asleep, fighting for her life.

"How much farther do we have to go?" Stevie stepped from around James's back and then glanced back down the road they'd just traveled. "I mean we've gone what? Ten miles or something?"

James remained in his kneeling position on the ground and glanced up at Stevie, whose shirt had soaked with sweat, clinging to his very lean frame. "Did you get any water?"

Stevie nodded. "Yeah, I got some from your pack." He stepped closer, undeterred by James's efforts to try and avoid his question. "So how much farther do we have to go?"

James knew that the truth might crush the man's spirits, and while he had no taste for lying, he decided to take use a particular well-worn tactic of diversion. "We've made good progress. We just need to keep up the pace."

James paused, studying the man, searching for any signs that he might quit on them during the rest of the trip.

But Stevie stood his ground, refusing to relinquish an inch. "Let's not kid ourselves about who's helping who here. We both have something to gain and something to lose. I'll get your wife to the vehicle, so long as there is still a spot for me and my wife inside."

Stevie returned to his wife, the pair whispering to one another, and Jake walked to his father.

"How's Mom?" Jake asked.

"She's hanging in there," James answered. "Did you get some water?"

Jake nodded, and then twisted his hands together the way he did whenever he was nervous.

"What's wrong?" James asked.

Jake shrugged and then crossed his arms, keeping his head bowed. "I ran."

James frowned. "What are you talking about?"

"After Mom was shot," Jake answered. "She told me to run and I did."

James glanced back to his wife, and then to his son,

making the connection. "Jake, look at me." He touched his son's shoulder. "Look at me, son."

Jake lifted his head, his eyes watering.

"You did exactly what your mother asked you to do," James said. "It's okay that you were scared. Everyone gets scared. It's what you do after you're scared that matters. And you came back, right?"

Jake nodded.

"That's right," James said. "And because you came back with those people, you were able to carry your mother to safety. You don't have anything to be ashamed about, okay?"

Tears rolled from Jake's eyes, and he nodded, then hugged his father as he sobbed into James's shoulder.

"It's all right," James said. "Everything is going—"

It was the rumble that pulled James's attention to the end of the alley. He let go of his son and picked up his rifle, aiming it at the road. When he neared the alley's entrance, James slowly craned his head around the corner to the south, his jaw dropping with surprise.

"Oh my god," James said.

A tsunami of bodies sprinted down the streets, propelled by a momentum that rolled them over cars and crashed into the side of buildings.

James spun around, running toward the others. "Get up, everyone, now."

Eyes turned to James in alarm, all of them rising to attention as James glanced back down to the end of the alley, expecting the bodies to roll past them at any moment. When James turned back around and found Stevie and Maya just standing there, he pointed to his wife on the stretcher.

"Pick her up, let's go!" The booming urgency of James's tone caught both of them off guard, and they quickly, and nervously, picked Mary off the concrete and followed James deeper into the alleyway. He knew that they wouldn't be able to fight against the crowds heading their way.

James managed to get all of them around the back corner of the building just as the flood of bodies passed the front of the alleyway. But just as a liquid fills whatever portions of its container it can fit, people broke away from the main pack, running into the alleyway and filling it up faster than James expected.

Unsure of where the alley ended, James followed it to a side street that ran north along the street parallel to the stampede. And as they passed intersections, James watched as more and more people spilled over to their side of the road, making it harder for him to keep his people together.

"Dad! Dad!" Jake screamed.

James pushed back against the crowd, most of them parting for him because of the rifle in his hands. "Jake!" He grabbed hold of his son's hand just as another wave of bodies rushed toward them, whisking them away in the crowd like a strong current.

Knowing that Jake could be easily trampled from the frantic pace, James flung the shoulder strap of the rifle over his shoulder and then scooped his boy in his arms, keeping his elbows out and moved with the crowd, searching for the rest of his group, including his unconscious wife.

"Stevie! Maya! Zi!" James shouted, but the moment the words left his lips, they were drowned out by the heavy pulse of the crowd.

James kept his head above water, searching for the rest of his party, trying to make sense of the mad dash and why people were running. Was it from the gunfire? He couldn't hear anything behind him.

But the frightened herd only followed the person directly in front of them, and everyone was heading north, blocked in by the makeshift wall that ran along the west side of the city. And the longer that James ran along with the crowd, holding Jake in his arms, still unable to locate his wife and the others from the sea of bodies rolling down the street, the more he realized what was happening.

The people weren't running, they were being herded. They were in a cattle shoot.

And when James saw the open patch ahead of them, looking as though they were going to escape into the promise land, to freedom beyond the imploding city, he saw the bodies already on the ground, people tripping over them without even looking at them.

James pushed his way to the side of the street, forcing the others out of his way and seeking the safety of the group's edge. Then he watched in horror as the bullets rained down over the crowd.

14

*G*unfire silenced the screams as James ducked into a nearby building, Jake clinging tightly to him as he pushed deeper into the building. A few others followed, but were gunned down before they made it through the door.

Jake whimpered into James's shoulder, and James ducked into the first room he could find. He set his son down and then slammed the door shut, the gunfire shaking the entire building.

The noise was impossibly loud. It was like being stuck under a tin roof in the middle of a hailstorm.

James turned back toward the door, rifle at the ready, prepared to make his last stand against whatever evil pushed their way through. But as the gunfire petered out, no one came to finish the job.

James lowered the rifle. He leaned his ear against the door but he heard nothing. He placed one hand on the door knob and looked back to Jake on the floor, holding up one finger to his lips, miming for him to be quiet, and he nodded in response.

The door offered no whine when James cracked it open,

and light spilled through the building's front windows, illu-minating the stack of bodies of those that had tried to follow James inside, but were a step too late.

James remained in the room, keeping the door cracked open and waited for any sign of movement among the dead in the streets. After a few minutes of nothing but still quiet, James stepped from the room, again gesturing for Jake to remain quiet and stay put.

Every step toward the front of the building was filled with hesitation. He had no idea where Stevie and Maya had disappeared to, but he hoped that if they did make it out, they had the decency to take his wife with them. Because God help them if they didn't and he saw them alive again before he left the city.

A few feet from the front windows which had been blown out, James raised the rifle's scope to his eye.

He moved the crosshairs slowly and swiftly over the bodies of the dead, everybody that he saw covered in the same blue clothing that Mary had worn, causing his stomach to flip inside out, only to have the moment pass when he realized it wasn't her.

After scanning the bodies and, thankfully, finding no signs of either his wife, Stevie, or Maya, James focused his attention to the buildings across the street. It was possible that they sought cover during the chaos just as he did, and he remembered seeing them being sucked in the opposite direc-tion before he lost them in the crowd.

James scanned the storefronts slowly, making sure to take his time. "C'mon." He had gone so far, come so close, he couldn't lose his family so near the end. They were almost out. They were almost—

James froze, shifting the scope of his rifle back over a section of window where he saw a person's head sticking over the top of the window's edge. It was Stevie.

James lowered the scope and then moved closer to the

window, picking up a piece of broken glass in the process as he sidled up next to the wall. He stuck the piece of glass out the window, keeping himself hidden, trying to catch Stevie's attention, who James could tell still had his head poking up through the window even without the use of the scope.

After a few tries, Stevie finally raised his hand, an acknowledgement of seeing James from his position. The pair were too far away to mouth anything and read lips, and James didn't want to risk shouting and pulling attention to either of them, so instead he retreated back into the building to find Jake.

"I'm going to get your mom," James said, and then removed a knife from his side and placed it in Jake's hand. "If anyone comes in this room besides me, then I want you to stick them with this, and then run as fast as you can. Get to the warehouse. Luis will be there waiting."

"Dad, I—"

"No," James said, shaking his head and not allowing his son to show any weakness. "This is what needs to happen, Jake. Understand?"

Jake's mouth quivered, and it took a few moments before he finally nodded and wiped the tears from his eyes.

"Good boy," James said. "I'll be back."

James closed the door behind him and then approached the front of the building, raising his scope to get a better look across the street, this time finding Maya and Zi with Stevie. He held up his hands to make sure that they knew to stay put.

He then checked the surrounding buildings to see if he could locate the gunmen that had opened fire on the crowd. He was betting that the enemy had some kind of heavy-caliber weapon or machine gun nests positioned on the roof. It would provide the most casualty without the need for good aim.

From James's current position, it was a thirty-yard dash

over the field of corpses to his wife across the street. It was a long way to run out in the open.

James adjusted his grip on the rifle as he approached the building's exit, the door propped open by the dead woman who had tried to follow James inside. He paused, drawing a few deep breaths and mapping out the most efficient path between this building and the one across the street. He shut his eyes, whispered one final prayer, and then opened his eyes and broke from the cover of the building.

Three steps into the street and James was chased down with gunfire, forcing him to hunch forward and use the vehicles as cover. Bullets ricocheted off the cars, shattered what glass remained in the windows, and added more lead to the corpses that lined the streets.

The bodies that lined the pavement made it difficult to run, James constantly having to leap over arms and legs, the asphalt slick with blood that collected and congealed in large patches over the blacktop.

With the gunfire becoming thicker the farther James ran, he leapt the last few feet, crashing through the building's open door, rolling a few rotations before slamming into a cluster of chairs.

Even after James was under the cover of the building, the gunfire continued for a few more seconds, but when it finally ended, he stood and glanced around the inside of the building, finding that it was the remains of a coffee shop.

A hand clamped down on James's shoulder, and he jerked around to find Zi staring down at him, sweat beading on her face, her eyes wide, and her pupils small and narrowed in the center of her eyes, making the white of her eyeball more prominent.

"She's back here," Zi said.

Maya and Stevie had set Mary down on a large steel table. Everyone looked unharmed, but James did a thorough check of his wife to make sure that no stray bullets had caught her unconscious body.

"What happened?" Stevie asked. "Why the fuck would they do that?"

"We need to get out of here," James said. "They know we're here, and they'll send someone to finish the job they started."

"And go where?" Stevie exploded, running his hands through his jet-black hair, slicking it backward until it lay flat. "We can't fucking move!" Stevie kicked a nearby trash can, spilling its contents over the floor.

"We can't lose our cool now," James answered, knowing that he still needed their help to get his wife out of this place alive, and he turned to Zi, the only one of the three not falling apart. "Is there a back exit?"

Zi stood by the door, watching the front, making sure that they didn't get ambushed. James was starting to like the woman more and more. "Maybe. I didn't check."

"Go look." James headed toward the front windows and searched for a car that he thought might work, but he found nothing, save for the soldiers marching down the street.

Zi returned, and kept her voice low. "No back exit. It just leads to the side alley that dead ends."

James slunk back into the building next to Zi, his expression alarmed.

"What?" Zi asked.

"Four-man team," James answered. "All with automatic weapons, Kevlar." He glanced down to the rifle in his hands, knowing that there was only one viable option. "I go out and distract them. My boy is in that building across the street. Once I have their attention, you get them over here and then work your way south down the street. I'll hold them off for as long as I can."

Zi frowned. "You're going to hold all of them off? What about the nest machine guns they have planted up there on the roofs?" She nodded. "Yeah, I saw them. They'd take us all out before we made it three feet from the building. You got lucky coming over because you were alone and had the element of surprise. How long do you think we'll last trying to get the rest of us out of this building moving your wife on that stretcher, plus your son?"

James cursed under his breath. He knew the woman was right. It was a suicide mission. He poked his head around the corner and saw the gunmen moving closer, zeroing in on their building.

They had run out of time.

But while James was contemplating his final moments, wanting to dart across the street back to his son, he heard a strange noise carry on the wind in the distance. It seemed impossible at first, but as the noise became louder, James stuck his head out just in time to see the Humvee speed down the sidewalk, avoiding the clogged streets, and knocking down the small trees and signs that lined the pavement, drawing the gunfire from both the ground party and the machine gun nests. The vehicle's armored plating repelled the bullets like water off a seal.

James turned back to Stevie and Maya, finding them at the door, staring out at the streets like they were lost in a dream. "Get the stretcher up here now!"

While Zi helped the shaking pair with Mary, James started picking off the shooters in the streets, providing some cover for Luis on his approach.

James flagged the Humvee down and Luis stopped in front of the building, parking the vehicle at an angle to use it as a natural shield from the machine gun nests.

Luis kept his head low as he stepped out of the door, and James embraced him in a hug, then punched his friend's arm. "I thought I told you to stay at the warehouse."

"What, and let you have all of the fun?" Luis asked,

shouting above the gunfire, but the smile faded when he saw Mary being carried out on the stretcher.

"Help me get her in the back," James answered.

Both Luis and James took the stretcher from Stevie and Maya's hands. Once she was secure, they piled the rest of them inside, leaving only Luis and James out of the Humvee, the threat of gunfire still raining down on them, though it had become more sporadic.

"I need to go and get Jake," James said, knowing that the road was too clogged to try and use the Humvee to cross the street.

"I will give you cover fire," Luis said, moving toward the back of the Humvee with his rifle.

"Me too." Zi climbed out of the car with her pistol, joining Luis at the bumper.

James moved toward the front of the Humvee, knowing that the lull in gunfire would end the moment he exposed himself from the cover of the vehicle. Just a little bit farther and they had a chance. He just had to stay alive long enough to make it happen.

"On my mark," James said. "Ready?"

Both Luis and Zi nodded, aiming toward the rooftops where the gunfire had been thickest.

"Now!" James darted from around the Humvee's hood, sprinting back across the field of corpses that he had moved over earlier, but now he was moving with a renewed sense of purpose, and before he realized it he was already across the street, opening the office door where he'd left Jake.

Jake lowered the knife, shaking as he sprinted toward his father, wrapping his arms around James's legs and squeezing tight.

James led his boy to the building's front, then pointed to the Humvee, which was less than thirty yards from their current position. Less than thirty yards away from freedom.

"We're going to run there as fast as we can, okay? Stay on my right side, close, and don't stop moving."

Luis and Zi continued their cover fire, and most of the bullets were now concentrated on the Humvee, the gunmen now focusing their efforts on the tires.

"Let's go!" James stepped from the cover of the building with Jake, and the world around him slowed. He was aware of every step he took, the bodies on the ground, holding his son's hand. He saw the bullets spark against the hoods and ceilings of the cars that he used as cover.

It was like he wasn't running on asphalt anymore, it was like he was floating, and it didn't stop until he reached the Humvee, shoving Jake inside and then jumping in himself.

"Go! Go! Go!"

Luis floored the accelerator, speeding back up the side-walk, the Humvee rattling from the gunfire, people scream-ing. James kept hold of his family, waiting out the storm until it passed and they were out of the city. They had made it. Now they just had to keep Mary alive.

he sun dipped lower into the west in front of them as they traveled down the road, and after the first hour, most everyone fell asleep. The rush of adrenaline that had propelled them to survive the city had run its course, and everyone's body needed to refuel.

But while others slept, James kept his attention on his wife, who was barely hanging on.

"We still need to head to town?" Luis asked, finding James's eyes through the rearview mirror.

"Yeah," James answered, keeping one hand on Mary's shoulder, her head in his lap, and her legs in Jake's lap. Stevie, Maya, and Zi had all fallen asleep in the back.

"What are we going to do with our new friends?" Luis asked.

James looked out to the passing landscape, hoping that he would be able to find answers in nature, but it only made him tired. "I don't know."

If they stayed on the ranch, it would be a big change for most of them, and James wasn't sure how everyone would adapt.

It was sunset when they reached the town of Ruckins, the

small strip of buildings in the same condition that he'd left it in, with one minor difference.

When James and Luis had passed through earlier, the streets and storefronts had been lined with people. But now it was empty. Only the vehicles that had been left behind remained.

Luis, undeterred by this fact, slowed when they reached Larry's gas station. "I'll get you as close to Doc's office as I can."

James turned to the gas station and saw something else that hadn't been there earlier in the day. A large semi-truck was parked next to the building.

"Do you want me to fill the Humvee up at Larr—"

"Stop," James said.

Luis hit the brakes at the same urgency as James's voice, jolting everyone awake.

"What's wrong?" Luis asked, scanning the town like a hawk, just as James had done.

"Where is everyone?" James asked.

Luis shrugged. "It's late, people are probably—"

"The ambush." James's voice was a whisper. This was the same set-up for the ambush in the city. "Luis, you have to get us out of here. Get off the road, head out into the fields."

Luis struggled to get the vehicle in reverse, his nerves just as shot as everyone else's from the hectic trip.

"Luis, now!" James roared, his voice snapping the sleep out of everyone's eyes.

"I'm trying!" Luis finally dropped down into reverse, but it was too late, and James covered his family with his body as the first heavy piece of artillery hit the Humvee, fracturing the bulletproof glass, but it didn't shatter, the material able to hold together for the moment.

Every eye inside the Humvee turned toward Ruckins, the evening light casting the town in a silhouette, masking the enemy hidden amongst a row of buildings.

Ducked low in the middle row of seats with his wife's head still resting in his lap, James kicked the back of Luis's seat. "Get us out of here now!"

Luis shifted the vehicle into reverse, gunfire chasing them on their retreat. The heavy barrage of artillery challenged the Humvee's armored plating, the impact sending vibrations through the vehicle.

"Get off the road and head out onto the fields!" James said.

Luis turned a hard right while still in reverse, exposing the passenger side before Luis shifted into drive and floored the accelerator as they moved from asphalt to grass, but not before an explosion rumbled beneath the Humvee, slanting the vehicle to the right.

"We've got a flat!" Luis said.

Bullets buckled the rear window inward, exposing their backside, but as Luis put distance between the Humvee and the town, the gunfire eventually faded.

James quickly checked his wife's vitals and then found his son's eyes, which were wide open, his cheeks pale in the dying light of day. "You okay?"

Jake nodded. "I-I think so." His voice was dry and cracked.

James peeked into the back row of seats where Zi, Stevie, and Maya had flattened themselves on top of one another. "You guys all right?"

"What the fuck was that?" Stevie exploded with anger, twisting his face into a snarl, his clothes dirty and stained with sweat from the long hike through San Antonio. "I thought we'd left all of those people back in the city? What are they doing all the way out here?"

"I don't know," James answered.

"Boss," Luis said, struggling to keep the wheel steady with both hands. "We aren't going to make it much farther with that tire."

The ride was getting worse, but James wanted to put more distance between themselves and the town. "It'll last long enough."

And while the Humvee limped along like a beaten dog, James knew that the only question that really mattered among the dozens that were whispered from worried lips was the first one that Stevie had asked. How did those terrorists make it to their small town of Ruckins?

James stared down at his wife's face, knowing that he'd have to find an answer, because he needed Nolan's help in stabilizing his wife. If the doctor was even still alive.

After night fell and the town was no longer in sight, James instructed Luis to stop so they could change the tire.

While Luis grabbed the spare, James stayed in the vehicle and placed two gentle fingers on Mary's slender neckline. The pulse was weak. And the fact that there was no exit wound meant the bullet was still inside. There was no telling what kind of damage it had done.

James opened the door while gently resting Mary's head on the seat, then looked at Jake. "Keep an eye on your mother."

Outside, James assessed the Humvee's damage. Aside from the busted tire, the armor plating was torn up and the windows looked one stiff wind from shattering into a million pieces.

James stood watch, his attention south in the direction of the town, while Luis replaced the tire. The enemy that had descended on their country was well-organized, and larger than he had originally calculated.

"Boss," Luis said, twisting the massive lug nuts on the new tire. "What are we looking at here? You think that the ranch is still going to be there when we get back?"

"I'm not worried about the ranch," James answered, unable to peel his gaze away from the town.

Luis grunted, securing the final nut on the tire before

dropping the iron into the dirt and releasing the massive jack that supported the beastly vehicle. He stepped right in front of James, disrupting his line of sight. "How's Mary?"

James finally looked Luis in the eye. "We need to get her home and stabilize her. But she'll need surgery to remove the bullet." He returned his attention to the town. "I need to get Nolan out of that town. If he's even still alive."

"Oh, he's still alive," Luis said, stepping back to the Humvee. "The old man is too stubborn to die."

While Luis climbed back into the Humvee, James lingered outside, wondering what the end game was for the enemy that had infected his country like a disease. He had expected the fight in San Antonio, but he hadn't expected it to follow him so close to the ranch. So close to home.

16

*T*he Humvee kicked up dirt and dust as Luis turned off the highway and onto the dirt road that marked the entrance to the Bowers Ranch.

A wrought iron arch curved over the dirt road at the midway point. James had asked his father once why the arch was in the middle of the road to the house instead of up by the highway.

"So visitors don't forget who they're coming to see," Stanley Bowers said. "And to remind us that it's important to meet in the middle with the people who come to visit."

James was ten when his father told him that, and it wasn't until he grew older that he understood the profound nature of his father's wisdom.

It was a way of life, an unofficial family creed. And it was a model that had brought his family much success. The Bowers family had been the keepers of over one thousand acres of Texas land, which they had nurtured and cultivated for the past four generations.

The dirt road ended at the ranch house, a two-story structure that James's great-grandfather had built and where five generations of Bowers had grown up.

Luis parked the Humvee as close to the front door as possible, and Zi helped James carry Mary inside.

In the bedroom, they gently laid Mary down on the fresh sheets, her head tilted delicately to the side, and she groaned as James slipped the IV needle into her arm, breaking the bag.

Liquid funneled down through the clear tube and into her system, the medicines and electrolytes combatting the effects of dehydration, pain, and injury.

"I was telling your son in the city that I was in nursing school," Zi said, staring at the bloodied bandages. "We need to clean her wound. If you don't want to do it—"

"No," James said. "I can do it."

James had never been squeamish. He had killed, skinned, and cleaned his fair share of animals over the years, and having been raised on the ranch, he was no stranger to death. But as James cleaned the gunshot wound, which had crusted with clotting powder and blood, and applied fresh gauze, he couldn't hide the tremble in his hands.

The area around the gunshot was red and inflamed, the first signs of infection, and James hoped that the antibiotics in the IV would help fight it. But there were more concerning signs of his wife's deteriorating condition.

"Her abdomen's swollen," Zi said, taking a closer look at Mary. "If the pressure gets too bad, her organs could shut down."

Finishing up with the bandage, James looked to Zi. "Could you get the bullet out?"

Zi shook her head.

James brushed his wife's hair back behind her ear. He thought about trying to get the bullet out himself, but this was beyond his first aid training, and he'd do more damage than good. He needed a doctor, and he prayed that Nolan was still alive. He squeezed her hand, her skin cold. "You're a fighter, Mary Bowers. You've always been that way. Even when the odds were stacked against us, you always pushed through." He leaned into her ear, whispering the words. "So keep fighting, Mary. Push through." He kissed her temple and then stepped out of the room.

James returned to the living room. Jake, Luis, Zi, Maya, and Stevie gathered around him, each of their faces covered in dust and sporting the vacant stare of exhaustion.

"My wife needs professional medical attention." James turned to Zi, Maya, and Stevie. "I know I promised you all a ride to your homes, but—"

"It's fine," Zi said, speaking for the group.

James smiled. "Thank you." He took a moment to gather his thoughts and then cleared his throat. "I'll ride back to the town and find Nolan. If he's still alive." He looked to Luis and Jake. "I need both of you to start preparing our defenses."

Luis stepped forward. "James—"

"If I don't come back, then you're in charge," James said, pointing at Luis. "Take care of my family while I'm gone."

James stepped outside, the cloudless night sky marked with millions of stars and a half moon that illuminated the path to the barn.

During the summer time, James let the animals sleep out under the stars. He had always thought the horses appreciated the sentiment.

Most of the animals trotted lazily around the penned enclosure, either munching on hay, drinking water from the trough, or laying in the cool dirt. But the moment James's mare caught his scent, she walked to him, pressing her nose into the palm of his hand as he opened the gate.

"Hey, girl," James brushed the long, muscular neck of the beast, who obediently followed James to the barn. "I hope you're up for a night ride."

Once the beast was saddled, James hooked a feed bag around her muzzle to keep her busy while he gathered his gear.

James loaded ammunition into magazines, making sure he had plenty should he get bogged down in a firefight.

In addition to the rifle and ammunition, James equipped himself with a few smoke and flash grenades, a suppressor, his .45 Smith and Wesson, and his hunting knife should he run out of bullets. He also stashed enough food and water for two days should things take a turn for the worse along with his standard first aid kit. But he hoped the Kevlar vest strapped around his torso would prevent him from needing such tools.

Packed and prepared for a variety of outcomes, James donned his backpack and walked over to the horse. He gently stroked the animal's neck, the hide smooth against his calloused hand. "We come home together. Deal?"

"Deal." Luis emerged from the darkness, rifle in hand, and the pack he wore from their trip into San Antonio on his back. "But I'd prefer not to carry you if I can help it. You still haven't lost your holiday weight from last Christmas."

James placed his foot into the stirrup and lifted himself onto the animal's back. "Luis, you should be—"

"Jake can handle it." Luis stood off to the horse's left, staring up at his boss. "Going back into that town alone is a mistake, and you know it."

James had never enjoyed admitting that Luis was right. The man had a bad habit of reminding you after it happened. "Wasn't sure if you wanted to come or not."

Luis laughed as he pulled another saddle from one of the barn stalls. "I don't know if *want* is the right word." Luis secured the saddle to the horse, and then mounted the animal.

"I don't know what we're about to walk into, but I know that it's going to get hairy any way we slice it," James said. "Based off of the damage they did to the Humvee, I'd say they're well-fortified. But nightfall should provide us cover."

Luis cocked one eyebrow up. "And what if they have

night vision goggles and they can see us coming from a mile away?"

James's mare whinnied, and he calmed the animal. "Then this will be a short trip."

$\mathcal{N}$ightfall brought no relief from the heat, and the hundred bodies crammed inside Ruckins First National Bank wasn't helping cool things down. It had been close to six hours since their town had been attacked and the gunmen forced everyone into the building, killing anyone who opposed them.

It had been hours since they'd heard the gunfire, but the spark from the conversation had yet to burn out.

Doctor Nolan Springer shifted on the tile, his back stiff and his knees aching. Everything ached at his age. He thought about trying to get up and stretch, but he didn't think he could stand without help, and he didn't want to draw any unwanted attention to himself.

Nolan leaned forward, his back cracking as he groaned in relief from the lack of pressure, then bent his knees, forming himself into a ball, choosing not to participate in the speculation of what people thought was going on and what would happen to them. He didn't want them to get their hopes up, only to have it dashed by his realist and sometimes nihilist opinions. But that didn't stop the spread of chatter from whispering lips in the darkness.

"I'm telling you, it was the military, probably a small platoon that was just on patrol."

"I don't know, man. You really think the military would turn tail like that? What if it was a big convoy or something? And these guys wiped them out. Christ, it sounded like there was a war going on out there."

"I'm telling you—"

The bank door opened, swinging inward violently. The whispers ended and the room drew in a collective breath as three men, all of them wearing masks and armed with rifles, entered, their figures silhouetted from the lanterns behind them.

One of the shadow men stepped near Nolan, but it was hard to tell in the darkness if he was staring at Nolan.

After a minute the shadow man returned to his cohorts, whispered something, and another pair of men moved toward Nolan. They were swift and purposeful as they placed both hands on the old man and picked him up from the ground like he was a rag doll and carried him outside.

Having been sitting down for hours, Nolan's legs were asleep and the gunmen that pulled him from the bank were forced to carry him. He saw that they had moved the vehicles in the streets, pushing them to either side of the town to form a kind of blockade for the town's entrances, leaving only a few cars in the middle.

Heading toward the east side of town, Nolan also saw a large number of gunmen by the gas station, and Nolan was surprised to find a semi-truck parked outside. It hadn't been there during the initial takeover, and he was surprised something so big, so mechanically inclined still working despite the power outage.

Nolan counted twenty armed men between the bank and the short walk to Mel's Hardware shop. Most of them were masked. Cowards.

The inside of Mel's had remained untouched. He

expected the violence to spread into looting, but he realized that these men hadn't demanded jewels or money from the people they locked up in the bank. Whatever their cause or their mission, it wasn't for monetary gain. It was something else.

When Nolan was carried into Mel's office, whose corpse lay in the hallway, what little strength returned to his legs disappeared and his knees buckled, but he didn't fall.

A man, who was not Mel, sat behind Mel's desk. He wore no mask, had no gun, and was hunched over a piece of paper, scribbling. Nolan noticed the man wore no mask, but did wear a pair of black gloves. And the man was American.

"Is this him?" the gloved man asked.

"Yes, sir," the man on the left answered.

The man continued to scribble and then ripped off the section of the paper he had been using before handing it to the man who'd answered. "I want everything secured before morning, and I want patrols set up around the clock."

Orders received, the men quickly exited the office, shutting the door behind them.

The man behind the desk leaned back, hands folded casually over his lap as he stared Nolan right in the eye, the expression almost clinical. "You're the town doctor."

"Feeling under the weather?" Nolan asked.

The man didn't smile, but Nolan didn't care.

"I was told that you have lived in this town all your life," the man said, his tone as cold and as calculating, his eyes so dark, it was like they were holes drilled into a skull.

"That's true." Nolan cleared his throat. "But if you're looking for any dinner recommendations, I'm afraid the food is better in San Antonio."

"San Antonio is burning," the man said. "Everything will burn when we're finished, but there are those that might survive should they prove themselves useful." He leaned forward. "I want to know about the man in the Humvee."

Nolan knew he was talking about James. He must have been the cause of the gunfire. And if they were still asking questions about him, then that meant James had survived the encounter, and he had hopefully rescued his wife and son from the city.

"He came through town earlier today, not long after the device was detonated," the man said. "I want to know where he lives."

Nolan glanced out the door and saw Mel's shoes sticking past the door's entrance. The guy must have asked Mel the same questions, his answers unsatisfactory. "I'm afraid there isn't anything that I can offer you that would be helpful."

The man at the desk retained his stoic glance, and Nolan wondered how they would kill him, and if they planned on doing it quickly.

But the man didn't reach for a gun, he didn't scream or shout, he simply opened one of the desk drawers and pulled out a file. A medical file.

"I was curious to see if I could get a head start on getting to know the townspeople," he said, opening the file on the desk. "You can learn a lot by studying a person's medical history. It provides insight into how they lived and what problems they might be facing down the road." The man continued to study the page. "Late stage lymphoma. It says here that it's spread to your bloodstream, which means you only have a few weeks left, maybe even less before your body starts to shut down." He left the file open but leaned back, returning to a relaxed position. "I'm sure you know what you're in for. The pain. The suffering. Whatever torture I could instruct my men to give you would pale in comparison to what you have waiting around the corner." He showed the first signs of a smile but repressed it quickly.

The door opened and another one of the armed terrorists stepped inside, paying no attention to Nolan as he addressed the man behind the desk in a foreign language. Nolan had spent enough time in border towns for volunteer work to know that it was Spanish, and he'd picked up enough to be able to follow the conversation loosely enough.

"We've finished unloading the supplies," the terrorist said.

"Everything was accounted for?"

"Three months' food for one thousand men."

"Keep all of it crated until it's time for distribution. More units will be arriving from the south."

"What do you want us to do with the truck?"

"Separate the trailer and park the vehicle on either side of the gas station," the gloved man answered. "I want full patrols around it and I want the doors locked inside."

The man nodded and the gloved man returned his attention back to Nolan.

"We're bigger than you can possibly imagine," he said. "I could tell you everything about our plan and it wouldn't make a difference. That's how strong we are, that's how dedicated we are, and that's how efficient the organization that I work for is."

"Not efficient enough to find some man in a Humvee," Nolan said.

The man stood and walked around the desk and slapped both palms onto Nolan's shoulders. "You tell me where to find him, and I'll help end your pain before it begins." He squeezed Nolan's shoulder harder. "But if you don't, then I'll keep you alive. Shove an IV into you myself if you won't eat or drink. And I'll make you feel every bit of pain and torture that's coming your way."

Nolan considered the offer, but only to buy him time. Because he knew that if he didn't give this man some information, then he'd just pull some other person from the bank who would give up James at the drop of a hat. At least Nolan would be able to lie. "What do you want to know?"

18

*J*ake sat in a chair next to his mother's bed, holding her hand, hoping and waiting for her to wake up, but he knew that wouldn't happen. He tried not to stare at the bandages that concealed the wound, more blood staining the white gauze, but it was hard not to look.

A knock at the bedroom door turned Jake's attention away from his mother, and he saw Zi standing in the doorway.

"Everything all right?" Zi asked.

Jake said nothing as he turned back toward his mother. Her hand was so cold. It had always been a warm touch, and he hated the fact that it had vanished. She was dying in front of him, and there was nothing he could do to stop it.

Zi entered and stood on the other side of the bed. She reached for Mary's wrist, and Jake grew defensive.

"Don't touch her," Jake said.

Zi glared at Jake. "I just want to make sure she's all right."

Jake rubbed his thumb against the inside of his mother's palm. "I already checked her pulse. She's still alive."

Zi released Mary's wrist and then crossed her arms. "Your

dad said we needed to get some things ready? I was hoping we could get started."

"Why?" Jake asked. "It doesn't matter. Nothing matters anymore."

Zi walked around the bed, then knelt by Jake. "Sometimes it's nice to have a distraction. So what do you say you help distract me and show me what your dad wanted us to get done? I'm going stir crazy just waiting around."

Jake saw her smile out of the corner of his eye. It was a nice smile, big, like his mother's.

"All right." Jake slid off the chair, and then carefully placed his mother's hand on the bed, his touch lingering, hoping for the return of that warmth that he always remembered her by, but the cold remained, and Jake let her go.

"So," Zi said, waiting near the door. "What do we need to do?"

Jake finally looked away from his mother. "If you're going to be staying here, then you should know a few things about the house." He moved toward his parents' closet and opened the door. "If we're ever in trouble, you want to come in here."

Zi walked over, glancing inside. "It's a little small, don't you think?"

Jake knelt and ran his fingers along the floorboards until he found the loose edge. When he lifted it up, he exposed a darkened space. "It's a tunnel. It runs from the house to the barn. It's in case we ever need to leave, but we can't use the back or front doors."

Zi leaned closer. "Oh my god. You built this?"

"My dad dug it," Jake answered, shutting the lid. "C'mon, I'll show you the rest."

Jake left the door open a crack and found Stevie and Maya in the kitchen, the pair looking half asleep at the table.

"Hey," Zi said. "Jake is showing us some things around the house."

"So?" Stevie snarled.

"So, maybe you should get up and listen," Zi said.

Stevie stood up quickly and knocked his chair down. "What the hell does it matter? The world is ending, and we're stuck in the middle of nowhere." He stormed off, heading down the hall, and they heard the slam of a bedroom door.

Maya, his wife, slowly stood. "I'm sorry about that. He's just tired." She slunk past Jake and Zi and disappeared down the hall into the spare bedroom.

Jake waited until he heard the close of the door, then walked to the wall that separated the kitchen and the living room. "This is for the spotlights on the roof." He opened a plastic covering, which revealed a switch. "We turn this on, and the lights turn on all around the house. It lets us easily see who's out there."

"I thought all of the power was shut off," Zi asked.

"We have solar panels on the roof," Jake answered. "They're hooked up to a spare battery where the power is stored."

"Smart," Zi said.

Jake smiled and backpedaled to the kitchen. "Then you're really going to like this." He walked toward the cabinets and opened the door next to the stove, pointing inside. "You see that plastic box?"

Zi got low and checked inside. "Yeah."

"That's one of our trump cards," Jake said. "We have mortars buried twenty yards out all around the house. If we are attacked, and we're overwhelmed, we flip the switch inside the box and BOOM!" He opened his eyes wide, making a little explosion with his hands.

Zi frowned. "There are explosives out there? Like, we've already stepped on them?"

"It's completely safe," Jake answered, closing the cabinet door. "So long as you don't flip on the switch." He stood and dusted his hands off. "We'll have to set up some trip wires around the house. I know my dad will want that done."

"Trip wires?"

"Yeah, c'mon, I'll show you." Jake headed for the door, but then stopped, remembering his mother. The distraction of showing Zi around had helped so much that he'd forgotten about her. He looked to Zi. "Do you think Maya will watch my mom? I just don't want to leave her alone."

Zi's expression was skeptical, but she tried to remain positive. "We can ask."

Jake followed Zi, and she knocked on the door. Unsurprisingly, it was Maya who answered, and she agreed to look over Mary while Jake took Zi outside.

But before they left, Jake told both of them to wait a moment, and he returned to his mother's room alone. He shut the door and quietly approached his mother's bedside. He picked up her hand again, finding it just as cold as before.

Jake knew that she couldn't hear him, but there were things that he wanted to say. Things he *needed* to say.

"I know that you said none of this was my fault," Jake said. "But I still feel guilty. Guilty because if it weren't for me, then we wouldn't have been in the city in the first place. And I know you wouldn't want me to say that, but it's true. I've always felt weak, Mom, and now that weakness hurt you." He wiped away a tear and then glanced at the door to make sure it was still closed. He stared down at his mother's lifeless hand and nodded. "I promise that I won't be weak anymore. No matter what. I won't let you down again." He kissed her hand and returned it to the bed.

When Jake left the room, Maya took a seat in the chair where Jake had been, giving her assurance that she would keep a close eye on Mary.

"So you ready to show me what's next?" Zi asked.

Jake nodded. "I'm ready."

19

*T*he horses' trot had become a hypnotic rhythm in the darkness. It was a sound that James had always enjoyed. And despite the gear on his back and the rifle in the saddle holster, he relished the wind on his face.

"Boss," Luis said, riding closer as he pointed ahead in the darkness.

James saw the glow of lights ahead. He slowed his mare on their approach and kept his distance. Sound carried far on the wind.

James waited until they were two hundred yards out before he dismounted, planting a stake in the dirt, tethering the animal in the open plains. Once Luis had done the same, the pair lingered in the darkness, preparing their weapons for their assault.

"We'll approach from the north," James said. "They'll probably have the bulk of their watch guards looking to the east and west on the roads."

"Right," Luis said. "So where do we start looking?"

James had given that some thought and figured that if the townspeople were still alive, then it would be easiest to control them by keeping them all together. "The only building big enough to hold everyone would be the bank. One entrance and exit. It'd be easy to guard." He wiped sweat dripping into his eyes. "I'll take a look around the perimeter and see what I can find. Stay here and I'll circle back around."

"You sure you want to go alone?" Luis asked.

"I'll be easier to move around with just me," James answered. "I won't be long. Just a quick look."

Before Luis protested any further, James darted off to the east side of the town, keeping low, moving quickly, eyes peeled for any threat in the darkness.

Along the way he saw only a few patrols, and James figured that the guards were overly confident about their fortifications. And when he made it to the east side, he saw why.

A fleet of old Humvees, like the one James arrived in, were parked near the Darvishes' gas station, along with a big rig and trailer. Two guards were stationed in that area, but James moved closer to get a better look.

Each of the Humvees was outfitted with a big fifty-caliber gun, and there were boxes of ammunition ready to be loaded should they need to be called into action. James knew that the moment they made any noise they'd immediately be screwed, and those vehicles were all terrain. Their horses were fast, but James wasn't in the mood to test their speed.

James stealthily snuck to the back of the gas station, near the old pump that he had Mavis install a few years ago. He paused, looking for a path toward the front, when he heard flies buzzing to his right.

James glanced over and saw a tarp covering two lumps on the ground, and next to the tarp was a wheelchair and oxygen tank.

James didn't need to lift the tarp to find out who lay beneath it. It was clear that it was Larry and Mavis Darvish. The father and son had run the gas station in town for years, and he'd seen both of them alive yesterday.

Still, knowing what he would find, James couldn't stop himself from walking over and lifting the tarp to find the dead pair of father and son lying side by side. Mavis was only recognizable by his big body, the bullet that killed him claiming half of his skull. Larry had a bullet wound in the chest, and both bodies were already well into the stages of decomposition. The Texas heat hadn't been doing them any favors.

James wondered what had happened, but he knew that Larry's mouth must have gotten them into trouble. The man never knew when to stay quiet. James covered their bodies with the tarp and then returned to the corner, fueled by a new hate for the people who had killed them.

James worked his way toward the front of the station, peeking around the corner to find both guards on a smoke break, their weapons propped up against the wall. James considered shooting them. He had a suppressor loaded on his rifle, but he didn't want to take the unnecessary risk. The best course of action was still evasion.

Aided by darkness, James slipped into the cluster of Humvees. He removed his blade and punctured the first tire that he came across. The air hissed quietly from the tire, but James waited to see if the guards heard anything.

Only when James was sure that they hadn't heard did he slice the next tires, slashing as many as he could without being seen.

Finished, he hurried back the way he came and into the fields where he found Luis waiting in the same spot as before.

"Well?" Luis asked.

"Guards are few and far between," James answered. "They don't seem to be too worried about an attack. I found two on a smoke break." He pointed toward the building. "We'll head through an alley near the back of the bank. I still think that's the best place to start looking."

"James," Luis said, clearing his throat. "Did you have to kill anyone when you were coming out of San Antonio?"

James was caught off guard by the question, and the moonlight revealed the worry on Luis's face. He cleared his throat and then nodded.

Luis exhaled and adjusted the grip on his rifle. "Okay then."

"Hey." James placed his hand on Luis's shoulder. "You can't hesitate on me." He pointed to the town. "The people that are doing this to us? They won't hesitate. Because killing us is their mission. Do you understand?"

"Yeah." Luis cleared his throat, looking calmer than he had before. "I won't let you down."

"Good." James looked to the town ahead, preparing himself mentally. "We keep quiet, stay low, and stay together until we know more about what we're dealing with."

James padded his feet quietly against the dirt and grass as they moved toward the backside of the buildings. Staying downwind, James smelled smoke before he saw the red dot from the cigarette. He quickly dropped, Luis doing the same, and pointed to the dark figure smoking.

The tall grass from the outside of the building provided enough cover for James and Luis to crawl without being seen, the wind blowing the tips of the grass in all directions, which also helped to mask his movements.

The tall grass ended fifteen yards from the terrorist, and because of the short distance, James knew it was an easy shot for him to make. But even with the rifle's suppressor there would be noise, and there wasn't any telling how many others might be inside that same building on the other side of the wall. Shooting the man now was a risk, but he might not get another chance.

James quietly and carefully positioned his rifle and peered through the scope as he lay on his stomach at the edge of the tall grass. He brought the man in his crosshairs, choosing to go for the head as he couldn't tell what kind of body armor the man was wearing.

And while James had hunted thousands of times before, he knew that this was different. He was about to kill a man, a defenseless man.

But all James had to do was remember the man who shot his wife, the same people who had destroyed this town, destroyed the city, put his son in danger. These weren't men. They were rabid animals. And rabid animals needed to be put down.

James placed his finger on the trigger when a back door flung open and another man stepped outside, calling the man with the cigarette.

A few brief words were exchanged and then both men returned inside, the smoker flinging the cigarette to the ground and the door slamming shut behind them.

James slowly exhaled and removed his finger from the trigger. He waited a little longer to make sure no one else was coming out, then emerged from the tall grass and positioned himself by the door that the pair of men had gone through.

James waved for Luis, and his right-hand man emerged from the tall grass and joined James's side.

"What now?" Luis asked.

James leaned closer to the door of the building and heard the foreigners talking inside. It sounded like there were more than two. "We'll stay to the back side of the buildings and then creep up to the bank by the alley."

James moved first, Luis falling in line behind him. Both were mindful for potential threats, but they reached the alley without incident.

James held up his hand, holding Luis back. "Stay here. I'll snake my way up front and then wave you up if it's clear."

"What happens if I spot someone?" Luis asked.

"You don't shoot unless it's absolutely necessary," James answered.

Luis nodded and then stood watch as James worked his way up the alley.

Voices echoed from the street, and James moved methodically toward the road. Slowly, James craned his head from the alley's exit, glancing in both directions as he hugged the bank's wall.

Old kerosene lanterns hung from the rafters and one guard stood watch at the bank's entrance, armed with an AK-47.

James shouldered his rifle, checking the streets to ensure the coast was clear, and then unsheathed his hunting blade. And even though James kept a tight grip on the knife's handle, he couldn't stop his arm from shaking.

James lingered at the edge of the alley, waiting for the right opportunity to strike. He knew that he was only going to get one shot at this.

When the guard walked toward the alley, James ducked behind the wall, his back flat against the worn wood.

The walkway boards groaned louder with every step the guard took toward James until the noises stopped just short of the alleyway.

James fought the urge to look and see what the guard was doing. Had he been seen? Was the guard waiting for something?

Another groan sounded, and James watched the shadow of the man turn. Now was his chance.

James stepped from the cover of the alleyway, the guard with his back to James as he took three silent footsteps and simultaneously placed his hand over the guard's mouth to muffle the scream and sliced the man's throat, holding him still until the life and fight drained from his body.

The blood that poured from the guard's neck was warm and slick, and blood splattered against the palm of James's hand as he kept it clamped tightly over the man's mouth. He wore gloves, but the guard bit through the tough leather.

Finally, the fight left the man and James gently lowered him to the ground. He stared at the blood on his hands and clothes and then stared at the body.

The guard gurgled the last few breaths, choking on his own blood. A thin red line marked the cut along his throat. James shut his eyes, but he still saw the man on the ground.

James placed the knife back in its sheath as he patted the dead man down, choosing not to look at the wound along the guard's throat. He found the keys in the left pants pocket and then moved to the door.

James waved Luis down, and with trembling hands, James managed to shove the key into the lock on the third try. He and Luis then carried the dead guard into the bank and shut the door behind them.

It was dark in the bank, the only light coming from the porch lantern spilling through the front windows, but when James turned to face the darkness, he could make out the shadowy figures huddled in the back.

James walked toward them, and collectively they drew back, all of them but one, and James was glad to see Nolan still alive, though his clothes had been bloodied.

"James," Nolan said, speaking the name with relief, the old man embracing James in a hug. "I didn't think I'd see you again."

It was James who pulled back, gripping Nolan by the shoulders. "Mary needs help. I have to get you out of here."

"How bad is it?"

"She was shot in the back. No exit wound."

"I have some of my old surgery tools back at the office," Nolan said. "I'll need them."

"Where are they?"

"The bottom drawer of the filing cabinet in my office. The key to that cabinet is in the middle drawer of my desk."

122

James nodded and then turned to Luis. "Get him to the horses and back to the ranch. If I don't make it back, then Nolan will just have to help Mary with what we have there—"

"Hey." The voice whispered loudly from the darkness, and both James and Nolan turned toward the silhouetted figure. "What about us?" The silhouetted figure walked to the edge of the light. "You have to get us out of here."

The man was a few years younger than James, but a little shorter and a little wider around the middle. He wore a business suit, pinstriped, with a white shirt that was stained with sweat. Whatever tie he'd worn had been removed and the top button of the shirt had been opened to allow for better airflow. Though James didn't understand why the guy didn't just take off the jacket.

"Please, I have family at home." A woman joined the man's side, her hands clutched together in a pleading gesture. She wore shorts and a faded green t-shirt. She was thin, almost all bones, but she couldn't have been older than twenty-five. The makeup she'd put on that morning had started to run, making her look like a poorly-drawn clown.

Slowly, one by one, the faces of the imprisoned emerged, each of them begging for help, each of them with problems that James couldn't solve.

"Get home," James said. "All of you, as fast as you can. Do anything but stay here."

Luis came from the window, spinning James around, his eyes wide. "People are coming."

James looked to the window and saw the moving lights heading toward their building, and he knew that they had run out of time.

Still surrounded and being hounded by the people that were trapped, James grabbed hold of Nolan and yanked him toward the door, both he and Luis on either side, guns up. He turned back to the crowd that had grown silent from his hasty movements. "You're only going to have a small window to escape, so run as fast as you can." James gripped the handle and then looked to Luis. "You ready?"

Luis nodded, and Nolan pushed up the glasses sliding down the bridge of his nose.

Shouts echoed in the street, and James peered out the window. Other terrorists had noticed the blood, and they had alerted the rest of the town. It was now or never. James flung the door open and opened fire.

20

Muzzle flashes brightened the darkness like lightning, quickly followed by the lingering thunder of gunshots. James hunched forward with his own rifle, returning gunfire and forcing the terrorists behind the remnants of the broken-down vehicles.

"Move!" James shoved Nolan down the alleyway, Luis guiding the old man while James provided as much cover fire for the others that poured out of the bank's doorway. But as fast and accurate as James's gunshots were, the enemy just had more bullets.

Bodies dropped, most of the casualties from the towns-people fleeing the bank, and the sight of the carnage was enough to keep others from trying to escape.

James held his position, giving Nolan and Luis enough time to get to the horses, and then sprinted down the alley, keeping to the back of the buildings and firing randomly down the alleys he passed in hopes of drawing the bulk of the forces toward him and away from Nolan.

And it worked.

By the time that James reached the west side of the town and peered down the street, he saw a dozen soldiers moving toward his position. And with Nolan's office on the other side of the street and in the middle of town, that presented a problem.

Four broken-down vehicles were spread out between James and the other side of the street, and while they were few and far between, he could use them as cover the way he did in the city.

James sprinted toward to the first sedan, his shadowy figure triggering more gunfire and screams just as he reached the hood of the car.

Bullets struck the vehicle, their vibrations traveling through the metal and against James's arm. Glass shattered overhead and James kept low, his nerves calm and his body still as he waited for a lull in gunfire.

When the time came, James emerged from the sedan, planted his elbows on the hood of the car, brought the shadowy figures into his scope, and squeezed the trigger.

The recoil of the assault rifle struck harshly against James's shoulder and created a rhythmic beat that began to match the same pounding of James's heart.

He provided enough cover fire for himself to sprint to the next car, repeating the process until he reached a truck, where the heavy barrage of bullets shot out the tires and shattered the windows, forcing James down into the protection of the engine block and the tire well where he knew the bullets wouldn't be able to penetrate.

By now, every terrorist in the town had been alerted, and a continuous stream of bullets were focused on the truck, tearing it to pieces.

James reached around to his pack and removed his one ace in the hole. He pulled the grenade's pin, keeping pressure on the handle. He flung the grenade in a high arc and covered his ears.

Screams replaced gunfire, but those ended with an explosion, sending shock waves through the ground.

James sprinted from the truck, stumbling behind the cover of the first building where the hasty momentum caused him to trip and crash face first into the dirt.

The gritty taste of soil on his lips, James hastily wiped his mouth with the back of his hand and then sprinted around the back of the buildings once more, the remaining terrorists in pursuit.

James found Nolan's building and disappeared inside before the terrorists saw. He caught his breath, and the walls muffled the shouting outside as the enemy continued their search.

James hurried into the nearest patient room and wheeled the bed out to block and barricade the door, wedging the corners of the bed tight into the walls.

Disoriented from the fight, James used the wall of the narrow hallway to keep himself upright. The adrenaline had hollowed out his body, and James knew he was running on empty, but he just had to push a little further.

After locating Nolan's personal office, James entered to a big mess. The terrorists had ransacked the office, tipping the desk to its side, the contents of the drawers spilled out onto the carpet, the computer that was on the desk smashed into pieces.

The pictures and frames that hung from the walls holding degrees and photographs of loved ones had been removed and smashed onto the floor. Stationary, papers, all of it covered every square inch of Nolan's office.

The file cabinet that Nolan had told him was lying horizontal on the back wall, all of the drawers opened save for the bottom one, which was still locked

James stepped over files and papers, kicking them aside as he searched for the key, trying the desk first, but the drawer's contents had already been emptied.

A heavy pounding sounded from the back door, and James knew his time was running out.

Unable to find the key, James aimed his rifle at the cabinet's lock and fired. He opened it and grabbed the black bag inside.

James emerged from the office, the back door buckling as the terrorists tried to break it down. He took a step toward the front door but stopped when he heard glass shatter and the thunder of boots rush inside.

James ducked into the nearest patient room and shut the door. With the enemies closing in and nowhere to go, he looked up and saw the old panels in the ceiling. He stepped up onto the cot and shoved one of the ceiling panels aside.

Voices echoed outside the door, coming from the front and the back. James was too big with the pack on his back, so he ditched it and then pulled himself through the ceiling, quickly replacing the panel as the door was kicked down.

Carefully and quietly, James stepped along the sturdy support beam, picking up the black medical bag along the way.

The wood groaned and James froze. He waited, listening to the chatter beneath him, and when the first gunshot was fired, he sprinted across the beam.

Bits of wood and insulation drifted through the air, making it dense and scratchy as James struggled for breath on his path toward the window.

The single pane glass shattered easily enough as James slammed the black bag through it. He brushed away the glass around the edges, the window barely wide enough for him to fit through as he climbed up and out of the attic and onto the roof.

James sprinted along the rooftop, the terrorists still shooting at the ceiling. He reached the end of the buildings and dangled off the side of the roof, then collapsed into the grass. He stumbled to his feet, sprinting into the darkness.

Relieved when James heard the whinny of his mare, he glanced back one last time to see the town still in an uproar.

He pulled the stake out of the ground and then stepped into the stirrups, slumping forward in the saddle as he secured the black surgical bag.

James kicked the beast and the horse raced across the plains, into the darkness and away from the shouts and gunfire of the town. Exhausted, he hoped the wind would keep him awake, and if he didn't, then he hoped his horse would remember the way back home.

21

*I*t was more open space than Zi had seen in her entire life. And it was so quiet. She'd never experienced such silence. At least not until the EMP. Sirens, trains, cars, planes, phones, it all stopped. But after a while, the sounds of machines were replaced with the terrifying screams of people fleeing from gunfire and the explosions.

Out here, Zi heard the breeze move the tall grass in the fields. She heard the steady patter of hooves from the cattle and horses that roamed the open space. And the only vibrations she felt were the steady beating of her own heart as she stood outside under the stars.

The sky had never looked so brilliant in the city. Thousands, no, millions of lights peppered the darkness. She had never seen the night look so crisp and so real.

"How big is this place?" Zi asked.

"Over one thousand acres," Jake answered. "The land was bought by my great-great-grandfather during the Great Depression." He pointed out into the darkness. "The east end of the property is marked by the Nueces River, and Highway 55 is to the west. North of us, we have a hundred-acre wooded area that's good for hunting and target practice."

Zi nodded, then glanced up at the sky again. "Is it always like this out here?"

"As long as there aren't any clouds," Jake answered. "C'mon. We need to start."

The pair walked back toward the barn where she helped Jake pick up some supplies.

"Have you ever been on a ranch before?" Jake asked.

"Nope," Zi answered. "I grew up in San Antonio. In fact, I think this is my first time out of the city in five years."

"Did you like it?" Jake asked.

Zi shrugged. "I didn't have much to compare it to." She glanced up at the stars. "I have to say that the view out here isn't half bad."

"I like it out here," Jake said. "But the city is fun too. There's always something to do, something to see, people to talk to. Not a lot of talking out here."

"Sounds like you have a lot of space out there to run around," Zi said.

"Yeah, but I don't go running too much." Jake opened the barn doors. "I read a lot though. It's about the only thing that I can do with my condition."

"Condition?"

"It's a heart thing, and it can make it hard for me to do physical activity sometimes."

Zi frowned. "Is that why you were in the city earlier today?"

Jake nodded. "I have to go every six months. I have AVS, aortic valve—"

"Stenosis," Zi said.

Jake stopped. "How do you know that?"

"I was friends with a girl in high school who had it," Zi said.

"Did she get worse as she got older?" Jake asked. "I've read a lot of what to expect down the line."

131

"She had a pretty bad case," Zi answered. "But I kind of lost touch with her after high school."

"I might have to get a heart transplant if it gets really bad, but those are rare cases," Jake said.

"Sounds like you've done your research," Mary said.

Jake flicked his flashlight to the left, illuminating some of the horses trotting back and forth behind the fence. "Most people don't like to know what's wrong with them. It's like they're afraid that if they give it a name, then it makes it real. What they don't realize is that it's always there, even if they recognize it or not. And it helps me know what to expect. And I can prepare. Just like how my dad prepared for all of this."

Once inside the barn, Jake led them to the last stall, which was filled with boxes.

Zi gazed at the stacks. "So your dad is what? Like, one of those end of the world people?"

"Preppers, survivalists, people give it all sorts of names," Jake answered. "My dad just likes to be able to take care of things himself."

Jake removed one of the boxes and set it on the ground. When he opened it, there were dozens of spiraling spools of wire, and Jake picked one up and handed it to Zi.

"What is it?" Zi asked, turning it over in her hands.

"Trip wire," Jake answered. "That's what we'll be setting around the house. And we attach it to this." He reached deeper into the box and removed a shotgun shell. "We create a taut line with the wire and then attach one end to the shotgun shell that is attached to one of these, um..." He searched through the box, looking for something, and then pulled it out when he found it. "Ah, this. It's like a little firing pin. It puts enough pressure on the shell to make it explode, which frightens whoever is trying to sneak onto our property, and at the same time alerts us that there is someone out there." He returned the supplies to the box but didn't close the lid. "Sound carries far out here, so we'll set the traps starting three hundred yards out in all directions from around the house."

"If the traps are all around the house, then how will we work around it?" Zi asked. "And what about the animals?"

"Animals are smarter than you think," Jake answered. "As for us, we'll create paths for ourselves where we'll know it's safe to move."

The pair carried the boxes to the north side of the house. Walking out into the field, Zi once again stared up at the starry night sky. "So have you guys done this before? Set traps?"

"Just for practice," Jake answered.

Zi sighed in relief when they put the boxes down in the dirt, and Jake walked her through the process.

To set the trip wire, a spike was driven into the ground and one end of the wire was tied to it and then pulled for six feet before attaching it to another spike, which had the firing pin to trigger the shotgun shell that would be hidden in the grass.

"You always want to keep it pointed down into the dirt," Jake said. "The idea is to alert us, not to kill anyone. Because the person that trips the wire could be friend or foe."

Both of them had their knees planted in the dirt, the soil moist and cool against Zi's fingertips. She smiled, feeling the dirt getting beneath her fingernails. "I don't suppose you guys still have showers during the apocalypse."

"We're completely self-sustaining," Jake answered, not picking up on the sarcasm. "We can grow our own food. We have water from the river. Solar panels for power to help with some smaller items around the house. Medical supplies. Weapons." Jake finished digging his small hole. "We can last a long time out here."

The pair worked in silence for a while, Jake helping Zi with the first few trip wires until she was confident that she wasn't going to blow her fingers off, then together they worked their way back toward the house.

It was nice working with Jake. He was one of those kids that was more adult than child. It was probably due to his condition. Most kids that grew up with some kind of trauma like that ended up maturing faster than other kids. She saw that growing up a lot in her own neighborhood. Not to mention her own trauma.

Zi had a younger brother growing up. She was Jake's age when he died, and despite their different skin colors, she saw a resemblance of her brother in Jake. Ty was quiet, smart, and kind.

At night, she still had nightmares of the day he died. It replayed in her memory so vividly it was like she was back on that river bank, trying to reach for her brother's hand. But the current was too strong, and she was too little.

"Zi?" Jake asked. "Are you all right?"

"Hmm?" Zi shook herself from the memory. "I'm fine. Mind if I use the bathroom?"

"It's on the west side of the house. First floor, second door on the left."

"Thanks." Zi wiped some of the dirt off on her jeans and tried to keep quiet on her walk up the front steps. She knew that Mary was resting and she didn't want to wake her.

Having come from a small apartment in the city, Mary was surprised at how large the house was. But even with the size, it was still cozy, and it brought back memories of her grandmother's house outside of San Antonio before her parents had put her in a home. Zi had volunteered to take care of Nana Greyson, but the old woman was stubborn.

"I'm not going to have you waste your days away with me," Nana said, patting her on the hand the way she did whenever she was finished speaking on the matter.

She was ninety-three when she finally passed. It happened in her sleep. The most peaceful way to go in Zi's opinion, and with everything that she'd seen over the past twelve hours, she realized how precious that kind of an end would be.

But Zi often wondered what Nana had thought about the night before as she laid her head down in that nursing home, surrounded by strangers, forced to lay in some bed that wasn't her own, staring up a ceiling that wasn't hers. She had hated that the woman was forced into a place like that, and she had gotten so angry that it created a rift between her and her parents so wide that they hadn't spoken since.

With the aid of the flashlight, Zi did her business. She washed her hands with a trickle of water and then dried them on the yellow towels that had small ducks embroidered at the ends.

Zi stepped out of the bathroom, but stopped when she heard the heated whispering coming from Mary's room down the hall. She approached slowly and leaned her ear toward the crack in the door, concentrating on their voices.

"We don't know these people," Stevie said.

"They saved us," Maya said, her tone calmer than her husband's. "They got us out of the city. We're safe here."

"And for how long?" Stevie asked. "How long before they work us to death or decide that they have one too many mouths to feed? Do you think that James is going to pick us over his family? No. He's already made that point very clear."

"They have so much," Maya answered. "More than enough to go around."

"Yeah," Stevie said. "So why don't we take what we need to, and then leave?"

Zi frowned and leaned away from the door, and Mary's tone matched the disgust on Zi's face as she leaned against the door again to continue her eavesdropping.

"You want to steal from them?" Maya asked.

"I want to keep us alive," Stevie answered. "How long do you think this is going to last, huh? How long until those people that attacked the city find their way here? You saw what happened to that little town we stopped at. Those terrorists are everywhere! We need to head farther north."

"Stevie—"

"We don't have a choice, Maya," Stevie said. "Look. I'll get one of the guns, we grab some food and water, maybe some of their medical supplies, and then we leave. We just go. They won't miss us, and even if we take some of their stuff, it's like you said, they have plenty. We have to do this. This is what survival looks like now."

Maya's silence was her consent, and Zi leaned away from the door but remained frozen in the hallway, processing what she'd overheard and suddenly wishing that she hadn't.

Zi quietly moved away from the door, unsure if she should tell Jake what she'd heard or if she should wait until James returned. But before she could think on it anymore, horses sounded outside, and she jogged to the front porch.

Luis and another man she didn't recognize dismounted a horse, both of them looking ragged and sweaty. Particularly the old man that was brought back, which Zi figured was the doctor from town.

"Where is she?" the old man asked, walking up the stairs.

"Down the hall," Mary answered. "Last bedroom on the left."

The old man darted past her, and Luis joined her on the porch, still catching his breath. "Did James come back yet?"

"No, he's not with you?" Zi looked out into the darkness, but saw nothing.

"We got separated," Luis answered. "Where's Jake?"

"Out back," Zi answered.

"Thanks."

Luis left, and Zi stood alone on the porch, glancing down the darkened dirt road where Luis had come, hoping that James would soon follow.

22

James lost consciousness twice during the ride back, and each time he woke from the horse's gyrating motions, he forgot where he was going. But the animal had found its way back to the road, somehow using that as a way to guide them home. Each time he woke, James stroked the animal's mane, whispering his thanks.

The final time James woke up, he managed to retain his consciousness all the way back to the ranch, breaking the animal into a full sprint down the dirt road, praying that Luis had made it back with Nolan without incident.

James didn't pull back on the reins until he was only a few feet from the front steps of his house and then slid his exhausted body down the saddle.

Before James even made it to the stairs, Luis bust through the door, coming down to help him into the house.

"He's already set up in the room," Luis answered.

"Is Mary—".

"She's still alive," Luis answered.

By the time James made it to the bedroom, he could barely stand on his own. He found Mary and Jake together and dropped to his knees. But while his son looked fine, Mary's face was pale and she was still unconscious.

Nolan picked up his black bag and started organizing his tools.

"Is it too late?" James asked.

"She'll need a blood transfusion," Nolan answered, looking only at his tools and not the man still on his knees holding his son. "Do you know her blood type?"

"Yes," James answered. "I'm a match."

"Good, does anyone here know how to draw blood?" Nolan asked. "I don't have enough time to do that and prep her for surgery."

"I can."

James turned to find Zi in the doorway.

"Good," Nolan said, then fished out a glass jar and extended it toward Zi, who took it. "Wash it, sterilize it, and then fill it up."

Zi took the items and disappeared while James and Jake remained by Mary's bedside. Still holding onto his son, James stood and then grabbed Mary's hand. It was cold and lifeless, and he feared that he had already lost her.

"It's best if you leave now," Nolan said, dropping his usual cordial tone.

James stared down at his son, whose eyes had watered, his lower lip trembling as he walked to Mary's bedside and delicately brushed the hair from her forehead.

"I love you, Mom," Jake said. "And I'll be right here waiting to take care of you when you wake up. I promise." He kissed her cheek and then sprinted out of the room.

James still had hold of her hand, and he gave it a reassuring squeeze, the way he always did whenever she had been nervous about something. And while there were a million things that he wanted to say, James only reminded her of the promise that they'd made to each other all of those years ago when they were married. "All the way. No matter what." He bent down and kissed her forehead, his lips lingering on her skin.

James left Nolan to his work, and he found Zi waiting for him just outside of the door.

"We can do it in the kitchen," James said.

Zi pulled up a pair of chairs for them, working the rubber tubing into the proper spots to funnel the blood into the container, and then dabbed at the crook of James's forearm to sterilize the area. James looked away when she finally stuck the needle into the flesh.

"You didn't strike me as the squeamish type," Zi said, giving the tube a few flicks to make sure that the blood was flowing.

James exhaled and then glanced at the jar where his blood was currently being collected. He stared at it, transfixed, unsure of why he couldn't stop staring at it, and then it suddenly dawned on him.

"It's the same color," James said.

Zi frowned, shaking her head, looking at the jar. "What do you mean?"

When James realized that he'd spoken aloud, he shook his head. "Nothing." But he couldn't look away from the jar slowly filling with blood. Blood the same color as the man he'd killed outside of the bank.

Blood the same color as the rivers he saw running red in the streets of San Antonio. That claret splashed over asphalt and concrete and clothes. Some of it shiny, some of it dried, some of it still slick and warm from the summer sun.

And all of that blood came from different people from different religions and different beliefs, different ethnicities. But everyone's blood was the same color.

"James," Zi said, her voice softly pulling him from the daze that he'd fallen into watching the blood drip into the jar. "I need to talk to you about something."

James pinched his eyebrows together. He was exhausted.

Zi rubbed her hands together nervously. "I heard something when I was helping Jake get the house ready."

James leaned forward, careful not to pull the needle from his arm and splash what little blood he had left onto the floor. "What?"

"It's probably nothing, just nervous chatter, but..." Zi pulled her lips into her mouth, struggling to finally spit it out. "Stevie and Maya were talking about stealing and then leaving." She lifted her gaze to meet James's eyes and leaned back, almost as if she thought she might be guilty of association because of what she had heard.

James chuckled, the laughter rolling out of him in waves that made him even more light-headed than before, and then slouched lazily in his chair.

The reaction caught Zi off guard. "I'm not making this up, James. I heard them talk about it while you were gone."

James waved his hand and then rubbed his calloused palm against his cheek, already starting to feel the rough grain of his beard creeping in. It grew quickly. Mary used to complain he would get a five o'clock shadow at nine o'clock in the morning. "I believe you. It's just..." James lowered his hand to his lap. "You try and do the right thing, give people the benefit of the doubt, and then they just end up burning you anyway." He glanced back to the blood that had now filled a quarter of the jar.

"So what should we do?" Zi asked.

James smiled when he found Zi's face. He liked how she was already speaking like they were a team. He adjusted himself in his seat, his eyelids starting to droop with fatigue. "We give them what they want. They don't have to steal. So long as their requests are reasonable. But after they sleep on it, they might feel different."

James was quiet for a moment, Zi's voice becoming nothing but distorted echoes that took a while to travel into his mind. He scrunched up his face when he looked at her again. "What?"

"I asked if you wanted me to keep an eye on them until morning," Zi said, repeating herself. "Are you all right, James?"

"Yeah. Fine." James shut his eyes, no longer having the strength to keep them open. "Keep an eye on them. I don't think they'll do anything... But... Keep.. Eye... them."

23

The blood still hadn't dried. The hot night air had kept it slimy. The slice from the blade was clean and narrow across Xavier's throat. His eyes still retained some of their golden amber, but they were lifeless.

Dillon Thompson adjusted his black gloves as he stared down at the fallen soldier. Dillon was taller than most of the fighters, thin and lean, his face covered with light brown scruff. His hair had receded, the hairline pushing back farther with every birthday, his baldness aging him well beyond his thirty-seven years.

Two fighters jogged up behind Dillon, both breathless from the journey. Both were decked out in tactical gear, covered in dust from the long trip. The shorter of the two stepped forward.

"We didn't find him." Emmanuel pulled down his bandana, exposing a patch beard of black and grey hairs that gave his face a rat quality to it. "There was a building, but it was abandoned."

Dillon snarled. He had sent Emmanuel and Dante to the location where the doctor had told him to find Bowers, which he now understood was a ruse. A wild goose chase to bide time, and now that time had cost Dillon some of his men.

The town had been easy to take. But this was Dillon's first taste of resistance, and it was a bitter medicine.

Dillon stood, leaving Xavier in the dirt. He would make sure the man had a hero's burial. It was important for the other men to see that, to know that their sacrifice hadn't been in vain.

One of the other fighters walked up to Dillon on his way to the bank, the pair weaving around the cars still lingering in the streets.

"Can we kill them?" Emmanuel smiled, exposing yellow, crooked teeth.

Like most fighters in their outfit, he had been pulled from the drug cartels in Central America. They were the easiest to transition to the makeshift army that had been constructed for their coordinated attack on the southern border.

"I want to question them first," Dillon answered, his long strides causing Emmanuel to nearly break out into a jog as he walked alongside him. "If they don't give me what I want to know, then you can have your fun."

Closer to the bank, Dillon saw the bodies of those that had tried to escape. Limbs, torsos, and heads were all overlapping with one another.

Emmanuel and the others had asked if they should move the dead and start burning them before they started to stink, but Dillon had told them to hold off. He wanted the people who were still in the bank to see them. He wanted them to remember what they fought back.

The front of the bank was covered in bullet holes, and the windows had been shattered, bits of glass twinkling under the light of the lanterns that hung from the roof overhang.

The townspeople that had been too frightened to run were still huddled in the back of the bank, in the darkness. They shivered and whimpered, unsure of what kind of punishment awaited them. It was the uncertainty that frightened them.

Dillon remained in the street, staring at the blood and the bodies that had yet to be moved. The heat would increase the rate of decomposition. He plucked a packet of cigarettes from his pocket and bit one between his teeth as he pulled it from the pack.

The Marlboro bounced on his lips as he exchanged the pack of smokes for a lighter, then cupped his hand around the red Bic as he brought it to the tip.

The flame illuminated a pair of focused dark eyes that stared down at the fire as if it had come from his very soul.

With the cigarette lit, Dillon took a long drag, pocketed the lighter, and then pondered how he could use this to his advantage.

Dillon motioned for Emmanuel to come closer, and the fighter did as he was told, waiting anxiously for his orders. Dillon knew that most of them wouldn't be able to provide much insight, and he didn't want to spend a lot of time with bullshit so he decided to speed things up a little bit.

"Bring me two of them," Dillon said.

Emmanuel disappeared into the bank and returned with two unwilling volunteers, shoving both of them to the ground by Dillon's feet. One was a man, middle-aged, trembling as he kept his head bowed, afraid to look up.

The second was a woman, but unlike her male counterpart, she lifted her eyes and stared at Dillon. She froze, unable to look anywhere but Dillon's eyes, even when he knelt and moved close enough to see the cracks of her makeup.

Dillon took a drag from the cigarette and then blew the smoke in her face. "Who came here today?"

The woman opened her mouth, but instead of words there were only muted gasps of air, and then she finally bowed her head. "I don't know."

Dillon turned to the man, his head still bowed, still trembling like a child. "Do you know?"

"I-I-I don't know either. I was just driving through for work when all of this happened." The man scrunched his face up, snot running from his nose as he started to cry. "I don't want to die. Please don't kill me."

Dillon stood, dropping the cigarette between the pair of sniveling cowards, and stepped on it with the toe of his boot. "Turn around. Both of you."

Neither moved, and instead looked at each other.

"I don't want to ask you again," Dillon said.

Slowly, the man and the woman turned, and Dillon squatted between them and pointed into the bank. "You see those people inside? All the way in the back? Every single one of them was hoping that you'd be able to answer my questions. That way they'd be safe. But you couldn't answer them, could you?"

"I don't fucking live here, man!" Spittle flew from the man's mouth as he clenched his fists at his side.

"No, you don't." Dillon stood, and then extended his hand to Emmanuel, who placed a pistol in his open palm. "But you're going to die here."

"NOO-"

The bullet sliced the top half of the man's head off. The woman screamed, but it ended with another pull of the trigger.

The pair both collapsed forward on their stomachs, and the blood seeping from their wounds pooled together between them to form a large puddle of darkness. Pistol in hand, Dillon looked up from the bodies and at the crowd huddled in the darkness. He stepped over the bodies and methodically worked his way into the bank.

Dillon's eyes adjusted quickly in the dark, and he saw all of the cowering faces huddled in the back.

"When I first came here, I told you that I didn't want

people to die," Dillon said, taking his time to fix each face he came across with a look that sized every person up, and Dillon was glad to find no heroes. "And in return, all I asked was for you to cooperate. To stay right here." He pointed toward the floor.

"We did," a woman said. She was crouched on the floor in the front row of the group. "We stayed. We didn't run."

"You didn't run because there were people shooting the ones that did," Dillon said, then pointed to the bodies near the door and out on the sidewalk. "But everyone dies. Death is the only reliable certainty in this world." He walked across the old bank floors, the polish gone from them years ago, then stopped in front of the woman who had spoken. He knelt, narrowing his eyes as he examined her, and she covered herself with her arms even though she was still clothed. He reached for a lock of hair and rubbed the red and blonde streaks between his fingers. He could still smell the shampoo she had used this morning. "Death always wins."

The woman shivered, looking away from Dillon, who only laughed in response. He stood, examining the rest of the group, and walked the empty space in front of their legs and shoes.

"I want to know who it was that came here," Dillon said. "And I want to know why he came here, and I want to know where he went."

"James Bowers!" The voice came from a man in the back. "He owns a ranch not far from here."

"Why was he here?" Dillon asked.

"He took Nolan," the man said, swallowing his fear.

Dillon tilted his head to the side, knowing that if this James Bowers had wanted the town doctor, then Bowers was in need of the doctor's services.

Dillon knew that James Bowers could prove problematic. If he had a Humvee and weapons, then he had provisions, and provisions would attract people. And if he had enough guns, then he could arm those people and come back to retake the town.

"Come with me," Dillon said, pointing to the man who spoke.

The man followed Dillon outside where his unit eagerly awaited their next move.

"There's a ranch west of here," Dillon said. "The man who gunned us down owns it."

Emmanuel smiled, an excited energy running from him through the rest of the group.

Dillon gestured to the man who he'd brought out. "He will tell you how to find it. Kill who you want, but bring the doctor back alive." Dillon had plans for the good doctor who had deceived him.

Emmanuel laughed and turned to his men, the group growing more excited as he relayed the orders in their native Portuguese, and then quickly dispersed.

Dillon reached for another smoke, letting this one dangle from his lips for a few minutes while he stared at the bodies of the fallen townspeople. He wondered how many piles of bodies were stacked in San Antonio, Dallas, New York, and Los Angeles. He imagined it was countless, more than he could have ever imagined.

Dillon flicked the lighter and brought the flame to the cigarette, knowing that there would be more piles added soon.

24

*T*he house creaked despite Maya and Stevie's careful steps. The wooden floors were just so old that it was impossible to remain completely silent, so they did their best to minimize the sound of their movements by staying in their socks and carrying their shoes until they made it outside into the early morning darkness.

"Maya," Stevie said, his voice a harsh whisper. "C'mon!" He waved his hand forward, and his wife nodded as she descended the stairs quickly, sliding on the pack filled with food that they'd swiped from the kitchen.

Stevie wanted to put as much distance between themselves and the ranch as possible before daybreak broke and the others realized what they stole.

It was enough for them for a few days on the road. Because Stevie had a plan, and it was better than the fantasy that James and the others had bought into.

"Do you really think the police will help?" Maya asked, raising her voice as the house grew smaller behind them.

Stevie nodded, sticking to their path along the dirt road. "I don't see how they couldn't. It's the best way for us to stay alive."

Stevie adjusted the backpack of food and then glanced up at the night, grimacing at the stars and moon. When they reached the road, he was forced to stop.

"I think I got a fricking rock in there." Stevie balanced on one foot while he dumped out the sediment he'd collected in his left shoe.

"It's so quiet." Maya watched the road ahead, a warm breeze brushing her hair back as she hugged herself. "I've never seen so much darkness before. I mean, it's like there's nothing out here."

"Why do you think I wanted to leave?" Stevie worked his shoe back on and then quickly tied the laces. "It's not safe for us out here."

Maya frowned, continuing to scan the darkness. "I want to go back."

Stevie straightened up, finished with his shoe. "What?"

Maya stepped closer to him, arms still squeezing herself tight. "It's not too late. I don't think anyone knows we left, what we did. People were still asleep." She gestured to the bags of food and other supplies they'd taken. "We can put this stuff back before anyone wakes up."

Stevie grabbed his wife's shoulders and shook his head. "We can't go back. I know this is scary, but we can't live here like this." He rubbed her arms in a reassuring gesture. "We'll go to the police, and they'll be able to help us." He pointed back toward the ranch. "Those people aren't the answer to our problems."

Maya drew in a breath and then exhaled. "Yeah. Okay."

"Good." Stevie kissed her forehead, but when he pulled back, he saw something in the darkness. He frowned, unable to make out the shapes in the road. And by the time he realized what they were, the blades had already cut their throats.

* * *

149

THE CANDLE that had been lit on the kitchen table had burned halfway down, wax dripping down the sides, in messy, Jackson Pollock-like strokes.

James opened his eyes, his vision blurred with sleep, and saw the flickering candles that had been lit in the kitchen. He was still in the same chair where Zi had taken his blood. A bandage covered the needle's puncture, and the jar that had collected his blood was gone.

James straightened up in his chair and saw the glass of water on the table. His fingers were numb and he struggled to bring the rim of the cup to his lips. He drank from it greedily, gulping half the glass before he took a break to come up for air. He rubbed his eyes, dry and filled with gunk as he squinted, struggling to keep them open.

No idea of the time, James finally managed to push himself up and out of the chair and stretched, his back popping with every twist of his waist.

The house was quiet, and James stepped carefully from the kitchen and into the living room, finding it empty and dark save for the moonlight that drifted through the front windows, the glow from the candle behind him in the kitchen causing his figure to silhouette.

James glanced down the hallway to his and Mary's bedroom and saw the door was cracked open. The cramped and narrow space of the hall bothered him on his walk down, but he stopped just short of the door, staring at the crack, afraid to open it, afraid of knowing what was really on the other side.

James slowly placed his hand on the door knob, the brass warm. He quietly opened the door, then stepped inside and saw his son asleep in a chair next to his mother's bed, who was also asleep. They were angelic, peaceful.

Like a ghost, James approached his family, kissing each of them, thankful that Mary was still alive.

With his back to the door, James didn't hear Nolan

approach and was startled when the old man touched his shoulder. Nolan pressed his finger to his lips and then motioned for James to follow him out of the room.

James nodded then scooped Jake from his chair and carried him to his room. He laid him down in his bed and then draped the bedsheets over his body.

With his son asleep, James found Nolan in the living room and then followed him to the front porch.

"I was able to get the bullet out," Nolan said, staring at the worn wooden floorboards in lieu of meeting James's gaze. "From what I could see, the bullet didn't strike any major organs, but I still have concerns."

James swallowed, but his voice didn't betray his nerves. "How bad?"

Nolan finally looked up at James. "Worst-case scenario is paralysis if the bullet damaged the spine, or one of her organs fails." He held out his hands in a helpless gesture sort of way, his shoulders slumped as his body seemed to cave and collapse inwards. "I just can't tell without any scan or x-ray. But I do know that the blood transfusion helped, along with the IV, and I think she has a good shot at recovery. She's a fighter, James. Your whole family is."

James should have felt better about Nolan's prognosis, but it was the old man's face that prevented James from the relief that his news brought. "What's wrong?"

The frown lines along Nolan's face deepened, and the old man looked one stiff wind from collapsing into nothing. He wiped the thin wisps of white hair back on his head, flattening them to his scalp, and took a deep breath that inflated his sloped shoulders and concave chest.

"If things go south, I won't be able to save her, James," Nolan said. "I know that's pessimistic, but it's the truth. I don't have the expertise to deal with the complications from surgery. Lord knows what I might have done to her on the operating table. And we won't know about the pregnancy until—"

"Pregnancy?" James frowned.

The moment Nolan looked at James, the old doctor realized he'd made a mistake. "I thought you knew."

James glanced back to the house. "Mary's pregnant?"

"She came to my office two weeks ago for a more official test," Nolan said. "Everything looked fine, both parties were healthy. I gave her a prescription for prenatal vitamins. I think she was getting them filled in San Antonio when—"

James held up his hand, and Nolan grew quiet. The floor was shifting beneath his feet and he leaned up against the wall to keep himself upright. He shut his eyes, shaking his head. "How far along?"

"Around eight weeks," Nolan answered.

"Eight weeks." James repeated the words to make sure they were real. He turned back to the doctor. "She didn't tell me. Why wouldn't she tell me?" James stepped back into the house, needing to find a chair before he collapsed.

James returned to the kitchen and sat down at the table. He shut his eyes and massaged his temples.

"James," Nolan said, appearing nearby. "I'm sure she had her reasons."

James rubbed his eyes and then lowered his hands from his face. When she had been pregnant with Jake, she told him the moment she found out. It was one of the happiest moments of their lives.

"It's not use going down the rabbit hole," Nolan said. "There will be plenty of time for that later." He joined James at the table. "Right now you need to start thinking long term."

James frowned. "I know that. We have enough—"

"Yes, yes, yes, you have food and water and medicine and land," Nolan said, rolling his hands forward in a swirling motion as he spoke. "But people are going to come to collect what you have."

"We have contingencies for that—"

"Not for what I'm talking about, you don't," Nolan said. "You're going to have to make a choice, James. A hard choice. People just weren't prepared for what happened."

James narrowed his eyes and then tilted his head to the side. "Nolan, I don't think—"

"Just let me finish." Nolan held up his hands, nodding quickly. "You have more than enough space for RVs and tents, even with all of the cattle. You have a chance to do something really special here, whether you realize or not." He lowered his hands, drawing in a deep breath that he exhaled, his shoulders slumping with him. "But this is your land. And I'm grateful and thankful for what you've done for me. But all of those people in town aren't bad folks. They just... weren't ready." He clapped James on the shoulder. "Take some time and think on it, okay?"

James nodded and Nolan headed to bed, leaving him alone at the table to contemplate.

Deep down he knew that there would be people who would come knocking on his door when things finally turned bad. But bringing on more people also meant bringing on more personalities, and people who he didn't know or understand.

Trust was important to James, because without trust, things fell apart. It was one of the reasons that the ranch had survived as long as it did. He trusted Nolan, and while he hadn't known her for very long, he was beginning to trust Zi.

But letting in more people also ran the risk of letting in more folks like Maya and Stevie. People who were so willing to rip his family off and steal from them even after James had pulled them out of the burning city and brought them into his home.

James checked the pocket watch and saw that it was a few

hours before dawn. He knew that he wouldn't be able to go back to sleep, so he walked back inside the house and into the kitchen, stepping slowly and carefully as the old house liked to alert those that slept to movement.

It was quiet in the house, as it was every morning when he woke to start his day. It was a time for him to reflect, and with everything that happened in the past twenty-four hours, he had plenty to reflect on.

Lost in thought, the quiet Texas morning was shattered with the sound of a gunshot that echoed from the front yard. A gunshot that was triggered from the trip wires that had been set up to detect intruders.

25

*B*y the time the second gunshot sounded, James had already flicked on the spotlights on top of the house. Light flooded the front yard, exposing the intruders.

James picked up his rifle from the kitchen and then opened the front door, firing at the fleeing enemy that was disoriented from the trip wires and lights. The five-man team split in half, three right, two left, both groups moving toward the back of the house.

James chased them with the rifle, dropping one on the right before the rest made it around the house, and he sprinted back through the kitchen, ducking just in time before a bullet shattered the windows.

Luis was the first one up, crouching low as he found James in the kitchen. "How many?"

"Five," James answered. "But I've already got one."

Glass shattered, and James saw the backyard darken as the enemy shot the roof spotlights.

"Get Mary and Jake into the hole!" James shouted, then fired into the backyard.

Zi was out next and joined James on the floor with the weapon that he'd given her earlier in the day.

More spotlights were shot out, but James managed to see a few of them within range of the buried mortars. It was now or never. He reached for the switches in the kitchen and braced himself. "Fire in the hole!"

James turned away from the back door as he flipped the switches, the explosions shaking the house's foundation.

His ears rang with a high-pitched din long after the explosions had finished, and he couldn't tell if the enemy outside had stopped firing or if he had just gone deaf.

Knowing that he wouldn't have much time, James stood, leaving Zi on the kitchen floor as he marched out into the darkness, searching for what remained of the enemy.

Movement to James's right caught his attention, and he pivoted, aiming at the silhouette on the ground. He fired, and the body suddenly fell still. With his ears still ringing, James neither heard the shadow's final cries or the gunshot that ended his life.

But as the ringing in James's ears subsided, it was slowly replaced with the gurgling moans of the enemy scrambling to their feet and trying to flee in the darkness.

James brought another one of them in his crosshairs and fired, dropping the man to the ground, who cried out in agony.

Only two remained.

The explosions from the mortars had upended the earth around the house, leaving the home on a tiny island of untouched land.

After a thorough sweep of the perimeter, James found one of the final two survivors, barely clinging to life as he crawled along the ground, blood spurting from a shrapnel wound on the back of his leg. James flipped him to his back, shoving the barrel of the gun into his face.

James ripped the terrorist's bandana down, unable to hide the surprise on his face as he saw that the man that had attacked him was American.

"Who are you?" James asked.

The terrorists wheezed labored breaths, even after lying still for some time. He shook his head, wincing in pain. "You cannot stop what we have started. It is the end of everything you love and everything that you took for granted."

James grimaced and then pressed his boot heel into the man's wound, causing the man to cry out in pain. He continued to apply pressure until the screams stopped, and the terrorist could only gasp in silence until James eased the pressure.

"Why did you come here?" James asked, repeating the question with fervor and haste.

"You killed our people," he said, sucking deep breaths between every few words, as if he were starved for oxygen. "And now we're here to kill yours."

"That didn't work out the way that you wanted it to now, did it?" Luis walked to the terrorist's head and aimed the rifle down at his face, his finger on the trigger.

Despite the fatigue and the pain from the gunshot wound, the terrorist laughed through choking coughs and sobs. "You will all die. Your family. Your friends. We will burn you all to the ground." He widened his eyes with madness and the cackling grew more violent. "We will cleanse you with the fires of hell!"

James had never considered himself a violent man, nor was he vengeful, but there was something about that man's laugh and the conviction in which he spoke that broke something loose in him, and he aimed the rifle at the man's face and pulled the trigger.

In the blink of an eye, the traitor's cackling ended, and James couldn't pull his eyes away from the gory hole of blood and brains that used to be the man's face. The force of the bullet caved the man's face inward, the deepest parts between the eyes where James had aimed the rifle when he squeezed the trigger.

The body jolted only once after James ended the man's life, and staring at the lifeless body, James felt something shift inside of him.

James had grown up hunting. He'd killed deer, hog, even butchered his own cattle. But since yesterday, he'd found himself hunting a different kind of beast, one that was far deadlier than any animal he'd hunted before.

"Dad?"

James spun around, his heart skipping a beat as he saw his own son staring down at the dead man. Both James and Jake were frozen, and it was Luis who came up from behind, guiding the boy away from the sight of the dead man.

"Go back inside, Jake," Luis said, giving Jake a shove toward the house. "Check on your mom. Make sure she's all right."

Jake followed Luis's direction but continued to look back at the body and his father, stumbling in a dream-like state toward the house, leaving James to wonder what his son saw and how he would explain what he had done.

Once the boy was out of earshot, Luis grabbed James's arm. He was saying something, but James couldn't hear him.

"What?" James asked.

"The bodies," Luis answered. "Once morning hits, they're going to roast faster than a pig on a spit. We can't leave them out here like that. It won't be sanitary. And I don't think that's something people will want to see with their morning oatmeal."

James nodded. "We'll bury them. Mass grave. I have some limestone we can put down." He took a step toward the barn, but Luis stopped him, pulling him back.

"You did what you had to do," Luis said. "We couldn't keep a hostage, and if we let him go, then he would have stumbled back toward the town and given them a rundown of everything we had here. You didn't have a choice, James. Remember that."

James nodded, and the pair of men walked back toward the barn in silence. James's mind was wild with worry, because he didn't think the men who came here tonight was the end of their confrontation. Plus, he saw a five-man team. And he only counted four bodies.

26

The first golden rays of dawn broke the darkness of night, and James planted the shovel into the dirt, wiping the sweat from his forehead with the back of his gloved hand, smearing more soot on his face as Luis added the final pile of dirt to the mass grave.

James had found Stevie and Maya's bodies on his search for the fifth man. Their throats had been sliced. At first he wanted to throw them in the grave with the others, but he buried them separately.

The night had been warm, but with the sun rising that heat was amplified, and it would only get hotter as the day grew longer.

"Good riddance to bad eggs." Luis planted his shovel in the dirt next to James, both men staring at the mound of dirt in silence before Luis couldn't take the quiet anymore. "You think they'll send more of them?"

James nodded. "But I don't know if we can fight them off again. They didn't use any of the heavy artillery we saw in the town. They underestimated us. If they come back, they won't make that mistake again."

Luis crossed his arms. "Well, I don't suppose that means we'll be enjoying a day off."

"Afraid not." James picked up his shovel from the dirt, and Luis did the same. "We'll need to reinforce the house, set more trip wires, mortars." He turned and glanced out toward the grave, looking past it to the bunker out in the distance. He faced forward again, the pair of men walking the same stride and picking up steam. "Jake and Zi will be able to help with some of the repairs, but I'll need you to take care of the duties on the ranch."

"You think the rest of the hands will come in this morning?" Luis asked.

James had hoped that they would show up, but he wasn't going to bank on it.

"I don't know," James answered.

Exhausted by the time they returned the house, James and Luis stepped into the back, finding Zi with Jake in the kitchen, both of them wide awake as if they'd never gone back to sleep. Which they probably hadn't.

"Hey, there are a bunch of people here," Zi said, looking concerned. "They're out front."

"I'll go and get them started," Luis said.

Zi lingered in the kitchen after Luis left. "What do you want me to do?"

James finally cleared his throat. "Go help Luis. He'll give you a rundown of some of the chores. Thanks, Zi."

Zi nodded, whispering something into Jake's ear before she disappeared.

With James and Jake alone, the pair of Bowers men lingered in silence, neither looking at one another, neither sure of what they should say.

But James knew that the silence would only make things worse the longer it went. "Have you checked on your mother?"

"Nolan is with her," Jake answered. "She's still sleeping."

James gestured inside and guided his son to the kitchen table, illuminated by the sun shining brightly through the broken window.

"I know you saw some things last night," James said once Jake finally took his seat on the opposite side of the table. "Things that I want to explain—"

"You killed him," Jake said, his eyes staring at some point on the wooden table, his expression stoic. "I know why you did it. And I understand." He raised his eyes to meet his father. "You did it to protect us. You didn't have a choice."

The answer should have made James feel better, but it sounded rehearsed. Jake spoke as if he wrestled with what to say all night, and this was the rational explanation of why he saw his father murder someone in their back yard.

"You're right," James said. "I was justified in killing those men, because they came here to kill all of us." James grabbed his son's hand. "But killing is a choice. No matter the circumstance. And it's the hardest choice you could ever make. And it should never be taken lightly. Death affects everyone involved."

Jake nodded, remaining silent, and then he slowly slid off the chair and walked around the table to James and hugged his father. "I understand."

James kissed the top of Jake's head. "Why don't you get breakfast ready for the troops?"

Jake nodded. "Yes, sir."

Once Jake was off to get the food started, James gathered the courage for what came next and chose to go ahead and hurry down the hall to Mary's room before he allowed his own doubts to make the trip harder than it was in reality.

James paused at the door, watching Nolan at Mary's bedside.

"You can come in, James," Nolan said, his back still to the door, finishing up his examination.

James stepped inside, the wood groaning from his weight,

and walked to the other side of the bed, reaching for his wife's hand.

Mary's face had grown paler, and her skin was ice cold. James engulfed her hand with his, hoping that his body heat would warm her. "How is she?"

Nolan finally removed his stethoscope from his neck and let it dangle precariously from his shoulders as he pocketed his hands, still wearing that white overcoat that he'd been taken hostage in. It was dirty with blotches of blood on it. Mary's blood. "She's fighting it."

After everything James had experienced, he was in no mood for guessing games. "Just give it to me straight, Nolan."

Nolan nodded and then drew in a big breath that raised his shoulders high and then down low again with the exhale. "She's not healing like she should. I was hoping that the antibiotics in the IV would have helped keep her afloat, but her vitals continue to decline, which could be a sign of internal bleeding. But without any x-rays or MRIs, I can't be certain."

James gently massaged Mary's hand, wondering if she could feel his touch in the deep unconscious state of her mind, knowing that Nolan was right. She wasn't a quitter. Never had been. But as tough and strong as she was, this might be more than she could handle.

"How long until we know for sure?" James asked.

Nolan rocked his head from side to side. "If it is internal bleeding, then she'll be gone by tomorrow morning. If it's an infection, the stronger antibiotic should help give her a fighting chance." Nolan finally looked up from Mary and at James. "Of all the people for this to have happened to, it's terrible that Mary should have gone through this." Nolan touched James's shoulder. "I'm very sorry, James."

"Me too," James said.

Nolan left the room, leaving James to think on everything that had happened, all they had gone through. Had he not prepared enough? Had he tried to help too many people? Perhaps. Or maybe he had lost sight of what was truly important.

James gently placed his hand over Mary's stomach and closed his eyes. He whispered a prayer, sending his hope to God with the humility of a man who needed help but felt ashamed to ask for it.

27

*W*ith one hand on the wheel and the second on the wound over his shoulder, Emmanuel struggled to stop the blood loss and keep the Humvee from crashing off the road. The old vehicle was a bear to handle with two hands, and only having one to maneuver made any sudden movements out of the question. If something stepped in front of Emmanuel's path now, it would die.

Blood continued to seep through the wound even though Emmanuel applied firm pressure. He was the last of five. Five fighters against one fucking farmer. He snarled at the thought and hoped he would be able to get stitched up and be a part of the second raiding party that returned and wiped the bastards off the face of the earth.

But the longer Emmanuel thought about the next move, the more he dreaded his return to the town. Because he knew what could be waiting for him on the way back.

Failure wasn't tolerated in their unit. But how were any of them to know about the traps waiting for them? How were they to know the farmer was that prepared?

Emmanuel paused, grimacing from a rush of pain in his

shoulder, knowing the answer to his own question. They should have never been caught off guard. They were sloppy.

Unable to maneuver the old Humvee around the blockade that they'd set up on the west side of town, Emmanuel was forced to park the Humvee and stumble into the checkpoint on foot.

With the help of his comrades, Emmanuel was brought to the doctor's office, the one that had escaped during the raid by the farmer. The place was trashed, turned upside down by their previous search for medicines and the firefight that happened during the massive jailbreak.

Two guards were placed outside of the room as the medic worked on Emmanuel. The wound was cleaned, treated for infection, and then bandaged. Finished, the medic collected his supplies and then walked out of the room, leaving Emmanuel to fend for himself against the coming inquisition.

The patient room had no windows, but Emmanuel saw the first glow of dawn stretch down the hallway from the front windows of the building.

A door opened at the front. The little bell attached to it jingled as if it were new, followed by slow, methodical footsteps.

Emmanuel kept his head down when Dillon entered the room. He attempted to keep himself from shaking, but the trembling only worsened the harder he tried to keep still. The silence was maddening.

"They blew us all to hell," Emmanuel said, blurting out the words. "It was like they knew we were coming. We went in using a standard formation, but there were trip wires set up —" He swallowed hard, the ball of fear going down stiff and slow.

"Five men," Dillon said, his voice smooth and calm. "Five men went to that ranch. But only one returned."

Emmanuel shuddered, shaking his head. "I can still finish our mission. I will do whatever it takes. I will—"

"If you had given all you could, then you wouldn't have come back," Dillon said.

Emmanuel cried, the tears coming involuntarily despite his attempt to keep them at bay. "I've done so much, and I know I can do more, just—please!" He wiped his eyes, forcing himself to regain his composure, and then cleared his throat. "I can make this right. I promise."

Dillon remained stoic, and the silence lingered for a long time until he removed one of his gloves, exposing a terribly scarred and disfigured hand. He placed his palm against Emmanuel's cheek and spoke with the gentleness of a father teaching a son. "Our cause is only as good as the people who serve it, Emmanuel. If one of us fails, then we all fail. Our success depends on our conviction. You have failed in your conviction." He repositioned that rough palm on the back of Emmanuel's head and pulled Emmanuel's face closer to his. "And there is only one outcome for that failure."

"No." Emmanuel squirmed, trying to free himself from the leader's hold. "No, please!"

The pair of soldiers entered the room as the leader kept him still, the cries transforming from a squirming nonsense to outright hysteria as Emmanuel's hands were tied behind his back and he was forced from the chair.

"No!" Emmanuel fought, using his body weight to try and keep him down, but his efforts were futile against the strength of both guards who pulled him out of the room, into the hallway, and into the light of early morning.

Emmanuel resisted even as he was brought out into the street where his fellow comrades had gathered, along with the prisoners of the town, none of whom understood what would happen. But Emmanuel did.

The pyre had already been constructed in the middle of the street, and Emmanuel was placed on it, tied to the wooden stake as he continued to scream, his grief giving way to anger as he pled for mercy.

"Don't do this!" Emmanuel's face reddened, and the veins along his neck bulged from the manic haste to break free before he was burned alive. "I can fight him again! I'll kill him! Just give me a chance!"

The gasoline burned his senses as it was doused over him and the wood at his feet. Emmanuel turned his head away, no longer able to open his eyes because of the burn from the fuel. "Please, I'm begging you, don't do this. You don't have to burn me, you don't have to—"

The first flash of heat stole Emmanuel's senses, and he drew in a breath that was all flames, burning his lungs.

The pain came quickly and all at once, and Emmanuel's scream remained lodged in his throat. He rocked from side to side, the flames devouring his skin, transforming it to blackened ash. It crackled and spit like a pig on a roast. His eyes shriveled up in his sockets, his tongue torched, the flames funneling down his open throat as the last bits of life drained from him.

And all the while, Emmanuel's comrades shed no tears because they understood that to betray was to be cleansed with the fire. It was the only way to be free of his sins and of his failure.

DILLON KEPT his attention away from the fire. But not because he couldn't stomach the sight of a man being burned alive. He wanted to see the reactions of the men. He wanted to ensure that they watched, because he wanted all of them to understand that there was no escape from the fires of truth.

The townspeople that had been brought out to watch offered a particularly amusing expression of horror and disgust. Three of them vomited, most of it just dry heaving after having gone an entire day without food or water.

Once the smell of burning flesh reached Dillon's nose, he turned away, heading for his post at the edge of town, knowing that he would be forced to retaliate. Such a distraction could prove troublesome should this rancher grow bolder after killing the squad that Dillon had sent.

Dillon stepped inside the small hardware store where he'd taken up residence and walked to the back office.

The room was small and crammed with more boxes than it was designed to hold. A small desk with a single chair and a computer from the late eighties sat on top of it, which was scattered with pens and papers, spreadsheets, and contracts.

Dillon enjoyed looking over the little notes that the owner had written. Memos, appointments, and reminders adorned the desk in a colorful and sporadic fashion.

The chair squeaked as Dillon sat down, leaning back in the same manner that he suspected the owner of the store did whenever he wanted to relax after a long day's work.

A small part inside Dillon envied the man who owned the shop. The simple life, the day in and day out routine of repetition, like a hamster on a wheel. He wished he could have a mind like that, but he had never been one to stay stationary for very long. No, he had to move, had to get places. And all those places brought him here.

Dillon stared down at his palms. The skin grafts that the doctors had done all of those years ago had been shoddy work, leaving behind a trail of scars that were as ugly as they were painful.

But those burns brought him to his current path. He had a purpose, a greater directive in this life than he could ever imagine.

"Sir?" Beckett stepped into the office. "What do you want to do with the body?"

Dillon drummed his fingers on the desk. "Leave him in

the streets. Let the fire smolder. I don't want this lesson in failure to be forgotten."

"Yes, sir. And the townspeople?"

Dillon flattened his palm against the wood and stared at one particular scar that ran the length of his index finger. "Leave them outside until the flames burn out."

Beckett left with a grin on his face, leaving Dillon to plan the death of James Bowers.

*T*he morning moved slowly, no matter how many chores James tried to busy himself with, and there were plenty to get done.

The detonations from the bombs had sent the cattle running into such a frenzy that they broke through the fence, and most of the morning was spent rounding up the herd while Zi, Jake, and James repaired the fence.

Mick and Ken's wives had joined them, and James had put them in charge of the house and barn, taking stock of the supplies that were brought in by Luis.

With their group slowly growing, James instructed Luis to dig up some of their caches and bring them back to the house to ensure that nothing had expired or gone bad. With the added people, James knew that they'd need the extra rations.

Mick rode over, slowing when they neared the work site, his shirt drenched in sweat. "We're only missing a half dozen, but we think they might have gone farther west along the river, maybe even tried crossing it if it was shallow enough and the water wasn't rushing. I sent Ken to check it out, but I told him not to spend longer than an hour. I'm not going to split hairs over six cattle."

James nodded, resting his forearms on one of the posts. "How are we looking with the rest of the herd? Any injured?"

"A few were fatigued and one had a limp, but I guess that just means we'll have good dinner for tonight," Mick said.

James glanced back to the fence and the progress they'd already made, then checked the time on his pocket watch, wondering how Mary was holding up.

"Dad!" Jake shouted from farther down the line and waved his hand. "We're out of water!" He lifted the cooler they'd brought out with them, Zi standing nearby, sweating and squinting from the sunlight.

"Head back," James said. "It's lunchtime anyway."

"What do you want us to do with the materials?" Zi asked. "And the tools?"

"Leave them. We'll finish up after lunch." James waited until both climbed into their saddles before he turned back to Mick. "You should head in too."

"You not eating, boss?" Mick asked.

"I'll be over in a minute."

Mick rode off, but it wasn't long before Luis rode over, staying on his mount as the horse munched on grass.

"Everything's accounted for at the house," Luis said. "Food, water, weapons, and medicine. Only found two of the caches had been compromised."

"That's good," James said. "We keep half out to use, and then bury the rest for safe keeping." He paused, and then added, "how's the mood?"

Luis shrugged, his horse fidgeting too. "Everyone's a little worried, but I think the work is helping to keep their minds off of it. None of them really think it's going to be like this for long. They're convinced that the power is coming back on and that someone is doing something about it. I didn't have the heart to tell them they're wrong. I figured there would be a time and place for that later."

James nodded. "No, you're right." But he knew that it would better to tell them sooner rather than later, making sure that everyone understood the gravity of their situation. "Head on back and ring the dinner bell. I just want to get things organized before I head in." James pushed himself off the post and dusted his hands. "Go on."

"You're the boss," Luis turned the animal toward the house and heeled it, rocketing himself over the open plains, quickly catching up to Jake and Zi, both of whom had chosen to take it slow on the way back.

James watched all three of them until the dust from the horses' hooves drifted back to the earth from which it came. He collected tools, putting them together, and added to the pile of unsalvageable materials. But even after he was done, James lingered behind, enjoying the silence and solitude.

He hadn't been able to enjoy the land like this since yesterday morning. He found it hard to believe that so much had happened in only one day. But he was thankful for today, and he'd be even more thankful for tomorrow.

Growing hungry, James finally mounted his mare and returned to the house.

Even before James stepped into the house, he could hear the chatter from inside, drifting through the open windows and back door. It was good to hear those voices, and James was glad to hear laughter.

Smiling faces turned to James when he stepped inside, half of them with food hanging out of their mouths. He saw the rations and supplies that Luis had dug up, and he became anxious when he saw everything piled together.

"Hope you don't mind peanut butter and jelly." Susan smiled from the counter, her fingers messy with the sandwiches ingredients as she placed another sandwich onto the pile. She was Ken's wife. She'd been Mary's friend, and she introduced the pair many years ago. Mary had always considered herself a prime matchmaker.

Ken slipped up from behind Susan and placed his hand on her backside, stealing the sandwich she just placed down, and she smacked him away as he laughed.

"Don't get handsy in front of company." Susan acted angry but was unable to repress her smile.

James cleared his throat, raising his voice. "If I could speak to everyone for a moment."

The chatter quieted down, and every head in the kitchen turned to him. But staring at the sunburnt and sweaty faces, eyes wide and attentive, James suddenly regretted stopping all of the fun. Because what he had to say would bring more sobriety to an already dire situation.

"You all know about the events yesterday," James said. "It's why we don't have power, it's why our cars don't work, and it's why I asked everyone here today." He paused, staring at each of them in turn, looking for any skeptical expressions. He found none. "Some of you might be wondering when this is going to stop and things will return to normal. The short answer to that question is: I don't know. The longer, more difficult answer, has to do with what I saw and experienced yesterday."

James went through a breakdown of everything that happened, what he saw, the terrorists, the military who retaliated, and the enemy that was so close to home in the nearby town, which drew the most nervous chatter.

"So what are you saying, James?" Ken asked, arms crossed and standing next to his wife. "This is permanent? That we'll be living here indefinitely?"

"That's not what I'm saying at all—"

"But you said the military was in the city." Mick stood from the kitchen table. "Doesn't that mean they have a handle on things?"

"And what about this group in the town," Susan said, stepping from behind Ken, smearing the peanut butter and jelly that was on her hands to her sleeves and arms. "You said they came here last night? What if they come back? Are we in danger?"

The worry quickly exploded into hysteria, people shouting over one another, and it wasn't until James raised his hands and Luis whistled that people quieted down.

"Let's take it easy!" Luis said, joining James's side. "You heard what James said. He doesn't have a crystal ball to see when all of this is going to end. So why don't we just all take a breath and focus on what we can control."

"Luis is right." James pointed out the back door. "We have enough resources here to support all of us for at least a year. But the only way this is going to work is if we work together. Not one of us can do it on our own."

The group relaxed, nodding.

"He's right," Ken said. "And I think I speak for all of us when I say how thankful we are to have you lead us through this."

The sentiments were echoed, and James removed his hat, wiping his sweaty bangs from his forehead as he bowed his head, hoping that he could blame his reddening cheeks on the heat.

"James?" Nolan asked, stepping into the kitchen.

The room fell silent.

Nolan smiled. "She's awake."

A collective sigh of relief filled the kitchen, and James was already in the hallway by the time he heard the dozens of congratulations that followed him all the way to her room.

Jake was already by Mary's side, holding his mother's hand, when James entered the room. Mary smiled weakly when she saw him, and before she had a chance to open her lips to speak, he kissed her.

"Hey." Mary's voice was sharp and raspy.

James dropped to one knee and gently pressed his forehead against hers. "Just take it easy."

"Yeah, Mom," Jake said, holding Mary's other hand. "You don't want to overdo it."

Mary nodded and then coughed. She glanced down at herself, rolling her eyes the way she always did whenever she was worried about the way she looked.

"You look fine," James said. "Jake, why don't you get your mother some breakfast?"

"Okay," Jake said. "I'll get some cinnamon rolls. I know they're your favorite."

"Just clear that with Nolan first," James said. "We don't want to give Mom anything she can't handle."

But as Jake started to leave, Mary reached for her son's wrist and pulled him back. He leaned close and Mary said, "I can always handle cinnamon rolls." She winked, and Jake's laughter trailed him out of the room.

Mary turned her head on the pillow, her hair gently falling along the sides of her face. But as relieved as he was to know she was alive, he was nervous about what came next.

"Nolan told me about the pregnancy," James said.

Mary's face slackened, but she didn't look away. She twisted the sheet on the bed, and her eyes started to water. "I'm sorry."

Of the million questions that ran through James's mind, there was only one that mattered to him. "Why didn't you tell me?"

Mary drew in a sharp breath, regaining her composure, and gently rocked her head from side to side. "It wasn't something I was expecting. I mean we weren't even trying."

James frowned. "Did you think I wouldn't be excited?"

Mary smiled sadly and then shook her head. "That's not why I didn't tell you." She squeezed his hand, and a tear rolled down her cheek. "I was afraid."

"Afraid?" James comforted her with a reassuring squeeze of his own hand. "Of what?"

Mary wiped away the rogue tear, her lower lip trembling. "Because I don't want another child to be sick." She covered her face with her palm, sobbing.

James kissed her cheek, tasting the wetness on her skin, the salt from her tears. "It's okay."

"It makes me feel like a bad mother, but I—" Mary dropped her palm, her face red from crying, and she held tight to his hands. "I feel like I failed Jake, that he's sick because of something that I did wrong, and I—" She paused, her lower lip quivering again. "And I just don't want to hurt another child, James."

The pair held onto one another for a long time, James waiting for Mary's tears to run their course, knowing that it was important for him to just be there, to hold her. Because sometimes the most important thing was just hanging on.

With red but dry eyes, Mary drew in a whimpering breath. James brushed the bangs off her forehead, the rest of her hair splayed out like a halo around her head on the pillow.

"I want you to listen to me," James said. "What happened with Jake, his condition, it had nothing to do with you. You are not a bad mother, and you're not broken."

Mary drew another sharp breath, nodding along with James.

James gently placed his hand on her stomach and then smiled. "Whatever life throws at us, we will always be able to handle it because we'll meet those challenges together. All the way. No matter what."

Mary placed her hand over James's and nodded, smiling again, wiping away the rest of the tears with her other free hand. "I'm sorry I wasn't the one to tell you. Did Nolan say anything was wrong with the baby after—"

The door swung open, and James expected to find Jake, but it was Luis. "Boss. Someone's coming."

James released Mary's hand, following Luis out of the room and to the front living room where the entire house had gathered, peering through the front windows. The group parted to make way for Luis and James, who stepped out onto the front porch, both of them taking slow steps onto the compacted gravel drive.

The bright sun reflected off the windshields of a convoy of vehicles that were traveling toward them in the distance. The dust that was kicked up behind their vehicles created a heavy, fog-like cloud around them as they turned from the highway and onto the gravel road of the drive that would lead them to the house.

"Did we get a chance to replenish our trip wires from last night?" James spun around, and his heart sank when he saw Luis shake his head. He then focused on the group of people in the house, half of them women and children. "Luis, get everyone to the bunker." James found Nolan in the kitchen. "Can we move Mary without causing too much harm to her or the baby?"

"Baby?" Jake asked, his inquiry ignored.

"It's hard to say," Nolan answered. "She's woken up, but that doesn't mean she can't go into a relapse from shock. Moving her isn't out of the question, but it's risky."

"Well, we don't have a choice." James spun around, raising his voice to garner the attention of the rest of the group. "Listen up! I'm going to send everyone in the house with Luis, who will take you out to the bunker! It's hidden and you'll be safe."

Everyone exchanged worried looks, whispering about what they had all feared from the very beginning. No place was truly safe.

29

Once the convoy reached the gravel road, they moved slowly but methodically. James probably figured that they were making sure they didn't run into the same type of traps that he'd laid before.

Mary was the first to be loaded into the ATV. Once his wife was secure, James turned to Jake, finding the boy with a gun in his hands.

"Son, you need to go with your mother," James said.

"I'm not leaving you here to fight alone," Jake said, struggling to keep his voice steady.

Had James more time, he would have told his son how proud he was to see him take such a stand, and how proud he was of the man he'd grown to become.

"I need you to protect her," James said. That's where you can do the most good. Understand?"

"Dad, I—"

"No." James clamped a hand over Jake's shoulder, and the boy grew rigid. "This is how you help the family. Your mother needs you. And I need you to be with her." He walked his son to the ATV where Mary had been loaded and sat him down. "You'll need to show everyone how to get inside the bunker." He looked to his wife and squeezed her hand.

"Just make sure you come back," Mary said.

"I will." James kissed her and then signaled to Ken, who was at the helm of the ATV, to leave. He didn't linger long, knowing that he didn't have much time, but when he turned back to the house, he found a surprise waiting for him inside.

"I didn't want to leave you here completely empty-handed." Luis adjusted the rifle in his hands.

James took one step toward him. "Luis, you don't—"

"Yes, I do." Luis shouldered the weapon and then met James halfway in the kitchen. "It's like you said earlier. Not one of us can do this alone."

James smirked. "Now you start listening to me."

"Better late than never," Luis said.

"We'll hold them here as long as we can," James said, walking to the living room and watching through the broken windows as the enemy passed the halfway point down the gravel road. "Give the others a chance to make it to the bunker before the bad guys have an opportunity to track them."

Luis nodded. "How many do you think they're bringing with them? More than last night?"

James had already counted a half dozen Humvees, and even from this distance, he could see the fifty-caliber mounted guns on the roofs. "Definitely more than last night."

The pair flipped couches, tables, and drew the curtains, putting as many layers between themselves and the bullets that would soon transform his childhood home into Swiss cheese.

With the living room turned upside down, James returned his focus to the enemy, and he could now make out the bugs that dotted the front grill of the lead Humvee that was making its way toward the house.

James headed toward the bedroom, his boots thumping

loudly in the hallway, and he opened a box in their closet. He reached toward the bottom of the box and removed the pair of Kevlar vests from inside and hurried back to the living room, tossing one to Luis.

"Put it on," James said, doing the same himself. "You'll thank me for it later."

"So what's the plan?" Luis asked, strapping the vest on. "We go down with the ship?"

"We give the group as much time as we can to get to the bunker," James said, securing his position by a window. "Then we use the tunnel from the house to the barn to get out." He glanced back to Luis. "You'll have a good lookout in the bedroom, but stay low." James focused his eyes on the caravan. "The Kevlar won't do us any good when those fifty-calibers open fire."

Once Luis was in position. James remained by the front window, watching the caravan of some evil army invade his front yard.

The Humvees sat idle for a moment, and the glare from the sun on the windows concealed just how many soldiers rode inside, but with the gunners on top of the roofs of each fifty-caliber weapon. James figured that each Humvee was packed with at least five soldiers, which would put their total count hovering near thirty. Thirty versus two.

The gunfire sounded like a freight train, and once the first heavy piece of artillery went through the house, James flattened himself against the floor, wood, glass, concrete, and debris raining over his back as the floor vibrated like there was an earthquake.

The debris piled up on his back so high that it took a jolt of strength to move it off of him and send it toppling down to the floor with the rest of it. He remained there on his hands and knees, staring down at the pile of rubble that had rained over him during the firefight.

His weapon was concealed beneath the rubble, and by the

time he unearthed it, both he and the soldier that had shouldered open the front door were surprised to see one another.

But with James already having the weapon aimed at the intruder and his finger on the trigger, he had the advantage. He squeezed the trigger and sent a round straight through the terrorist's chest, knocking him backward and out the door.

Retaliatory gunfire forced James below the window again, and he knew that it was a waste of time to stick around for much longer. He scrambled on all fours to the bedroom while the gunfire reigned overhead. He found Luis on the ground, still alive. "We need to get to the tunnel."

More fighters circled around the back, boxing James and Luis inside. Footsteps and voices entered the house, and James led Luis through the rubble, toward his bedroom.

Gunfire chased both of them, though the enemy had the same difficult path to walk as they did, and it slowed them down.

James moved toward the closet, ripping the door off the hinges as Luis watched the door, firing at the pair of soldiers that reached the room first. James opened the hidden hatch and hollered at Luis. "C'mon!"

Luis fired two more shots before he ran over and then jumped into the hole. James was quick to follow and once inside he shut the lid, locking the top.

"Go!" James said.

The pair crawled forward in the darkness until they reached the end of the tunnel, which dumped them inside the barn.

Fatigued from the journey and still partially deaf, James was quick to head to the barn doors to see what kind of destruction had befallen his house, which had been circled by the enemy.

Luis moved close, panting and catching his breath. "So what do we do now?"

James turned back toward the barn. The animals inside were in a frenzy and James opened all of their stalls, letting them prance around the inside of the barn, then grabbed Luis.

"We ride out in a stampede and we'll split up," James said. "You head east, and I'll go north. Just keep riding as fast and as far as you can, and then at nightfall head to the bunker."

James maneuvered Luis to one of the horses, his friend nodding along, disoriented. Then he grabbed his own horse, forgoing the saddle, and mounted the beast.

The rise of gunfire caused the horse to become even more agitated, and James struggled to balance the reins and the weapon as the beast made it difficult to keep hold of both. He shouldered the rifle and then nodded to Luis.

"Good luck, brother," James said.

"You too," Luis said.

James hesitated a moment but then burst out of the barn doors, riding hard north as fast as he could.

The stampede of horses and cattle flooded from the barn, and the terrorists took notice immediately, firing wildly at both Luis and James on their hasty retreat.

James kept low, glancing over at Luis, thankful as he watched his friend safely put distance between himself and the enemy, but James's mood shifted when he saw the Humvee chasing him with that big fifty-caliber gun.

"C'mon!" James cracked the reins and smacked his heels into the animal's ribs, rocketing both of them forward.

Gunfire chased him, but the rough terrain slowed the Humvee and gave James and the animal just enough time to make it to the river.

The horse wanted to stop, but James forced the beast forward, refusing to let it slow. He was close to the river. He just had to make it a little farther before the Humvee closed the gap.

James saw the rushing water before he heard it, and

artillery fire forced the horse to veer a harsh right, nearly throwing James from its back, but he gripped the neck, forcing himself upright, and then turned the beast back toward the river.

In that short stretch of land, James truly believed that he was going to die. Time slowed, and he became only aware of his heartbeat and the beast between his legs.

The shoreline was less than twenty yards away, but before the next hoof hit the ground, the earth erupted beneath the animal and flung James forward and through the air, propelling into the water where he splashed, the animal landing on top of him.

*J*ames floated in darkness until he choked for air and was thrust into the light. He coughed up water as he lay in the mud on the riverbank. He flipped to his back, and glanced up at the sky, which had faded into the pinks and oranges of sunset.

Exhausted, James lay on the riverbank, the water behind him running smoothly and quietly downstream. He lay there for a moment, catching his breath until he sat up, pressing his hand against the mud, which sank from his weight.

Arms and legs shaking by the time he was completely out of the water, James collapsed onto the grass, basking in its lingering warmth from baking in the sun all day.

He shut his eyes, trying to remember what happened, and he caught glimpses of the gunmen, the explosion of the house, and then, like a bolt of lightning, he remembered his family.

"Mary. Jake." Speaking their names aloud provided him the needed strength to stand. He took one step, then another, repeating the process until he looked around and the river was behind him. He stopped himself, wondering how far he'd drifted, finding no landmarks that he recognized.

James trudged through the open plains, the sun sinking lower in the west. He walked so far that his clothes dried, only to be soaked with sweat. His lips had dried and cracked, and his tongue felt like sandpaper on the inside of his mouth. He kept to the river, not trusting his navigation in his haggard state, and periodically walked over to take little sips.

James knew that it could be contaminated, but he'd built up his immunity over the years by increasing the amount of unfiltered water that he drank so should the time come when he would need to drink something that didn't come from a faucet, it wouldn't be a shock to his system. But he made sure to only take small sips. He didn't want to push his luck.

The sun finally sank below the horizon, but it was another flicker that caught his attention in the distance. James lifted his weary head and saw a bright orange ball. It was his home. The bastards had set fire to it along with the barn.

James finally reached the fence along the perimeter of his property, his joints cracking from the movement, and he landed hard on his boot heels.

Above, the sky was blanketed with clouds, casting the land into a black dark that caused James to stumble along the way. But while he couldn't see, he heard the buzz of flies that pulled his focus back to the river.

James stopped, staring at the blackness where the sounds were coming from. The buzz grew louder, as if there were an army of flies circling overhead, and then that familiar stench of death hit him.

James stumbled toward the smell, fearing what he would find rotting in the darkness. He envisioned his family and friends sprawled out across the grass, their bodies twisted and bloody. He envisioned their lifeless eyes, like the bodies he'd seen in the city.

Trembling by the time he reached the first corpse on the ground, James couldn't muster the courage to look down.

But he couldn't ignore it forever, so he turned left, staring at the black mound which at first struck him as a pile of bodies, and his blood ran cold.

But the longer he stared, the more he realized it wasn't a pile of bodies. It was too smooth and round at the top. It was one of his cattle.

The steer had been riddled with bullets and left to rot. He looked from that lifeless cattle to the other mounds in the darkness where the rest of his herd had been gunned down.

James stumbled through the graveyard, shocked at the number of cattle that the terrorists had slaughtered and left to rot. "They didn't even bother to take the meat."

Once past the rotting field, James press forward. Even in the darkness, James knew exactly how to find the bunker. He knew every blade of grass on his land. He could walk the ranch blindfolded and be able to find any spot you asked him to. This was his turf, and it was the only reason that his family wasn't dead.

James found the bunker and then knocked three times, paused, and then knocked three more times to let his family down below know that it was him.

The door unlocked and the old steel hinges groaned as James lifted the lid and descended into the bunker, finding everyone huddled together in his underground shelter.

Jake immediately rushed toward his father, wrapping his arms around James's waist. He squeezed tight, his eyes shut, breathing sporadically.

Luis walked up next, rifle over his shoulder and smiling as he clapped his friend and boss on the shoulder. "Took you long enough."

"How's Mary?" James asked.

Nolan wiped his glasses. "She's still stable."

Jake peeled his face off his father's chest and James stepped away from his boy and toward his wife.

Mary's hand was cold as James scooped it up in his own.

He gently rubbed his thumb against her palm, the diamond of her wedding ring sparkling under the fluorescent lighting that was already beginning to dim.

Once James had confirmed that his family had survived, he turned to face the nearly two dozen people that had been waiting for his return and to answer the questions that all of them were dying to have answered.

The heat from all the extra bodies had transformed the inside of the bunker into a steam room, and James knew that this wasn't going to work as a long-term solution.

"So what now?" Ken asked, stepping away from his wife, Susan, both of whom were huddled together close in the back. "We just stay down here until they leave?"

"When will that happen?"

"What about food? Water?"

"Is there enough for everyone?"

And there it was. The only question that mattered when push came to shove. The bunker was only designed to hold three people with enough rations for three months. James counted nine faces in the dark, ten including himself.

"They torched everything," James said, then shook his head when he remembered the caches that had been dug up and left in the house. "And I only have enough here to last a couple of weeks."

"That's it?" Susan asked. "We're supposed to stay down here for three weeks? It's like a sardine can. And what happens when the food runs out?"

"I might be able to help with that." Nolan raised his old, weathered hand, standing near the front of the bunker. "There are supplies in the town."

James stepped forward. "What kind of supplies?"

"At first I just thought it was weapons," Nolan answered. "More bullets and guns, but there was food. Water. Medicine." He glanced to Mary when he said that last word, and then aimed his old and watery eyes back to James. "It was enough to feed an army."

James paused, waiting for Nolan to continue, and then nodded. "And I'm guessing that you remember where all of these supplies are located?"

Nolan nodded. "And I doubt they moved them. It looked like they were getting ready to ship them again, seeing as how they didn't take them out of the packaging."

"And how are we supposed to move all of those supplies?" Luis asked, joining the inner circle. "We can't carry them."

"The semi-truck," James said, talking to himself. "That's what they loaded in that trailer."

James ran through the scenarios in his mind. He glanced to the eager faces, looking to him to make the hard decision. But not everyone had the tactical training needed to pull this off, and he would need more than just himself and Luis to pull this off.

But Zi had come into her own as a fighter, and what was more, James trusted her. And the others didn't necessarily need to fight as much as they could load the truck. But even if they managed to infiltrate the town, locate the supplies, load them onto the truck, and then drive the truck out of town, they would still have to deal with the repercussions of the enemy.

Which meant that the only way for this to work was to not just beat the enemy, but to wipe them off the face of the planet.

31

---

*I*t had taken some time, but James thought he had come up with a plan that gave them a fighting chance. With Nolan's help and James's understanding of the town, they had a good idea of what to expect from their enemy.

The plan boiled down to three components. The first was locating the food and supplies that Nolan had overheard their leader talking about that was stashed near the gas station, which James kicked himself for not noticing on his first visit.

The second component was rescuing the townspeople, who were hopefully still being held in the bank.

And the final component, which was the most difficult, would be making sure that they managed to evacuate both the supplies, and the townspeople, from Ruckins without the enemy following, which meant making sure there weren't any of them left to follow.

But in order to fight the enemy, they needed weapons, and while the bunker provided enough rifles to arm everyone, they didn't have enough to go toe-to-toe with these people, so James resorted to the tried and true method of guerilla warfare and a little shock and awe.

"We're going to take a page out of their book," James said, looking to the group. "Once we have secured both the supplies and the people, we'll be setting off explosions to clear the roadblocks that they have set up on each end of town and setting fire to the buildings. The townspeople will be loaded into the semi-truck with the supplies, and everyone else will escape on horses. I'll also be rigging their Humvees with explosives so they won't be able to follow. Once the shooting starts, we kill as many of them as we can, and I'll set fire to the town. Now, does everyone understand their role?"

Luis and Zi were charged with recovering the townspeople. While they were breaking the others out, Mick and Ken would be loading the semi with the supplies from the gas station. And James would be charged with setting the explosives, preparing the fires, and one last personal mission.

James turned to Nolan, wanting the doctor to go over what he saw one last time. "And you're sure that their leader stays in Mel's Hardware?"

"I'm sure," Nolan answered.

To help ensure that the enemy didn't try and chase them back down, James wanted to chop the head off the snake, operating under the premise that if their leader was dead, then the others would turn tail and run.

James nodded. "Our big advantage is that they think we're on the run. And I don't think they'd expect us to strike back as quickly and as strongly as what we're about to do. But we treat this as if they're expecting us and hit them right before dawn." James stood, glancing to the faces turned toward him. "Let's get ready."

The group broke apart, and James returned to his wife's bedside and took a knee, the pair having a rare moment where neither were pulled in the other direction.

"How are you feeling?" James asked.

"Tired," Mary answered, then shut her eyes, swallowing hard. She was quiet for a while and then drew a deep breath, her voice and expression almost returning to normal as if she weren't injured. "I can't believe it's all gone."

"It's not all gone," James said. "We're still here. That's what's important."

Mary cried, and the tears surprised James. But her expression softened and she brought his hand to her lips and kissed it. "You're a good man, James Bowers. And I want to make sure that you don't forget that."

"James," Nolan said, interrupting the moment. "I need to speak to you."

The old doctor waved a finger that beckoned James away from his wife and the others and to the very back of the bunker. The old man crossed his arms over his chest and remained hunched forward in that permanent stoop, his brow creased in hard lines.

"I didn't want to say anything before when tensions seemed to be a bit high, but you should know something about me," Nolan said, drawing in a breath, working his mouth to speak, but only managing a few unintelligible noises before he finally spit it out. "I have cancer."

The news didn't seem real, and it took James a moment to realize that Nolan was being serious. "What?"

"It's terminal," Nolan answered, then pointed to his lower abdomen. "Started in the pancreas and got into the bloodstream. Found out last week."

James studied the man who had looked old, but still fit. "Are you okay? Do you need—"

Nolan uncrossed his arms and waved his hands. "It's done. I made my peace with it, but... well. I wanted to make sure you knew in case... I became too much of a burden."

James placed a comforting hand on the old doctor's shoulder. "You'll stay here until the end, Doc."

"Thank you, James." Nolan smiled, and then walked away.

James remained in the back of the bunker for a moment, reflecting on Nolan's words and what Mary had told him. Sometimes it was hard to understand why things happened the way the did in this world. Maybe James just wasn't meant to understand.

James grabbed the rest of his supplies, making sure that he had everything he needed for the detonations and to start the fire, and he barely had enough. With the collection of all of his caches at the house when it blew, most of his spare weapons had been destroyed along with his food and medical supplies. It had been an error on his part, and he was more than paying for that now.

After handing out the rifles he kept in the bunker to everyone else, James was left with his trusty .306 Winchester. It had belonged in the Bowers family for generations and was just as trusty now as it was when his grandfather had used it to hunt.

"Dad?" Jake joined his father in the back.

"Hey, son, what—" James stopped, studying his son's attire, and he saw that he wore a pistol and holster, along with boots and a jacket.

"I want to help," Jake said.

"No, it's too dangerous."

"Dad, I can help—"

"I said no, Jacob!" James's voice shook the bunker, silencing everyone. "Now is not the time. You will stay here and that is final."

Jake kept his head bowed and then wiped at his eyes. He said nothing as he turned away from his father and sat on the edge of his bunk, then turned his back to everyone in the bunker.

James lingered in the back, watching all of the eyes staring at him. He had been harsh with his son, he under-stood that, but sometimes that was necessary to protect the people that he loved. And now he would travel back to that town, to stop the spread of evil from touching anyone else. He just hoped he'd survive to see the fruits of their labor.

32

*P*acked and confident in their plan, James, Luis, Zi, Ken, and Mick saddled five horses and started the long ride into town a few hours before sunrise.

While the rest of the folks were still riding off the flood of adrenaline, James was forced to pop a caffeine pill to keep him awake. He was running on fumes.

Before James even saw the town, he heard the caw of birds in the air. He looked up toward the sky and saw the dark wings circling above in the distance. Even in the darkness, James knew that they were buzzards, because the place they were heading was filled with death.

When the lights of town came into view, James slowed their pace and set them on a course to head for the east end of town first. He wanted to make sure that the semi was still there and that they'd be able to get it running before the rest of the plan went into motion. It all hinged on making sure that they could get the supplies, and the people, out of there before the enemy knew they were there.

James kept the group one hundred yards from the gas station, then he and Luis moved closer to investigate.

"If there are guards, then you take the one on the left, and

I take the one on the right," James said, keeping his voice to a whisper. "I'll shoot first."

They approached slowly, crawling through the tall grass, and sure enough spotted the pair of sentries on patrol around the station, which helped confirm that they still had the supplies inside. No reason for them to guard an empty building.

Suppressors had been applied to both rifles, and while James knew the weapon would still make some noise, the garage was isolated away from the rest of the town and he was confident that the shot wouldn't be heard. So long as he didn't miss.

If the bullet hit glass or the side of the building, then the guards would be alerted and their plan would end before it began. But both men were skilled hunters. He was confident they could make their shots.

James steadied his hand as he brought the crosshairs over his target, waiting until Luis was ready. They would need to squeeze the trigger quickly after one another.

The sentries wore no masks, and James didn't recognize either of them from the raid on the ranch.

There was a light breeze on the air, and James waited for it to pass. The men turned the corner to head up the side of the building toward the front, and James had his target dead center of his crosshairs. But just before James squeezed the trigger, both of them ducked behind the trailer.

James lowered the rifle, gritting his teeth. "Shit."

"I didn't have a good shot anyway," Luis said. "So how much longer do you want to wait?"

"We're not waiting." James unsheathed his hunting blade, showing it to Luis who did the same, and then followed his boss to the backside of the garage, the pair quickly chasing the two guards around to the front of the station, where they ensured the coast was clear.

By the time the pair of guards had walked back around to the backside of the building again, James and Luis had crept silently up behind them. It was different than the first time, and James wasn't nervous. It was just a part of the job, part of their mission.

James placed the knife against the guard's throat as Luis did the same. He pressed his palm over the terrorist's mouth to muffle the scream, then sliced. And then it was done. Only a few seconds. So quick. So easy.

James and Luis dragged the dead men deep into the tall grass where they couldn't be seen.

Once both bodies were concealed in the tall fields, James and Luis returned to the gas station, confirming that their needed supplies were still inside.

Massive pallets with crates filled the inside of the station, and James and Luis worked their way inside to confirm it was the rations that Nolan believed it to be.

"If there isn't any food in here, what are we going to do?" Luis asked, standing next to one of the crates, crowbar in hand.

"We'll cross that bridge when we come to it." James stared down at his own hand, still covered in that man's blood. It was shaking. He forced the hand steady by using it to pry open the nearest box.

"What are they?" Luis asked, plucking one of the packages from the crate.

"MREs," James answered, whispering as he stared at the three big letters that meant their salvation. He set it down and then searched through the rest of the crate. The box was filled with hundreds of them. If all of the crates were packed full with these, then they'd have enough rations to feed everyone for the next two years. "Put the lids back on."

Finished at the station, James and Luis returned to the group.

"The truck is there," James said. "Along with the supplies.

Load them into the back as fast as you can." He looked to Mick. "You're sure you can hotwire it?"

Mick nodded.

"All right." James nodded, knowing that they needed this to work. "Everyone knows their job." He looked to Ken and Mick. "Load the truck." He glanced to Zi and Luis. "Get the townspeople." He addressed all of them. "And for the love of God, do it quietly. The faster we can get this done without drawing attention to ourselves, the better."

* * *

IT HAD TAKEN A WHILE, but Jake finally managed to leave the bunker, convincing both Nolan and his mother that he just needed some fresh air. He took one of the rifles with him, telling his mother that it was better to have protection on him after what happened, and she didn't argue.

But the moment Jake was topside, he grabbed one of the horses and sprinted away from the bunker, heading into the darkness.

Jake had spent a lifetime having to sit on the sidelines. Because of his AVS, people thought he couldn't handle himself, but they were wrong. His father was wrong. And he was going to prove it to him.

Eventually, Jake saw the town, but he made sure to keep his distance. Not wanting to draw attention to himself and knowing that the sound carried on the wind in the plains, Jake rode to the south side of the town, downwind close to two hundred yards, and chose to move the rest of the way on foot.

He brought his rifle with him, and he was embarrassed at how much his arms were shaking. He stopped several times on his approach to the town to try and keep himself calm.

Jake had gone hunting with his father before, and that's

all this was. Except this time, what he was hunting could shoot back.

The only building he recognized from the rear was Nolan's office, so he used that as his point of entry into the town. He felt better going into a place he was familiar with.

Jake slipped to the back door, and he poked his finger through some of the bullet holes as he peeked inside and confirmed that there was no one inside.

But even with the coast clear, Jake didn't take the open area for granted. The hallway had patient rooms on either side, and Jake stopped before each one, clearing it before he moved on. He probably could have made it down the hallway safe enough, but his father had always taught him to be thorough.

Once the hallway was cleared, Jake moved swiftly through the waiting room and posted up on the left side of the door, peering out through the shattered glass.

The street was dark, and there were cars littered sporadically along the streets. Jake studied the layout, looking for anything out of the ordinary.

His eyes adjusting to the darkness, Jake saw something move in one of the cars. It was nothing more than a shifting shadow, but with the stillness of the town, Jake knew that it was a sign to stay off the street.

From his position at the doctor's office, Jake spied the hardware store. Just beyond that at the east side of town, he saw the vehicle blockade. If he snaked around the back of the buildings, he could use the blockade to get to the other side at the hardware store.

That's where Nolan had said the leader lived. And if Jake could kill the leader, then he could end all of this.

Jake glanced down in the opposite direction and saw another blockade of vehicles on the west side of town. It would be a longer route, but he figured that it would less guarded than the east side.

Jake moved quickly along the backside of the buildings, staying low, eyes peeled for any other traps. He managed to cross to the other side of main street without incident using the cars in the blockade as cover.

Again keeping to the backside of the building, Jake moved quickly through the grass, making sure that the coast was clear as he made his way to the back of the hardware store where whispers escaped, growing louder. He ducked down a side alley just before a patrol unit passed by.

Jake aimed his rifle at the alley's back entrance, his finger on the trigger and unable to keep his body still. The tip of the rifle wavered back and forth, and Jake shut his eyes, trying to calm himself. But the adrenaline running through his nerves was too much.

The voice grew louder, and just when they sounded as though they were going to turn down the alleyway, they grew softer.

Jake exhaled, the tip of the rifle lowering from its aimed position. With the moment of danger gone, Jake inched toward the rear of the alley. His muscles turned to jelly, and he saw that the coast was clear.

Jake sprinted the rest of the distance to Mel's Hardware and burst inside before his courage vanished. He found it empty.

Jake lowered his weapon and placed his hands on his knees to catch his breath, his face covered with sweat, most of it dripping down his neck or off the tip of his nose.

But as he stood there hunched over on his knees, catching his breath, he caught the scent of something rotten.

Jake sidestepped toward the wall, moving away from the back door, but the scent only grew stronger. He kept to the wall, moving slowly until he finally stepped on the slimy remains of what had died on the hallway floor.

The substance was slick and sticky beneath his shoes, and while Jake was glad that the body had been moved, he still couldn't work up enough courage to actually stare down at the remains of what he had stepped in. He could only take so much.

Jake then slowly moved down the hall toward the front of the store, stopping to check Mel's office only to find it empty, he froze when a door opened. Jake backpedaled, but then slipped in the grime on the floor, hitting the ground hard.

The noise caused the people in the front of the store to hurry into the back, restraining Jake before he had a chance to fight back.

The first man led with the flashlight, illuminating Jake as he reached for his rifle, and before he could reach over for it, another man snatched him away, spinning him around in a hold and placing a gun to his head.

Jake tried to scream, but his cries were muffled by the man's palm, which was rough and sweaty against his mouth. He could taste the grain and dirt that had accumulated.

The man with the flashlight kept the beam pointed at Jake's face, blinding him and forcing Jake to turn his head away.

"It's a boy," the man with the flashlight said. He stepped closer, keeping that bright light on Jake's face as Jake continued to fight against the man's hold, even though he knew that he couldn't break free.

The light was lowered slightly. Jake turned back toward the man who had shined it in his face, but his vision still hadn't adjusted from the blinding light, and there was nothing but darkness. But through the darkness, he heard a voice, a voice that made his skin crawl and an icy sensation run up the back of his spine.

And when Jake's vision finally adjusted to the light, he was able to see the man who held the flashlight wearing a pair of black gloves.

33

*W*hile the others headed toward the gas station, Luis and Zi kept to the tall grass as they snaked their way to the back of the bank building. Both kept hunched low on their trek through the surrounding fields, keeping an eye out for any more guards on patrol.

Luis had expected heavier security and was surprised to find it so light.

Once they were lined up with the back of the bank, Luis forced both himself and Zi to wait. He wanted to make sure that they wouldn't get any surprises on their approach. The moment their cover was blown, their job would become infinitely harder.

While they lingered in the tall grass, Luis looked to the woman that James had brought back from San Antonio. She was good looking, though a little younger than Luis normally got himself involved with. Most girls he knew that age were too busy posting on their social media platforms than actually living a life or having a real relationship.

Luis had felt like he'd always been between generations. He wasn't old enough to have completely missed the technological revolution, but not young enough to have been fully immersed in it all. And a part of him was glad about that. Not that it mattered anymore.

"How long do you want to wait out here like sitting ducks?" Zi asked.

Luis rolled his eyes, keeping his attention on the backside of the bank. "We're not sitting ducks. Not so long as we stay hidden."

"So we're hidden ducks," Zi said.

Luis repressed the smirk, refusing to give the woman any satisfaction. "I want to make sure we're not walking into a trap. We need the element of surprise on our side, and if there are patrols coming around on the backside of the buildings, then I want to know when they come and how many there are."

Zi sighed, shifting uncomfortably in the grass, but she didn't move despite her disagreement.

Luis kept his attention on the building and finally saw what he was waiting for as a pair of guards emerged from a nearby alley.

The guards were armed and more vigilant than the last time Luis and James had come into town. One of them walked to the edge of the field where they were hidden, glancing out into the darkness.

"I know I heard something," the man at the edge of the grassy field said. "I heard voices."

"It was probably just a weird echo from the inside of the bank," the second soldier said. "They've all been whispering since the convoy came back and Dillon starting shooting them one at a time."

Luis frowned, remaining frozen in the grass, but noticed that Zi's breathing was growing more labored and noisier, drawing unwanted attention. He slowly reached his hand over and placed it over her forearm, and she jerked toward him, but the breathing stopped just as the wind died down.

"Go back and get a light," the man at the edge said, taking

another bold step into the tall grass where Luis and Zi were hidden. "I want to clear the area before we head back inside."

There was a reluctant groan, but Luis watched the man's partner disappear back to the front of the building while the second sentry remained vigilant in the darkness.

It was the worst-case scenario for Luis and Zi, and he knew that once the cover of darkness was broken, so was their chance of using the element of surprise against the enemy. They were stuck between a rock and a hard place. If they moved, they'd be seen. If they waited for the second man to return with the light, then they'd be seen. In both instances, they would die.

Luis slowly returned his hand from Zi's arm to the barrel of his rifle. He was crouched on his knees, ducked forward with his elbows in the dirt. He also had a straight shot at the man on the edge of the field, the one so certain that there were spies hidden amongst the grass.

The second sentry returned, flashlight already in hand, and Luis knew that his opening was closing. He steadied his hand, prepared to take his shot, when the flashlight was exchanged.

"Took you long enough," the first sentry said, taking the flashlight. "I could have been—"

Luis emerged from the tall grass, drawing the attention of both men, but with their guard down, he had enough time to squeeze the trigger and take down the sentry with the light, which bathed the field in the harsh glow of the flashlight. He then pivoted his aim toward the second sentry, squeezing the trigger and sending one through his skull, which dropped him to the ground with his friend.

Both shots were fired within half a second of one another, and after it was done Luis remained frozen, standing in the tall grass, his weapon now aimed at the exit of the alley by the bank, waiting for the storm of other soldiers that were sure to follow.

But no one came.

Zi emerged from the tall grass and shook Luis free from his paralysis. "Good shot."

Luis didn't lower his weapon, but he relaxed, forcing his muscles to give him room to breathe. "We'll head down the alley where they came from. Stay close behind me, and only step where I step."

The pair kept their guards up as they emerged from the grass, passing the pair of bodies on the dirt, both of whom had landed on their backs, forcing both Luis and Zi to stare at them on their way past.

Luis clicked off the flashlight, making sure that he didn't leave anything behind to draw unneeded attention to what he'd done.

He kept close to the bank's wall down the alleyway, and unlike their trip here before, he saw no lanterns burning in the streets, which he thought would work in their favor, but he was willing to bet that a new security protocol had been put into place and that the monsters preferred to hunt in the darkness.

On their trek toward the main street and the front of the bank building, which they would have to enter since the other doors had been closed off, the wind blew a hot, foul stench down the alley.

Both Luis and Zi covered their noses; the stench of death wasn't something that you forgot. With his nose buried in the crook of his elbow, Luis slowly stepped from the alley, being mindful to keep everything that he could hidden in the shadows of the alley. He paused, searching for any threats, but found none.

Barely poking his head around the corner, Luis checked the street, which was still littered with broken-down cars.

Directly in front of the bank were the remains of the townspeople that had been gunned down during their first attempt to rescue Nolan. Each one of those bodies had spent the past day rotting in the sun, exposed out in the open like that as if they were roadkill.

He was unable to keep his eyes focused on the mangled bodies, the blood still shiny and fresh from the heat of the day, most of the corpses picked at by the birds and vultures that they'd seen circling the town on their ride in, some of which were still snacking on the remains.

But aside from the dead and the birds, Luis found no signs of any other guards in the area, which felt wrong, and some unexplainable force continued to pull Luis back to the vehicles that had been left in the street. There was something ominous about the way that those cars were laid out, as if they had been moved again. And then, as Luis continued his thorough scan, he saw the remains of a pyre in the middle of town.

Most of it had burned down, but the pole still remained, holding up what was left of the person that they had burned.

With his stomach lurching, Luis retreated back into the alleyway, his heart suddenly pounding, and then he shut his eyes, trying to get a grip before he lost his mind.

A nudge from Zi prompted him to finally open his eyes, and when he did, he saw her staring at him with a questioning glance.

Knowing he wouldn't have time to explain, Luis simply shook his head and then leaned close to whisper. "I don't see anyone. Stay behind me and keep your eyes peeled."

With eyes wide as saucers, Zi nodded quickly and then Luis faced forward again, performing one final scan of the area before he stepped into the open.

Luis planted his foot onto the wooden walkway in front of the bank, keeping his shoulder close to the wall, and the moment that both Luis and Zi were exposed, the first gunshot was fired.

Zi was knocked to the ground, rotating clockwise as she fell, the force of the shot so violent and so fast that she was already on her back by the time that Luis had dropped to a knee and opened fire, shooting blindly into the street.

Heart pounding, flooded with adrenaline, Luis didn't feel Zi pounding on his shoulder until she started screaming in his ear.

"Get inside!" Zi pushed him toward the door, the pair of them providing cover fire for themselves as they stumbled awkwardly over the dead and into the depths of the bank, the gunfire growing worse once they were inside and then shutting off completely.

Luis turned to Zi, unable to make out her features in the darkness. "Are you all right?"

"Fine." Zi coughed, clearing her throat. "I think it just grazed me. Got lucky. You?"

"I'm fine." Luis returned his attention to the front door, which was open. The entrance, combined with the broken windows, provided more than enough opportunities for the enemy to come and end their lives. "We need to move." He glanced behind him in the darkness, unable to see anyone. "Hello?"

Zi kept close, but while Luis scoured the depths of the bank, she kept her attention focused on the front of the bank, making sure that they had time to get anyone that was still alive in the bank out.

With their cover already blown, Luis knew that they had to move quickly, and if they couldn't get out of the bank, then the very least he could do would be to pull the gunfire toward him and Zi to allow the others to finish their mission.

More gunfire erupted from the streets, and Luis and Zi climbed over the teller stations, the protective structures having been removed, and jumping behind them for cover.

Luis landed on something, and he heard a yelp as he scrambled to sit himself upright. With his eyes still adjusting to the new level of pitch-black darkness as opposed to the outside, Luis could only hear the person scramble away from him.

"Hello?" Luis asked.

Zi's gunfire deafened Luis to any response, but she paused to reload. "Luis, they're at the door!"

Luis moved deeper toward the back where he saw shadows moving. "It's all right!" He stretched out his hands, groping the darkness until he felt cloth on his fingertips. He gripped the cloth hard and yanked it close enough for him to see the whites of the eyes of the woman whom he grabbed hold. Blood covered her face and body, the stench of death on her like the others even though she was alive.

When there was a break in gunfire and he was finally able to hear what she kept repeating to herself over and over again, he wished that she would have just stayed quiet.

"They're going to kill us all."

34

*J*ames was at the east end of the town by the blockade, setting the charges to blow the cars to smithereens for when the semi-truck needed to make their way through the town. He'd already set the charges by the Humvees and dumped gasoline on the first two buildings.

The town's buildings were clustered close together, and he knew that once the first two caught fire, the rest would follow shortly. It had been a particularly dry summer.

Engulfed in the quiet for so long, the sound of gunfire made him jump and he ducked back behind the cover of the front building, thinking that it was directed at him.

When he'd finally had a moment to recover, James realized that the gunfight was farther down the street. Near the bank. Near Luis and Zi.

Once the gunfight began, the forces that had remained hidden burst from the buildings and the vehicles and rushed toward where the action was located.

James counted nine fighters, all of them heading toward Luis and Zi. He finished setting the charges and then quickly moved toward the gunfight.

He glanced back to the gas station, where he hoped that the guys were still loading the supplies despite the sudden change in plans, and then kept to the street, darting between the cars and staying low as he approached the fighting by the bank. He stopped twenty yards from the bank, the random pops of the gunfire dying down.

James poked his head up from behind the back of the sedan, the muzzle flashes giving away the enemy's position in the darkness. He saw that three of the seven fighters were clustered together near a van by the bank's entrance. He plucked one of the three grenades he'd brought with him.

James pulled the pin, squeezing the lever of the grenade tightly, and then arched it high, watching it land at the heels of the enemy, who turned in time to release one scream before the grenade erupted.

The explosion triggered the fighters pressing on the bank's front steps to turn, and by the time they realized what had happened, James was already on top of them, forcing them back behind the cover of vehicles while he took up position near the three dead soldiers the grenade had taken out.

The harsh scent of smoke, dirt, blood, and charred flesh caught in his nostrils, and James frowned as he looked at the charred remains of a pyre. They had burned someone at the stake, and the position in front of the bank made James think that they had made their hostages watch.

"James!"

James looked to the bank, and he saw tufts of hair through the window. It was Luis. He quickly emerged from behind the van and fired at the enemy he'd driven from the front steps of the bank, giving the people inside a chance to escape.

Luis and Zi worked in tandem with James to provide cover fire for the fleeing hostages. It was slow going, and they only managed to get two or three out at a time until Luis gave a thumbs up to James that they'd all gotten out.

Once Luis and Zi had escaped, James plucked another one of his grenades and crouched low as he moved to the other end of the van. He peered around the side and spotted the three more terrorists clustered together. He pulled the pin and chucked the grenade, but his aim was too short as it hit the front side of the car.

But the explosion provided the needed distraction to give James time to escape, and he sprinted toward the east side of town, knowing that he'd have to blow the charges and then torch the buildings.

Bullets chased James down the road as he weaved between the vehicles. Between his fatigue, the bullets, the gunfire, and the darkness, James was forced to dart into Mel's Hardware.

Once inside the darkened store, James did a very quick scan of the interior before setting his gaze back into the street and locating the goon squad currently chasing him. He fired a few shots out into the street to ensure that they knew he was still a threat, but he also understood that he'd have to work fast if he was going to make it out of this alive. They'd be swarming the back entrance soon, and once he was surrounded, it would make his attempted escape that much more difficult.

Keeping an eye on the front of the store, James worked his way to the back, but stopped when he neared Mel's office.

"Hey, let me go!"

James pivoted his rifle toward the open door of the office, but when Jake was placed in the narrow hallway with a gun to his head, every ounce of color in his face vanished and was replaced with a sickly white.

The tip of the rifle dipped and James's legs turned to jelly. Sweat stung James's eyes as he tried to blink away the nightmare that was currently plaguing his vision. It was impossible for his boy to be standing there with that gun aimed at his head. Jake was back at the ranch. He was tucked away in the bunker, safe and sound with his mother. He couldn't be here.

Jake was sweaty, and he scrunched up his face in defeat and shame as his eyes watered. "I'm sorry, Dad."

With the nightmare refusing to end, James forced himself back to his feet, swallowed his fear, and then cleared the anxiousness from his throat. "Let him go."

"I don't think I will," the man said. "I think you're going to toss all your weapons down the hallway, and then you're going to slowly walk with your son to the front doors, where you'll instruct the rest of your men to stand down."

James kept his eyes on Jake. The gunmen had tied a rope around Jake's waist and was hiding in the office, only the gun exposed. No flesh.

With the rifle still held limply in his hands, James reaffirmed his grip on the weapon.

"I'm not going to be patient, James," the voice said. "Comply, or I will kill your son."

James looked to his boy and saw the rope and chain tied around the waist, and then slowly and quietly raised his rifle.

"Do it now, James!" The voice thundered and Jake trembled, standing alone in the hallway as the gun was flush against Jake's temple.

James's stared down at his Winchester. The weapon was unique in the fact that it was a good balance of power and precision. It could bring down big game, and the high-caliber bullet meant that there was more force thrust behind the weapon, which allowed for more stopping power.

James slowly aimed the rifle away from Jake and toward the wall. Based off of the barrel of the rifle near Jake's temple, it told James that the gunman was about two feet to the right of Jake, and he aimed the weapon accordingly.

With a bullet already in the chamber, James kept his

finger on the trigger and raised the rifle's stock to his shoulder.

"One!"

Jake shut his eyes.

"Two!"

Jake trembled.

James knew that if he missed, or if he gave the man any chance to try and retaliate, then his son would die. But after everything he'd witnessed from the group and the others, James knew that the man wasn't bluffing. They didn't care about who they killed, or why. They were absolute in their mission. He was sure of that. And James wasn't going to let his son fall victim to their cause.

"Three!"

Jake screamed, but his son's voice was quickly drowned out by the gunshot that blasted from James's Winchester, blowing a hole through the wall, and the rope holding Jake dropped.

Jake sprinted toward his father, and James pulled both of them out of the hallway just as the gunmen charged from the office, firing wildly on his escape toward the back door.

Once they were out of harm's way, James returned to the hallway, but the gunman was already gone.

Before James had time to react, more fighters charged through the front door, and James grabbed hold of Jake, pulling him toward the back door. When they were in the hallway, two more fighters barged through their only exit.

James pulled both himself and Jake into Mel's office, slamming the door shut behind him as gunfire filled the hallway.

"Get to the back corner!" James reached for the desk, heaving it from the middle of the room and against the door. He then toppled the shelves and cabinets over that to help fortify the loose structure further and then joined his son in the back corner. "Stay behind me."

JAMES HUNT

James aimed the rifle at the barricade, positioning himself between the door and his son. He glanced up at the ceiling, which was drywall instead of the ceiling tiles like he used in Nolan's office to escape.

No other windows, the only door to their freedom currently blocked. They were trapped with the worst of humanity coming to kill both of them without mercy or prejudice.

"Dad?" Jake asked, his tone growing more worried the longer he lingered behind his father.

"We're okay, Jake," James answered, feigning confidence. "We just have to hold them off."

Hold them off until what? Until they ran out of bullets? Until they broke through that door and overwhelmed them? James flexed his grip on the rifle.

He still had one of the grenades, but because the office was so small, the moment it blew up, it'd take anything that was inside the office with it. The only chance he'd have would be to provide kill shots for anyone that busted through the door, which would be difficult.

James made sure that he kept his position between the door and his son. They were coming for them. This was it, this was the final stand.

More shouts, and then screams, and then an explosion of gunfire that sounded like hail striking a tin roof. But something was wrong. The gunfire sounded like they were pointed in the wrong direction.

The hail storm ended, and then there were only a handful of sporadic shots spaced out between a few of the gunfire, and then there was silence.

"James?" Luis asked. "You in there?"

James lowered the weapon and then shoved the desk and cabinets aside, opening the door to find both Luis and Zi in the hallway, a string of dead terrorists behind him, both of them wide-eyed and panting. "The plan was to have you take everyone back to the ranch."

"We weren't leaving you behind," Luis said.

Zi stepped forward. "We need to move quick."

The four of them maneuvered carefully to the back of the buildings. On the way back to the gas station, James set fire to the buildings, the gas igniting quickly. He then double-checked with Mick to make sure everything was loaded and then detonated the explosives, blowing the Humvees and the blockade in the same sweep.

Mick jolted forward, moving through the town quickly as it caught fire, while James, Ken, Luis, Zi, and Jake headed back toward their horses, riding fast, shooting any of the enemy that ran from the burning town.

When they were done, and the glow of the fires behind them were challenged by the first rays of dawn, James was glad to be gone. But he couldn't help but look over his shoulder at the smoldering town behind him. He hoped that this would be the end, but the hope was marred by the tingling sensation running up his spine.

othing but smiles and hugs greeted the group upon their triumphant return to the ranch, and everyone was glad to see the pallets of supplies stored in the truck. With the water sourced from the river, they would be set for a very long time.

"We'll need to unload everything and get it organized," James said, speaking to the group. "Proper storage will be important to ensure that our supplies don't spoil. And we'll want to make sure that we keep our resources spaced out, so in the event that one location is compromised, we'll still have multiple sites that we can pull from."

"Boss, we got this," Luis said. "Go and check on Mary."

James smiled. "Thanks." He left Luis in charge as he descended back into the bunker, slipping from the morning sunlight to the darkened subterranean layer that the enemy and circumstances had forced them into.

Nolan was still by Mary's side, and he smiled when he walked over, answering his question before he even had a chance to ask it. "She's doing very well." He looked back to Mary and winked. "Tough broad."

"Texas doesn't make 'em weak, Nolan," Mary said, managing a smile.

"No, they don't." Nolan clapped James on the shoulder as he passed and then ascended the ladder, leaving Mary and James the only two in the bunker.

The door to the bunker closed with a heavy thunk, and James knelt by Mary's bedside, taking her hand in his own, and then kissed her lips.

When he pulled back, she smiled. "You look terrible."

James cocked his left eyebrow up and chuckled. "Look who's talking."

"I got shot," Mary said. "What's your excuse?"

The pair smirked, and Mary sighed.

"Everything go all right?" Mary asked.

James nodded. "We have enough supplies to feed everyone for at least a year. And by then we'll have crops in the ground, and I'm hoping I can find some livestock that survived the slaughter. And we can still hunt and fish, and—"

"Hey," Mary said, locking eyes with her husband, who had a tendency to drift whenever he was talking about work. "You did good."

James relaxed, letting his head hang between his shoulders. He'd only ever been able to be vulnerable around her. To really let his guard down. It was hard work running a ranch, and there wasn't room for a lack of will and determination.

A hard life typically bred a hard man. And a hard man that continued to harden over time, growing rougher and coarser, well, eventually that man was too rough to even touch, and he ended up hurting the people that he cared about.

"You did what needed to be done," Mary said. "What about the town?"

James gave her a brief rundown of what transpired,

choosing to leave out the part about Jake and the group's leader.

"Do you really think he's going to come back?" Mary asked, her voice equal parts of fear and skepticism. Over the past twenty years, the pair had been able to know what the other was thinking without even having to speak the words out loud, and when James didn't answer, Mary simply nodded. "Well. We'll be ready for them if they do."

James smirked. "Planning on becoming a one-woman wrecking crew, darling?" He added an overly sweet tone to hammer the point home, but she punched his arm.

"You know how good of a shot I am." Mary pointed at him, and then closed one eye and then shaped her finger and thumb like a weapon. "Besides, I know that you'll get everyone in shape by the time they regroup." She reached for his collar and pulled him just short of her lips. "They won't know what hit them."

James smiled, glad to see the strength returning to his wife. He hadn't realized how much he'd missed it, and just before he brought his lips to hers, the bunker door flung open, a beam of light spreading into the bunker and over-taking the false lighting from the fluorescent bulbs.

"James! Get up here!" Luis said.

The panic in his friend's voice caused James to grab his rifle as he quickly ascended the ladder, reaching the surface and expecting to find an army marching toward them from the south, tanks rolling, terrorists screaming, an unstoppable force of death.

But when James returned with Luis to the crumbled remains of the farmhouse and the barn where they'd parked the semi, there was no enemy.

Luis dismounted the horse and waved James forward. "C'mon."

Still confused, James lingered a few seconds before he dismounted and followed Luis to the back of the trailer.

"Luis, what is going on?" James asked.

"You'll see," Luis answered.

Half the trailer had been emptied, but one of the crates had been opened, and he saw both Ken and Mick standing on either side of the large crate and staring inside.

Luis climbed in the back, and still sensing no danger, James propped the rifle up against the bumper and climbed inside to see what the commotion was about.

"So we were going through everything like you said, and we found something that wasn't rations." Luis gripped the side of the crate and gestured for James to look inside.

James approached the crate warily, unsure of what he would find, but when he finally peeked over the side, the fear was replaced with confusion and more questions. "What is this?"

Luis tossed it over to Mick, who adjusted his grip on the edge of the crate and leaned forward. "It's a cooling device. I saw them a lot when I did power plant inspections." He stared at James as he said this, and while James heard him, it took a moment for the words to sink in.

"Is it radioactive?" James asked.

"There's no plutonium," Mick answered. "But I can tell it's been used. Restored, but used." He pointed to some of the markings inside the concaves of the device.

James frowned, staring at the device. "They have a cooling motor for a nuclear power plant." He tossed a look to Luis, who nodded at Mick to continue.

"There are some applications that I was trained to look for when inspecting the devices at the plants," Mick said, his eyes on the device. "They were to make sure that the operations hadn't been compromised or attempted to be converted to a bomb."

James rubbed his eyes together, trying to gather his thoughts. "God." He stared into the back of the trailer and the remaining crates that they hadn't gone through yet. "And this is the first thing we've seen that hasn't been MREs or other food supplies?"

Everyone nodded. But if James had just stolen a piece of the enemy's bomb, he was confident that others would come looking for it. The only question was, how many?

36

The ringing in Dillon's ears didn't stop for the first few miles of wandering south, and he didn't look behind him until the sun came up. By then the town was miles away, barely a glint in his eye.

He snarled, clenching his fists. Anger boiled his cheeks red, which would stay permanent after a few hours in the sun.

Dillon had departed the town unprepared, but he knew that was no excuse. The rancher had caught him off guard, and he had no choice but to flee.

Still, even though he had convinced himself of the retreat, he felt a cold sense of dread spreading from the pit of his stomach to the rest of him as he wondered what it would be like when he was forced to speak to his superiors.

Dillon walked, continuing his trek south, finding nothing along his path save for open spaces and the occasional bird that circled overhead. It made him think of the buzzards that had circled the town when the dead had been sprawled out over the streets and left to rot there under the sun because of his orders.

The birds pecked at them immediately, snacking on the

bodies all day, and with that imagery in his mind and the birds flying overhead, Dillon quickly looked away from the bird and down at the ground. He wasn't going to allow himself to become a meal.

Unaware of how much time passed, Dillon slowly disrobed, the day growing hotter. He knew that it would be a full day's hike to the nearest post, but he had underestimated the Texas heat. He had underestimated quite a few things about Texas.

It was better when the sun went down, but the temperature dropped slightly, and because he'd gone practically the entire day without any water, his lips were parched and cracked and he stopped, collapsing to his knees in the sand and dirt. He landed forward with his palms touching the grit of the cool earth.

His strength left him and he shut his eyes, trying to catch his breath. He should have reached the outpost by now. At least that's what he thought. His mind was so jumbled and confused that he couldn't be sure what was right and what was wrong, and his sudden indecision had caused doubt to creep in, doubt he had fought so hard to eradicate.

Had he veered too far east or west? Had he missed it already and would have to retrace his steps? Dillon lifted his head and glanced up at the sky, and he was so absorbed and concerned with trying to figure out where he was that it wasn't until he heard the click of the safety and felt the muzzle of the rifle against the back of his head that he realized he wasn't alone.

"My name is Dillon Thompson," he said, slowly raising his arms by this head. "I'm from post twenty-seven."

"Up, Gringo."

The rifle was removed and Dillon stood, spinning around to find the pair of men completely clothed in black, save for the single red stripe that was wrapped around their right bicep. It was the symbol of their cause.

Neither of the men introduced himself, and the pair walked for another ten minutes to the west. It turned out that Dillon had overshot the trajectory, and when he finally saw the outpost, he knew that something was different from his previous visit.

The security had been elevated, but why it was increased, he didn't know.

The outpost had been an old Mexican border town for traffickers coming into the city. It was off grid and self-sufficient, and there were no roads that led to it, at least none that were paved. Unless you knew where it was that you were looking for, you never would have known it existed. It was where Dillon had been trained. It was the epicenter of their regional coordination attempts to spread across the southwest.

But the last time Dillon was here, they didn't have this kind of manpower, and he saw people that he'd never seen before. The location had exploded with new folks, and Dillon wondered if they had pushed up the date of their next phase. If they had, Dillon hadn't been told, and that made him nervous. It wasn't good when you weren't told things. It meant that you had lost favor. And to lose favor in an organization like this…

Dillon passed men busy cleaning their weapons, the entire camp in a commotion, buzzing about their duties with a harried attitude, as if they were heading out today.

Eventually Dillon was brought to the center of the village and forced into one of the huts where their lieutenants gathered for briefings. Dillon shielded his face to guard himself against the long reeds that acted as a makeshift door that hung from the entrance. They were scratchy and old, one of them cutting a line across his cheek that stung from the harsh burn he received from his wandering across the southern Texas landscape.

Torches on the walls flickered with flames, casting their

moving light around the small mud hut. Dillon saw the shadowed faces of the men at the center table, all of whom were in mid-discussion when he walked in, and all of whom fell silent when he set their eyes upon them.

And when Dillon saw their leader amongst the other lieutenants, Dillon's heart caught in his throat and he immediately dropped to his hands and knees, bowing in humility.

"Khan," Dillon said.

Silence lingered while Dillon kept to his position on his hands and knees. The longer no one spoke, the more visible Dillon's trembling became. Finally, hands roughly grabbed his shoulder, picking him up and off the ground and stood him closer to the table, keeping their hands on him so he either wouldn't run, or he wouldn't bow again.

Dillon didn't dare try and make eye contact with Khan in fear that it would be the last thing he would see in this world.

"Why are you here?" Khan asked, his English slightly broken, his voice like gravel being chewed up in a garbage disposal. His voice was deep, and his words always lingered long after he had finished speaking. It was like some illusionist's trick, a terrible echo that he couldn't get rid of no matter how hard he tried.

Dillon stared at the tips of his worn and dusty boots, embarrassed that the pair of guards that were holding him could still feel his trembling. It wasn't right. It wasn't fair.

"The town was attacked," Dillon said, his voice wavering despite the effort to keep it still. "We lost our position." He lifted his gaze just quick enough to see the other lieutenants at the table exchange a few glances, but he still didn't dare look Khan in the eye. He didn't have a death wish. "We were overrun—"

"I gave you forty men," Khan said, keeping his tone even. "Humvees, armor, weapons, all of it to deal with the threat that you said needed to be eradicated. And the last transmission you sent was confirmation of that eradication."

Because the only light was by firelight, Dillon couldn't be sure what exactly the stain on the ground was made up of, but from the darkened color, he knew it was probably dried blood. Blood from some idiot who had misspoke, mis-stepped, or done something unforgivable.

Dillon had spent his entire life trying not to misstep or mis-speak, doing his best to fulfill his mission, his purpose. And he knew that if he screwed up here that he'd only be making that little blotch on the floor bigger.

"I take full responsibility for the failure of my platoon. But I knew that it was important for me to come back here and inform you of the failure, so you could prepare accordingly." Dillon lifted his eyes up from the stain on the ground and stared at the wall, still refusing to look Khan in the eye. "I now await my punishment."

Dillon remained still and rigid, arms at his side, still staring at the wall. He was getting in his own head now, and he could have sworn that he could smell the stain of blood on the ground. It smelled fresh.

He knew what happened to people who came back to this place with their tail between their legs. But he hoped that keeping some pivotal information to himself about who had bested him might provide useful as leverage to keep himself alive long enough to prove himself once more.

Khan stood, and the rest of the lieutenants stood at attention. He walked around the table and over to where Dillon stood. He wasn't a big man, only slightly taller than Dillon. But he was thick as a boulder.

Dillon had heard stories about the man long before he met him. How Khan had pulled together different factions in South America with sheer will and strength. He would walk into those groups and challenge the leader, forcing him to fight. And he would kill them. Every time. And then he'd kill anyone who didn't accept him as their new leader.

In only eight months, Khan had grown from obscurity to

the top of the CIA's watchlist for terrorist leaders of threatening organizations. And his people moved with such precision and accuracy that it was nearly impossible to keep up with all of his movements. He had built an army from sheer brute force, and those that had survived his culling throughout his conquering of groups had remained incredibly loyal to him. Because everyone knew the price of betrayal.

But like most of the people that had joined Khan's cause, they knew little of the man he was before he became a conqueror. It was the reason he had earned the name "Khan," like the great Mongolians conquerors of Asia.

Dillon thought that because of the man's massive build there might also be some physical correlation, what with the bald head. Though he lacked the long facial hair that Dillon remembered from the history books.

But even with Khan standing directly in front of him, looking him in the eye, Dillon didn't dare try to return the gaze. Not until he was spoken to.

"I remember you," Khan said. "From training. We've met before."

"Yes, Khan," Dillon answered. "For a humble recruit, it was a great honor." He finally looked at Khan in the eyes and then offered a light bow.

Khan nodded. "Bottom of your class during the physical requirements of your training. Poor use of weaponry. When I saw you in the mud pits, I remember thinking that I would have to kill one of my recruiters for allowing such a weakling to enter the ranks of our officer's training. But then I saw you in the strategy portion of the training and you dominated the other recruits. It was the best work I'd ever seen, and I came over to you and shook your hand." He grimaced. "Your grip was weak. There is no room for weakness in our cause. I have made that expectation clear from the beginning."

"You are a wise and—"

Khan gripped Dillon's throat, squeezing tight, choking the words from his lips. A steady pressure built up in his head, but Dillon did his best not to squirm and show any sign of the weakness that Khan despised.

Dillon's cheeks turned from red to purple, and his vision tunneled as the airflow was cut off from his brain. His knees buckled but Khan held him up with his one arm, further choking Dillon.

Khan released Dillon and he dropped to the floor on his knees, gasping for breath. The pinhole of his vision widened, and his eyes immediately found the blood stain.

Khan kicked Dillon's ribs, knocking him to the side. Dillon whimpered and curled up in the fetal position.

After a few more seconds of wallowing in pain, Dillon was lifted from the ground and was kept upright by the pair of sentries that had plucked him from the desert.

Khan once again stepped into Dillon's face, his expression of contempt carved out of granite and marble. "If you were as clever as you thought you were, then you wouldn't have come back here unless you thought you had something to give me. So what it is? What have you brought to bargain for your life?"

Even with two men keeping him upright, Dillon couldn't straighten his back all the way. The pain in his ribs kept him hunched forward, and when he opened his mouth to answer, there was only raspy noises that escaped. It was like Khan had cracked his vocal chords.

Khan landed a hard punch across Dillon's body that knocked him back to the ground. The pain was bright and hot against his cheek, and his vision exploded with a bright light, then flashed darkness. His vision slowly returned, with bright spots dancing across the ground like shooting stars.

Dillon had always prided himself because he feared no

man. But as Khan stopped directly in front of Dillon, staring him down with those dark, soulless eyes, that pride vanished.

"I can fix this," Dillon said.

"You can fix nothing," Khan said, his voice a terrifying whisper. "You can only atone for your failures, and you above all people understand that only fire can absolve you of your sins."

Dillon rubbed his fingertips together, the charred and disfigured flesh that had been burned away by war. A constant reminder of the betrayal that was the foundation for his fight against the very country that he had sworn to protect and defend, the scars that propelled him to seek out Khan and enact his vengeance.

"I atone through my sins only by the destruction of my enemy," Dillon said, finding the strength in his voice. "You and I have the same enemy." He raised his hands next to his face, exposing the scars. He gestured to the pyre. "You burn me and you burn all the information about your enemy—"

Khan snatched Dillon's throat, the strike quick as a cobra, Khan tightening his hand around Dillon's throat like a vise.

The pressure in Dillon's head bulged his eyes from his sockets and turned his cheeks purple and with one arm, Khan lifted Dillon effortlessly off the ground.

"You do not tell me what I can and cannot do," Khan said. "You think you have suffered? You think that you're entitled to some revenge because of broken promises to you?"

Dillon kicked his feet desperately, and just when he thought that his head might explode from the pressure, Khan let go.

Dillon crumpled to the ground and gasped for air.

"I believe you do not fear the fire because you have forgotten what it feels like." He turned back to Dillon, then gestured to the burned and charred hands. "The flames dancing across your skin, the shock from the pain, and the beauty the fire leaves behind on the canvas of your body."

Khan reached for Dillon's cuff and yanked the sleeve up his arm, exposing the line between charred skin and the fresh, untouched flesh. "And look at all of the canvas that your body still has to offer the fire."

One snap of Khan's fingers summoned three others from the circle, and Dillon was restrained to the ground, his clothes stripped from his body, and then he was carried over to the pyre where his hands were tied behind his back.

Dillon didn't scream, he didn't cry, because he knew that both were useless. A calmness had blanketed his frayed nerves. And when he was finally secured to the post, the people who bound his hands together stepped backward and handed a torch to Khan as he approached the pyre. The light from the flame was swallowed whole in Khan's eyes.

"The fire will burn what is not needed," Khan said. "The fire will purge you of your failure. But you will not die, comrade. You will live. And you will suffer, as those who fail are meant to suffer."

Khan stepped closer and slowly brought the flame toward Dillon's skin, and Dillon remained calm until the fire finally touched his flesh. And then he screamed.

37

The river babbled softly, the stream steady as it flowed toward the Gulf in the same winding path that it had done for centuries.

The sun rose in the east the same way it always did even before the world transformed into darkness and despair. Before civilization collapsed. Before the EMP.

But the sun was a constant. No matter what happened to humanity, the sun would still rise, and that brought an unexpected comfort to James Bowers. The knowledge that in a constantly evolving world, there still remained a few absolutes.

After graduating high school, James had taken a few courses at San Antonio's community college. He hadn't wanted to go, but his mother wanted him to brush up on the business aspects of ranching.

James wasn't dumb, but he had never had the patience for a classroom. And while he picked up a few things in those classes, he didn't stick around for very long.

But during his time at college, James had met one student in the cafeteria. He was smart as a whip, but friendly.

The guy's name was Bernie, and he was majoring in

astrophysics. He said he wanted to work for NASA one day and help advance the space program. During their lunches together, Bernie would tell James all these facts about the universe and their solar system. And he told James that one day the sun would burn out, and that gave James new meaning to the phrase "everything has a beginning and an end." But Bernie also told him that the universe was always expanding, and would continue to expand, which meant that the whole journey of beginning and end was constantly repeating itself.

"Life might end here one day, but that just means it's started somewhere else," Bernie said. "Isn't that amazing?"

And while James didn't share the same level of excitement about the end of the world and life as they knew it, there was something oddly comforting about what Bernie had said.

As a Christian, James had always thought that just because God created man didn't mean he had *only* created man. If he had made the universe such a big place, then James figured it would be a waste only fill it with rocks and dust.

Once the sun and risen swiftly into the light blue sky, James stood, dusted the dirt from his pants, and secured his Stetson to his head.

James climbed onto his horse and headed toward the bunker, knowing that people wanted answers and knowing that he was the only person who could provide them.

When he arrived he saw Nolan, Luis, and Zi conversing with one another, but it was his son, Jake, who walked up to him first.

"Mom's up," Jake said. "She wants to talk to you."

James placed his palm on the top of his son's head and then looked to the bunker where everyone had stayed the night. "Is she all right?"

Jake nodded. "I think she just misses you."

James smiled. "All right." He looked past his son and to his trusted confidants, who looked to him with eagerness. "Why don't you go tell Luis and Zi I'll be over in a minute. You're in charge till I come back."

Jake scoffed, showing those teenage emotions that were starting to creep in. "Yeah, right, like they'd ever listen to me."

"Hey." The sternness in James's voice surprised his son, who snapped to attention. "You act like that and no one will ever listen to you." He placed a firm hand on his son's shoulder. "If you don't believe you can do it, then no one else will. Understand?"

Jake nodded, tilting his chin up a little higher and dropping his voice an octave. "Yes, sir." He spun around and marched toward the others.

James watched him leave, unsure if the boy was being sarcastic. He'd never done well in trying to pick that kind of thing up.

The bunker had emptied, and the only person left inside was his wife, Mary. It was infinitely roomier with only her inside, but a damp warmth clung to the air, the kind that lingered after a large room had been cleared out.

Mary smiled as James approached, and he felt the returned strength in her touch as she grabbed his hand. "So?"

James pulled over a stool and sat by his wife's bed, still holding her hand. He sighed, shaking his head. "I don't think they'd leave something so valuable behind and not come look for it." He rubbed his calloused thumb over her smooth skin. He had already told her what he found, and he had gone to the river to decide what to do about it.

Mary nodded and then clutched the blanket, balling it up with her fists in tiny bunches. "Okay." She looked to him, and he could tell that her mind was already churning over the different ideas in her head, going through the scenarios, preparing for the possible outcomes.

James reached for her hand once more and held it gently in both of his. He massaged her palm and then glanced down at the wedding ring still sparkling on her hand. He remembered when he gave that to her all those years ago. He remembered how nervous he was and how calm she seemed. She was always the calm one. Now it was time for him to return the favor. "We're going to figure it out."

Mary finally exhaled, relaxing. "You're right."

James drifted his eyes from Mary's hand to her stomach, and the life that he prayed was still growing inside. "Did Nolan say anything?"

"He still doesn't know," Mary said.

James nodded, then kissed her hand and stood, returning the stool out of the pathway in the bunker's only walkway. "Do you want someone to stay down here with you, or do you want some time to rest? I doubt you slept well down here last night."

"It was like sleeping in a sauna," Mary said. "I'll just rest. Thank you."

James pressed his finger to his lips and then transferred the kiss to her fingers as he walked away, and then she touched her fingers to her lips. It was their way of saying goodbye without actually saying goodbye. It was a word that neither of them liked. Goodbye always seemed to sever the moment, while a touch made it linger long after it passed.

Topside, the quiet morning murmur had transformed into a roar of questions. They were questions born from fear and the unknown.

Once the chatter had quieted, James placed his hands on his hips while Zi, Luis, and Nolan stood alongside him.

"I know we've all gone through a lot over the past forty-eight hours." James scanned the crowd, Ken, Mick, and their families, along with the people they had rescued from the town. Most of them were still covered in blood. Their gaze was unsettled, yet attentive, like a man listening to the judge who would hand out their punishment.

"But we are alive," James said, his voice thundering with

that same confidence he'd spoken to his son about. "And we are going to stay that way so long as we continue to fight."

"And what good is fighting going to do us?" The question came from a man in the back, who stepped forward when every head turned to him. He was one of the bloodied towns-people, some of the blood starting to run again from the heat and their sweat. "There's nothing out here except for some dead cattle."

"And how are we supposed to protect ourselves if those people come back?" One of the women stepped forward, again from the town, looking like Carrie from Stephen King's novel after she was crowned prom queen.

James stepped forward. "I know you're scared. And you have a right to be. But we can show you how to protect yourselves. Right now, our greatest strength is our numbers, and if we start squabbling amongst ourselves, then we lose that advantage. A unit is only as strong as its weakest link. We don't just survive for ourselves. We do it for each other."

James studied the group, including the two townsfolks that had spoken up, and they nodded as they slunk back into the crowd.

"Now," James said. "Here's what we're going to do."

James broke them off into groups and had Mick and Ken show folks the day-to-day jobs of the ranch. Everyone worked. That was part of the deal if people wanted to stay. No one objected.

Once the groups were squared away, James turned to his trusted advisors - Luis, Nolan, and Zi.

It was quiet for a moment, and then Luis arched his eyebrows and lifted his arms. "So, I guess no one is going to address the elephant in the room?" He pointed back in the direction of the barn. "We've got a piece of a nuclear bomb just sitting in the back of a truck trailer." His eyes grew even wider. "*A nuclear bomb.*"

"We heard you the first time," Zi said, crossing her arms,

then looked to James. "Do you think they'll come back for it?"

"If they don't have a replacement, or if they think it will give away the rest of their plan, then they'll come back for it," James said, nodding as he came to the conclusion. "We need to be prepared for them if they do."

"Prepared?" Luis asked. "James, we need to get rid of that thing. We don't know where they plan on detonating, or if they have another one. Something like that goes off, and it completely changes the game. We can't stick around if half of Texas is a radioactive wasteland."

James understood the risks. But what the others didn't know was the community of individuals that James had come to know as a prepper. There were others out there like him, and while he wasn't sure they would help him, he had to try.

"There's a man I know," James said. "He doesn't live too far from here. He's a survivalist, he built a community off grid. I don't know the exact location, but I know the general area."

"Are you talking about Banks?" Luis asked. "That guy is just as likely to shoot you as he would help you."

"If more of those people come back, then we need more people to fight them," James said. "Banks is the closest thing to help we can get."

"And why would he help us?" Luis asked.

"Because of what I can tell him," James answered. "Because of what we found. It should buy us some good faith. I hope."

"I think it's a good idea," Zi said.

James looked for any further objections, but found none. "Good. Now, we need to figure out housing. We can't keep everyone in the bunker again for much longer. It's too small, and the summer is only going to get hotter. We need shelter."

Luis hooked his thumbs in his beltloops by his hips and

cocked his right hip to the side. "Harry's junkyard had some campers in it last time I visited. Some of those might help."

"Good," James said. "You and Zi can go. Take the semi and the trailer and bring them back in it. They should fit so long as they're not too big. Pack a go-bag with at least two days rations. And make sure you're armed. Rifles and handguns for each of you."

James and Zi departed, heading toward their horses that were munching on the grass around the outskirts of the bunker.

"How's Mary?" Nolan asked.

"She's fine." James looked to the old doctor. "And you?"

Nolan smiled. "Good." He drew in a breath and sighed. "For now at least."

"You sure?"

Nolan touched his forehead. "Just have a headache is all." He lowered his hand and squinted, looking up at the sky. "Probably the heat." He looked at James and smirked. "And the cancer."

"Why don't you go to the bunker and lie down," James said. "Mary needs the company anyway."

Nolan nodded. "Yeah, that's a good idea."

James watched as Nolan walked away and wondered how much more time the old man really had. Nolan was a realist, and that tended to make him slightly more pessimistic, but James didn't think Nolan had downplayed the severity of his condition.

But the old doctor wasn't the only one suffering from a disease, and James knew it was time to go and check on his son.

* * *

SHOVELS WORKED their way through the dirt, the trench they were digging from the bunker to the river wide and deep enough to keep the pipeline buried. While most of the townspeople provided the manual labor, Jake acted as the supervisor, a role which he fell into easily enough.

Because Jake was the only one in the group that understood the process of laying irrigation, he was charged with overseeing the more technical matters of the process. It wasn't hard, but Jake would have been lying if he hadn't made it out to be a bigger deal than it actually was.

But not one to slouch, Jake also helped with the digging when he wasn't connecting the pieces of PVC pipe that the water would flow through. He was forced to take several breaks, more than the others, and he grew worried about his condition.

"Good work, everyone," Jake said, again feeling that spat of dizziness taking over, but he was able to fight through it this time. "I want everyone to take a quick water break." The group headed for the trough that had been set up in the shade of the tree to keep the water cool.

Jake pressed his hand against his chest and over his heart. He knew what the dizziness meant, along with the small pains pulsating from his head and his arms.

"Jake!"

He turned at the sound of his father's voice and saw him ride toward him, alone. He dismounted and kept hold of the horse's reins as he glanced over to the group of townspeople that had huddled by the water trough, drinking greedily in the shade.

"How's it going?" James asked.

"Good," Jake answered. "Just taking a break now."

James looked from the group and to his son. "How are you holding up?"

Jake hoped that he didn't look bad, and that his symptoms hadn't become noticeable, because he knew he'd be confined to the bunker the moment he showed any signs of weakness.

"I'm fine," Jake answered.

James studied the boy, examining him with a careful eye. After a pause that seemed to stretch for eternity, his father finally nodded. "All right. What do you have planned next for them?"

"I was going to show them the filtration process, and then—"

"Hey!" One of the townspeople stepped away from the water and shade, wiping his mouth with the back of his hand and squinting as he barged his way into the conversation. "How much longer are we going to be out here?"

Jake noticed that the question was directed toward his father and not him.

"We work sun up to sun down," James answered.

The man, who Jake remembered his name was Benny, kept his hands planted on his hips and didn't back down. "And is that what you're doing?" He gestured to the horse. "Working?"

Jake stood between both men like a spectator at a bullfight. He could tell that his father was getting angry, he'd seen that look on his face before.

But there was no outburst, no threats. His father simply stared the man down until Benny finally stepped backward.

"If you have any problems with the way I run my land, or if at any point in time I discover that you have caused problems for the operations here, you will find yourself on your own." James kept his tone even-keeled and calm, which Jake found even more frightening. "And you've already seen what happens when you're out on your own."

Again, James held his gaze until Benny finally walked away. When he was gone, James dismounted the horse and placed a hand on Jake's shoulder. His father's hand was heavy, the arm attached to it thick with muscle, and the palm itself easily engulfing the entirety of his shoulder.

"I'm going to see Banks," James said. "I'm taking the piece of the bomb we found, and I'm going to try and convince them to help us if those people come back." He paused, and Jake sensed that there was more his father wanted to say, but he didn't.

"Dad?" Jake asked, trying to prod. "What's wrong?"

James stared at Jake, and he watched his father's expression soften, and just when he thought that his father was going to leave, he spoke again. "You're going to get worse." He tapped Jake's chest, right over his heart. "Do not hide it from us, okay? If it gets bad while I'm gone, Nolan can perform the procedure."

"Okay," Jake said, unable to stand the silence. "How long will you be gone?"

"Hopefully not long," James answered. He then patted his son on the shoulder and stood, moving back to the horse quickly. "Just keep working with the group, and make sure that everyone stays hydrated and eats." He reached for the animal's reins. "Don't push them too hard."

One quick flick of the wrist and his father and his horse were off, galloping toward the road, back to the remnants of the barn and the house. It still amazed Jake how his father and his horse seemed to always be one entity. It was like his father controlled the beast by telepathy, as if he could let go of the reins and the animal would know exactly where to go and what to do.

James had told Jake that it was the ultimate form of trust and one of the cornerstones of their family's success. It was why they had survived the buyouts from the bigger ranches. It was what people had come to call the Bowers Standard.

Jake had spent his entire life trying to live up to that standard, and he did so with the disadvantage of his illness. There were times when he wished that he would have never been born instead of having to live with the pain and embarrassment that the illness provided.

It was something he never quit understood, but something he never questioned. It was an instinct, and every time he got close to quitting, that instinct would push him a little bit further, just far enough to get him past the hard stuff, to regroup. Jake could never be sure, but he hoped that he and his father shared that trait, because he'd never seen his dad fail. He always came through. And that's what Jake would do.

38

*T*he first half mile from the ranch was bumpy, the big semi-rig jerking forward along the road as Luis struggled to get a handle on it.

"Good thing I put on my seatbelt," Zi said.

Luis blushed. "It's just been a while." Fueled by embarrassment, he forced himself to drive smoother, and by the time the first mile ticked past on the odometer, he succeeded.

"God," Zi said, rolling down her window. "We finally get a car that works and the A/C is busted." She tilted her head out the window, her tightly-curled hair flung wildly in the breeze as she shut her eyes.

Luis snuck a few glances her way while she had her attention focused on cooling herself, and he noticed the way the sun reflected off her skin, making it glisten. He cleared his throat and adjusted his hands on the steering wheel as he weaved around a sedan that had broken down on the road. "So, what did you do in San Antonio?"

"I was a waitress," Zi answered.

"Where at?"

"At a café in the lobby of a Marriot downtown."

"How long have you been working there?"

"Are we playing twenty questions?"

Luis raised his hands passively. "Just trying to pass the time."

It was quiet for a long time, and then Zi finally leaned over. "I'm just working there while I'm going to school." She raised an eyebrow. "*Was* going to school, I guess."

"What were you studying?" Luis asked.

"Nursing." Zi smiled as she answered, but it faded. "Not that it matters anymore."

"You don't know that," Luis answered.

Zi scoffed. "You really think that things are going to go back to normal after all of this? Have you not seen what's been happening over the past few days?"

"People will start to get a hold on things," Luis answered, shrugging off the doubt. "That's what we're doing, aren't we?"

Zi laughed. "I don't know if I'd call driving a semi-truck to a junkyard to pick up some old rusted campers my normal." She looked at him. "Probably just another Saturday for you, huh?"

"I'm just saying that people fight their way through," Luis said. "People have gone through bad batches before, and we've always made it out the other side. Sometimes it takes a while, but we usually figure it out and turn it around. We're creatures of comfort and habit, and once those are disrupted, we tend to give those that caused the disruption a lot of trouble."

Zi jutted her jaw forward and nodded as she stared out the window. "It's just that everything is so different now. The world has gone off the rails and we're stuck trying to piece everything back together again. It's bullshit. It makes me want to take that piece of bomb and nuke the people that did this to us. Wipe them off the map."

Luis was quiet for a moment and then nodded. "They'll get theirs. If history has taught me anything, it's that the bad guys eventually lose. Call it a balance of the universe, call it God, call it whatever you want. But so long as there's life, then anything that threatens to take that life won't last. Because once life is gone, what's left?"

The words lingered in the cabin, nothing but the hum of the diesel engine between them, but it was Zi who finally broke the silence.

"Hopefully us," Zi said.

The road remained clear for most of the trip. There wasn't much traffic to begin with out in these parts, but Luis was thankful not to have to avoid too many obstacles on the road.

The brakes squealed as they pulled into the junkyard parking lot. It was a large piece of property that sat alone in the middle of nowhere, the whole thing surrounded by a tall fence with barbed wire spiraled around the top.

"Big wall for such a bunch of junk," Zi said.

Luis parked, shut off the engine, and the big semi lurched forward. He shrugged. "One man's trash is another man's treasure."

"You think anyone is home?" Zi asked.

"No. Harry's in Houston. Been there since May." Luis opened the door and landed hard on the soles of his boots. He left his pack in the cab, but made sure to bring his pistol and rifle as Zi joined him at the front of the truck. "So, I know how to get in, but we'll need to be careful because if we've decided to come and pick the meat off the rest of this carcass, then chances are there might be others with the same idea. And anyone in that junkyard just heard both of us pull up due to our ten-ton pickup behind us." He tucked the rifle's stock into his shoulder, holding the weapon comfortably in his hand.

Zi nodded. "I'll follow your lead."

Luis moved toward the gates, muttering under his breath. "We'll see how long that lasts."

The main gate was chained shut, but Luis knew where the spare key was hidden inside the small building, which was always unlocked. Old Harry Finster relied solely on the security system sticker in the window, which he did not own. But he'd always told Luis that there wasn't anything of value to steal inside the building. He kept his cash at the bank.

Inside, the place had already been ransacked. Not that it was very organized to begin with, but Luis had visited the place enough times to know that it had been looted.

But the key was still in its secret place, hidden amongst hundreds of others in a jar that had been shattered. It was Harry's cruel joke to any burglars, giving them the key to what they wanted in plain sight, but them having no clue of which key it really was. But Luis knew what to look for, and he located the correct key quickly.

Key in hand, Luis headed toward the front gate, unlocked the heavy chain, and then slid it open, exposing both of them to the piles of junk that stretched for miles.

Luis looked to Zi. "Shall we?"

The junkyard was an intricate series of pathways that Harry Finster had left between the massive piles of scrap that he'd accumulated over the past forty years.

"Last time I was here, I saw the campers in the back-right corner," Luis said, keeping his eyes peeled for any movement.

"How many did you see?" Zi asked, staying alert like Luis. It was impressive how quickly she had taken to the life of fighting.

"At least a dozen," Luis answered, the paths growing narrower the deeper they moved into the junkyard. "We should be able to move most of them with one of the ATVs that Harry left lying around. We can chain them up and—"

The gunshot ricocheted the bullet off an old radiator with a twang as Zi and Luis ducked behind one of the coves in the trash piles for cover.

Luis kept one hand back to keep Zi still, using himself as a human shield. "Did you see where it came from?"

"I can't see anything if you don't move." Zi shoved his arm off of her and quickly jettisoned across the path to another pile of trash that provided cover, her quick motion triggering another gunshot.

When she was settled, Luis glared at her, and she wrinkled her eyebrows together as she moved carefully toward the front to get a better look.

When another bullet was fired from somewhere in the junk piles, Zi jumped backward and held up two fingers, signaling that she saw at least two shooters, and then pointed up, letting him know that they were high up.

Luis braced himself for what came next, knowing that he'd have to move fast. He held up his own hand, extending all five fingers, and then counted down from five. Four. Three. Two. One.

Luis spun from the edge of cover and planted a knee on the ground so he could steady the rifle in his hands. Through the scope, he quickly located the first shooter, but he didn't line up the shot properly and the bullet missed wide left.

While Luis was realigning his next shot, Zi provided cover fire, but her assault pushed both shooters back into hiding, not giving Luis a chance to adjust his aim.

Luis peeled his eye off the scope and moved forward quickly, waving for Zi to follow. He kept both eyes on the pair of shooters ahead and waited for them to show themselves. When the tops of their heads appeared above the piles of trash, Luis returned fire, his assault unrelenting as both he and Zi charged forward.

The trash pile where the two shooters were located had a

fork in the road. When they reached the pile, Luis turned right and signaled for Zi to go left.

Bullets chased them along the path, but eventually the same pile of junk that gave the shooters the high ground provided cover for Luis and Zi, and that gave Luis time to charge up the trash pile.

It was dangerous climbing, every piece of junk precariously stacked against one another. One wrong move could spell disaster and send Luis tumbling down.

Muscles burning by the time he reached the top, Luis worked his way back to where the shooters were positioned, but he found nothing but trash.

"Drop the rifle."

Luis froze, and then, keeping the weapon in his hand, he slowly turned around.

One of the shooters had gotten hold of Zi and had positioned themselves in front of her, using her like a human shield with a pistol to her head.

"I said drop it!" The voice barked the demand once more, but Luis knew the moment the gun left his hands, they'd be finished.

Luis didn't move. He found Zi's eyes, which were unafraid of the circumstances, and when she glanced just past his left shoulder, Luis knew what was coming.

Luis ducked, spinning around in the same motion as he swung the rifle around, the barrel cracking against the shin of the second shooter who had stealthily snuck up on him. But when Luis aimed the weapon at his attacker, Luis was surprised to see a kid.

A boy that couldn't have been much older than Jake, his face dirtied and sunburnt, his hair disheveled and a mess, wearing clothes that swallowed him up. He thrust his hands up to protect himself, but Luis also saw that the boy had no weapon.

"Get away from him!" The man puffed his chest and placed the pistol beneath Zi's chin. "I'll do it! I swear I will!"

Before Luis could act, Zi jerked away from her captor, separating her head and the pistol, and elbowed the man in the ribs, buckling him forward and then twisted the man's wrist, causing him to drop the pistol, which she quickly picked up and aimed at him.

Wincing and now on his knees and weaponless, the man slowly raised his hands in defense. "Please. I'm sorry."

"A little late for that now," Zi said.

Luis picked up the kid from the ground and then pushed him toward his father, the pair hugging in a tight embrace. "What are you doing here?"

The father stood, moving his son behind him, and then cleared his throat. He was dirty like his boy, his clothes worn and torn, rougher around the edges than his son, and Luis got the impression that the pair had been in a bad spot since even before the EMP. "We've been hiding here."

"Since when?" Luis asked.

"A while," the father answered, swallowing, and running his tongue over burned and chapped lips. "I thought you might have been those people again."

"What people?" Zi asked.

"They had guns, like yours, but they wore masks," he answered, touching his face, which was covered in a mangy beard. "They tore the place up last time they were here."

"How long have you been here?" Zi asked.

The man wiped his eyes and then sniffled, drawing in a breath. "Long time. We worked out a deal with Harry before he left. Said we could look after the place, stay in the building while we did." He stared down at the junk scattered around their feet. "He was a good man."

Luis looked at the old man and his son. They were even in worse condition than the people they rescued from the town.

And Luis suspected that they had been in this condition for a long time. "Listen. We're here to grab some of the RVs that Harry has lying around. We're taking them back to the Bowers Ranch."

The father nodded. "I've heard of the family. Harry talked about them."

"We have plenty—"

Zi grabbed Luis's arm, leaning close. "Can I talk to you for a moment?" She stepped away from the father and son, and Luis followed suit. When they were alone and away from the others, she lowered her voice. "What are you thinking?"

"Zi, they—"

"They were just shooting at us only a few seconds ago," Zi said, struggling to keep her voice at a whisper. "We don't know them at all, and I don't think James would want us bringing back more people to feed and shelter. That problem brought us here in the first place."

Surprised by her reaction, Luis studied her and shook his head. "We can help them. Just like we did with the people from town. I mean look at them, Zi. They don't have anything."

"I just think that it's a bad idea to invite someone you hardly—what?" Zi frowned, cocking her head to the side.

But while Zi maintained her hardline stance, Luis only shook his head. "And what would have happened to you if James had used that same line of thinking in the city?"

"I didn't try and shoot James." Zi thrust a finger in his face. "This is different, and you know it. I don't know about you, but I think we have enough people to worry about shooting us in the back of the head without bringing on others that sleep in the same area as us." She huffed out the last few words and then drew a deep breath, which calmed her down a bit. "Is it really worth the risk to bring them just to make your conscience feel better?"

Luis knew that it might be foolish to bring them, and he understood the risks, but he still couldn't push the thought out of his head. "People make mistakes, Zi. That doesn't mean they don't deserve a second chance or an opportunity to make things right. None of us get it right the first time." And after that, he walked back toward the father and son, asking if they could show him where the campers were parked and hoping that his words resonated with Zi.

39

*a*fter one hour into James's ride to the west, he still hadn't come up with a good plan of how to convince Banks to get his people involved. The man was notoriously reclusive, and the only reason that James knew about him and his operation was because the pair bought MREs from the same company.

James arrived to pick up his flat of prepackaged food, and Banks happened to arrive and pick some up at the same time. The pair started to talk, and every few months, the pair would meet up to talk shop at a neutral location.

Even though Mary believed in prepping and being a survivalist, she was always skeptical of Banks because of the way he was so reclusive. She had said he was too paranoid about who he trusted. And while James didn't disagree with his wife, he doubted that Banks was having any regret about taking that line in the sand now that the world was falling to pieces.

James stuck to the highway for as long as he could, using it to guide him, and then when he passed mile marker eight-ninety-two he veered north, breaking the horse into a gallop and stayed as true north as he could muster.

Banks had purchased more southern Texas land over the past two decades than any real estate developer in the entire state. He got most of it cheap, seeing as how there wasn't anything resembling civilization for miles in any direction. But that was just the way Banks had wanted it.

Banks had transformed all of his thousands of acres into a compound with a thriving community that lived completely off grid. It was a safe haven for anyone that Banks trusted, or could help him, and those individuals were few and far between.

James pulled back on the reins, the horse shaking his head back and forth to protest the sudden stop. James turned the animal in half circles in every direction, trying to find a landmark to catch his bearings, anything that he remembered from his previous conversations with Banks. But nothing came to mind.

A wind blew from the northwest and the horse stomped its hooves, growing restless and alarmed. James glanced in the direction of the wind, squinting, but seeing nothing but shrubs and grass.

Still, the animal flung its head back and forth, jumping on its hind legs, trying to buck James off as he struggled to regain control of the animal. "Hey!" He pulled back on the reins, trying to steer the animal to be still. "Easy! Easy." He placed one hand on the horse's neck, hoping to soothe her through touch. "There we go."

The wind died down, and so did the animal's tantrum. James once again glanced in the direction of the wind, squinting, looking for anything out of the ordinary, and while he couldn't see it, he did start to feel it as the horse did.

The hairs on the back of his neck stood up, and he broke out in a cold sweat, his heartrate elevated as he reached for the pistol at his hip. He unholstered the weapon, waiting for any sign of movement, but the longer he stared, the more it all just blended together.

Finally, when there was nothing, James motioned the animal forward again, but he kept the weapon drawn, hoping that it would be a deterrent if there really was anything out there.

One thing that James hadn't considered was that if Banks's compound had already been attacked. It wasn't likely, but it wasn't impossible. And because he'd never even been to the compound, James needed to consider every angle.

After all, the man valued his privacy. What little information he fed to James could have just been misinformation. And just when he thought about turning around, a gunshot shattered the quiet afternoon air.

The horse jumped, and so did James. He turned around, noticing that the gunshot had come from behind them. In the same motion that James fired his pistol, he heeled the horse and the pair rocketed forward.

Still unable to locate the shooter, James only fired once, then ducked low on the horse, trying to make himself as small a target as he possibly could. The rush of wind blew past his ears, a faint ringing lingering because of the gunfire.

A geyser of dirt and grass erupted ten yards ahead and the horse reared, bucking James from the saddle and onto his back. The contact from the landing knocked the wind out of him, and he gasped for air, disoriented as he gazed up at the sky.

Knowing that he was a sitting duck out in the open, James rolled to his stomach, reaching for the pistol at the holster, then realizing he'd dropped it when the horse had bucked him off. He crawled on all fours, scouring the ground for his weapon, a high-pitched din ringing in his ears.

The horse had trotted off, galloping away, and just when James had his fingers on the weapon, he was quickly tackled from behind and face planted into the dirt.

"Stay on the ground! Don't move!" The orders were

barked angrily as the man who tackled him attempted to pin James's hands behind his back, but he wouldn't let go of the weapon. "Drop the pistol! Do it now!"

James thrust his head backward and felt his skull connect against the man's nose, who quickly cursed, and then twisted James's wrist until the weapon was dropped. James felt the cold steel of handcuffs clamp around his wrists.

James thrashed back and forth, but the swinging of his shoulders was useless.

"Enough!" The man who had handcuffed James slammed him onto the ground, and because James couldn't use his arms to brace for the impact, he hit it hard.

The front side of James's body exploded with pain the moment he made contact, and his body went limp, his vision fading as more boots stepped around him.

"What do you want to do with him?"

"We should get rid of him now, save everyone the trouble."

"What if he's not one of the terrorists?"

"I know he's not a terrorist!"

"Then why don't we take him back?"

"You really want to lug his body all the way to the compound from here?"

James struggled to speak, nothing but raspy whispers passing over his tongue.

"Shut up!" The order was followed by a swift kick in the ribs, and the deliberation continued. "I say we get his horse, and we finish him now. Bury them in the sand, and no one is the wiser."

It was quiet for a moment, and the longer the silence lingered, James knew that his chances of survival were waning. He finally coughed and managed to spit out a word. "Banks!" He coughed again, his senses slowly returning after the assault. "I know Banks."

James was lifted off the ground and stood upright, and the barrel of a pistol was pressed against his right cheek.

"You know Banks?" The man with the pistol had a thick, matted beard. It was covered in dust, along with most of his face. In fact, James noticed that the man's attire was nothing but camouflage gear, matching the surrounding fields. It was why James hadn't been able to spot the shooter before.

"I'm James Bowers. I know him. And he knows me."

The second man, dressed in similar attire minus the beard, pushed the pistol out of James's face and studied him with a hard glare. "If you know Banks, then you know that he doesn't like unexpected visitors."

"I know," James said, the pain in his body starting to numb. "But he'll want to see what I brought him. He needs to know what's coming."

The pair of men exchanged a glance, and the bearded one shrugged.

"I'll need my horse," James said, looking at the bearded man. "If you wouldn't mind."

"You son of a—"

"Get him his horse." The second man pushed James forward, and the pair started walking. "I'll meet you at the gate."

"Are you kidding me?" the bearded man asked. "You're really going to listen to this clown?"

Neither James or the man's partner answered, and then the bearded man grumbled as he started off to find James's mare.

The walk was long, and hot, and the world blurred. James's head lolled from side to side like a bowling ball, and the man behind him kept a firm grip on the restraints at all times.

"I hope you have something good for Banks on that horse," the man said, finally breaking the silence. "Gibbons

254

will make sure you have a bad time if he chased that animal down for nothing."

"Believe me," James said. "If I had a choice of either facing Gibbons or finding what was in my horse's saddle, I'd pick Gibbons."

After what felt like an eternity walking under the hot sun, James finally caught his first glimmer of the compound on the horizon. At first it just shimmered like a desert mirage, and James wondered if it was really even there, but the longer he stared and the close they moved, the more detailed the compound became.

"Stop." The man tugged back on the restraint.

James turned around to see what the man was doing, but before he could see what was happening, the world around him went dark as the bag was placed over his head. "Is this really necessary?"

"It's protocol," the man said. "No one sees the inside of the compound unless you're a member. And I don't remember seeing you at last week's meeting. Now move."

James stumbled forward, guided by the man who had cuffed him. With the world dark, he relied on his hearing, and the closer he moved to the compound, the louder the world became.

A gate opened, its gears grinding. Chatter fluttered past, James's captor shouting a few words to whoever opened the gate. More whispers and talking, a few gunshots far away that James figured was firearm training. He was turned left, then right, then left again. More doors opened, more chatter, more greetings, and the one final door and then James was shoved into a chair and the bag was ripped off his head.

The brightness of sunlight blinded James and he turned his face away. His arms were still cuffed behind him in the chair, which forced him to sit on the very edge. Two men stood in front of him, both of them different than the men who had caught him out in the open.

They were dressed in tactical gear, arms crossed over their chests, each of them providing a thousand-yard stare that James suspected worked on most folks.

"I need to speak with Banks," James said.

"And you need to give us a good reason why we shouldn't gut you where you sit," the man on the left spoke first and dropped his arms. He stepped closer, and James saw a beard that was tripped short. He was well groomed. "You're lucky my guys didn't blow your head off."

The second man stopped forward. He was bald, clean-shaven, shorter than his friend. But he had a scar that worked its way along the jawline. It was so seamless that James almost didn't notice it was there at all. "Why do you need to speak with Banks?"

"My name is James Bowers," he said, his voice raspy, but he cleared it and the strength returned. "My family has owned ranchland east of here for decades. I came here to tell him that his compound might no longer be secure."

The bald man arched his eyebrows and he leaned forward, flaring his nostrils. He tilted his head to the side. "Why?"

"Ruckins," James answered. "The town was overrun with those terrorists. There were probably over two dozen of them, and they were toting some heavy artillery, I'm talking military-grade weapons."

"And what makes you say that?" Beard asked.

"Let's just say I got an up-close look," James answered.

Baldy clenched his jaw.

"I had the item we found on my horse," James said. "But you guys set off that bomb and scared him off. The animal needs to be recovered if—"

"This is bullshit." Baldy turned toward his bearded comrade. "Do you really want to deal with this right now? We can't take him to Banks, he'll think we've lost our mind."

"It's not bullshit," James said. "It's a piece of a bomb. A piece of a nuclear bomb."

James knew that dropping that knowledge on the pair of men was a Hail Mary, but he didn't want to waste any more time.

"The same people who detonated the EMP are going to detonate a nuclear bomb," James said. "I don't know where, but I have a piece of it, and that means there are most likely groups with other pieces and they're going to come looking for it."

James studied the two men, hoping that he was able to reach them in some way, and judging by the look in their eyes, he thought that he might have, but he was wrong.

"Take him to the cell," Baldy said. "Banks will decide what to do with him when he comes back."

"Hey, wait!" James protested, but it did little to do anything as he was ripped from his chair and black-bagged once more. "We don't have time for this!"

James's voice was ignored as he was whisked away. Again, he was directed in several directions until he was finally shoved forward, the bag ripped off his head, and a heavy clang echoing behind him as the caged door was closed.

James hurried toward the door, gripping the bars. "They're going to come back! Hey!" He pounded his fist against the bars, the dull thud echoing as he watched the guards disappear.

The bunker was surprisingly cool, and despite the claustrophobic fears that had kept Nolan aboveground for most of his life, he figured that he'd need to get used to being six feet under sooner or later. The lights were dim, giving everything a dull, vanishing look. Including the people.

Nolan didn't mind the folks, but he didn't want to answer questions. He was too tired. It might have been a selfish thought, but he was old and dying and he thought that he deserved a few selfish thoughts. Because if he couldn't have them now, then when in the hell could he have them?

"You can't avoid them forever," Mary said, keeping her voice to a whisper.

"Watch me," Nolan said, pretending to check Mary's bandages.

Mary laughed, and he smirked as he removed the thick, coke-bottle lens glasses and leaned back in his chair, trying to straighten out a back that didn't seem to want to be straight anymore. He took a deep breath and then folded his hands over the book and papers in his lap.

"How are you holding up?" Mary asked.

Nolan did a little tsk, tsk, tsk, clucking his tongue in the same motion, and then shook his head. "You're the patient, not the doctor."

"Nolan." Mary reached for his arm and wrapped her fingers over his wrist, her touch warm.

"I'm fine," Nolan said, hoping he hadn't lost his touch for false reassurances. "Really."

Mary studied his face for a moment and then finally released his wrist. "James said you might only have a couple of weeks?"

Nolan shrugged. "Could be more, could be less."

"And... Is it going to be—"

"Yes," Nolan said. "It will be very painful, but it will be quick. It's an aggressive cancer. I just need a good place to lay down once it gets really bad." He examined the bed she currently occupied. "How's this one?"

"Nolan," Mary said, forcing herself not to smile. "You can't make jokes."

"Why not? Laughter is the most powerful medicine. And it makes me feel in control over something I can't change."

"Your right," Mary said. "I'm sorry." She held up a finger in the way that all mothers did whenever they wanted to ensure their point was understood. "But you're also old, and a doctor, so you're a bit of a know-it-all, so don't forget that you can ask for help." She tilted her head to the side. "Got it?"

"Yes, ma'am." Nolan grimaced from a pain in his abdomen. He clutched his stomach, rubbing the point of contention. His first thought, as with any sudden outbreak of pain that he felt throughout his body, was that it was due to the cancer slowly eating his insides, and he wondered if there was anything worse than rotting from the inside out.

But the rumbling in his stomach stopped and he remembered that he didn't have anything to eat this morning. Hell, he hadn't had anything to eat since yesterday.

"You all right?" Mary asked.

"Yeah." Nolan patted his stomach and laughed. "Just hungry."

"Are you scared?" Mary asked.

Nolan raised his eyebrows. "Of dying?"

Mary nodded.

Nolan considered his answer. The truth was he hadn't really given himself time to think about the afterworld and what came next. He had been busy with work, and then after the EMP was detonated, he had been in a constant state of duress that hadn't allowed much time for reflection.

"I don't know," Nolan finally said. "I think I might be more scared of the pain that comes right before I die. I've seen this disease before. I've seen what it can do, and the havoc it wreaks on the body." He glanced down to his person and then cleared his throat. "Like what it's doing to me right now, at this very moment. Slowly eroding what still works. Which isn't much to begin with." He rubbed his eyes and chuckled. "I've never been a religious man, never thought that there was a higher power at work, but... He dropped his hands and readjusted his glasses, smiling at Mary, who was hanging onto his every word. "I guess I just thought I'd have some kind of epiphany by now, something that would lead me toward a better understanding of what was possible."

"Nolan, I don't want to be rude, or intruding, but..." Mary fidgeted anxiously in her bed, then cleared her throat and spoke with more confidence. "I wanted to ask if I could say the Lord's Prayer with you?"

Nolan had never been someone who had believed in God, but sitting in the bunker, holding Mary's hand, he found himself wanting to find Him and was glad for the help.

"I would like that," Nolan said.

Nolan sat quietly and patiently as Mary took his hand. The pair closed their eyes. Mary asked the Lord to watch over him, to keep the pain at bay for as long as possible, and to accept him into His arms when the time came for him to be called home.

When Mary finished, she kissed Nolan's hand, and when Nolan opened his eyes, he felt a single tear on his cheek. It was unexpected, and he wiped it away quickly.

"Thank you," Nolan said. "That was... more than I deserved."

"You're a good man," Mary said. "And He'll remember that when you're called home again."

"I hope so," Nolan said.

The pair lingered in silence for a moment, Nolan still basking in the glow of prayer, when one of the townspeople came over and interrupted the peaceful silence.

"I was wondering if you know when they'll be back?"

Nolan shook his head. "I'm not sure. I bet it won't be long though."

Another person came over, expressing the same concern, and before Nolan realized, there were a dozen people around him asking questions, all of them concerned.

Eventually Nolan was forced to stand, raising his arms and his voice as he shouted above the crowd. "Everyone, please!"

The crowd finally quieted down, and Nolan lowered his hands, the eyes staring back at him so focused and intense that he thought they were going to drill holes right through his soul.

"I don't know when they're coming back," Nolan said. "We're all dealing with a lot of uncertainties right now, but the most important thing is to stick together and not to go down all of the rabbit holes of what if's and—" Nolan stopped, his mind suddenly pulsing, and he shut his eyes. He swallowed, trying to shake off the pain. His body broke out into a cold sweat and when he opened his eyes again, the people in front of him were staring at him like something was wrong, but Nolan tried to push through. "What's important is..." he staggered, and a pair of hands steadied him.

Lightheaded, Nolan sat down. The lights, the people, the sound, all of it blurred together, and he raised his fingers to touch something warm on his upper lip. When he examined the tip of his finger, he saw blood, and then he passed out.

* * *

THE SUN REACHED its highest point in the sky, and with the trench at the halfway mark toward the river, Jake decided that it was time for lunch.

"Okay, everyone," Jake said. "Go ahead and pick up your shovels, and we'll walk back toward the bunker and have ourselves some food."

A mixture of relief and complaints were whispered between breaths as everyone collected their gear and started the long trek back toward the bunker.

Jake was beginning to understand what his father was trying to tell him about people. Not everyone had the ability to push through the pain and fatigue.

"Gah." Jake stopped, lurching forward, and he clutched his chest. He shut his eyes, and two cold spots formed in each of his cheeks. The pain grew so intense that Jake's entire body felt like it was hollow, and if even the slightest breeze was blown his way then he would dissolve like a pile of dust.

"Hey, you all right?"

Jake didn't look up to see who it was, but he held up his hand. "Just catching my breath. I'll meet up with you." There was no follow up and when Jake finally lifted his head, he saw that the group was well ahead of him.

Slowly, Jake forced himself to take a step, and it required every amount of effort and strength that he had. But he wasn't going to give into his illness. He wasn't going to become a burden to his family. There was still too much to do, and Jake knew that if he couldn't carry his own weight, then there wouldn't be anyone else that could do it for him.

Jake straightened up and walked. And while every step seemed to add another twenty pounds of pressure to his chest, he didn't stop.

By the time he made it to the bunker, he saw a cluster of people around the top. Starting to become dazed and delirious himself, Jake frowned, wondering what could have been so important.

Jake stumbled left, then collapsed into the dirt. The pressure in his chest kept him pinned down.

On his back, Jake squinted his eyes as he looked up into the sky. He heard mumbled shouts, and it didn't take long before he saw faces above him and felt himself being picked up and carried.

Jake had wanted to try and help, and he wanted to tell them that he could do it himself, but the words wouldn't form on his tongue. It was suddenly becoming harder to breathe, harder to hear, harder to see, and the light blue sky slowly faded to black.

Zi kept her distance from the father and son, who she and Luis learned were Terry and Mark. She hung back while Luis spoke to Terry, Mark leading the pack. She hated that Luis's words lingered in her mind, because it only worsened the guilt. But the longer she flipped them over, the more she realized that he was right and she was wrong.

Fear was getting the best of her, and Zi vowed a long time ago to never let fear control her life. It had done that too much already.

"That's what you're looking for, right?" Terry pointed toward the campers, his son in tow, who sprinted ahead of them. "Well, there they are."

Zi nudged Luis with her elbow. "I thought you said they're in good condition?"

"Well," Luis said, struggling to find a silver lining. "You haven't seen the inside yet."

The group walked toward the dilapidated structures, and Mark dove into one of the campers. Zi and Luis poked their heads inside and found him jumping up and down on an old mattress that was covered in stains and dirt.

"Yeah," Zi said. "It's much better on the inside."

"We can fix them up," Luis said. "I'm handier than I look." He stepped closer, the space between them growing more intimate. "I recognize that this isn't the ideal situation. But people are going to have to make do with what we're giving them. It's not like we have a lot of options right now."

Zi shifted her weight from side to side, her hips rocking back and forth, and she tossed her hands up in the air and shook her head. "I mean is this it now? Is this what everyone has to look forward to?" She shut her eyes and took a few deep breaths, trying to regain her composure, but it wasn't until Luis placed his hand on her cheek that she finally relaxed.

"We'll have things to look forward to again one day," Luis said.

Zi smiled sadly. "Not everyone thinks the way you do. Not everyone tries to make things better. Just look at the people who did this. You can't just wish for evil to go away."

"No," Luis said. "But that doesn't mean we give up hoping for a better world. And it won't make me stop trying to build one." He stepped back, giving her some room.

Zi watched him head back over to the trailers, where he started walking through them with Terry and Mark. She admired him. She really did. And while his words were meant to make her feel better, she just couldn't get herself over that emotional hump.

Maybe it was because of how hard she'd fought to get out of those bad neighborhoods that she grew up in. It was an uphill battle, all the way, and her family didn't make it any easier.

Zi never wanted to live like that. She never wanted to be that person, it was the reason why she had decided to become a nurse, because she wanted to help people that were in a bad situation and put them on the road to recovery. And now the world had changed, but it still needed help.

Zi rejoined Luis and the others at the front of one of the campers. It was the smallest one, maybe big enough for two so long as the pair living together didn't mind sleeping on top of one another. "So how are we going to pull them up front?"

"We won't have to." Luis stood up after examining one of the hitches, then pointed around the bend of one of the trash piles. "There's an old access point that I can pull the truck around and load it using winches and pulleys. Piece of cake." He grinned, his teeth surprisingly white against his dark tan and thick spread of stubble that ran down to his Adam's apple.

It gave him a more rugged look, and while Zi had never imagined herself with a cowboy, she was beginning to warm to the idea.

"I'll go pull it around," Luis said, already walking away. "Why don't you go with Terry and Mark. He'll need some help opening the back door."

Before she answered, Luis had already disappeared down one of the paths and Mark was tugging at her hand, smiling up at her as he pulled her down the path past the campers and the other junk that acted as the little boy's home.

The "hidden access point" that Terry had told them about was about as accessible as a locked door. What used to be another entrance point to the junkyard had been chained over with fencing. They found some bolt cutters and started opening the space up.

Because the original space was wide enough to have trucks dump off large pieces of cargo, Luis was able to back the vehicle up and into the junkyard. It took some time and a lot of turns at the hand crank for the winch, but they managed to fit all but two of the campers in the trailer.

"Good work," Luis said, giving Mark a high five, and then faked that the boy had hit his hand so hard that he'd hurt him. "Ow, easy, Tex. No need to get rough with me."

Mark smiled, and seeing the boy smile made Zi smile too. Finished, Zi knew that Luis was going to invite the pair back to the ranch, and Zi wanted to extend the offer herself. "Listen, I know that—"

"It was really nice meeting both of you." Terry lunged forward, shaking Zi's hand quickly and then shaking Luis's hand. He grabbed his boy's arm and started to pull him away. "Say goodbye, Mark."

Confused by the sudden change in behavior, Zi tossed a look to Luis, who raised his hands in the same stupor that Zi was in. She broke into a jog, cutting Terry off before he disappeared farther into the junkyard. "Wait, we wanted—"

"No," Terry said, immediately waving his hands and trying to step around Zi. "I know what you're going to say, and it's best that we don't get involved." He glanced down at his son. "C'mon, Mark."

"But you don't have to stay here," Zi said. "We want you to come back to the ranch."

Terry spun around and became aggressive. "You mean the same ranch that you said was nearly blown off the map? The same ranch that doesn't have enough shelter for the people that they already have? We don't need that kind of trouble. Thank you, but no." He started forward again to charge past Zi, but this time it was Mark who pulled his father back.

"Why can't we go?" Mark asked.

"Not now," Terry barked harshly at his son and then yanked him forward harder, but Mark stood his ground, squirming out from his father's hold. "Mark!"

"No!" Mark screamed, tears in his eyes as he moved away from his father, backtracking toward the trailer. "I don't want to stay here with you! I don't want to be here anymore! I want to leave! I want to go!" He screamed the last note and then sprinted away from everyone. Away from his father, away from the trailer, away from having to stand to face a final decision.

Terry started after him, but Luis held up a hand and jogged to follow instead. The old homeless man stumbled forward a few steps after both of them were out of sight, and then stopped. He hung his head and his shoulders slumped.

Zi watched him stand there for a long time, so many questions running through her head, and unsure of where she should start, or if she should begin at all.

Finally, Terry turned, his cheeks wet from the tears that poured down his face. He wiped at his eyes, but it only smeared dirt around on his cheek. "Just go."

Zi recognized that brokenness in him, the same brokenness that she had felt for most of her life. "It's okay." She moved toward him slowly, even when he shook his head and sobbed harder. "You don't have to stay here alone. I know that you think you do, but you don't have to. This isn't the life that you want for yourself, and this isn't the life that you want for Mark."

"And what are we supposed to do?" Terry asked. "People don't understand. They don't forgive. I failed, and it's a failure that I've never been able to overcome. All those people at your ranch? Those are the same faces I've seen all my life. The faces that toss me a glance and a quarter and tell me to go and get a job. The same faces that ask me how could I let my child live like this and tell me I should be ashamed for not being able to put a roof over my kid's head." He pounded his chest. "I give everything I have to my boy. I make sure that he never goes hungry, even if that means I do. I might not look like much, but I know that I'm a good father."

Without a word, Zi reached for the old man's hand and held it between both of her palms. She squeezed his hand. "Come with us."

Luis returned with Mark, the little boy wiping his eyes, and then ran to his father, who scooped him up in his arms, the pair holding onto one another like they were the only two people in the world.

"I'm sorry," Terry said.

"Me too," Mark replied.

Zi looked past the father and son and to Luis. Things could get better, and for the first time in a long time, she knew that she was exactly where she needed to be to shape that future.

_T_he temperature in James's cage had risen steadily since he was locked away. He had no idea of how long he'd been away, but he'd shed most of his clothing, and after the amount of sweat that had been squeezed from his body, he was shocked to discover that more was coming out. Another hour and he'd be a raisin.

During his time under lock and key, James had made some discoveries about his imprisonment. He examined the floors, walls, and ceiling of his cage, and realized that it was the inside of an old shipping container. He could tell by the large boxed shape and the ribbed ceiling that was the trademark of those containers.

It had been refurbished a little bit, having a window cut out near the top with more rebar covering it so no one could escape. Although if they wanted to try, they'd have to be about as thin as a pencil to squeeze through it. At the rate James was losing water, he just might fit.

James suspected that was what most of the compound was made out of. He had heard of people using them to build houses, and they were usually cheap to purchase, stackable, and easy to transport. It was a smart idea.

But while James admired Banks's ingenuity, he couldn't help but laugh over the fact that the one time he'd been caught had been the one time where he had gone to seek help. He had escaped the clutches of evil, only to walk into a friend's home and be locked up.

James shut his eyes and then flung more sweat from his face, the water quickly disappearing into the floor. He counted the seconds that it took for the water stain to completely disappear. It was so hot that even the concrete was thirsty.

James stood, forcing himself to move around to keep the blood flow moving even though all he wanted to do was lie down in a pool of his own sweat. He needed to stay awake. He needed to keep moving, keep engaged, keep thinking of any other way out of this than trying to break out. Because that really wasn't an option. Or a last resort.

After pacing the small square room back and forth, sufficiently getting his blood pumping, which required less and less effort as his body grew more dehydrated, forcing his heart to work harder to pump his blood through to his extremities, James sat in the corner and leaned back against the wall, his shoulders rolling forward in exhaustion.

James thought of the ranch and he thought of his wife and son, one of whom was getting sicker and the other getting better. There was always a balance to life. Every action has an opposite and equal reaction. It was the most basic cycle of humanity, and of life in general.

James stared at his calloused palms, covered with grime and sweat. He rubbed his fingertips together, his skin slick from sweat.

A cramp bit into James's left leg, breaking him from the monotony of his thoughts, and he curled forward, clutching the hamstring that had tightened up. With strained effort he straightened the leg, keeping it still as the slow burn of the cramp faded away and he caught his breath.

"Damn," James said, his voice cracking.

After a minute of stretching, James stood and limped a few steps as he felt the muscle want to seize again. He managed to push through the pain, and after a few short trips from the door to the back of the cell and to the door again, it dissipated. It wasn't much of a track, but it helped provide enough distraction until the cramp passed.

James stopped in the center of the cell, knowing that it was inevitable that another one would come to ravage his body unless he got some water in his system. He moved toward the door, the surge of adrenaline triggered by his survival instincts and the need for water. He pounded on the bars. "Hey!" He shouted, his voice bouncing back in his face from yelling at the door. "I need water!" He pounded on the door again, longer and harder than the first go around. "Open this door! Open this door right now! They're coming! You hear me? They're coming, and they won't stop until they've blown everything away!" His strength faded and James backed away from the bars, his heart pounding in his head, the room starting to spin. He backed against the wall and shut his eyes.

When the floor finally stopped moving and James was confident he was on level ground again, he opened his eyes. He was on his own.

James slid to the floor, exhausted from his outburst, and he slumped his shoulders forward, his head hung low. Sweat dripped from the tip of his nose, splashing against the same point on the floor, hitting the same spot again and again and again, and for a moment James watched the sweat collect on the floor. He was hypnotized by the fact that he had not moved, and he wondered if he was going to die, or if he had already died. But those thoughts were interrupted by the door hinges to his cell, and he lifted his head, staring at a man blurred from his own fatigue.

"I'll be damned."

James blinked, the figure still out of focus.

"When my people told me that James Bowers had come to see me, I told them that they must have misheard." The man stepped forward, his boots thumping against the inside of the shipping container, his figure still silhouetted from the open door behind him. "Because the James Bowers that I know would never come knocking on my door after the shit hit the fan, since we both made a deal a long time ago to make sure we gave each other space."

Banks leaned against the cell bars, staring down at James between the iron poles, shaking his head as if he still didn't believe what he was seeing.

"You must have one hell of a good reason to be here, amigo," Banks said.

James wanted to stand, but he was too exhausted. "We're in for a fight, Banks. Both of us. And we can't run from it."

Banks scratched the back of his head. He wore a simple outfit. Grey shirt, dark jeans, and boots. He had a holster on his right hip with a pistol inside, and James remembered that Banks had told him he like to cross draw since he was a lefty. "James, I don't think you understand what's happening. The world has gone to shit, and we both agreed to let bygones be bygones when that happened. Now, whatever trouble that you might find yourself in, I am truly sorry. But it doesn't have anything to do with me." He turned back toward the door. "I'll get you out of there and send you on your way."

"Did they tell you?" James shouted. Even with the effort, his voice didn't carry very far, but Banks stopped. "Did your people tell you what I said?"

Banks spun around. "They told me you were crazy."

"They're building a bomb, Banks," James said, and pushed himself off the ground. "A nuclear bomb. I found a piece of it, and they're going to come looking for it." He stopped at the bars, curling his hands around the rusted iron. "And if that thing goes off, even you won't be able to survive it. Not even all the way out here."

Banks stepped closer and cocked an eyebrow, challenging James's assumption. "You sure you want to test that theory, partner?"

"I just need five minutes," James answered. "You listen to what I have to tell you, and then you can make up your own mind. But hear it from me."

Banks chewed on his lower lip and narrowed his eyes. He was quiet for a long time and then sighed, shaking his head. "All right, James." He turned back around and headed for the door. "This better be good."

Two other men entered, and James gathered his clothes and dressed. This time, when he was taken out of the cell, he was not black-bagged, and he caught his first real glimpses of the compound that Banks had built. And it was more impressive than James had imagined.

James's assessment of the shipping containers had been correct. The compound was filled with them. There were stacked, side by side, and stand-alone containers everywhere. Banks had built a small city with them.

But what was even more surprising than the size and structure of the place was the number of people that he passed. And they weren't all just fighters and guards. Women and children walked around, most of them armed, but it was a much more casual atmosphere than James would have expected, and he realized that this place was more than just a compound. It was a community.

James was brought to another container, this one set up like a command room, and he found Banks waiting inside flanked by the pair of men that had found James earlier in the day. James sat down and then greedily and unabashedly drank the two bottles of water that sat on the table.

When James was finished, he crumpled the plastic up and

then leaned back in his chair, eyes closed. He'd never been so exhausted in his life.

"So, what's this all about, James?" Banks asked.

James straightened up his chair and cleared his throat. The water helped clear his mind, and he felt more awake the longer the water had time to funnel through his system. "I know everyone here understands what happened, why the power shut down."

"EMP," Banks said. "We've been ready for that for years."

"I know," James said. "But the people who did this have something more planned for us. Did you find my horse?"

Banks glanced up at the bearded man, who he remembered had been called Gibbons. "Well?"

"I found the horse," Gibbons answered, his eyes locked on James. "And I found the piece you were talking about. Didn't look like a bomb to me."

"It's a piece of a bomb," James said. "And to be more factual, it's a piece of a nuclear reactor."

Banks cocked his eyebrows up, touching the tips of his hands together. "James, I still fail to see why this is—"

"Why would someone detonate an EMP?" James asked. "They're looking to cripple us, put us down on the canvas, but that's not the final move. It can't be. People would eventually figure out what was happening, so what happens next?" He glanced around the room like a teacher waiting to hear an answer. "What do you do?"

"You finish the job." It was the second man who brought James in, the one who kept Gibbons from blowing James's head off. "It's like a blitzkrieg."

"Exactly." James leaned forward. "The people who detonated the EMP didn't just want to cripple us, they want to destroy us, and if they get their hands on that piece of the bomb, then they'll have the capacity to do so."

James waited for someone to speak, and as the silence was dragged out, James felt like he was losing them.

"Banks, I think the organization who did this has people everywhere," James said. "And that network of people will start looking for that bomb and it will lead them to our back door."

Banks leaned back in his chair and crossed his arms. "And what do you want me to do about it, James? Am I supposed to take my men and go fight a war all on our own?"

"I have people at the ranch," James said. "Good people, but they're folks who won't stand a chance if another wave of fighters decides to march on us. I need more manpower."

Banks laughed, then rubbed his jaw like it was sore. "You are one fool hardy son of a bitch."

"I'm not talking about going off to war," James said. "I'm just talking about trying to save some people who weren't prepared. People that I—"

"People that you decided to take care of," Banks said, thrusting a finger in James's face. "That was your choice, James, not mine." He grimaced and then gestured around him. "How do you think I built this place? Do you think I decided to bring people over here because we were friends? Because I wanted the company? No. I brought people here who I knew were valuable. People I knew who could provide skills and knowledge whenever the shit hit the fan."

"Banks, please, I'm not—"

"Get him out of here." Banks stood and then walked toward the door. "I don't have time for handouts."

"Then what do you want?" James shouted, jumping from his chair, and the aggressiveness brought Banks to a halt. "You want to barter? You want to trade? Name your price."

Banks kept his back to James for a while, and when he finally did turn, he did it slowly. "My price?" He stepped closer toward James, the pair the same height, able to look at one another eye to eye. "What can you offer?"

"After we drove out the enemy in Ruckins, we ransacked their supplies," James said. "MREs, weapons, medicine, we got it all. It's enough for an army." He glanced around the room. "And it looks like you could use a little insurance in case this conflict lasts longer than you think."

Banks ground his teeth, and then nodded. "What's the volume?"

"Five pallets of MREs and one pallet of .223 ammunition," James answered.

Banks scoffed. "That for a trade to potentially feed even more mouths? No. I'd need at least double that."

James didn't have that much to spare. They'd only found eight pallets of MREs, and that was all the ammunition. But he stood his ground. "Eight pallets of MREs and the ammunition stays the same." He glanced at the two guards. "Your boys are already well armed."

Banks laughed. "You're not in a good position to start making demands, James. You're the one who needs my help. Not the other way around."

"You're wrong." James stepped closer, knowing that he was already on thin ice, but if he was going to push this over the edge, then he needed to do something drastic. "And I know that you're wrong firsthand." He glanced around, nodding. "Your place, this community, it's impressive." He slowly turned in a circle. "Lots of guards, in the middle of nowhere. Able to grow your own food I presume, probably even have some livestock stashed away somewhere." He stopped when he turned around. "But because you picked the middle of nowhere, you don't have any game to hunt if food runs out. And the last I checked, the only water source was several miles north. And if something happens, if you end up needing help, you're even farther from trying to seek anyone out." He shrugged. "Maybe those people will never find you, but this isn't pretend anymore, Banks. This isn't theoretical, or hypothetical. An army is coming to wipe us off the face of the earth, and if we're going to stop it, then we need each other. It's the only way to survive. Whether you like it or not."

Having spoken his piece, James stepped back, returning to his chair, where he sat down with his back toward Banks. For a long time, he heard no movement, and James hoped that it had worked.

Finally, Banks returned to the table, sitting across the other side, and James knew that it had worked. The man had finally understood what he had.

"Your people can stay here," Banks said. "For the pallets we discussed."

James tried not to reveal how much he was relieved, but it was hard not to show any emotion. "Thank you, Banks—"

"But." Banks held up a finger. "I'm not fighting this war for you. Because even if these people do end up coming here, the moment we poke our heads out of the sand, then we become a target. Just like you became a target the moment you interfered with the town. I'm not putting my people at risk."

"Banks," James said, leaning forward. "We can do this. If we band together—"

"I'm not finished," Banks said. He took a moment to gather his thoughts and then rubbed his palms together. "I need guarantees that when your people come here, there won't be a chance that they're followed. Which means I need someone to stay behind and make sure that if your ranch is attacked again, this organization is thrown off the trail. And it needs to be someone I trust will get the job done."

James had done enough deals with buyers for his cattle to know how to read between the lines, and it was no different here. But instead of bartering for price per pound, he was fighting for how many lives could be saved against the cost of how many would be lost. But if Banks only required James to stay behind, James knew that was a deal he couldn't turn down.

"All right," James said. "I'll stay behind. I'll throw them off your trail, make sure it doesn't get back to you."

"Good," Banks said. "Then we have a deal."

Banks stretched his arm across the table, and the men shook hands, and just like that it was done. James had successfully negotiated safe passage for his family and the rest of his people.

"I'm going to send a man back with you to confirm the details," Banks said. "So long as you're able to do what was said, then your people will return with my man."

Banks left, and James was once again quarantined at the room until they had given him his horse and the rest of his weapons.

But James knew that he had a daunting task ahead of him when he returned to the ranch. Not everyone would be thrilled about the deal he struck up. And he spent the entire ride back trying to figure out how to convince Mary and Jake to leave him behind.

Mary pressed the cool cloth against Jake's forehead, the water gently rolling down his temples and into his hair. She knew that she should be resting herself, but she couldn't stand to leave him alone. And when he cracked his eyes open, she brought a cup of water to his lips.

"Drink," Mary said.

Without question, Jake drank from the cup. When he finished, he leaned his head back onto the pillow and glanced around confusingly at his surroundings. "What happened?"

"You passed out," Mary said. "The others helped bring you down." She sighed, the lines on her forehead wrinkled together in worry. "You shouldn't have been out there in the heat like that working."

"Mom, I'm fine," Jake said.

"No, you're not," Mary relied. "You're sick."

"I know that," Jake said, turning away. "It's not like I haven't known that all my life."

Mary placed her hand on his shoulder. She knew that he knew. And she didn't know why she felt the need to remind him. Jake's entire life had been nothing but one long, strenuous effort, and the boy had always tried to make it through with a smile on his face.

When he was little and the condition was really bad, Jake would be bedridden for weeks at a time. It was a very boring time, but Mary and James tried to make him feel as normal as possible.

They gave him books and games, but what he loved most was the telescope that his father had given him that he used to chart the constellations, and anytime he finished charting a new system, he would pin it to the roof of his room so he could gaze up at them before he fell asleep.

When Mary had asked him why he liked the stars so much, he had told her that it was reassuring to know that in a world where his condition was changing, or getting worse, there were somethings that wouldn't change. The North star would always shine bright. Orion's Belt would always be there even when he couldn't see it. The Big and Little Dipper too. All of that helped Jake through those rough years when doctors were still trying to figure out the best way to treat him.

Faith had always been an important staple in the lives of the Bowers clan, but seeing her son like this, seeing what had become of her home, she questioned how a just God could do all of this. And while she still didn't have answers to those questions, she knew that it was still her job to protect him. No matter what.

Finally, Jake turned back to his mother. "Mom, if I don't make it—"

"Hey," Mary said. "Don't you talk like that, understand?" The anger was misdirected, and she wiped her nose, shaking her head. "You're too strong. Stronger than you realize."

"Mom, just listen," Jake said, his voice eerily calm. "If something does happen, if the unthinkable—"

"It won't," Mary said. "Your father is going to come back, you'll have the procedure done, and you'll be fine—"

Jake tightened his grip on his mother's hand. "I want to be buried at night, beneath the stars."

Mary wept, and no matter how hard she tried, she couldn't make the tears stop, and then Jake began to cry as well.

"Mom?" Jake asked. "Promise me. I want to hear you say it."

Mary kept her head bowed, her face still scrunched up and her lower lip still quivering. She stayed like that for a little bit, but after a few moments, she regained her composure, and with tears in her eyes, she nodded. "Okay. Yes, I promise."

Jake smiled. "Thank you."

Mary gently laid down by her son's side, stroking his hair, but it felt like he was holding her more than she was holding him.

"I love you more than anything," Mary said, unable to see Jake's face. "From the moment I felt you growing inside of me, I loved you with all my heart and soul. And I will always love you." She shut her eyes, and a light vibration struck her cheek. "Jake?"

Mary lifted her head and saw that Jake was having a seizure, his eyes shut, and his body rigid as his muscles convulsed. She quickly stood and flipped him to his side so he wouldn't choke on his own spit. She glanced back to Nolan who was still passed out and knew that she was on her own.

The seizures were due to the pressure growing in his system. The blood was getting backed up in the heart, and now it was affecting his brain functionality. There wasn't anything that she could do until it passed, but she kept a close eye on him, making sure he was all right.

He had never gotten this bad before, but between the escape from the city and the work at the ranch, he had pushed his body too far, and Mary kicked herself for letting him do it.

The seizure finally ended, and Mary rolled Jake onto his back. She brushed the bangs from his face, trying to soothe him, and then she noticed how still he was. Too still. And then his cheeks transformed from a pale white to blue, then purple.

"Oh my God." Mary quickly adjusted her son's mouth and blew air into his lungs. She then checked for a pulse and felt nothing.

Mary performed CPR, pressing her son's chest fifteen times, and then puffed air into his lungs. "No, no, no, no." She repeated the process, and after several rounds, she felt herself growing tired. But she knew that she was his only hope, and that she had to keep him alive until James returned. She just prayed that it would happen sooner rather than later.

---

*L*eading the front, Khan was the first to see the shimmer of the setting sun against the windows on the buildings of Ruckins.

The line of Khan's caravan stretched as far as he could see. It was a mixture of old army vehicles, horses, and men who had marched on foot. Men who were loyal to him, and only to him. In this clan, in this army, in this organization, he was the only authority. His word was law.

By sheer might and determination, Khan had brought together a group of fighters that could rival any army on the planet. But it was here they would be tested, and it was here where they would find their glory, their absolution, the end to the beginning they had started all of those years ago.

For too long, people with weak minds and wills were fed by the silver spoon while the rest of the world was forced to fight for the scraps that fell from the table they couldn't reach.

But while others were squabbling over what couldn't be theirs, Khan was working on something else, something that would bring them to the source. Because that was the only way that the shift in balance would occur.

Once in the street, Khan saw the damage done by the fires that had consumed the town, and he stopped the caravan when they reached the pile of ashes where a pyre had been constructed for the burnings.

Khan stepped out of the vehicle, his boots crunching against the dirt and gravel that had blown onto the asphalt. It had only been a few days, but nature was already starting to reclaim what man had taken from her, and Khan knew that it would only demand more once it had the taste of its property again. Because everything belonged to the earth. It was the only reason any of them were even still here, and Khan knew better than most that when the earth decided it was time to reclaim what it had lost, there was no stopping it. Nature was one of those absolutes. In fact, it might be the only absolute. And that was why Khan respected it so much.

At the edge of the ash pile, Khan dropped to a knee and dipped his fingertips into the ash that hadn't been blown away. He rubbed the silky contents between his fingers, closing his eyes as he imagined the slow and agonizing burn of those that were consumed by the flames.

He wished that people could be touched by the fire for longer, but it only lasted a few seconds. The pain became so overwhelming that they felt nothing. The fire consumed them and then transformed their worthless bodies to fodder for the earth to grow new life. It gave them a purpose, and it was a purpose that Khan would fulfill with everyone who didn't join his cause, and a few that would require the sacrifice for their mission to be fulfilled.

Doors opened and shut, and there was a heavy groan as a body was pulled from one of the caravans and was brought to the edge of the burnt circle where Dillon was dropped at Khan's feet.

Dillon's face had been beaten to a pulp, both eyes swollen shut, and his body bruised and covered in dried blood. The burns Khan had inflicted on him were crusted and infected, causing excruciating pain.

Khan stepped into the circle of burnt ashes. "Where is this ranch?"

"On the road west," Dillon said, spitting the words out as if holding them in any longer would make the pain worse. "There is a sign down a dirt road. There were traps last time. He'll probably have more."

Khan smirked. He was beginning to like this Bowers man. It was a shame he would have to kill him. "Bring me Carlos and Samuel."

The orders were carried down the line and soon after, a pair of men emerged from the pack. Carlos was short and stout like Khan, his face thick with beard though his head was shaved. His skin was tanned so dark it was nearly black, which only made the green in his eyes more brilliantly sinister. He had been a policeman in a corrupt precinct in Venezuela. He had been one of Khan's first recruits, and had given his lost soul a purpose.

Samuel was an American who had heard whisperings of Khan's group through a few cells planted around the United States. Lost and wandering, and with an ache of violence in his heart, he sold everything he owned and sought out Khan.

"I want recon on this Bowers man," Khan said. "Go to the ranch. Tell me what you find."

"Should we kill him?" Samuel asked, his voice void of any emotion.

Carlos smiled. "We'd like to kill him, Khan."

Khan felt the pride rush through him as he heard those words. He knew that these men were the best, better than Dillon, because they were the simplest forms of power and focus. They were the sharpened point of a surgical tool, and it was because of men like them that Khan had been able to bring the world to its knees. "Kill everyone but his family, if you can find them. But if the opportunity presents itself, and you're able to do what an entire platoon of men could not..." He glanced down at Dillon and snarled. "Then yes, I want you to kill them." He glanced back up at the scouts. "Locate the piece of the bomb and bring it to me. If you can't find the bomb, then bring me back someone who knows where I can find it. Do not be seen. No failure. Go."

Both Carlos and Samuel jogged off into the west, neither wasting the resources of their horses or fuel of their vehicles to track the place down. They didn't ask how far it was or how long it would take them, and that was the level of loyalty and commitment that Khan required of his soldiers. No questions, only solutions and action.

Khan returned his attention to Dillon, who still lay on his side next to the pile of ashes. He was such a pitiful sight, fallen so far from the pedestal that he had built for himself. But that was Dillon's first mistake. His reach had exceeded his grasp. And men like those were always brought down in the end by men like Khan.

Khan stepped close enough to Dillon that the tips of his boots touched his lower back, and Dillon shuddered, looking up at Khan but unable to see him. "Have you told me everything?"

Dillon nodded his head quickly. "Yes, I-I have. I swear to you."

Khan pressed the heel of his boot into one of the fresh burned marks on Dillon's back, his heel sliding on top of the loose skin and muscles that had transformed into a scab, causing a green ooze to spill from his side and a blood-curdling scream to jettison from his lips.

"Are you sure?" Khan asked, applying more pressure.

But Dillon couldn't speak, his mind lost in the pain, and Khan was forced to remove his heel and wait for the weakling's hysteria to end. "I'm sure." His voice was small and cold, no longer human. He trembled, dissolved into a shaking pile of muscles. "I'm sure."

Khan knew that the man was telling the truth. Because Dillon knew what would happen next, and the man was in so much agonizing pain that he wanted it to end.

"Dillon," Khan said. "You will not be granted the freedom of the fire. I will spill your blood and leave your corpse to rot and fester until the earth has decided to slowly reclaim you as its own." He lifted his eyes to look to the caravan, every man and soldier watching at attention. "There is no greater failure than to waste one's life! Even in death we can serve a purpose, and no man under my command will ever forget that!"

A sword was brought to Khan, and Dillon's head was placed on the chopping block. He raised the blade high, swinging down with all of his strength.

The head rolled only a few inches as the body slumped and blood spilled from the severed body. Khan watched the blood slowly stain the pavement and then slowly mixed with the ash to form a dark black mud.

Khan picked up Dillon's head and held it up for the caravan to see, triggering a unanimous cry of victory. He walked along the caravan, the men still cheering at the sight of death, because it was death that drove them, it was death that made them powerful, and it was in death that they found purpose. It was witnessing the balance of the equation, it was witnessing something perfect.

Khan was handed a spike, and when he reached the edge of town, he firmly planted the stake in the ground and then stuck the head through the spike.

The lifeless stump didn't look like a face anymore. It was as far from a face as anything could be, but he knew that people would understand.

And as Khan turned to head back to the front of his pack and set up camp for the night, the cheers continued, and he wanted the excitement to linger a little bit longer. He wanted them to feel the power, to feel the rage, because they would need to keep up momentum for the fight to come. Because they had yet to be tested. They had yet to be truly pushed, and what came next would force them to discover more of themselves than they'd ever known.

But Khan would be sure to set up more spikes. He'd build an entire wall with nothing but spikes and heads. He would layer the foundation of the new world with the bones of the old. And his world would last, because his world would be balanced back to zero.

45

*T*he man that Banks had sent with him didn't say much during the ride, but James didn't mind the silence. It gave him time to think about how he was going to break the news to his wife about the deal that he'd struck with Banks.

There wasn't a fiber in James's being that didn't believe she was going to try and stay, but he knew that he would be able to convince her to go. Because if she stayed, then she'd be putting both of their children in danger.

Both.

James hadn't thought about the baby much since he found out. It was hard to think about the life of a child James hadn't met yet, but he prayed that the child survived. All James had to do was make sure there was still a world for her to grow up in after the baby was born.

When James saw the west perimeter of the ranch's fence line, he kicked the horse into a full gallop, speeding across the grass, dirt flying behind him.

Even when James saw the skeletal remains of the house, he didn't slow his horse, picking up steam once the beast's hooves touched the ranch's familiar soil, the only home it had ever known. And while the sight of both the charred house and the barn were sobering, nothing could erase the sweet moment of happiness of returning home.

James saw Mick out on patrol, and both men exchanged a quick wave to one another.

The burned house and ranch were more than just a symbol of the times, they were a reminder that even after something was destroyed, even after it had been burned to the ground, it could still be rebuilt. Like a phoenix rising from the ashes, James had no doubt in his mind that they would be able to return the Bowers Ranch to its former glory.

James's family had survived other hardships, and they would survive this one. It wasn't going to be easy, but it wasn't impossible. Because life was never truly gone. It always existed somewhere, just like how Bernie told him the universe was always expanding. It was an absolute.

His ranch hands had finished wrangling up what remained of the herd, and James raised a hand as he passed them, which they returned in kind. He counted twenty cattle, more than he expected to find after the massacre. It was something to build upon.

Nearing the bunker at the property's center, James frowned when he saw people standing outside, huddled together and chatting. And the moment that all of them turned toward him and he saw their expressions of fear and concern, James knew something had happened.

As the golden evening light gave way to the fluorescent coloring of the bunker's lighting, James found Mary over Jake's body, performing CPR while Nolan was passed out on the cot.

"He's getting worse," Mary said, her voice hysterical. "He stopped breathing a little while ago, and I had to do CPR and—"

James placed his hand on her shoulders. "You did the

right thing." He hurried past his wife and grabbed the medical kit that had the tools for Jake's procedure. "Just keep pumping his heart!" He brought the equipment over, trying to keep his hands steady. He searched the first aid bag for the adrenaline and syringes. He found both and quickly filled the syringe, spurting some of the adrenaline out of the needle's tip to ensure there was no air bubbles.

"What are you doing?" Mary asked.

"I can't perform the procedure if his heart is stopped," James answered. "The adrenaline should give him a kick start."

James felt along the sternum and then walked his fingers to the location over the heart where the doctors had told him to place the needle should he ever need to administer the medicine himself. Because the chambers in Jake's heart had filled with blood, there wasn't enough room for more blood to get through, causing it to clog and stop. So far, they'd never had to administer a shot because they'd been able to keep his condition stable through the procedures.

James waited until he was sure he was over the heart, then drove the needle into the flesh, pressing the syringe down in the same motion.

Once the syringe was emptied, James removed the needle and waited for the medicine to work, holding his boy while Mary continued to pump air into their son's lungs.

Time slowed as James waited. He still had so much to show his son, so much to tell him. He just needed a few more moments, and just when he thought that the hourglass had finally run out, the seconds dripping away like sweat from a hot summer day, James felt a heartbeat. "I have a pulse."

Mary kissed Jake's cheek, which was cold and pale, and she hugged her son, trying not to cry, but the tears coming regardless. She didn't keep him long, knowing that he needed his rest, and James glanced to Nolan, the old man barely able to keep his eyes open.

Jake lay still, unconscious but alive. Mary was nearby, and Nolan was fading in and out of consciousness. The instructions for the procedure were laid out on a nearby table, but James had already committed them to memory. He knew them backwards and forwards.

But the steps to the procedure provided little comfort because up until now, they had all been theoretical.

James applied the local anesthetic to Jake's wrist, which he pinched delicately between his fingers. He then cut an incision in the wrist, wiping away the blood that seeped through, and picked up the catheter that held the balloon that would be used to relieve the blockage in Jake's left heart valve.

He brought the tip of the catheter to the entry point, but stopped. His hand wouldn't stop shaking. He closed his eyes and took a breath.

Mary placed her hand on his shoulder. "You can do this."

James nodded, and when he opened his eyes again, his hand was steady. Normally, a doctor would have a team around him and the aid of a camera that helped direct him toward the valve and let him know when he was close.

But James would be going in blind, and while inserting through the wrist was less invasive than going through the groin, that didn't guarantee success. All it took was for the vein to pop, or Jake to suddenly wake and panic during the procedure, or panic and go into shock, or a dozen other worst-case scenarios, and the routine procedure would transform into the untimely death of his only child.

James double-checked to ensure that the balloon was attached to the catheter securely and then slowly, and carefully, brought the pointed tip to the vein.

With the tip of the catheter inserted, James carefully navigated into the vein, watching inch after inch of the tubing disappear into his son's body. More blood welled up from the wound, and James wiped it away quickly.

Throughout the process, James continued to monitor Jake's vitals, checking his pulse and making sure he was still breathing. He would check every minute or so, then return to feeding the catheter into the vein.

When James couldn't push the catheter any farther, he knew that he had reached the heart chamber that was blocked. With the balloon in place, James inflated, repeating the motion to allow the blocked chamber to open and release the backed up blood creating the pressure.

Falling into a rhythm, James checked his son's pulse once more, but while he waited for the bump against his fingers, none came.

James let go of the catheter. "No." He checked for a pulse again, pausing, hoping that he was wrong, but there was still nothing. "No, no, no."

Mary started to cry, covering her mouth as James placed his hands over his son's chest, pressing down so hard that he heard the crack of ribs.

"C'mon, Jake!" James continued the CPR, hoping that he would be able to restart the heart, but after several rounds of pumping and checking for a pulse, there was still nothing. He shut his eyes, whispering a prayer, unsure of what else he could do. "Start his heart again. Don't let him die here. I'll do whatever you ask. Just don't let him die here." He bit the inside of his cheek, and then he opened his eyes.

James pressed his fingers against Jake's neck for a pulse, and the moment stretched for an eternity, until James's heart skipped a beat.

"He has a pulse," James said, his voice breathless.

Mary cried, and James continued to squeeze the balloon, relieving the pressure, thanking God for saving his son.

46

Wind rustled some of the tall grass near the front of the property and cooled the back of Mick's neck. The brutal summer Texas heat rarely took a break, even during the night, and he was thankful for the reprieve. He glanced up at the sky.

"Nice night." Mick smiled and continued his steady and methodical pace around the property, thankful for the stars that provided a little extra light for him to find his way. He adjusted the rifle in his hands, still not used to carrying the weapon instead of the normal ranch supplies.

Mick stopped once he reached the fence's perimeter and then gazed out at the endless horizon. He hadn't been a Texas native. He was originally from Iowa, and while his home state had big stretches of land, there was something entrancing about Texas.

After ten years of working at the Bowers Ranch, Mick couldn't see himself anywhere else. This was his home as much as it was his job. And it was the only reason he was still alive.

When he was first hired on, James was upfront about his lifestyle, prepping and all of that. He said that people looked at him funny because of it, but that didn't make him any less dedicated. Mick supposed that all of those people who'd made fun of James were the same people wishing they'd spent more time listening to what he had to say.

James had become like a brother to Mick. He had given him his first job down in Texas, helped him find his way, and showed him how to move on after the tragedy that he was running from in Iowa. Because while James had been able to protect his family, to take care of them in times of chaos and distress, Mick hadn't been able to do the same.

Even now, after almost twelve years, Mick couldn't keep the shame from welling up inside of him and burning his cheeks red hot at just the thought of it. But he handled it better now than he used to.

Before, he would have needed a fifth of Jack Daniels.

After about half a mile sticking to the western side of the property fence line, Mick took a ninety-degree turn east and started back on his path.

But staring out into the blackness, something pricked the hairs on the back of Mick's neck, and he froze after planting his left foot on the grass.

Mick dropped to a knee, aiming into the darkness. The night was still, and even though the sky was clear and the stars gave him some light to see, there were still nothing but shadows on the land.

He waited for a sign, waited for something to tell him that evil was near, and just when Mick thought that he might be letting his mind get the better of him, he heard the faint pop of a muffled gunshot, the bullet connecting into his upper right shoulder and slamming him onto his back and gasping for air.

The pain from the gunshot stole his voice, but after a few seconds, he managed to roll onto his side and then made it three inches before another muffled pop triggered more pain in his leg. This time he managed to scream, sending the verbal warning up into the night sky, but it was too weak to be heard.

So, instead, Mick fumbled into his pack trying to find the flare gun that was given to him to warn about an intrusion. But the bullet in his shoulder had rendered his right arm useless, and the blood loss and pain were a terrible cocktail that limited his coordination.

He managed to get his fingers on the pocket of his pack where the gun was stored, and then he heard hurried footsteps from somewhere in the darkness.

Mick hastened his pace, fighting off the lingering darkness that was stealing his vision. The black spots spread, but he could still feel with his fingertips, and he felt around until he touched the flare gun and managed to wrap his fingers around the handle.

Voices grew louder in the darkness, and Mick raised his hand with the flare, hoping that he was aiming it up high, and just before he squeezed the trigger, it was kicked from his hand and flew somewhere into the grass.

Mick turned in time to see the figures standing above him, one of them with a rifle aimed at Mick's chest, and he saw the smile spread across the face of evil as he pulled the trigger.

The impact of the bullet into Mick's chest paralyzed him, but while he seemed to have lost control over his body, the pain that had been numbed returned in full force, and Mick drew in a breath, which caused him to choke on his own blood that spilled over the front of his clothes.

Large black circles dotted his vision, but between the massive circles, he saw the stars in the sky above and he couldn't hear anything.

Slowly, Mick craned his head around him and between the large pieces of black, he saw the bright orange of the flare gun nestled in the grass. The sight of the gun, fueled by his determination to save his adoptive family, gave him the energy to flip to his stomach, and he started the slow crawl toward the plastic orange gun sticking up out of the grass.

Blood trailed Mick's slow movements, a brilliant streak of dark red left in his wake that shimmered from the stars and moonlight. Every muscle in his body caught fire as he moved over the rough grass. He didn't think he was going to make it when a breeze caught his back, offering a brief reprieve from the pain that plagued his body.

With only one good elbow and one good leg, Mick shimmied his way toward the orange. Twice he collapsed on his face, and the pain seemed to grow worse the closer he moved toward the flare gun, challenging him, daring him.

The pain reached a crescendo when he wrapped his fingers around the handle, but when he tried to lift his hand, the weapon fell from his grip. Mick grunted and tried again, but this time while he could keep the grip, he couldn't raise his arm.

Mick lay there in the grass, wallowing in his own blood, and he whimpered to himself. He felt death crawling over him.

Knowing that he didn't have much time left, Mick readjusted his grip around the flare's handle, and as he drew in a slow breath, he watched his arm raise into the sky. His arm trembled. He exhaled, and in that moment, he knew it was his final breath, and every ounce of life that remained to him was sent to his finger and he squeezed the trigger, passing out on the grass as the flare jettisoned into the night sky.

47

When James stepped out of the bunker, only Luis and Zi were up top and waiting for him, everyone else having claimed their camper and trying to figure out how to make it habitable.

"It worked?" Zi asked.

James nodded. "Blood pressure is normal. He's sleeping now."

"How's Nolan?" Luis asked.

James shook his head, Luis and Zi remaining silent for a moment. And while he was sad about Nolan, for the first time since he got his family out of San Antonio, James thought that things were turning around.

"James." The voice was deep, commanding authority, and Trunks appeared, weapon still in hand. "I need to get confirmation on those supplies."

"Right," James said. "Hey, Ken!"

Ken popped his head out of the camper that had a blue stripe across the side and jogged over. "What's up, boss?"

"I need you to show this guy our MRE pallets," James said.

"Sure thing, boss."

As Ken led Trunks away from the group, both Luis and Zi scrunched their faces up in confusion.

"What was that about?" Luis asked.

"Nothing," James answered.

"So, what now?" Zi asked. "How long will Jake need to recover?"

"Normally it's just a day, but it could be longer." James looked back at the bunker, then cleared his throat and kept his head bowed. "I don't know how much longer Nolan is going to last. The way he keeps passing out, I think it might be as little as days."

"I could take a look at him," Zi said, and then stumbled over her words when she realized that she might have bitten off a little more than she could chew. "I mean, I know I'm still in the nursing program, but I might be able to help narrow down a few things, and if Nolan is coherent, then I'm sure he could help guide me to make him feel better. Give me some pointers."

"That's very thoughtful, but..." James shook his head, unsure of how much he should actually share about their resident doctor and his wishes to die as quickly as possible. "He wasn't going through any treatments. This isn't something he wants to fight."

"Oh." Zi's expression matched the surprised tone in her voice. "I didn't realize—"

"It's fine," James said. "But if the pain starts to kick in and gets even worse, then I think that having something ready to take the edge off might be a pretty good idea."

"I'll go and check the stash." Zi took one step forward before stopping herself, realizing that Mary and Jake were still down below. "Is it all right if I—"

"It's fine," James said, and then placed a hand on her shoulder before she passed. "And thank you. For everything."

Zi smiled and then headed toward the bunker,

descending quickly and quietly, leaving James and Luis alone.

But James had turned back around faster than Luis had, and he caught Luis's lingering gaze as Zi walked away and even after she disappeared into the bunker. James crossed his arms, waiting for Luis to realize that James was watching him in his little daydream, and when he did, Luis became immediately defensive.

"What?" Luis asked, but was unable to hide his smile.

"Nothing," James answered. "Just wondering how that trip to the junkyard went."

Luis crossed his arms as the pair headed toward the campers that they'd parked farther south on the property. "I don't know what you're talking about."

James laughed, and then after giving Luis the needed time to let the teasing roll off of him, Luis finally spoke up.

"She's a good woman," Luis said. "But she's young. Maybe too young."

"Hey," James said, nudging Luis with his elbow. "It's not like you have snow on top of the mountain. And besides, you're younger than I am."

Luis chuckled. "Yeah. I do have that going for me."

"Mary and I are twelve years apart," James said. "We turned out all right."

"That's true," Luis said.

The campers came into view ahead of them. A few of them already had the glow of candlelight. "Looks like folks are already making themselves at home." He changed the subject, getting the hint that Luis didn't want to talk about whatever budding romance was happening between him and Zi.

"We tried to pick the ones that were in the best condition, but pretty much all of them had something wrong with them." Luis nodded, convincing himself that it really wasn't that bad. "We might be able to get some considerable time out of those things." He then stopped, letting James walk a few paces ahead before he stopped, looking back at his oldest and most trusted friend.

"What is it?" James asked.

"We found a father and son living in the junkyard," Luis answered. "He knew Harry. And he shot at us." He held up both hands before James could protest. "I'm fine, and so is Zi. But we talked to the guy, got to know him a little bit. He'd been going through a pretty rough time even before the EMP went off, and he helped us out with loading those campers so I thought that—"

James placed his hand on his friend's shoulder, Luis so lost in his explanation that he didn't even see James until he actually touched him. "It's fine. People are a resource, remember?"

Luis smiled. "Yes. They are."

Luis and James were nearly to the campers when a streak of red caught James's attention out of the corner of his eye, and both he and Luis turned in the same instant, knowing what lay beyond. James rushed toward the flare while Luis corralled everyone who stepped outside to stare and started pounding on the doors for those who hadn't.

"Everyone out! C'mon, let's go! To the bunker! Everyone get to the bunker! Now! Now! Now!" Once everyone was out, Luis turned around to find James already twenty yards toward the direction of flare. "James!"

James twisted at the waist, slowing a little bit, but never stopping his movement toward the flare. "It's in the southwest quadrant! By the house!"

Luis caught up to him, handing James a weapon. "Mick's on patrol."

James nodded, his answer just as breathless as Luis's question. "I didn't hear any shots, did you?"

"No," Luis answered.

No gunfire made things unclear, and the uncertainty

made James nervous. Had Mick just seen something? Had he been spooked?

Sweating and nearly on the brink of collapse, James and Luis arrived at the barn.

"You see anything?" James asked, raising the rifle into a defensible position.

"I've got nothing," Luis answered.

James took the lead and kept them both close to the barn at first, wanting to keep cover until he was absolutely sure that there was no chance of an ambush.

"We need to get to Mick," Luis said, stepping away from cover. "We need to—"

The sound of the gunshot and Luis dropping to the grass happened instantaneously, and it took James a moment to realize that his best friend had just been shot.

"Luis!" James lunged for Luis, grabbing his ankles and pulling him back behind the cover of the barn. "Oh no. Oh God, no."

Luis trembled, his body going into shock. The bullet had entered his gut, and blood covered the front of his shirt, the liquid so dark that it was black under the moon and stars. James pressed his hands against the wound, trying to stop the bleeding.

"It's all right," James said. "Just keep pressure on it."

James pressed down, but the blood just seeped up between his fingers. Luis's face grew pale white, and the trembling stopped, his body growing still and his eyes wandering, looking for something in the sky. James placed his palm to the back of Luis's head and lifted up so James could look him in the eye.

"Fight it." James took his free hand and placed Luis's hands over the wound, pressing down, but there was no strength in Luis's arms.

Blood collected in Luis's mouth and he shut his eyes, wincing, choking on the blood in his lungs, and the spasm triggered Luis to fight what came next. He grabbed hold of James's shirt, staining it with blood. He gasped for air, and then choked, the airflow cut off. And then his body went limp.

"No." James gently shook Luis, hoping that he could wake the man up, but it did nothing. "Luis." He placed the body on the ground and then tried CPR, but it only caused more blood to seep from the wound on Luis's stomach.

James fell to the ground and then leaned back against the barn walls, staring at Luis's body and listening to the footfalls of the men who'd shot him grow closer. But the shock that paralyzed James wouldn't go away.

No matter how hard he tried, his legs wouldn't move, and he sat there transfixed on Luis's eyes. They were still pointed upward, gazing at the sky, but they were just like the dead eyes that he'd seen in San Antonio when he walked the streets.

How many more would have to die? How many more would it take before the evil spreading across their land finally ended?

The crunch of a boot in the grass thrust James back to the moment. Before the first gunman turned the corner, James leapt from behind the barn walls, shooting the first man in the back and then tackling the second gunman to the ground.

James and the second gunman grappled, fighting for their weapons. They rolled over the grass, punching, kneeing, thrashing like wild animals.

The gunmen had his hands around James's throat, and James had his hands around the gunman's throat, but he also had the upper hand, managing to get himself on top. The pair of men were locked in, neither relinquishing their hold, both struggling to hold on.

Blood rushed to James's head, his pulse pounding like a sledgehammer. His airway was slowly closing, but between the black spots of his fading vision, he saw the gunman's eyes bulge from his skull, his cheeks turning purple.

James looked over to where Luis's body lay, and their twenty years of friendship flooded through his mind, the images of them together striking his mind like lightning.

The exhaustion that James had felt from the past two days suddenly vanished, replaced by a rage that he couldn't control, that he didn't want to control, and with his last remaining bits of strength, he crushed the man's windpipe, the crunch killing the man instantly.

The brute's hands dropped from James's neck and James gasped for air, collapsing to his side as his own strength left him.

With this right cheek against the cool grass, James was close to Luis's body, but as he slowly regained consciousness, he stood up and saw that the body of the man he'd shot was gone.

James crept toward the front edge of the barn, picking up the rifle along the way, and peered around the corner.

A quiet snap came from inside the barn, and James immediately shot the burnt barn wall. He spread out his firing pattern, hoping that it would give him more of a range to hit his target. Bits of charred wood broke away from the wall, and James worked his way toward the barn's front, ceasing his assault as he waited and listened at the barn doors.

The entire structure was consumed in black ash, and what part of the roof hadn't collapsed was sagging, the structure practically leaning in on itself. It could collapse at any moment.

James kept the rifle square against his shoulder, and old bits of wood crunched beneath his boots. He followed the shallow breaths and coughs and found the terrorist had been shot in the leg. He lay clutching the wound, unarmed.

James could now see that the first bullet hadn't killed him because he had been wearing Kevlar. But one of the bullets caught him in the leg, and he sat there waiting for James to kill him. But James didn't pull the trigger.

He stood there for a while, watching over the dead man like the Grim Reaper. He stared at the rifle at his side, wondering if this was his life now, if this was the only future that he would have. Had the days of ranching gone? Would he never ride his land beneath the warm sun, herding cattle that he raised from calves?

All James had ever wanted was to leave the world a little better than the way he found it. And he tried to accomplish that in the way he lived his life, in the way that he treated others, and the way that he conducted his business on the ranch.

What was happening now went against everything that James had tried to do throughout his life, and as he gazed down at the dead man in the barn that had been reduced to a pile of charred sticks, a part of him knew that he wouldn't be the same even if he could pull himself out of it. He had gone too far down the rabbit hole now, and the only way out was tunneling deeper into the unknown.

James needed to know what kind of trouble was coming their way, and he wanted to know what the other dead man couldn't tell him.

*T*he terrorist was lying down next to his dead friend in the barn, restrained. The rope configuration was a simple one that James used on cattle. It was designed to train the cattle from struggling whenever it was placed in a confined space. The more it moved, the tighter the rope became, causing discomfort around the legs.

But James had made a slight modification for the terrorist, which caused the rope to tighten around his neck the more he struggled. It would never get tight enough to kill him, but it would get tight enough for him to wish that he was dead.

Trunks stood nearby with a bucket of cold water from the river. James hadn't asked him to be there, but since the man wouldn't leave, James put him to use, and when James nodded, Trunks splashed the man's face.

The terrorist gasped, his movement causing the rope to tighten, and he choked for air.

James dropped to a knee so he could get a better look at the man's face, and so the pair were eye to eye. He wanted to make sure that there were no delusions about who was in control.

"Where did you come from?" James asked.

With his hands and feet tied behind his back and the rope still digging into the soft flesh of his throat, the terrorist snarled and then spit in James's face.

James wiped the mixture of blood and saliva from his cheek and then tightened the rope, choking the terrorist until his eyes rolled back and his cheeks turned blue. He held it there for a few more seconds before finally letting go.

The man coughed and hacked, his expression dazed and confused, wondering how the hunter had become the hunted, and the sensation was as disorienting to him as the noose around his neck.

"Where did you come from?" James asked.

This time the man didn't spit. "The town."

"How many are with your group?" After a few seconds of silence, James reached for the rope again.

"Wait!" The man barked, his voice hoarse. "Wait." He coughed and then caught his breath, waiting for a moment to either gather the strength to speak or try and remember how many more terrorists he had marched into town with. "One."

James frowned. "One what? Hundred? Thousand?" With still no answer, James pulled on the rope and it tightened, choking the man.

The man squirmed in what little room was available to him, the motions he was making looking more like seizures than anything else.

James released the pressure of the rope and then waited for the man to catch his breath again. "How many of you are there? How many did you bring!"

The man kept his head slung low, his breathing slow and methodical, and he started to laugh. "We are one."

James stood, stepping back as the man continued to laugh, repeating the same phrase.

"We are one! We are one! We are one!"

James stepped out of the barn, but even outside, he could still hear the screams.

"James," Trunks said, joining James outside. "He's not going to tell us anything useful, no matter how much we try and torture him."

James stopped his pacing and looked toward the barn where the enemy was still screaming, and it finally occurred to James that they had been going about this the wrong way. They had been treating the enemy like people, but they weren't people.

"James?" Trunks took a few short steps as James headed back toward the barn. "He won't talk!"

James picked up the rifle as he entered the barn. Without giving himself time to think it over, he placed the end of the barrel against the man's head.

The screaming stopped, and the terrorist turned his bloodshot eyes up toward James, which were bulging from his skull with madness. "You won't stop us, because you don't know how to stop us. We will march until there is no one left to fight. You cannot win, because we don't know how to lose."

James placed his finger on the trigger and squeezed.

The man's body went slack but remained upright because of the rope, making him look like a dead spider that had fallen on his back, its stiff legs raised toward the sky.

James stared at the body for a while, then turned to find Luis at the barn's entrance, frozen.

"Jesus," Trunks said.

James walked toward Trunks. "My people leave tonight. You can take everything but a few weapons." He shoved Trunks into the darkness. "Get the people ready."

James walked toward the house and then grabbed the wheelbarrow that had been used earlier in the day. He finally understood what these people were. They were animals. Rabid animals. And they needed to be put down.

JAMES HUNT

James loaded the terrorist's bodies into the wheelbarrow and then pushed it toward the front of the ranch. He dumped the bodies at the front, then tied it to a post at the front gates. The body was limp, and the head hung to the side, but it stayed upright on the post by the time that James was finished. After the second body was tied up, James found some old tarps and covered Luis and Mick's bodies.

James saw the group and immediately bypassed them. He couldn't handle speaking to them now. He needed to see Mary, and Jake, and remember why he was doing all of this.

In the bunker, James found Mary by Jake's bedside. Their son was still asleep. She held his hand, gently massaging his palm in both of her hands.

"Mary," James said. "We need to talk."

When she didn't respond, James knelt by her side and saw the transfixed stare on her face. James placed his hand on her shoulder, but she still didn't budge.

"Mary?" James asked.

Finally, Mary looked at her husband, and in that knowing glance she saw something that frightened her. "James, what—"

"I made a deal with Banks. The man who came here with me, Trunks, he's going to take everyone in the semi along with our supplies and take you to the compound." He turned to leave and Mary pounded her fist against the metal post at the foot of Jake's cot.

"James, what are you—Stop!" Mary shouted. "When will you be able to just walk away? When can you just leave it? How much farther do you have to go before there isn't anything left? Do you want to die? Is that it? Look at me, goddamnit!"

James turned. "Luis is dead." He watched her reaction, and her expression morphed between surprise and horror. "They killed him, Mary. And they're going to keep killing unless someone does something."

"I know how much you love this place, but it's just a piece of land." Mary trembled as she walked to her husband. "And I know how much Luis meant to you and—" She covered her mouth. "Christ." She shut her eyes and tears leaked out. She shook her head and looked at James. "He wouldn't want you to stay. This isn't worth losing your life."

"I know that," James said, and then, calmer than he expected himself to be, he walked to his wife, and the moment he touched her, the trembling ended. "But this isn't about the land. It isn't about the ranch. It isn't about Luis. It's about standing up for what's right. It's about taking the fight to the enemy. It's making sure that no one has to endure what we've endured. They can torch the land. They can kill all of my cattle. They can take every last thing I own until I've got nothing but the clothes on my back, but I swear under the oath of my Lord and Savior that I will not let them steal my freedom to choose my fate. I will not let them take that away from me. Because if we can't choose our own fate, then what the hell are we doing out here? What was it all for?"

Mary placed her hands on his cheeks and then pulled him close, her face bunched up like she was about to cry, but she wouldn't let the tears fall. "It's to see our boy grow up." She reached for his hand and placed it on her stomach. "To raise our next child. That's what it's all for. I'm begging you. Please. Don't stay. I already know how strong you are, but this is one fight that you won't win."

"It's not about winning, Mary." James gently removed her hands from his cheeks. "It's about letting the enemy know that we won't run."

The lines on Mary's face slacked, realizing that there was nothing that she could tell him to try and convince him that this was the wrong choice, that this was folly. She only nodded and reached for Jake's hand again. "Just let me know when you're ready to move him."

Before James could exit the bunker, Zi came in, breathless from her hustle down. She dusted her hands off and then frowned when she saw the state of James and Mary. "What happened? Everyone's up there wondering what—" She realized someone was missing. "Where's Luis?"

James didn't answer.

Zi grew emotional, her eyes reddening and her mouth trembling. "Where is he, James?" She hunched forward, starting to cry. "James, where is he?" She slowly stumbled to the bunker wall for support, and the tears fell.

James never said the words out loud as he walked past her and climbed back to the surface where he addressed the crowd. He told them about the community, about the deal that he had made. They were worried, but no one objected to leaving.

James kept his distance from everyone else while he prepared for what came next.

"I'm staying."

James turned from his rifle and saw Zi. "I'm not asking you to."

"And I'm not asking for permission," Zi said, stepping forward. "I'm staying. I'm fighting."

"Me too." Ken appeared to his left.

James wasn't looking for volunteers, but he wasn't going to stop anyone from staying behind if that was their choice. "Grab a gun. Start loading magazines."

Their work was silent, and before they had a chance to finish, Trunks informed James that everything was loaded and ready to go.

James found Mary by the truck, and while she had warmed a little from her previously cold demeanor, she still wasn't happy.

"Survive," Mary said. "No matter what you have to do. Make sure you're still here when I come back for you." She walked toward the truck, hands on her stomach as she turned around. "I love you."

"I love you too," James said.

The truck started, and James lingered behind, waiting until he couldn't see the truck anymore and long after he couldn't hear the rumble of its engine. When he turned around, he saw Ken and Zi standing there, waiting for him.

"So, what now?" Ken asked.

It was dark, but they had less than ten hours before dawn, and they'd need every second of the darkness to prepare for the fight that was heading their way. "We get ready."

49

The cancer affected everything about Nolan's existence, even the way that he dreamed. Whenever Nolan dreamed as a boy, he could always tell when he was dreaming. He had read somewhere that some individuals could actually control that part of their brain, and once they had the ability to recognize that they were dreaming, they could harness that dream and do whatever they wanted, like they were creating an alternate reality.

Nolan was in his teens when he finally managed to master that muscle of the mind, and while it came in useful for all of the pubescent and adolescent urges that were making his limbs too big for his body and the hair too wild on his face and chest, he'd also use it to think his way out of problems that he was having in real life.

Because while Nolan had always been smart, he had never been creative, and there was something about the space in his dreams where he could harness untapped creative potential.

Over time those skills sharpened, and every time Nolan turned out the lights and crawled into bed, he actually looked forward to clocking in for his night job, because that world he would enter was full of endless and infinite possibilities. Nothing was impossible.

But the cancer cells that were eating away at his body had finally made their way into the one organ that he valued and still worked even though the rest of his body had decayed and slowly shut down with age.

Nolan tossed and turned in the nightmare, unable to control or even comprehend the reality of the dream world that he'd fallen into as he was chased by monsters with claws and fangs, and he was harassed by the corpses of the dead that had risen from the earth.

Fire and brimstone rained down from a blood-red sky, and Nolan was always too slow to evade the evils of the world that he couldn't escape. And while the monsters were these faceless creatures, the people that had risen from the dead were always people that Nolan knew. They were friends, family, and finally his beloved wife who had passed six years ago in her sleep.

The moment Nolan saw her, the world around him suddenly transformed into the bedroom of his house, and he was lying in bed, his wife beside him, with her eyes closed as she slept still and calm.

Nolan glanced around the room, every detail exactly the same, and for a moment he thought he'd finally woken up, but as he lay there in bed, he felt something warm touch the side of his leg. It was liquid and spreading down his leg and up his side.

Nolan ripped off the sheets and saw a black ooze running from beneath his beloved Betty, and he quickly reached over with both hands to try and shake her awake. "Betty! Betty, darling, wake up!"

But she wouldn't stir, and the more he tried to stir her awake, the more that black ooze continued to run from beneath her body and she was sinking into the stuff, which Nolan now recognized as blood.

JAMES HUNT

"Betty, no!" Nolan reached for her hand as Betty sank into the liquid, eyes closed and oblivious to her husband's pleas. "No!" He cried harder when her face disappeared and she vanished beneath the surface of the darkness and all that was left was the hand that he held, but now it was going under and it was pulling Nolan with it.

Nolan didn't fight it anymore, and he cried as he held tight to his beloved wife's hand as she was sucked deeper into the darkness and the abyss. He shut his eyes, his body sick and cold and ready for the sweet release of the torture.

And then it was nothing but blackness, and in that blackness, he heard his wife whisper in his ear, her breath tickling his skin the way it did whenever she tried to wake him up in the morning. She had always been an early riser, raised on a farm and up before the sun.

It was a habit that she had instilled in Nolan, though Betty still managed to "beat him to the sunrise" as she used to say despite his efforts. And she never once used an alarm clock. She'd simply wake up and whisper a 'good morning' in his ear. But when she whispered now, it was loveless.

"You're a weak old man," Betty said. "You're a failure and a coward."

Nolan tossed and turned, and it was only after he heard himself screaming that he woke.

After his eyes adjusted to the dim light, he realized that they were no longer in the bunker. When he opened his mouth to call for help, there was nothing but the gasping sensation of breathing in raspy gulps of air. It was like every muscle in his body had seized up and were being stabbed by thousands of tiny needles.

The pain continued for a few minutes, but when it finally subsided, he collapsed back onto the sweat-soaked sheets and pillow and then finally found his voice, which cracked a few times before he was able to finally speak any coherent words. "Jake? Mary?"

Whispers and murmurs were followed by shuffling feet and then Mary was beside him.

"How are you holding up?" Mary asked.

Nolan groaned, and then after a concentrated effort and a few breaths, he shook his head. "How long have I been out?"

"A few hours," Mary answered, and then handed Nolan a bottle of water. "Here, drink."

Mary had already unscrewed the top off the bottle, Nolan thankful for the gesture so he didn't have to try and work the cap off himself, because he wasn't even sure he had the strength to do that. Hands shaking, he brought the rim of the bottle to his lips and drank.

The water rolled down either side of Nolan's mouth as he slowly drained half the bottle before lowering it to his side and taking deep breaths, shutting his eyes, not realizing how thirsty he had been. But when the sensation of hunger didn't follow, Nolan knew that his condition had worsened. Time was running out.

"They came back," Mary said. "Those fighters we dealt with in the town. They came back."

Nolan looked past Mary and saw all of the faces inside… whatever they were inside.

"We're in the semi-trailer," Mary said. "James struck a deal with Banks. He stayed behind." She lowered her eyes. "Not everyone survived the last attack."

It didn't take long for Nolan to connect the dots. "Luis."

Mary nodded. "I didn't want him to stay, but he wouldn't listen."

"He's a strong man, Mary," Nolan said, trying to be supportive. "He'll make it through."

And while Mary nodded, Nolan sensed that she didn't think that was true.

Nolan wondered why James had stayed. He had never been a vengeful man, never someone who sought an eye for an eye and thought that dying in a blaze of glory would absolve the loss of losing a friend. But perhaps there were some things that were beyond revenge and hate. Perhaps too much blood had been spilt.

* * *

THE LANTERN RATTLED against the floor of the trailer, providing a false light that everyone huddled around to avoid the darkness that filled the trailer's corners.

The inside of the trailer was huge, but all of them were drawn to one another by some deep embedded instinct in their DNA that told them survival was more likely in groups, and that the only way for them to fight against the growing threat was to stay together. It was such a simple concept, but one that was forgotten when times were good.

Mary stroked Jake's hair, his head in her lap, doing her best to keep him cool in the hot box. She thought of James back at the ranch, still upset about his decision. The man had always walked his own path, and it was a path that he would continue to walk no matter what stood in his way.

Mary glanced down at their son, and then to her stomach where she prayed that there was still life growing inside. And while she had first been nervous about the pregnancy, what with the complications that she had with Jake, she now desperately wanted to have the baby, no matter its health or condition. She just wanted to bring life back into the world that had been so darkened by death and destruction.

"You don't have anything to worry about," Nolan said.

"You don't know that," Mary replied, and then glanced around, noticing that everyone else was eavesdropping on the conversation. Not that there was much room to have any privacy.

"What are you worried about?" a woman asked, tucking her knees into her chest. "Are we in trouble again?"

"No," Mary answered, casting her reassurance to every

member of the group. "No one is in danger." She glared back at Nolan for bringing it up in the first place.

"Then what's the matter?" another woman asked. "Is it Jake?"

"She's pregnant," Nolan said.

Mouths dropped, and even Mary couldn't hide her surprise over the fact that Nolan had spoken so openly about her private life, but when he started to laugh, she couldn't suppress the smile.

Congratulations were given, and Mary thanked them for their kind words.

"How far along are you?" the woman asked.

"About two months," Mary answered.

And just like that, the conversation transformed from something so dreary and lifeless to the hope that a child brought the world. Maybe it was because a child represented a blank slate, a fresh start, a chance to do something good again, but for whatever reason, Mary was glad to have the conversation shift from survival to life.

With all of the talk shifting to babies and memories of family and childhood, the rest of the trip passed quickly and it wasn't until the trailer slowed to a stop that the chatter ended and they were taken out of their reprieve from life on the run.

The engine continued to idle, and Mary wondered if they should try and get out, but she knew that it would be better for them if they stayed inside. She didn't want to cause any more trouble or concern.

Finally, the back doors opened and the early gray of dawn lightened the darkness of the trailer. Even though the sun hadn't fully risen, the light was still incredibly blinding and it wasn't until her eyes adjusted that Mary saw a dozen rifles aimed into the trailer.

"All right," one of the men said. "I want everyone out. Nice and slow."

"We have people who need to be carried," Mary said.

Two men were sent inside to collect Jake and Nolan.

"Careful with him," Mary said, her joints cracking and screaming at her as she stood. "He just had a procedure." She kept hold of Jake's hand until his fingers slipped away from her own and was carried away.

Nolan was carried away next, and then the rest of the survivors were marched outside along the side of the truck, Mary joining the others as she was the last person out.

"We came here because of my husband," Mary said after a time when no one was speaking. "He said that there was safe passage for us here."

None of the men answered, and their leader simply stared at Mary as if she were speaking a foreign language.

"He was the one who brought you the piece of the bomb!" Mary screamed and stepped toward the men, who raised their weapons at the sign of aggression. "He was the one who told you about the enemy that's coming your way! He was the one who told you about what's coming! And he needs your help!"

"Ma'am, you need to step back with your group," the man said.

But Mary refused to back down, and she refused to be ignored. "He said he made a deal with you! He said that you would help us!"

The leader took an aggressive step forward. "Ma'am, I'm warning you one last time—"

"Stand down!"

The order barked came from the front of the truck and the weapons were immediately lowered, the soldiers standing at attention as Mary watched another officer make his way toward the group.

The man was tall, around James's age, but more muscular and clean-cut. A brief conversation was held, and after their sidebar was over, the group leader stepped forward.

"You all will follow my men inside where you will be given food and a medical examination," he said, then turned toward Mary. "Ma'am, you will stay here for a moment longer."

Mary's group looked at her for confirmation that it was okay to leave, and it was only after she nodded that they followed the men.

"Mary Bowers, I presume?" he asked.

Mary shook her head, confused. "Should I know you?"

"Jonathan Banks." He extended his hand, and Mary shook it.

"You're... not what I expected."

Banks laughed. "We can talk inside."

Mary shook her head, breaking herself from the trance, knowing that they had already wasted too much time. "James needs help."

"Mrs. Bowers, I—"

"The people who did this? The people who wanted to build that bomb? They're already on their way to the ranch. James stayed behind to fight them off, but they're going to kill him. Do you understand me? He's out there by himself fighting a goddamn war!"

Mary waited for an answer from him, but Banks just stood there with his gaping maw, and Mary nearly broke down into tears. But she forced herself to stay strong and then turned back toward the road they'd traveled, back toward her home.

"He's alone," Mary said. "And he needs help."

"Mary," Banks said. "Your husband and I made an arrangement. I keep you safe, and he leads the enemy away. It's the only reason why you're here."

Infuriated, Mary refused to back down. "And how much longer do you think it will be before those men come knocking on your door? How much longer do you think you can hide?"

50

$\mathcal{K}$han mobilized his men before the sun broke over the horizon. The march of boots thundered like a brewing storm, and Khan basked in the orchestra of power that trailed him. He knew of no greater rush than war. And as all great leaders and generals had done during their conquests, Khan made sure to lead from the front.

The fact that the scouts hadn't returned from their mission told him that the man they were charging into battle to meet was stronger and more cunning than anyone he'd faced before. And for a man like Khan, it was refreshing to finally meet an equal.

It hadn't been since he started out as a young man when he had tried so hard to build an empire that he had anticipated a battle like this one.

Of course, he knew that no matter what force was waiting for them at this ranch, he would crush the enemy by sheer force. He could lose half of his men, three quarters, all of them, so long as he was victorious.

It was dawn when Khan saw the buzzards circling overhead in the distance. He knew that they were approaching their destination, and he brought the convoy to a stop when they reached the dirt road that Dillon had described.

The entrance had been marked with the bodies of his scouts, both of them tied up, festering in the early morning sun. Some of the buzzards had already started to feast. Nature wasted no time in taking back what was rightfully theirs.

"He's only a man." Khan looked past the bodies and onto the dirt road that stretched onto the property. He smiled, excited for a challenge as he returned to his vehicle. "Forward."

The driver hesitated, looking to the pair of men that were still strung up by the poles. "Sir, shouldn't we try and take them down? They're—"

Khan pressed the pistol against the driver's head and squeezed the trigger, blowing the man's brains across the window.

The inside of the Humvee had gone silent, but Khan sat there, saying nothing. Eventually, one of the men from the back seat moved behind the wheel.

"The dead only slow us down," Khan said after the vehicle was moving again.

* * *

JAMES HAD GROWN STIFF WAITING near the house all night, but when he noticed the sky lighten from a dark black to a dull grey, his heart pumped faster. He knew that it was almost time, and while James and the others had prepared, he secretly hoped that he would see nothing. He hoped that the morning would fade into afternoon without a single drop of blood.

And when the sun burned away the muddy grey and transformed the sky into a brilliant blue, cloudless morning, his wishful hopes were shattered when he saw the metallic glint of a car and the caravan marching slowly and steadily toward the ranch's entrance.

James counted a dozen Humvees, and between each vehicle were close to twenty men, putting the fighting force somewhere close to one hundred and twenty soldiers. And James could see that every one of them was armed with automatic assault rifles. Mostly AK-47s by the color and shape, though he saw a few M-16s scattered about.

Only a few of the soldiers had body armor, but in addition to the automatic weapons, each of the Humvees were outfitted with a fifty-caliber gun mounted on the roof, each of them manned.

It was a convoy meant for one thing and one thing only, to wipe out anything in its path. But what was even more concerning was the organization of the units. The men that were marching were doing so in formations, in rhythm, and in step with the man beside them.

The fighters weren't just some ragtag team that had come together in hopes of sparking rebellions, these were men who had come to win.

James removed his eye from the scope and glanced over to Zi, who was standing guard at the other end of the house, or at least what was left of it.

"You didn't have to stay," James said.

Zi turned her eye from her scope to James, the lines on her face hardened as she squinted from the sun. "Yes. I did."

James had mixed feelings about her staying, because he knew that Luis had felt something for her, that there had been a growing chemistry between them. And James knew that Luis would want her to survive all of this.

"He was a good man," James said. "The best."

Zi's expression softened, but only for a moment, and she masked her grief by returning her eye to the scope. "I wish I could have known him better."

James nodded, returning his attention to the enemy, the progression slow and steady.

All that was left to do was kill as many of them as they could. And while James Bowers had spent a lifetime preparing himself to survive the worst that the world could throw at him, he knew that every ounce of his will and strength would be tested in this fight. And he hoped that he could pass the test. Because while he wanted to stop the war, he didn't want to die.

Once the Humvees passed the halfway mark, James and Zi retreated to their rendezvous points with Ken who had dug themselves into trenches as they awaited their fate.

After wiring and burying explosives, they'd spent the majority of the night digging trenches from their current position all the way to the woods that would act as their last stand.

"They've got tanks," Ken said, unable to hide the trembling in his voice.

"They're just Humvees," James said. "We stick to the plan, force them to fight us on our terms." He studied their formations and saw the chink in their armor. "They're too close together."

"Huh?" Ken asked.

"Their marching formations," James answered. "They're too close to the units in front and behind them."

"We can jam them up," Zi said, following James's line of thinking.

It wasn't much of a break, because James knew that they didn't have enough explosives to wipe all of them out, but it was better than nothing. "We'll wait till the end of the convoy is past the house and the barn."

"Won't that put them close to us?" Ken asked.

James nodded. "You've always had bad aim anyway, Ken."

There was silence at first, but then Ken chuckled, followed by Zi and lastly James. And while it might have seemed like madness to laugh in such times, it helped lighten the mood, and it reminded all of them that they were human, and that it was their very humanity that they were trying to save.

The laughter finally died out when the front of the convoy reached the house, their forward progress painfully slow. The heat bore down on the back of their necks, and as James stole a quick glance down the line of trenches, he thought how odd it was that only three days ago he was riding these lands on his mare, chasing down stray cattle, with his biggest worry being if his latest buyer had dropped out. "Mary's pregnant."

He knew the statement was oddly timed, and everyone in the trench with him glanced around at one another, unsure of how they were supposed to react to such news.

"At least she was," James said, needing to speak the words aloud before the fight began. "We don't know if she lost the baby when she was shot. We won't know for a long time now, I guess." He cleared his throat and then adjusted his grip on the rifle as he kept his attention on the enemy. "I just needed to say that aloud, I guess."

It was quiet for a while, but it was Zi who spoke first.

"Congratulations, James," Zi said.

"Yeah," Ken said. "Congrats, boss."

James smiled. "Thanks."

And for some unknown reason, James felt an odd shift in the mood and body language of the fighters beside him. They were fighting for something other than themselves, something more abstract. They were fighting for the future, even if they might not live to see it.

With less than twenty yards separating them from the enemy, James reached for the detonator to the explosive devices, his hand steady as a rock, and he flipped the switch.

The explosions erupted by the house and barn, chopping

off the tail of the caravan, shaking the ground and tearing into the heart of the terrorist army.

The aftermath of the explosion caused everyone in the trench to lose their footing, but while the explosions might have rocked James and the rest of the group, it took the terrorists by surprise and momentarily halted their slow progression forward as grown men scrambled to find a safe place to wait out the storm.

However, with the enemy on its heels, James knew that now was the perfect time to strike, and unable to hear his own commands, he shouted for his people to open fire and started picking off the enemy one by one.

The stunned army fired randomly, their shots missing as they struggled to regroup. But their chaos was James's opportunity, and he used it to bring down as many terrorists as he could bring into his crosshairs.

But when the front Humvee lurched forward again, James started his slow and steady retreat through the trenches and toward the forest.

"Keep moving!" James remained crouched even when he wasn't in the safety of the trenches, and while they put more distance between themselves and the enemy, James knew that they had to keep moving, they had to make the enemy chase them.

The enemy recovered faster than James would have liked, but they didn't let up on their assault.

After the fifth trench, James reached for the detonator once more and flicked the switch, but instead of a boom going off, there was nothing.

"The trigger's dead!" James shouted while the other two fired into the encroaching enemy, who had now regained some of their lost momentum as they approached the first trench.

Enemy gunfire forced James back down into the hole for cover, but he managed to sneak a peek at the front line, where the enemy had organized the Humvees into a wall of armor to protect their fighters and the big fifty-caliber guns mounted on top of the vehicles were being unleashed.

The plan was unraveling.

"Run for the woods! Go!" James led the charge, making sure that everyone made it to the next trench before he moved on, the three of them working together on their retreat, the thunder of the fifty-caliber weapons sounding like the explosions of C-4 that they had set to charge before the battle.

With James and company in full retreat, the enemy grew wise to their plan and weaved around the trenches to avoid the Humvees getting stuck, but the small maneuver gave James and the others the needed time to head into the woods.

Branches smacked James's face as he led all of them into the thick foliage. "Just keep moving!" James made sure to keep everyone in front of him, not wanting to lose anyone, and eventually the gunfire faded.

Sweaty, exhausted, the three of them hunched over to catch their breath, and James checked his ammunition. "I've got three magazines left."

"Two," Ken said.

"One," Zi said.

It was quiet for a moment, the silence finally interrupted by the rumbling of the Humvees nearing the woods.

"Anyone who wants to make it to the river," James said. "Now's the time to go." He looked at each of them in turn. "We've done what we can."

Ken winced, grimacing as he clutched his side. "I'm staying with you, boss."

James smiled and when he turned to Zi, she had tears in her eyes.

"Luis would have stayed," Zi said. "I'm staying for him."

"Thank you," James said. "Thank you for this."

328

The roar of the enemy grew louder, the first fighters entering the woods.

"This is it," James said. "Fan out. Keep moving. And do not let them capture you."

While the others spread out, James picked a spot a few yards ahead of where they had stopped and brought the rifle's scope to his eye, waiting for his first shot.

The world narrowed through the high-powered lens of the scope, thrusting James toward the enemy until he could see the whites of their eyes. He spied three fighters marching their way through the foliage. He knew that he wouldn't have enough bullets to take down the entire army, but he wasn't going to try and beat them all, he just needed to remember why he was fighting in the first place. He was doing it to win, to beat the people who had hurt and killed so many innocent lives, who had changed the future to a world cloaked in blood and fear.

James wanted to put fear into those that harnessed it as a weapon. He wanted to prove that the enemy that had brought the country he loved to its knees could be destroyed and that there was a future for those that still believed in good triumphing over evil.

James took a breath, his finger over the trigger. The moment he squeezed it, there would be no turning back. But all James had to do to harden his resolve was to remember Luis, and how he had given his life to protect this place, to protect his family. And that was all the courage James needed.

The first bullet went through the terrorist's neck, dropping him instantly while the other two fired randomly, unable to determine where the shots were fired from, giving James time to line up his next shot.

The second bullet entered the target's chest, right over the heart, knocking him to his back, where he lay still.

James swept his rifle over the woods smoothly, falling

into a trance-like state in which his movements were guided by the perfect combination of instinct and skill.

Every fighter that came into his crosshairs was brought down. He emptied the first clip of his remaining three and never missed a shot.

More fighters flooded into the woods, the Humvees forced to stop since they couldn't make it through the dense woods, and it bought them just a little more time.

The pop of gunfire thickened as Zi and Ken both fired from their positions from deeper into the woods, and it didn't take long before the forest was alive with gunfire. Gunpowder and lead poisoned the world, but James remained steady, bringing down fighter after fighter, and with each body that he dropped to the forest floor, two more took the dead man's place.

And slowly, inch by inch, the enemy pushed forward by the simple fact that James couldn't reload fast enough to bring the men down. The only reason he knew how many men he killed was because of the fact that he knew how many bullets he had left, and James hadn't missed a shot since he started firing from behind the tree.

Shells stacked up around James's ankles, the recoil of the rifle against his shoulder becoming as steady and rhythmic as the beating of his heart. And he knew that the moment the pounding ended against his shoulder, so did his pulse. Because the two were connected now, each needing the other to survive.

James loaded his last magazine into the rifle, and he felt the feeling in his hands start to numb. He wondered if the others were still alive. He hoped they were, and he suddenly regretted them staying. They didn't have to stick around to fight, but that was their choice. And just as James made his own choice to stay, so they made theirs.

One of the fighters managed to move within ten yards of James, and he didn't see him until the terrorist already had an opportunity to shoot. The bullet only grazed James, but it was enough to cost James his momentum. The fighter lunged forward, tackling James to the ground.

The fighter wedged the rifle against James's throat, pressing down hard, choking him. James struggled to fight back. The man was strong, and he was so tired, but somewhere deep within him erupted that primal strength that was only used whenever life was nearly gone.

James thrust the man off of him then unholstered his side arm, shooting the man down, and then a second that appeared from out of nowhere. He emptied the pistol, then picked up the rifle again. But before he could get a firm hold, another fighter appeared, and James was surrounded.

The rifle was kicked from James's hands, and instead of bullets, a hail of fists rained over him, the punishment relentless. And somewhere between the fists and the boots, James rolled to his back, no longer able to defend himself against the assault.

But between the heads of the men that were beating him to death, James saw a glimmer of the blue sky above. It was clear, cloudless. And even in the midst of such savagery and death, James was reminded that the universe was always expanding, and that while his life was about to end, others would start. Like his unborn child.

"Enough!"

The voice thundered through the woods and the beating stopped, though James was already too far gone to feel anything now. He was limp and broken. At least that was how it felt. But, with the beating reaching a momentary pause, James managed to roll to his right and he sat up, leaning on his elbow, which was starting to regain some of its feeling.

"Is it you?"

Wincing, his vision blurred, James turned toward the voice that had ended the beating. Blood dripped from his lip, his cheeks were beginning to swell, and when he bent his left leg, his knee made a terrible grinding sound.

"The other man I found said he was not James Bowers." The man who spoke was squat and muscular, and wide as a barn. He had soulless eyes and a mechanical movement to him, as if he were a robot posing as a man. "Are you him?"

James forced himself to his hands and knees, and then with what remained of his strength, he stood, slowly straightening out his back, so he looked down on the man who spoke. "I am."

A devious smile spread over the man's face, and he spread his arms wide. The fighters that had circled them stepped back, creating a space.

"I have been waiting to see you," he said. "My name is Khan, James Bowers. And I am the root of everything that has happened to this place, to this country." He removed his armor and his weapons and finally his shirt, revealing a physique that could rival Mr. Olympia. "You have caused me great trouble. I instructed my men to keep you alive until I could kill you myself." He tilted his head to the side, examining James's beaten figure. "I'm disappointed they didn't leave me more to work with."

James was convinced that he had at least two ribs broken, and the pain in his left arm had gotten worse. He couldn't even move it now. His left eye was beginning to swell shut. "Still more than enough to deal with you, I think."

Khan was quiet for a moment, and then that smile spread even wider, followed by a laugh so deep it shook the trees. "I had hoped you would still put up a fight." He raised his boulder-sized fists and stepped forward.

James kept his distance at first, testing his legs to see what he was working with. His right arm was fine, but his entire left side was exposed, making it an easy target. But if the man in front of him was in charge of the army, then James finally had the head of the snake within reach, and he had no plans of letting it get by him without a fight.

Khan made the first move, moving in quickly with a stiff jab to James's face, which he didn't land fully, James able to bob out of the way before it connected fully.

"Fast," Khan said, hands still up and circling James like a tiger. "But so am I."

The next punch that came was so quick James didn't even see it, but he felt the pain light up his left side, his body wanting to cave inward. His knees buckled, but he remained upright, refusing to go down so quickly.

"Yes!" Khan shouted, continuing his dance around James. "He's not given up yet!"

The next few minutes were nothing more than Khan toying with James, landing blow after powerful blow into James's face and body until James couldn't even keep his one good arm up anymore for defense or offense.

But that fighting spirit, that defiance forced James to remain upright. Even if all he could do was stand, it would at least keep the fighting away from the others. That was his mission. And he would see it through until the end.

Khan landed a final blow square on James's chin, knocking James to the ground and sending him into a spinning world of stars.

"You are a weak man, James Bowers," Khan said.

James struggled to get off his stomach. The world just wouldn't stop spinning, and his vision was fading. He didn't think he'd be awake for much longer.

"And weak men die," Khan said. "It's why I've brought my army, my people. We will purge this world of weakness through the truth of fire and blood."

James flattened to his stomach for good this time, and he drew in a few wheezing gasps.

"Do you hear me, James Bowers?" Khan knelt and grabbed hold of James's chin, James unable to keep his eyes focused on any one spot. "I will burn you all. And I know that you have family. I will burn them too. I will burn your friends, your neighbors. I will march across this land until everything behind me has been scorched to dust."

Staring at Khan, James saw the same madness in his eyes that he saw in Dillon's and in all of the fighters that he'd met. There was dedication and conviction in those eyes. But they lacked humanity, they lacked any semblance of life, and James remembered the universe.

"Death might win the fight," James said, forcing a smile. "But it will never win the war. Because of people like me. They won't kneel, and they won't stop. You can only torture people for so long before they fight back. Life pushes forward." He thought of Mary. "All the way. No matter what."

James watched the smugness in Khan's expression fade, and when he stepped back and was handed a firearm, James prayed that Banks was ready for the fight that was coming.

And when the pistol was aimed at James's face, he only saw his wife and son. He would meet them again someday, along with the unborn child he had yet to meet. It would be a hard world to live in when she was born, but she would be a Bowers. And Bowers never quit.

Suddenly, James smiled, laughing to himself, realizing what he'd just thought. "It'll be a girl. Mary's going to have a girl." No, James thought, still smiling. *We're going to have a girl.*

The gunfire that came next was far too loud to have been the product of the pistol in Khan's hand, but nevertheless the world erupted in heavy machine-gun fire.

At first James thought that it must have been Zi or Ken coming over to join James in his last stand, but as the shouting continued and the war raged on, James managed to retain a conscious awareness that it was something else. Something bigger.

* * *

FOR A LONG TIME, James's senses drifted in and out of consciousness, and he couldn't tell what was reality and what were dreams and nightmares. For a while he thought that he had died, and he was in the fires of hell.

Heat blasted James's face, and a terrible pain ran through his body, making everything hurt something fierce. But then, slowly, the heat subsided and the pain dulled, and he drifted from a world of war and into the soft throes of clouds and weightlessness until he finally woke.

Expecting to find himself either in the woods or the inside of a coffin, James was surprised to see that he was back in the bunker. His bunker. On his cot with an IV hooked up to his arm.

"The girl put that in you." Banks appeared from the back of the bunker and moved up toward the bed. "She looked like she knew what she was doing, so I didn't stop her."

James stared up at Banks, unable to speak from the shock.

"Surprised?"

"What are you doing here?" James asked.

Banks found a chair and sat down. He wasn't armed, and they were the only two in the bunker. He rubbed his palm over the rough stubble on his shaved head. "Saving your ass." He leaned back in his chair, examining James in the bed. "Though I can't say you might not be better off dead."

"My wife—"

"You can thank her when we get back to the compound," Banks said. "She was the one who convinced me to come over here." He tilted his head to the side, smirking. "Well, she called me a coward, and I filled in the blanks myself."

Of all the people to come, Banks was the last person James expected to show up. "What happened?"

"You did good work leveling the playing field," Banks said. "We came up from behind, commandeered some of the Humvees, and unloaded on the rest. A few of them surrendered when they realized there wasn't a way out, and the handful that talked to us we kept alive. This was the bulk of their forces, but they have other pockets around the country. And they only had the one bomb. Looks to me like the worst is over."

James lay still for a moment, trying to wrap his head around what the guy had just told him. It didn't seem real.

"What happened to Khan?" James asked.

"Who?"

"He was their leader. He was the one who worked me over and put me in my current spot."

"Oh, the big one." Banks drew in a breath. "He was taken out by one of the heavy artillery rounds we dumped into the forest. One of his people identified the body."

"I want to see it."

With Banks's help, James slowly moved out of bed and then carefully climbed the ladder out of the bunker, the sun blinding him as he stepped out onto the grass.

When his vision finally adjusted, James saw the smoldering wreckage that was Khan's army, and he saw the hundred fighters that Banks had brought with him. The dead were being moved, buried, or burned, depending on which side they represented.

In all the years that James had worked and lived on the ranch, he had never seen so much death. "How many did you lose?"

"Forty-two," Banks answered.

James turned and walked over to the man who had saved him, saved his land, and potentially saved millions of others across the country. "Thank you, Banks. You didn't have to do this."

"Yes," Banks said. "I did." He looked past James and to the bodies being moved. "I didn't realize how bad things have gotten. Probably because I've stayed on my own land for too long. It's important to have perspective. I'm just glad I didn't find it too late."

"James?" Zi pushed herself between two of Banks's guys, then sprinted toward him and wrapped her arms around his neck. "Thank God." She stepped back, frowning. "What are you doing up? You should be in bed, resting." She cast Banks a hard glare, but James calmed her down.

"I just needed to see Khan's body," James said.

Zi walked with James, helping him over to the hole in the ground where they were putting the dead terrorists, but there was one body that was set aside. Khan was on his back, a hole in his chest the size of a grapefruit, those same pair of maddening eyes staring up at the blue sky.

"Yeah," James said, nodding. "That was him."

With his curiosity sated, James became suddenly exhausted, and Zi helped him back into the bunker, where she hooked the IV back into his arm.

"Maybe this time you'll stay asleep," Zi said, tucking James in like he was a child.

"I'm sorry about Luis," James said. "I know you liked him. And he liked you too."

Zi's lower lip trembled, but she didn't cry. "I'm sorry too. He was a good man."

"He was the best man." A tightness formed in James's chest, and he drew in a sharp breath that caused his ribs to ache. "I couldn't save him. I wanted to, but the wound was—"

Zi grabbed James's hand. "It wasn't your fault, James."

It was the first time that James had allowed himself to grieve and as the tears came, he was thankful that Zi was there, because the guilt that plagued him over Luis's death was magnified over the fact that he had torn apart two people who had grown to care for one another. And it was something that he could never make right.

* * *

EVERYONE from the ranch had been confined to the same

337

space, which was growing more cramped the longer that they were stuck together. The mood swayed between fear, desperation, and anger, but Mary did her best to ignore all of that and instead focused on Jake.

She gently brushed her fingers through his hair, praying that he would wake up soon. She needed something to hold onto, something to give her strength as she awaited to hear the fate of her husband.

Banks had left hours ago, and while Mary was thankful the man had decided to go help, she was worried that the effort might have been too little and too late.

Jake groaned and rocked his head from side to side, slowly awakening. He cracked his eyes open. "Mom?"

Mary kissed Jake's forehead. "Hey."

Jake glanced around, becoming alarmed once he realized that they were no longer at the ranch, but Mary was quick to calm him.

"We're safe," Mary said.

Still weary, Jake nodded. "Dad did the procedure?"

"He did," Mary answered, smiling with tears of joy. "He saved you."

"Where is he?"

Mary hesitated, unsure of how much she should tell him in his fragile state. But deep down, she knew that the truth was the only way. "We had to leave the ranch. Those people that were in the town, the same ones that attacked us, your father believed they were coming back for the piece of the bomb. He wanted to make sure that we were safe, so he made a deal with the other prepper community."

Jake frowned. "What deal?" He sat up, shaking his head. "What are you talking about?"

"Jake, you need to listen to me—"

"Where's Dad?"

The rest of the group was looking back at Mary and Jake's growing outburst. Mary grabbed both of Jake's hands and forced her son still. "Hey, listen to me." She waited until he was still and quiet and then looked into his eyes. "He stayed behind. To protect us. To save our family. And we have to accept that, no matter how much it hurts." Tears formed in her own eyes now. "But no matter what happens, we are still a family."

Jake nodded, and then sniffled. "I just want to go home."

Mary lunged forward and wrapped her son in a hug. She rocked him gently, both of them crying now. "Me too, baby. Me too."

"Me three."

Mary froze, but her heart swelled in her chest. She spun around, finding James standing in the hut, the others clearing out and giving the family a moment to reunite in private. With the light behind James, Mary thought that he might just be a figment of her imagination, but the longer she stared, the more she realized that he was really there.

Before he vanished into smoke, Mary hobbled toward him, moving as fast as her healing body allowed, then hugged him tight. But when he winced, she pulled back, getting a better look at him now that she was closer.

"Oh my God." Mary gently touched the bruises and cuts along his body. "What happened?"

"It's over," James answered. "Banks wiped the rest of them out."

"Did we lose anyone?"

James nodded. "Ken. He's gone."

And while Mary knew that she should have mourned for someone who was more family than friend, she was just thankful that James was alive, and that he was well. And as James walked over to their son, the pair embracing, she believed that they could make it through tomorrow. She touched her stomach and looked down. No matter what happened.

51

ONE YEAR LATER

*J*ames pounded the last post into the hole and poured the filler dirt to keep it in place. Sweat dripped from his nose and chin, and he wiped it away with his sleeve. The Stetson shielded his face from the sun, but James found himself constantly looking up at the beautiful summer sky.

The past three days had brought constant rain. And while it was needed, it had made work on the ranch uncomfortable for anyone who was working outside. The rain may have been a reprieve from the heat, but James had never minded the sweat.

He rolled out the last bit of fence, then hammered the chained mesh into place on the final post, finishing his last project for the day. He stepped back, planted his fists on his hips, and admired the one hundred yards of new fence on the western perimeter.

It was one of the last projects that James had given himself that marked the end of the repairs from what happened last summer during the EMP. For the most part, life had returned to normal, and the world was slowly transforming back into the independent society that it was before the disaster. There was less death than last summer, less fighting. And for that, James was grateful.

According to the news, there were only a few smaller factions remaining in the U.S., and officials were close to snuffing out the rest of them. Power had been restored to all major metropolitan areas, and to most rural areas.

And most importantly, James was back in the saddle and working his family's land once more. It had been a long road to recovery, and even longer to rebuild what had been torched to the ground, but the long journey had been worth it. Never in his life had James been more thankful for the phrase, 'back to normal.'

After James packed up his gear, he mounted his mare, the horse protesting the added weight with a stomp and whinny.

"I'm still getting back into shape," James said. "No need to keep reminding me." He stroked the animal's neck and it calmed.

James gave her a little nudge with his heels and the pair galloped across the open plains. The wind whipped his face, his sweaty shirt clinging to his body, and he smiled. He had missed this, and not just the riding, but the end of the day. He had worked hard, and waiting back at the house was his reward. He couldn't wait to see them.

The only thing that remained in the house after the fire was the foundation, and James had built something new. In a way, it was nice to have such a fresh start, and he was glad to have family and friends to start over with.

James stayed in the barn for a little while longer, finishing up with the animal, reflecting on how the world had pulled itself out.

And he didn't take that lightly, because he still remembered what happened. The nightmares came every night. He saw the dead bodies in San Antonio. He saw Luis. He saw Nolan, who passed away shortly after Khan and his people were defeated.

Those images replayed in his head every night like a highlight reel. But he bore it and pushed through, because as horrific as those events were, and how terrible it was to have experienced all of those atrocities, it reminded him of what was important and to cherish every day. Because the world could always fall into despair again. But just like before, he'd be ready.

Once the horse finished its feed, James removed the bag and shut the stall doors. He then headed to the house, which had transformed into a one-story structure. It was Mary's idea. She wanted to make it easier for them to get around once they were old and grey.

But James still made sure that it had a walk-around porch, and he entered through the back door where there was still a kitchen. And while the paint, the walls, the rooms, the whole house had changed, the people in it hadn't changed at all.

"Hey, Dad." Jake looked up from his book at the kitchen table, smiling. "How'd it go today?"

James walked over and kissed the top of his son's head. "It was great. Where's Mom?"

"Here." Mary entered, holding their three-month-old baby Rosie in her arms, her cheeks red from crying. "Someone didn't want to take a nap today, so she's a little cranky."

James smiled, tickling Rosie's toes, and then picked her up from Mary's arms, planting a kiss on each cheek before leaning over to kiss Mary.

"Whew," Mary said, leaning back. "You stink."

"Are you sure it's me?" James lifted Rosie and sniffed her butt, then nodded. "Yeah. It's me." He smiled, and Mary slapped his arm playfully while Rosie squirmed.

"Zi's coming by for dinner with Banks," Mary said, grabbing meat out of the fridge. "Should be here in a few hours. I was thinking we could…"

James listened to his wife as he held Rosie, then looked back to Jake who was still buried in his book, and he couldn't wipe the smile off his face even if he tried. Because this was what a good life looked like. He was sure of it. And he was so glad that Rosie had come into the picture, their little, completely healthy, baby girl.

James had always believed in second chances, because he knew people normally didn't do things right the first time. And while he was ready to die that day last year when he stayed behind and faced the wrath of the devil's army that knocked down his front door, he couldn't imagine missing this life.

"Hey," Mary said, pointing a spatula at him. "Are you listening?"

James smiled. "Yes. Everything sounds perfect."

Made in the USA
Monee, IL
26 February 2025

13027422R00193